What People Are Saying about the Left Behind Series

"This is the most successful Christian-fiction series ever."
Publishers Weekly

"Tim LaHaye and Jerry B. Jenkins . . . are doing for Christian fiction what John Grisham did for courtroom thrillers."
TIME

"The authors' style continues to be thoroughly captivating and keeps the reader glued to the book, wondering what will happen next. And it leaves the reader hungry for more."
Christian Retailing

"Combines Tom Clancy–like suspense with touches of romance, high-tech flash and Biblical references."
The New York Times

"It's not your mama's Christian fiction anymore."
The Dallas Morning News

"Wildly popular—and highly controversial."
USA Today

"Bible teacher LaHaye and master storyteller Jenkins have created a believable story of what could happen after the Rapture. They present the gospel clearly without being preachy, the characters have depth, and the plot keeps the reader turning pages."
Moody Magazine

"Christian thriller. Prophecy-based fiction. Juiced-up morality tale. Call it what you like, the Left Behind series . . . now has a label its creators could never have predicted: blockbuster success."
Entertainment Weekly

Tyndale House books by Tim LaHaye and Jerry B. Jenkins

The Left Behind series
Left Behind®
Tribulation Force
Nicolae
Soul Harvest
Apollyon
Assassins
The Indwelling
The Mark
Book 9—available summer 2001

Left Behind®: The Kids
#1: The Vanishings
#2: Second Chance
#3: Through the Flames
#4: Facing the Future
#5: Nicolae High
#6: The Underground
#7: Busted!
#8: Death Strike
#9: The Search
#10: On the Run
#11: Into the Storm
#12: Earthquake!

Tyndale House books by Tim LaHaye
Are We Living in the End Times?
How to Be Happy Though Married
Spirit-Controlled Temperament
Transformed Temperaments
Why You Act the Way You Do

Tyndale House books by Jerry B. Jenkins
And Then Came You
As You Leave Home
Still the One

THE RISE OF ANTICHRIST

NICOLAE

TIM LaHaye

JERRY B. JENKINS

Tyndale House Publishers, Inc.
WHEATON, ILLINOIS

Visit Tyndale's exciting Web site at www.tyndale.com

For the latest Left Behind news visit the Left Behind Web site at www.leftbehind.com

Left Behind series designed by Catherine Bergstrom
Cover photo illustration by Brian Eterno and Paul Christenson
Edited by Rick Blanchette

Published in association with the literary agency of Alive Communications, Inc.,
7680 Goddard Street, Suite 200, Colorado Springs, CO 80920.

Scripture taken from the New King James Version. Copyright © 1979, 1980, 1982 by Thomas Nelson, Inc. Used by permission. All rights reserved.

Left Behind is a registered trademark of Tyndale House Publishers, Inc.

Library of Congress Cataloging-in-Publication Data

LaHaye, Tim F.
   Nicolae : the rise of antichrist / Tim LaHaye, Jerry B. Jenkins.
     p. cm.
   ISBN 0-8423-2914-5 (hardcover)
   ISBN 0-8423-2924-2 (softcover)
   I. Jenkins, Jerry B. II. Title.
   PS3562.A315N53 1997
813'.54—dc21   97-20356

Printed in the United States of America

05 04 03 02 01 00
31 30 29 28 27 26 25 24 23

To Beverly and to Dianna

PROLOGUE

What Has Gone Before . . .

IT has been nearly two years since the mass disappearances. In one cataclysmic instant, millions all over the globe had vanished, leaving behind everything but flesh and bone.

Airline pilot Captain Rayford Steele had guided his jumbo jet back to Chicago, along with three hundred terror-filled passengers and crew. The plane had been fully loaded upon takeoff, but suddenly more than one hundred seats were empty, save for clothes, jewelry, eyeglasses, shoes, and socks.

Steele lost his wife and twelve-year-old son in the vanishings. He and his college-age daughter Chloe were left behind.

Cameron "Buck" Williams, senior writer for a weekly news magazine, had been on Rayford's plane. Like the pilot, he launched a frantic search for the truth.

Rayford, Chloe, and Buck, along with their mentor— young pastor Bruce Barnes—become believers in Christ,

calling themselves the Tribulation Force, determined to
stand against the new world leader. Nicolae Carpathia of
Romania becomes head of the United Nations seemingly
overnight. And while he charms much of the world, the
Tribulation Force believes Nicolae is Antichrist himself.

Through a bizarre set of circumstances, both Rayford
and Buck become employees of Carpathia—Rayford his
pilot; Buck, publisher of *Global Community Weekly*.
Carpathia knows that Rayford and his new wife,
Amanda, are believers, but he remains unaware of
Buck's relationship with them or of Buck's faith.

The Tribulation Force schedules a reunion in Chicago.
Rayford pilots Global Community Potentate Nicolae
Carpathia from New Babylon to Washington D.C. (with
Amanda on board). Aware of an insurrection plot,
Carpathia announces conflicting and intricate itineraries
to make himself hard to locate. Meanwhile, Rayford
took Amanda on *Global Community One* to Chicago
for the rendezvous with Buck, Chloe, and Bruce.

They discover that Bruce is in the hospital, but on
their way to visit him, global war erupts. American
militia factions, under the clandestine leadership of
Carpathia-emasculated President Gerald Fitzhugh, had
joined forces with the United States of Britain and the
former sovereign state of Egypt, now part of the newly
formed Middle Eastern Commonwealth. American East
Coast militia forces have attacked Washington, which
lies in ruin.

Carpathia, whose hotel was leveled, is spirited away
safely. His Global Community forces retaliate by attack-

ing a former Nike base in suburban Chicago, within sight of the hospital where Bruce Barnes was suffering from a deadly virus. An assault on New Babylon is quickly thwarted, and London is attacked by Global Community forces in retaliation for Britain's collusion with the American militia.

During all this, Rayford asks his former boss, Earl Halliday, to fly *Global Community One* to New York, where Rayford had assumed he himself would be asked to rendezvous with Carpathia. But as Global Community forces marshal in New York, Rayford fears he has sent his old friend to his death.

Rayford, Amanda, Buck, and Chloe frantically try to get to the ailing Bruce Barnes at Northwest Community Hospital in Arlington Heights, Illinois, when they hear a live broadcast from the Global Community Potentate:

"Loyal citizens of the Global Community, I come to you today with a broken heart, unable to tell you even from where I speak. For more than a year we have worked to draw this Global Community together under a banner of peace and harmony. Today, unfortunately, we have been reminded again that there are still those among us who would pull us apart.

"It is no secret that I am, always have been, and always will be, a pacifist. I do not believe in war. I do not believe in weaponry. I do not believe in bloodshed. On the other hand, I feel responsible for you, my brother or my sister in this global village.

"Global Community peacekeeping forces have already crushed the resistance. The death of innocent civilians weighs heavy on me, but I pledge immediate judgment upon all enemies of peace. The beautiful capital of the United States of North America has been laid waste, and you will hear stories of more destruction and death. Our goal remains peace and reconstruction. I will be back at the secure headquarters in New Babylon in due time and will communicate with you frequently.

"Above all, do not fear. Live in confidence that no threat to global tranquility will be tolerated, and no enemy of peace will survive."

As Rayford looked for a route that would get him near Northwest Community Hospital, the Cable News Network/Global Community Network correspondent came back on. "This late word: Anti–Global Community militia forces have threatened nuclear war on New York City, primarily Kennedy International Airport. Civilians are fleeing the area and causing one of the worst pedestrian and auto traffic jams in that city's history. Peacekeeping forces say they have the ability and technology to intercept missiles but are worried about residual damage to outlying areas.

"And this now from London: A one-hundred-megaton bomb has destroyed Heathrow Airport and radiation fallout threatens the populace for miles. The bomb was apparently dropped by peacekeeping forces after contraband Egyptian and British fighter-bombers were discovered rallying from a closed military airstrip near

Heathrow. The warships, which have all been shot from the sky, were reportedly nuclear-equipped and en route to Baghdad and New Babylon."

"It's the end of the world," Chloe whispered. "God help us."

Rayford remained desperate to check on Bruce in the hospital. A passerby told him Northwest Community was "through that field and over the rise. But I don't know how close they'll let you get to what's left of it."

"It was hit?"

"Was it hit? Mister, it's just up the road and across the street from the old Nike base. Most people think it got hit first."

Rayford's heart sank as he walked alone over the rise and saw the hospital. It was mostly rubble.

"Halt!" a guard called out. "This is a restricted area!"

"I have clearance!" Rayford shouted, waving his ID wallet.

When he got to Rayford, the guard took the wallet and studied it, comparing the photo to Rayford's face. "Wow! Clearance level 2-A. You work for Carpathia himself?"

Rayford nodded and headed toward what had been the front of the building. Body after body was laid out in a neat row and covered. "Any survivors?" Rayford asked an emergency medical technician.

"We hear voices," the man said. "But we haven't gotten to anyone in time yet."

"Help or get out of the way," a heavyset woman said as she brushed past Rayford.

"I'm looking for a Bruce Barnes," Rayford said.

The woman checked her clipboard. "Check over there," she said, pointing to six bodies. "Relative?"

"Closer than a brother."

"You want I should check for you?"

Rayford's face contorted and he could hardly speak. "I'd be grateful," he said.

She knelt by the bodies one by one, checking, as a sob rose in Rayford's throat. At the fourth body, she began to lift the sheet when she hesitated and checked the still intact wristband. She looked back at Rayford, and he knew. The tears began to roll. The woman slowly pulled back the sheet, revealing Bruce, eyes open, but otherwise still. Rayford fought for composure, his chest heaving. He reached to close Bruce's eyes, but the woman said, "I can't let you do that. I'll do it."

"Could you check for a pulse?" Rayford managed.

"Oh, sir," she said, deep sympathy in her voice, "they don't bring them out here unless they've been pronounced."

"Please," he whispered, crying openly now. "For me."

And as Rayford stood in the bluster of suburban Chicago's early afternoon, his hands to his face, a stranger placed a thumb and forefinger at the pressure points under his pastor's jaw. Without looking at Rayford, she took her hand away, replaced the sheet over Bruce Barnes's head, and went back about her business. Rayford's knees buckled, and he knelt on the muddy pavement. Sirens blared in the distance, emergency lights flashed all around him, and his family waited less than half a mile away. It was just him and them now. No teacher. No mentor. Just them.

As he rose and trudged back down the rise with his awful news, Rayford heard the Emergency Broadcast System station from every vehicle he passed. Washington had been obliterated. Heathrow was gone. There had been death in the Egyptian desert and in the skies over London. New York was on alert.

The Red Horse of the Apocalypse was on the rampage.

ONE

It was the worst of times; it was the worst of times.

Rayford Steele's knees ached as he sat behind the wheel of the rented Lincoln. He had dropped to the pavement at the crushing realization of his pastor's death. The physical pain, though it would stay with him for days, would prove minor compared to the mental anguish of having yet again lost one of the dearest people in his life.

Rayford felt Amanda's eyes on him. She laid one comforting hand on his thigh. In the backseat his daughter, Chloe, and her husband, Buck, each had a hand on his shoulder.

What now? Rayford wondered. *What do we do without Bruce? Where do we go?*

The Emergency Broadcast System station droned on with the news of chaos, devastation, terror, and destruction throughout the world. Unable to speak over the

1

lump in his throat, Rayford busied himself maneuvering his way through the incongruous traffic jams. Why were people out? What did they expect to see? Weren't they afraid of more bombs, or fallout?

"I need to get to the Chicago bureau office," Buck said.

"You can use the car after we get to the church," Rayford managed. "I need to get the word out about Bruce."

Global Community peacekeeping forces supervised local police and emergency relief personnel directing traffic and trying to get people to return to their homes. Rayford relied on his many years in the Chicago area to use back roads and side streets to get around the major thoroughfares, which were hopelessly clogged.

Rayford wondered if he should have taken Buck up on his offer to drive. But Rayford had not wanted to appear weak. He shook his head. *There's no limit to the pilot's ego!* He felt as if he could curl into a ball and cry himself to sleep.

Nearly two years since the vanishing of his wife and son, along with millions of others, Rayford no longer harbored illusions about his life in the twilight of history. He had been devastated. He lived with deep pain and regret. This was so hard. . . .

Rayford knew his life could be even worse. Suppose he had not become a believer in Christ and was still lost forever. Suppose he had not found a new love and was alone. Suppose Chloe had also vanished. Or he had never met Buck. There was much to be grateful for.

Were it not for the physical touch of the other three in that car, Rayford wondered if he would have had the will to go on.

He could hardly imagine not having come to know and love Bruce Barnes. He had learned more and been enlightened and inspired more by Bruce than anyone else he'd ever met. And it wasn't just Bruce's knowledge and teaching that made the difference. It was his passion. Here was a man who immediately and clearly saw that he had missed the greatest truth ever communicated to mankind, and he was not about to repeat the mistake.

"Daddy, those two guards by the overpass seem to be waving at you," Chloe said.

"I'm trying to ignore them," Rayford said. "All these nobodies-trying-to-be-somebodies think they have a better idea about where the traffic should go. If we listen to them, we'll be here for hours. I just want to get to the church."

"He's hollering at you with a bullhorn," Amanda said, and she lowered her window a few inches.

"You in the white Lincoln!" came the booming voice. Rayford quickly turned off the radio. "Are you Rayford Steele?"

"How would they know that?" Buck said.

"Is there any limit to the Global Community intelligence network?" Rayford said, disgusted.

"If you're Rayford Steele," came the voice again, "please pull your vehicle to the shoulder!"

Rayford considered ignoring even that but thought

better of it. There would be no outrunning these people if they knew who he was. But how did they know?

He pulled over.

Buck Williams pulled his hand from Rayford's shoulder and craned his neck to see two uniformed soldiers scampering down the embankment. He had no idea how Global Community forces had tracked down Rayford, but one thing was certain: it would not be good for Buck to be discovered with Carpathia's pilot.

"Ray," he said quickly, "I've got one set of phony IDs in the name of Herb Katz. Tell 'em I'm a pilot friend of yours or something."

"OK," Rayford said, "but my guess is they'll be deferential to me. Obviously, Nicolae is merely trying to reconnect with me."

Buck hoped Rayford was right. It made sense that Carpathia would want to make sure his pilot was all right and could somehow get him back to New Babylon. The two uniforms now stood behind the Lincoln, one speaking into a walkie-talkie, the other on a cell phone. Buck decided to go on the offensive and opened his door.

"Please remain in the vehicle," Walkie-Talkie said.

Buck slumped back into his seat and switched his phony papers with his real ones. Chloe looked terrified. Buck put his arm around her and drew her close. "Carpathia must have put out an all points bulletin. He knew your dad had to rent a car, so it didn't take long to track him down."

Buck had no idea what the two GC men were doing

behind the car. All he knew was that his entire perspective on the next five years had changed in an instant. When global war broke out an hour before, he wondered if he and Chloe would survive the rest of the Tribulation. Now with the news of Bruce's death, Buck wondered if they *wanted* to survive. The prospect of heaven and being with Christ sure seemed better than living in whatever remained of this world, even if Buck had to die to get there.

Walkie-Talkie approached the driver's-side window. Rayford lowered it. "You *are* Rayford Steele, are you not?"

"Depends on who's asking," Rayford said.

"This car, with this license number, was rented at O'Hare by someone claiming to be Rayford Steele. If that's not you, you're in deep trouble."

"Wouldn't you agree," Rayford said, "that regardless who I am, we're all in deep trouble?"

Buck was amused at Rayford's feistiness, in light of the situation.

"Sir, I need to know if you are Rayford Steele."

"I am."

"Can you prove that, sir?"

Rayford appeared as agitated as Buck had ever seen him. "You flag me down and holler at me through a bullhorn and tell me I'm driving Rayford Steele's rental car, and now you want me to prove to you that I'm who you think I am?"

"Sir, you must understand the position I'm in. I have Global Community potentate Carpathia himself patched through to a secure cell phone here. I don't even know where he's calling from. If I put someone on the phone and tell the potentate it's Rayford Steele, it had blamed better be Rayford Steele."

Buck was grateful that Rayford's cat-and-mouse game had taken the spotlight off the others in the car, but that didn't last. Rayford slipped from his breast pocket his ID wallet, and as the GC man studied it, he asked idly, "And the others?"

"Family and friends," Rayford said. "Let's not keep the potentate waiting."

"I'm going to have to ask you to take this call outside the car, sir. You understand the security risks."

Rayford sighed and left the car. Buck wished Walkie-Talkie would disappear too, but he merely stepped out of Rayford's way and pointed him toward his partner, the one with the phone. Then he leaned in and spoke to Buck. "Sir, in the event that we transport Captain Steele to a rendezvous point, would you be able to handle the disposition of this vehicle?"

Do all uniformed people talk this way? Buck wondered. "Sure."

Amanda leaned over. "I'm Mrs. Steele," she said. "Wherever Mr. Steele is going, I'm going."

"That will be up to the potentate," the guard said, "and providing there's room in the chopper."

"Yes sir," Rayford said into the phone, "I'll see you soon then."

Rayford handed the cell phone to the second guard. "How will we get to wherever we're supposed to go?"

"A copter should be here momentarily."

Rayford motioned for Amanda to pop the trunk but to stay in the car. As he shouldered both their bags, he leaned in her window and whispered. "Amanda and I have to rendezvous with Carpathia, but he couldn't even tell me where he was or where we would meet. That phone is only so secure. I get the feeling it's not far away, unless they're coptering us to an airfield from which we'll fly somewhere else. Buck, you'd better get this car back to the rental company soon. It'll be too easy to connect you with me otherwise."

Five minutes later Rayford and Amanda were airborne. "Any idea where we're going?" Rayford shouted to one of the Global Community guards.

The guard clapped the chopper pilot on the shoulder and shouted, "Are we at liberty to say where we're going?"

"Glenview!" the pilot hollered.

"Glenview Naval Air Station has been closed for years," Rayford said.

The chopper pilot turned to look at him. "The big runway's still open! The man's there now!"

Amanda leaned close to Rayford. "Carpathia's in Illinois already?"

"He must have been out of Washington before the attack. I thought they might have taken him to one of the bomb shelters at the Pentagon or the National Security Administration, but his intelligence people must have figured those would be the first places the militia would attack."

"This reminds me of when we were first married," Buck said as Chloe snuggled close to him.

"What do you mean 'when we were first married'? We're still newlyweds!"

"Shh!" Buck said quickly. "What're they saying about New York City?"

Chloe turned up the radio. ". . . devastating carnage everywhere here in the heart of Manhattan. Bombed-out buildings, emergency vehicles picking their way through debris, Civil Defense workers pleading with people over loudspeakers to stay underground."

Buck heard the panic in the reporter's voice as he continued. "I'm seeking shelter myself now, probably too late to avoid the effects of radiation. No one knows for certain if the warheads were nuclear, but everyone is being urged to take no risks. Damage estimates will be in the billions of dollars. Life as we know it here may never be the same. There's devastation as far as the eye can see.

"All major transportation centers have been closed if not destroyed. Huge traffic jams have snarled the Lincoln Tunnel, the Triborough Bridge, and every major artery out of New York City. What has been known as the capital of the world looks like the set of a disaster movie. Now back to the Cable News/Global Community News Network in Atlanta."

"Buck," Chloe said, "our home. Where will we live?"

Buck didn't answer. He stared at the traffic and wondered at the billowing clouds of black smoke and intermittent balls of orange flame that seemed to hover directly over Mt. Prospect. It was like Chloe to worry about her home. Buck was less concerned about that. He could live anywhere and seemed to *have* lived everywhere. As long as he had Chloe and shelter, he was all right. But she had made their ridiculously expensive Fifth Avenue penthouse flat her own.

Finally, Buck spoke. "They won't let anybody back into New York for days, maybe longer. Even our vehicles, if they survived, won't be available to us."

"What are we going to do, Buck?"

Buck wished he knew what to say. He usually had an answer. Resourcefulness had been the trademark of his career. Regardless of the obstacle, he had somehow made do in every imaginable situation or venue in the world at one time or another. Now, with his new, young wife beside him, not knowing where she would live or how they would manage, he was at a loss. All he wanted to do was to make sure his father-in-law and Amanda were safe, in spite of the danger of Rayford's work, and to somehow get to Mt. Prospect to assess what was happening to the people of New Hope Village Church and to inform them of the tragedy that had befallen their beloved pastor.

Buck had never had patience for traffic jams, but this was ridiculous. His jaw tightened and his neck stiffened as his palms squeezed the wheel. The late-model car was a smooth ride, but inching along in near gridlock made the huge automotive power plant feel like a stallion that wanted to run free.

Suddenly an explosion rocked their car and nearly lifted it off its tires. Buck wouldn't have been surprised had the windows blown in around them. Chloe shrieked and buried her head in Buck's chest. Buck scanned the horizon for what might have caused the concussion. Several cars around them quickly pulled off the road. In the rearview mirror Buck saw a mushroom cloud slowly rise and assumed it was in the neighborhood of O'Hare International Airport, several miles away.

CNN/GCN radio almost immediately reported the blast. "This from Chicago: Our news base there has been taken out by a huge blast. No word yet on whether this was an attack by militia forces or a Global Community retaliatory strike. We have so many reports of warfare, bloodshed, devastation, and death in so many major cities around the globe that it will be impossible for us to keep up with all of it. . . ."

Buck looked quickly behind him and out both side windows. As soon as the car ahead gave him room, he whipped the wheel left and punched the accelerator. Chloe gasped as the car jumped the curb and went down through a culvert and up the other side. Buck drove on a parkway and passed long lines of creeping vehicles.

"What are you doing, Buck?" Chloe said, bracing herself on the dashboard.

"I don't know what I'm doing, babe, but I know one thing I'm not doing: I'm not poking along in a traffic jam while the world goes to hell."

The guard who had flagged down Rayford from the
overpass now lugged his and Amanda's baggage out
of the helicopter. He led the Steeles, ducking under
the whirring blades, across a short tarmac and into
a single-story brick building at the edge of a long airstrip. Weeds grew between the cracks in the runway.
A small Learjet sat at the end of the strip close to the
chopper, but Rayford noticed no one in the cockpit
and no exhaust from the engine. "I hope they don't
expect me to fly that thing!" he hollered at Amanda
as they hurried inside.

"Don't worry about that," their escort said. "The guy
who flew it here will get you as far as Dallas and the big
plane you'll be flying."

Rayford and Amanda were ushered to garishly colored
plastic chairs in a small, shabbily appointed military
office, decorated in early Air Force. Rayford sat, gingerly
massaging his knees. Amanda paced, stopping only when
their escort motioned that she should sit down. "I am
free to stand, am I not?" she said.

"Suit yourself. Please wait here a few moments for the
potentate."

Buck was waved at, pointed at, and hollered at by traffic
cops, and he was honked at and obscenely gestured at by
other motorists. He was not deterred. "Where are you
going?" Chloe insisted.

"I need a new car," he said. "Something tells me it's going to be our only chance to survive."

"What are you talking about?"

"Don't you see, Chlo'?" he said. "This war has just broken out. It's not going to end soon. It's going to be impossible to drive a normal vehicle anywhere."

"So what're you gonna do, buy a tank?"

"If it wasn't so conspicuous, I just might."

Buck cut across a huge grassy field, through a parking lot, and beside a sprawling suburban high school. He drove between tennis courts and across soccer and football fields, throwing mud and sod in the air as the big car fishtailed. Radio reports continued from around the world with news of casualties and mayhem while Buck Williams and his bride careened on, speeding through yield signs and sliding around curves. Buck hoped he was somehow pointed in the right direction. He wanted to wind up on Northwest Highway, where a series of car dealerships comprised a ghetto of commercialism.

A last sweeping turn led Buck out of the subdivision, and he saw what his favorite traffic reporter always said was "heavy, slow, stop-and-go" traffic all along Northwest Highway. He was in a mood and in a groove, so he just kept going. Pulling around angry drivers, he rode along a soft shoulder for more than a mile until he came upon those car dealerships. "Bingo!" he said.

Rayford was stunned, and he could tell Amanda was too, at the demeanor of Nicolae Carpathia. The dashing young man, now in his mid-thirties, had seemingly been thrust to world leadership against his own will over-night. He had gone from being nearly an unknown in the lower house of Romanian government to president of that country, then almost immediately had displaced the secretary-general of the United Nations. After nearly two years of peace and a largely successful campaign to charm the masses following the terror-filled chaos of the global vanishings, Carpathia now faced significant oppo-sition for the first time.

Rayford had not known what to expect from his boss. Would Carpathia be hurt, offended, enraged? He seemed none of the above. Ushered by Leon Fortunato, a syco-phant from the New Babylon office, into the long-unused administrative office at the former Glenview Naval Air Station, Carpathia seemed excited, high.

"Captain Steele!" Carpathia exalted. "Al—, uh, An—, uh, Mrs. Steele, how good to see you both and to know that you are well!"

"It's Amanda," Amanda said.

"Forgive me, Amanda," Carpathia said, reaching for her hand with both of his. Rayford noticed how slow she was to respond. "In all the excitement, you under-stand . . ."

The excitement, Rayford thought. *Somehow World War III seems more than excitement.*

Carpathia's eyes were ablaze, and he rubbed his hands

together, as if thrilled with what was going on. "Well, people," he said, "we need to get headed home."

Rayford knew Carpathia meant home to New Babylon, home to Hattie Durham, home to Suite 216, the potentate's entire floor of luxuriously appointed offices in the extravagant and sparkling Global Community headquarters. Despite Rayford and Amanda's sprawling, two-story condo within the same four-block complex, neither had ever remotely considered New Babylon home.

Still rubbing his hands as if he could barely contain himself, Carpathia turned to the guard with the walkie-talkie. "What is the latest?"

The uniformed GC officer had a wire plugged in his ear and appeared startled that he had been addressed directly by Carpathia himself. He yanked out the earplug and stammered, "What? I mean, pardon me, Mr. Potentate, sir."

Carpathia leveled his eyes at the man. "What is the news? What is happening?"

"Uh, nothing much different, sir. Lots of activity and destruction in many major cities."

It seemed to Rayford that Carpathia was having trouble manufacturing a look of pain. "Is this activity largely centered in the Midwest and East Coast?" the potentate asked.

The guard nodded. "And some in the South," he added.

"Virtually nothing on the West Coast then," Carpathia said, more a statement than a question. The guard nodded. Rayford wondered if anyone other than those who believed Carpathia was Antichrist himself would have interpreted Carpathia's look as one of satisfaction, almost glee. "How about Dallas/Ft. Worth?" Carpathia asked.

"DFW suffered a hit," the guard said. "Only one major runway is still open. Nothing's coming in, but lots of planes are heading out of there."

Carpathia glanced at Rayford. "And the military strip nearby, where my pilot was certified on the 757?"

"I believe that's still operational, sir," the guard said.

"All right then, very good," Carpathia said. He turned to Fortunato. "I am certain no one knows our whereabouts, but just in case, what do you have for me?"

The man opened a canvas bag that seemed incongruous to Rayford. Apparently he had gathered Air Force leftovers for a disguise for Carpathia. He produced a cap that didn't match a huge, dress overcoat. Carpathia quickly donned the getup and motioned that the four others in the room should gather around him. "The jet pilot is where?" he asked.

"Waiting just outside the door, per your instructions, sir," Fortunato said.

Carpathia pointed to the armed guard. "Thank you for your service. You may return to your post via the helicopter. Mr. Fortunato and the Steeles and I will be flown to a new plane, on which Captain Steele will transport me back to New Babylon."

Rayford spoke up. "And that is in—?"

Carpathia raised a hand to silence him. "Let us not

give our young friend here any information he would have to be responsible for," he said, smiling at the uniformed guard. "You may go." As the man hurried away, Carpathia spoke quietly to Rayford. "The Condor 216 awaits us near Dallas. We will then fly west to go east, if you know what I mean."

"I've never heard of a Condor 216," Rayford said. "It's unlikely I'm qualified to—"

"I have been assured," Carpathia interrupted, "that you are more than qualified."

"But what *is* a Condor 2—"

"A hybrid I designed and named myself," Carpathia said. "Surely you do not think what has happened here today was a surprise to me."

"I'm learning," Rayford said, sneaking a glance at Amanda, who appeared to be seething.

"You are learning," Carpathia repeated, smiling broadly. "I like that. Come, let me tell you about my spectacular new aircraft as we travel."

Fortunato raised a forefinger. "Sir, my recommendation is that you and I run together to the end of the airstrip and board the jet. The Steeles should follow when they see us get on board."

Carpathia held the oversized hat down onto his styled hair and slipped in behind Fortunato as the aide opened the door and nodded to the waiting jet pilot. The pilot immediately took off running toward the Learjet as Fortunato and Carpathia jogged several yards behind. Rayford slipped an arm around Amanda's waist and drew her close.

"Rayford," Amanda said, "have you ever once in your life heard Nicolae Carpathia misspeak?"

"Misspeak?"

"Stutter, stammer, have to repeat a word, forget a name?"

Rayford suppressed a smile, amazed he could find anything humorous on what could easily be the last day of his life on earth. "Besides your name, in other words?"

"He does that on purpose, and you know it," she said.

Rayford shrugged. "You're probably right. But with what motive?"

"I have no idea," she said.

"Hon, do you see no irony in your being offended by the man we're convinced is the Antichrist?" Amanda stared at him. "I mean," he continued, "listen to yourself. You expect common courtesy and decency from the most evil man in the history of the universe?"

Amanda shook her head and looked away. "When you put it that way," she muttered, "I suppose I am being oversensitive."

Buck sat in the sales manager's office of a Land Rover dealership. "You never cease to amaze me," Chloe whispered.

"I've never been conventional, have I?"

"Hardly, and now I suppose any hope of normalcy is out the window."

"I don't need any excuse for being unique," he said,

"but everyone everywhere will be acting impulsively soon enough."

The sales manager, who had busied himself with paperwork and figuring a price, turned the documents and slid them across the desk toward Buck. "You're not trading the Lincoln, then?"

"No, that's a rental," Buck said. "But I am going to ask you to return that to O'Hare for me." Buck looked up at the man without regard to the documents.

"That's highly unusual," the sales manager said. "I'd have to send two of my people and an extra vehicle so they could get back."

Buck stood. "I suppose I am asking too much. Another dealer will be willing to go the extra mile to sell me a vehicle, I'm sure, especially when no one knows what tomorrow may bring."

"Sit back down, Mr. Williams. I won't have any trouble getting my district manager to sign off on throwing in that little errand for you. As you can see, you're going to be able to drive your fully loaded Range Rover out of here within an hour for under six figures."

"Make it half an hour," Buck said, "and we've got a deal."

The sales manager rose and thrust out his hand. "Deal."

TWO

THE Learjet was a six-seater. Carpathia and Fortunato, deep in conversation, ignored Rayford and Amanda as the couple passed. The Steeles ducked into the last two seats and held hands. Rayford knew global terror was entirely new to Amanda. It was new to *him*. On this scale, it was new to everyone. She gripped his hands so tight his fingers turned white. She was shuddering.

Carpathia turned in his seat to face them. He had that fighting-a-grin look Rayford found so maddening in light of the situation. "I know you are not certified on these little speedsters," Carpathia said, "but you might learn something in the copilot's chair."

Rayford was much more worried about the plane he would be expected to fly out of Dallas, something he had never seen or even heard of. He looked at Amanda, hoping she would plead with him to stay with her, but she quickly let go of his hand and nodded. Rayford climbed toward the cockpit, which was separated from the other seats by a thin panel. He strapped himself in and looked apologetically at the pilot, who offered his hand and said, "Chico Hernandez, Captain Steele. Don't worry, I've already done the preflight check, and I don't really need any help."

"I wouldn't be of any help anyway," Rayford said. "I haven't flown anything smaller than a 707 for years."

"Compared to what you usually fly," Hernandez said, "this will seem like a motorbike."

And that's exactly what it seemed to Rayford. The Learjet screamed and whined as Hernandez carefully lined it up on the runway. They seemed to hit top ground speed in seconds and quickly lifted off, banking hard to the right and setting a course for Dallas. "What tower do you connect with?" Rayford asked.

"The tower's empty at Glenview," Hernandez said.

"I noticed."

"I'll let a few towers know I'm coming along the way. The weather people tell us we're clear all the way, and Global Community intelligence spots no enemy aircraft between here and touchdown."

Enemy aircraft, Rayford thought. *There's an interesting way to refer to American militia forces.* He recalled not liking the militias, not understanding them, assuming them criminals. But that had been when the American government was also their enemy. Now they were allies of lame duck United States President Gerald Fitzhugh, and their enemy was Rayford's enemy—his boss, of all things, but his enemy nonetheless. Rayford had no idea where Hernandez came from, what his background was, whether he was sympathetic and loyal to Carpathia or had been pressed into reluctant service as Rayford himself had. Rayford slipped on earphones and found the proper dials so he could communicate to the pilot without allowing for anyone else to hear. "This is your pretend first officer," he said softly. "Do you read me?"

"Loud and clear, 'Copilot'," Hernandez said. And as if reading Rayford's mind, Hernandez added, "This channel is secure."

Rayford took that to mean that no one else, inside or outside the plane, could hear their conversation. That made sense. But why had Hernandez said that? Had he realized that Rayford wanted to talk? And how comfortable would Rayford be talking to a stranger? Just because they were fellow pilots didn't mean he could bare his soul to this man. "I'm curious about *Global Community One*," Rayford said.

"You haven't heard?" Hernandez asked.

"Negative."

Hernandez shot a glance behind him at Carpathia and Fortunato. Rayford chose not to turn, so as not to arouse any suspicion. Apparently, Hernandez had found Carpathia and Fortunato in earnest discussions again, because he told what he knew about Rayford's former plane.

"I suppose the potentate would have told you himself if he had had the chance," Hernandez said. "There's not good news out of New York."

"I heard that," Rayford said. "But I hadn't heard how widespread the damage was at the major airports."

"Just about total destruction, I understand. We know for sure that the hangar where she was located was virtually vaporized."

"And the pilot?"

"Earl Halliday? He was long gone by the time of the attack."

"He's safe then?" Rayford said. "That's a relief! Do you know him?"

"Not personally," Hernandez said. "But I've heard a lot about him in the past few weeks."

"From Carpathia?" Rayford said.

"No. From the North American delegation to the Global Community."

Rayford was lost, but he didn't want to admit it. Why would the North American delegation be talking about Earl Halliday? Carpathia had asked Rayford to find someone to fly the *Global Community One* 757 to New York while Rayford and Amanda were taking a brief vacation in Chicago. Carpathia was to spend a few days confusing the press and the insurrectionists (President Fitzhugh and several American militia groups) by ignoring his published itinerary and being shuttled from place to place. When the militia attacked and the Global Community retaliated, Rayford had assumed that at least the timing was a surprise. He also assumed that his selection of his old friend and boss at Pan-Continental Airlines as the one to ferry the empty 757 to New York was of little consequence to Nicolae Carpathia. But apparently Carpathia and the North American delegation had known exactly whom he would choose. What was the point of that? And how did Halliday know to get out of New York in time to avoid being killed?

"Where is Halliday now?" Rayford asked.

"You'll see him in Dallas."

Rayford squinted, trying to make it all compute. "I will?"

"Who did you think was going to take you through the paces of the new aircraft?"

When Carpathia had told Rayford he might learn a few things by sitting in the copilot's chair, Rayford had had no idea it would entail more than a few interesting tidbits about this quick, small jet. "Let me get this straight," he said. "Earl Halliday knew about the new plane and is conversant enough to teach me to drive it?"

Hernandez smiled as he scanned the horizon and maneuvered the Learjet. "Earl Halliday practically built the Condor 216 himself. He helped design it. He made sure anyone who was certified on a seven-five-seven would be able to fly it, even though it's much bigger and a whole sight more sophisticated than *Global Community One.*"

Rayford felt an ironic emotion rise within him. He hated Carpathia and knew precisely who he was. But as strange as his wife's taking offense at Carpathia's insistence on getting her name wrong, Rayford suddenly felt left out of the loop. "I wonder why I would not have been informed of a new plane, especially if I am supposed to be its pilot," he said.

"I can't say for sure," Hernandez said, "but you know the potentate tends to be very wary, very careful, and very calculating."

Don't I know it? Rayford thought. *Conniving and scheming is more like it.* "So he apparently doesn't trust me."

"I'm not sure he trusts anyone," Hernandez said. "If I were in his shoes, I wouldn't either. Would you?"

"Would I what?"

"Would you trust anyone if you were Carpathia?" Hernandez said.

Rayford did not respond.

"Do you feel like you just spent the devil's money?" Chloe asked Buck as he carefully pulled the beautiful, new, earth-toned Range Rover out of the dealership and into traffic.

"I *know* I did," Buck said. "And the Antichrist has never invested a better dollar for the cause of God."

"You consider spending almost a hundred thousand dollars on a toy like this an investment in our cause?"

"Chloe," Buck said carefully, "look at this rig. It has everything. It will go anywhere. It's indestructible. It comes with a phone. It comes with a citizen's band radio. It comes with a fire extinguisher, a survival kit, flares, you name it. It has four-wheel drive, all-wheel drive, independent suspension, a CD player that plays those new two-inch jobs, electrical outlets in the dashboard that allow you to connect whatever you want directly to the battery."

"But Buck, you slapped down your *Global Community Weekly* credit card as if it were your own. What kind of a limit do you have on that thing?"

"Most of the cards Carpathia issues like this have a quarter-of-a-million-dollar limit," Buck said. "But those of us at senior levels have a special code built into ours. They're unlimited."

"Literally unlimited?"

"Didn't you see the eyes of that sales manager when he phoned for verification?"

"All I saw," Chloe said, "was a smile and a done deal."

"There you go."

"But doesn't somebody have to approve purchases like that?"

"I report directly to Carpathia. He might want to know why I bought a Range Rover. But it should certainly be easy enough to explain, what with the loss of our apartment, our vehicles, and the need to be able to get wherever we have to go."

Once again, Buck soon grew impatient with the traffic. This time, when he left the road and made his way through ditches, gullies, parkways, alleys, and yards, the ride was sure and, if not smooth, purposeful. That vehicle was made for this kind of driving.

"Look what else this baby has," Buck said. "You can switch between automatic or manual transmission."

Chloe leaned down to look at the floorboard. "What do you do with the clutch when you're in automatic?"

"You ignore it," Buck said. "You ever drive a stick?"

"A friend in college had a little foreign sports car with a stick shift," she said. "I loved it."

"You wanna drive?"

"Not on your life. At least not now. Let's just get to the church."

"Anything else I should know about what we're going to encounter in Dallas?" Rayford asked Hernandez.

"You're gonna be ferrying a lot of VIPs back to Iraq," Hernandez said. "But that's nothing new for you, is it?"

"Nope. I'm afraid it's lost its luster by now."

"Well, for what it's worth, I envy you."

Rayford was stunned to silence. Here he was, what Bruce Barnes referred to as a tribulation saint, a believer in Christ during the most horrifying period in human history, serving Antichrist himself against his own will and certainly at the peril of his wife, his daughter, her husband, and himself. And yet he was envied.

"Don't envy me, Captain Hernandez. Whatever you do, don't envy me."

As Buck neared the church, he noticed yards full of people. They stared at the sky and listened to radios and

TVs that blared from inside their houses. Buck was surprised to see one lone car in the parking lot at New Hope. It belonged to Loretta, Bruce's assistant.

"I don't look forward to this," Chloe said.

"I hear you," Buck said.

They found the woman, now nearly seventy, sitting stiffly in the outer office staring at the television. Two balled-up tissues rested in her lap, and she riffled a third in her bony fingers. Her reading glasses rode low on her nose, and she peered over the top of them at the television. She did not seem to look Buck and Chloe's way as they entered, but it soon became clear she knew they were there. From the inner office, Buck heard a computer printer producing page after page after page.

Loretta had been a southern belle in her day. Now she sat red-eyed and sniffling, fingers working that tissue as if creating some piece of art. Buck glanced up to see a helicopter view of the bombed-out Northwest Community Hospital. "People been callin'," Loretta said. "I don't know what to tell 'em. He couldn't survive that, could he? Pastor Bruce, I mean. He couldn't still be alive now, could he? Did y'all see him?"

"We didn't see him," Chloe said carefully, kneeling next to the old woman. "But my dad did."

Loretta turned quickly to stare at her. "Mr. Steele saw him? And is he all right?"

Chloe shook her head. "I'm sorry, ma'am, he's not. Bruce is gone."

Loretta lowered her chin to her chest. Tears gathered and pooled in her half-glasses. She spoke hoarsely.

"Would y'all mind turnin' that off then, please. I was just praying I'd catch a glimpse of Pastor Bruce. But if he's under one of those sheets, I don't care to see that."

Buck turned off the TV as Chloe embraced the old woman. Loretta broke down and sobbed. "That young man was like family to me, you know."

"We know," Chloe said, crying herself now. "He was family to us, too."

Loretta pulled back to look at Chloe. "But he was my *only* family. You know my story, don't you?"

"Yes, ma'am—"

"You know I lost everybody."

"Yes, ma'am."

"I mean, everybody. I lost every living relative I had. More than a hundred. I came from one of the most devout, spiritual heritages a woman could come from. I was considered a pillar of this church. I was active in everythin', a church woman. I just never really knew the Lord."

Chloe held her close and cried with her.

"That young man taught me everythin'," Loretta continued. "I learned more from him in two years than I learned in more than sixty years in Sunday school and church before that. I'm not blamin' anybody but myself. I was deaf and blind spiritually. My daddy had gone on before, but I lost Mama, all six of my brothers and sisters, all of their kids, their kids' husbands and wives. I lost my own children and grandchildren. Everybody. If somebody had made a list of who in this church would be most likely to go to heaven when they died, I would

28

have been at the top of the list, right up there with the pastor."

This was as painful for Buck as it seemed for Chloe and Loretta. He would grieve in his own way and his own time, but for now he didn't want to dwell on the tragedy. "What're you working on in the office, ma'am?" he said.

Loretta cleared her throat. "Bruce's stuff, of course," she managed.

"What is it?"

"Well, you know when he got back from that big teaching trip of his in Indonesia, he had some sort of a virus or something. One of the men rushed him to the hospital so fast that he left his laptop computer here. You know he took that thing with him everywhere he went."

"I know he did," Chloe said.

"Well, as soon as he was settled into that hospital, he called me. He asked me to bring that laptop to him if I could. I would've done anythin' for Bruce, of course. I was on my way out the door with it when the phone rang again. Bruce told me they were taking him out of the emergency room and straight to intensive care, so he wouldn't be able to have any visitors for a while. I think he had a premonition."

"A premonition?" Buck said.

"I think he knew he might die," she said. "He told me to keep in touch with the hospital for when he could have visitors. He was fond of me, but I know he wanted that laptop more than he wanted to see me."

"I'm not so sure about that," Chloe said. "He loved you like a mother."

"I know that's true," Loretta said. "He told me that more than once. Anyway, he asked if I would print out everything he had on his hard drive off his computer, you know, everything except what he called program files and all that."

"What?" Chloe asked. "His own Bible studies and sermon preparation, stuff like that?"

"I guess," Loretta said. "He told me to make sure I had plenty of paper. I thought he meant like just a ream or something."

"It's taken more than that?" Buck said.

"Oh, yes sir, much more than that. I stood there feeding that machine every two hundred pages or so until I'd finished up two reams. I'm scared to death of those computers, but Bruce talked me through how to print out everything that had a file name that began with his initials. He told me if I just typed in 'Print BB*.*' that it should spit out everything he wanted. I sure hope I did the right thing. It's given him more than he could ever want. I suppose I should just shut it down now."

"You've got a third ream going in there?" Chloe said.

"No. I got some help from Donny."

"The phone guy?" Buck said.

"Oh, Donny Moore is a whole lot more than just a phone guy," Loretta said. "There's hardly anything electronic he can't fix or make better. He showed me how I can use those old boxes of continuous-feed computer paper in our laser printer. He just hauled a box out and fed it in one end and it comes out the other so I don't have to keep feeding it."

"I didn't know you could do that," Buck said.

"Neither did I," Loretta said. "There's a lot of stuff Donny knows that I don't. He said our printer was pretty new and fancy and should be kicking out close to fifteen pages a minute."

"And you've been doing this how long?" Chloe said.

"Just about ever since I talked to Bruce from the hospital this morning. There was probably a five- or ten-minute break after those first two reams and before Donny helped me get that big box of paper under there."

Buck slipped into the inner office and stood watching in amazement as the high-tech printer drew page after page from the paper box through its innards and out the other side into a stack that was threatening to topple. He straightened the stack and stared at the box. The first two reams of printed material, all single-spaced, lay neatly on Bruce's desk. The old paper box, the likes of which Buck hadn't seen in years, noted that it contained five thousand sheets. He guessed that it had already used 80 percent of its total. Surely, there must be some mistake. Could Bruce have produced more than five thousand pages of notes? Perhaps there was a glitch and Loretta had mistakenly printed everything, including program files, Bibles and concordances, dictionaries, and the like.

But there had been no glitch. Buck casually fanned through first one ream and then the other, looking for something other than Bruce's own notes. Every page

Buck glanced at contained personal writing from Bruce. This included his own commentary on Bible passages, sermon notes, devotional thoughts, and letters to friends and relatives and churchmen from around the globe. At first Buck felt guilty, as if he were invading Bruce's privacy. And yet why had Bruce urged Loretta to print all this stuff? Was he afraid he might be gone? Had he wanted to leave it for their use?

Buck bent over the fast-rising stack of continuous-feed sheets. He lifted it from the bottom and allowed the pages to drop before his eyes one at a time. Again, page after page of single-spaced copy, all from Bruce. He must have written several pages a day for more than two years.

When Buck rejoined Chloe and Loretta, Loretta said again, "We might as well shut it off and throw the pages away. He'll have no use for all that stuff now."

Chloe had risen and now sat, looking exhausted, in a side chair. It was Buck's turn to kneel before Loretta. He placed his hands on her shoulders and spoke earnestly. "Loretta, you can still serve the Lord by serving Bruce." She began to protest, but he continued. "He's gone, yes, but we can rejoice that he's with his family again, can't we?" Loretta pressed her lips together and nodded. Buck continued. "I need your help on a big project. There's a gold mine in that room. From just glancing at those pages, I can see that Bruce is still with us. His knowl-edge, his teaching, his love and compassion, they are all there. The best we can do for this little flock that has lost its shepherd is to get those pages reproduced. I don't know what this place will do for a pastor or a teacher, but in the meantime, people need access to what Bruce has written. Maybe they've heard him preach it, maybe they've seen it in other forms before. But this is a treasure that everyone can use."

Chloe spoke up. "Buck, shouldn't you try to edit it or shape it into some sort of book form first?"

"I'll take a look at it, Chloe, but there's a certain beauty in simply reproducing it in the form it's in. This was Bruce off-the-cuff, in the middle of his study, writing to fellow believers, writing to friends and loved ones, writing to himself. I think Loretta ought to take all those pages to a quick-print shop and get them started. We need a thousand copies of all that stuff, printed on two sides and bound simply."

"That'll cost a fortune," Loretta said.

"Don't worry about that now," Buck said. "I can't think of a better investment."

As the Learjet made its initial descent into the Dallas/Ft. Worth area, Fortunato ducked into the cockpit and knelt between Hernandez and Rayford. Each slipped the headphone off the ear closest to Carpathia's aide. "Anybody hungry?" he said.

Rayford hadn't even thought of food. For all he knew, the world was blowing itself to bits and no one would survive this war. The very mention of hunger, however, triggered something in him. He realized he was famished.

He knew Amanda would be as well. She was a light eater, and he often had to make sure she remembered to eat.

"I could eat," Hernandez said. "In fact, I could eat a lot."

"Potentate Carpathia would like you to contact DFW tower and have something nice waiting for us."

Hernandez suddenly looked panicky. "What do you think he means by 'something nice'?"

"I'm sure you'll arrange for something appropriate, Captain Hernandez."

Fortunato backed out of the cockpit and Hernandez rolled his eyes at Rayford. "DFW tower, this is *Global Community Three,* over."

Rayford glanced back as Fortunato took his seat. Carpathia had swung around and was in deep conversation with Amanda.

———

Chloe worked with Loretta in fashioning a terse, two-sentence statement that was sent out by phone to the six names at the top of the prayer chain list. Each would call others who would call others, and the news would quickly spread throughout the New Hope body. Meanwhile, Buck recorded a brief message on the answering machine that simply said: "The tragic news of Pastor Bruce's death is true. Elder Rayford Steele saw him and believes he may have died before any explosives hit the hospital. Please do not come to the church, as there will be no meetings or services or further announcements until Sunday at the regular time." Buck turned the ringer off on the phone and directed all calls to the answering machine, which soon began clicking every few minutes, as more and more parishioners called in for confirmation. Buck knew Sunday morning's meeting would be packed.

Chloe agreed to follow Loretta home and make sure she was all right while Buck was calling Donny Moore. "Donny," Buck said, "I need your advice, and I need it right away."

"Mr. Williams, sir," came Donny's characteristic staccato delivery, "advice is my middle name. And as you know, I work at home, so I can come to you or you can come to me and we can talk whenever you want."

"Donny, I'm not mobile just now, so if you could find your way clear to visiting me at the church, I'd sure appreciate it."

"I'll be right over, Mr. Williams, but could you tell me something first? Did Loretta have the phones off the hook there for a while?"

"Yes, I believe she did. She didn't have answers for people who were calling about Pastor Bruce. With nothing to tell people, she just turned off the phones.

"That's a relief," Donny said. "I just got her set up with a new system a few weeks ago, so I hope nothing was wrong. How is Bruce, by the way?"

"I'll tell you all about that when you get here, Donny, OK?"

———————

Rayford saw billowing black clouds over the Dallas/ Ft. Worth commercial airport and thought of the many times he had landed big craft on those long runways. How long would it take to rebuild here? Captain Hernandez guided the Learjet to a nearby military strip, the one Rayford had visited so recently. He saw no other aircraft on the ground. Clearly, someone had moved all the planes to keep the strip from being a target.

Hernandez landed the Learjet as smoothly as a man can land a plane that small, and they immediately taxied to the end of the runway and directly into a large hangar. Rayford was surprised that, indeed, the rest of the hangar was empty, too. Hernandez shut down the engines, and they deplaned. As soon as Carpathia had room, he put back on his disguise. He whispered something to Fortunato, who asked Hernandez where they would find the food. "Hangar three," Hernandez said. "We're in hangar one. The plane's in hangar four."

The disguise proved unnecessary. There was not much space between the hangars, and the small contingent moved quickly into and out of small doors at the sides of the buildings. Hangars two and three were also empty, except for a table piled with catered lunches near the side door that led to hangar four.

They approached the tables, and Carpathia turned to Rayford. "Say good-bye to Captain Hernandez," he said. "After he has eaten, he will be on assignment for me near the old National Security Agency building in Maryland.

It is unlikely you will see him again. He flies only the small craft."

It was all Rayford could do to keep from shrugging. What did he care? He had just met the man. Why was it so important for Carpathia to keep him updated on personnel? He had not told Rayford of Earl Halliday's involvement in helping design a new plane. He had not told Rayford that he expected to need a new plane. He had not even sought Rayford's input about the plane he would be flying. Rayford would never understand the man.

Rayford ate ravenously and tried to encourage Amanda to eat more than usual. She did not. As the group made its last move between hangars, Rayford heard the characteristic whine of the Learjet and realized Hernandez was already airborne. Interestingly, Fortunato disappeared soon after they entered hangar four. There, standing at attention in a neat row, were four of the ten international ambassadors who represented huge land masses and populations and reported directly to Carpathia. Rayford had no idea where they had been or how they had gotten here. All he knew was that it was his job to get them all to New Babylon for emergency meetings in light of the outbreak of World War III.

At the end of the row was Earl Halliday, standing stiffly and staring straight ahead. Carpathia shook hands with each of the four ambassadors in turn and ignored Halliday, who seemed to expect that. Rayford walked directly to Halliday and stuck out his hand. Halliday ignored it and spoke under his breath. "Get away from me, Steele, you scum!"

"Earl!"

"I mean it, Rayford. I have to bring you up to speed on this plane, but I don't have to pretend to like it."

Rayford backed away, feeling awkward, and joined Amanda, who had been left alone and looked out of place herself.

"Rayford, what in the world is Earl doing here?" she asked.

"I'll tell you later. He's not happy, I can tell you that. What was Carpathia talking to you about on the plane?"

"He wanted to know what I wanted to eat, of all things. That man!"

Two aides from New Babylon entered and greeted Carpathia with embraces. One motioned for Earl and Rayford to join him in a corner of the hangar as far from the Condor 216 as they could get. Rayford had purposely avoided staring at the monstrous aircraft. Though it sat facing the door that would open to the runway and was more than 150 feet from where they stood, still the Condor seemed to dominate the hangar. Rayford had known from a glance that here was a plane that had been in development for years, not just months. It was clearly the biggest passenger plane he had ever seen, and it was painted such a brilliant white that it seemed to disappear against the light walls in the dimly lit hangar. He could only imagine how difficult it would be to spot in the sky.

Carpathia's aide, dressed just like Carpathia in a

natty black suit, white shirt, and bloodred tie with a gold stickpin, leaned in close to Rayford and Earl and spoke earnestly. "Potentate Carpathia would like to be airborne as soon as possible. Can you give us an estimated time of departure?"

"I've never even seen this plane," Rayford said, "and I have no idea—"

"Rayford," Earl interrupted, "I'm telling you, you can fly this plane within half an hour. I know you; I know planes. So trust me."

"Well, that's interesting, Earl, but I won't make any promises until I've been put through the paces."

The Carpathia wanna-be turned to Halliday. "Are you available to fly this plane, at least until Steele here feels he's—"

"No sir, I am not!" Halliday said. "Just let me have Steele for thirty minutes and then let me get back to Chicago."

Donny Moore proved more of a talker than Buck appreciated, but he decided feigning interest was a small price for the man's expertise. "So, you're a phone systems guy, but you sell computers—"

"On the side, right, yes sir. Just about double my income that way. Got a trunk full of catalogs, you know."

"I'd like to see those," Buck said.

Donny grinned. "I thought you might." He opened his briefcase and pulled out a stack, apparently one of each of the manufacturers he represented. He spread six out before Buck on the coffee table.

"Whoa," Buck said, "I can see already there are going to be too many choices. Why don't you just let me tell you what I'm looking for, and you tell me if you can deliver?"

"I can tell you right now I can deliver," Donny said. "Last week I sold a guy thirty sub-notebooks with more power than any desktop anywhere, and—"

"Excuse me a moment, Donny," Buck said. "Did you hear that printer quit?"

"I sure did. It just stopped now. It's either out of paper, out of ink, or done with whatever it was doing. I sold that machine to Bruce, you know. Top of the line. Prints regular paper, continuous feed—whatever you need."

"Let me just check on it," Buck said. He rose and peeked into the inner office. The screen on Bruce's laptop had already suspended itself. No warning lights on the printer told of shortages of ink or paper. Buck pushed a button on the laptop and the screen came alive. It indicated the print job was finally over. Buck guessed there were about a hundred pages left from the five-thousand-page box Loretta had run through the printer. *What a treasure,* Buck thought.

"When's Bruce gonna be back here?" Buck heard Donny ask from the other room.

Rayford and Earl boarded the Condor alone. Earl held a finger to his lips and Rayford assumed he was looking for bugs. He checked the intercom system thoroughly before speaking. "You never know," he said.

"Tell me about it," Rayford said.

"*You* tell *me* about it, Rayford!"

"Earl, I'm much more in the dark than you are. I didn't even know you were involved in this project. I had no idea you were working for Carpathia. You knew I was, so why didn't you tell me?"

"I'm not working for Carpathia, Rayford. I was pressed into service. I'm still a Pan-Con chief pilot at O'Hare, but when duty calls—"

"Why didn't Carpathia tell me he was aware of you?" Rayford said. "He asked me to find somebody to fly *Global Community One* into New York. He didn't know I would choose you."

"He must have," Earl said. "Who else would you pick? I was asked to help design this new plane, and I thought it would be fun just to test it a little bit. Then I get asked to fly the original plane to New York. Since the request came from you, I was flattered and honored. It was only when I got on the ground and realized the plane and I were targets that I got out of New York and headed back to Chicago as fast as I could. I never got there. I got word from Carpathia's people while I was in the air that I was needed in Dallas to brief you on this plane."

"I'm lost," Rayford said.

"Well, I don't know much either," Earl said. "But it's clear Carpathia wanted my going to New York and winding up dead to look like your decision, not his."

"Why would he want you dead?"

"Maybe I know too much."

"I've been flying him all over the place," Rayford said. "I have to know more than you, and yet I don't sense he's thinking about doing me in."

"Just watch your back, Rayford. I've heard enough to know this is not all what it seems to be and that this man does not have the world's best interests at heart."

There's the understatement of the ages, Rayford thought.

"I don't know how you got me into this, Rayford, but—"

"*I* got *you* into this? Earl, you have a short memory. You're the one who encouraged me to become the pilot of *Air Force One.* I wasn't looking for that job, and I certainly never dreamed it would turn into this."

"Piloting *Air Force One* was a plum assignment," Earl said, "whether you recognized that at the time or not. How was I to know what would come of it?"

"Let's stop blaming each other and decide what we're supposed to do now."

"Ray, I'm gonna bring you up to speed on this plane, but then I think I'm a dead man. Would you tell my wife that—"

"Earl, what are you talking about? Why do you think you won't make it back to Chicago?"

"I have no idea, Ray. All I know is that I was supposed to be in New York with that plane when it got obliterated. I don't see myself as any threat to the Carpathia administration, but if they cared a whit about me, they would have gotten me out of New York before I had the idea I'd better get out of there."

"Can't you get yourself some sort of emergency assignment at DFW? There has to be a huge need for Pan-Con personnel over there, in light of everything."

"Carpathia's people have arranged a ride back to Chicago for me. I just have this feeling I'm not safe."

"Tell them you don't want to put them out. Tell them you've got plenty of work to do at DFW."

"I'll try. Meanwhile, let me show you this rig. And Ray, as an old friend, I want you to promise me that if anything does happen to me—"

"Nothing is going to happen to you, Earl. But of course I'll keep in touch with your wife either way."

Donny Moore fell silent at the tragic news. He sat staring, eyes wide, seemingly unable to form words. Buck busied himself leafing through the catalogs. He couldn't concentrate. He knew there would be more questions. He didn't know what to tell Donny. And he needed this man's help.

Donny's voice came hoarse with emotion. "What's gonna happen to this church?"

"I know this sounds like a cliché," Buck said, "but I believe God will provide."

"How will God provide anybody like Pastor Bruce?"

"I know what you mean, Donny. Whoever it is won't be another Pastor Bruce. He was unique."

"I'm still having trouble believing it," Donny said. "But I don't guess anything should surprise me anymore."

———————

Rayford sat behind the controls of the Condor 216. "What am I supposed to do for a first officer?" he asked Earl.

"They've got somebody on his way over from one of the other airlines. He'll fly with you as far as San Francisco, where McCullum will join you."

"McCullum? He copiloted for me from New Babylon to Washington, Earl. When I went to Chicago, he was supposed to go back to Iraq."

"I only know what I'm told, Rayford."

"And why are we flying west to go east, as Carpathia says?"

"I have no idea what's going on here, Rayford. I'm new to this. Maybe you know better than I do. The fact is, most of the war and devastation seems to be east of the Mississippi. Have you noticed that? It's almost as if it was planned. This plane was designed and built here in Dallas, but not at DFW where it might have been destroyed. It's ready for you just when you need it. As you can see it has the controls of a seven-five-seven and yet it's a much bigger plane. If you can fly a 'fifty-seven, you can fly this. You just need to get used to the size of it. The people you need are where you need them when you need them. Figure it out, boy. None of this seems a surprise to Carpathia, does it?"

Rayford had no idea what to say. It didn't take long to catch on.

Halliday continued, "You'll fly on a straight line from Dallas to San Francisco, and my guess is you won't see any devastation from the air, and you won't be threatened from attack heading that way either. There might be militia people somewhere out west who would like to shoot rockets at Carpathia, but there are precious few people who know he's heading that way. You'll stop in San Francisco just long enough to get rid of this copilot and pick up your usual one."

———

Buck touched Donny's arm, as if rousing him from sleep. Donny looked at him blankly. "Mr. Williams, this has all been hard enough even with Pastor Bruce here. I don't know what we're going to do now."

"Donny," Buck said gravely, "you have an opportunity here to do something for God, and it's the greatest memorial tribute you could ever give to Bruce Barnes."

"Well then, sir, whatever it is, I want to do it."

"First, Donny, let me assure you that money is no object."

"I don't want any profit off something that will help the church and God and Bruce's memory."

"Fine. Whatever profit you build in or don't build in is up to you. I'm just telling you that I need five of the absolute best, top-of-the-line computers, as small and compact as they can be, but with as much power and memory and speed and communications abilities as you can wire into them."

"You're talking my language, Mr. Williams."

"I hope so, Donny, because I want a computer with virtually no limitations. I want to be able to take it anywhere, keep it reasonably concealed, store everything I want on it, and most of all, be able to connect with anyone anywhere without the transmission being traced. Is that doable?"

"Well, sir, I can put together something for you like those computers that scientists use in the jungle or in the desert when there's no place to plug in or hook up to."

"Yeah," Buck said. "Some of our reporters use those in remote areas. What do they have, built-in satellite dishes?"

"Believe it or not, it *is* something like that. And I can add another feature for you, too."

"What's that?"

"Video conferencing."

"You mean I can see the person I'm talking to while I'm talking to him?"

"Yes, if he has the same technology on his machine."

"I want all of it, Donny. And I want it fast. And I need you to keep this confidential."

"Mr. Williams, these machines could run you more than twenty thousand dollars apiece."

Buck had thought money would be no object, but this was one expense he could not lay off on Carpathia. He sat back and whistled through his teeth.

THREE

"CALL it a hunch, Rayford, but I put something in here just for you."

Rayford and Earl were finished in the cockpit. He trusted Earl. He knew that if Earl thought he could fly this thing, then he could. He still was going to insist on his and his temporary first officer's taking off, staging, and landing before he risked flying anyone else. It wouldn't have bothered Rayford to crash and kill himself along with the Antichrist, but he didn't want to be responsible for innocent lives, particularly that of his own wife.

"So, what did you do for me, Earl?"

"Just look at this," Earl said. He pointed to the button that allowed the captain to speak to the passengers.

"Captain's intercom," Rayford said. "So what?"

"Reach under your seat with your left hand and run

your fingers along the side edge of the bottom of your chair," Earl said.

"I feel a button."

"I'm going to step back into the cabin now," Earl said. "You mash the normal intercom button and make an announcement. Wait for a count of three, and then push that button under your seat. Make sure your headphones are still on."

Rayford waited until Halliday had left and latched the cockpit door. Rayford got on the intercom. "Hello, hello, hey Earl yada yada yada." Rayford counted silently to himself, then pushed the button under his seat. He was amazed to hear through his earphones Earl Halliday speaking in just above a whisper. "Rayford, you can tell I'm speaking in lower than even conversational tones. If I did my job right, you can hear me plain as day from all over this plane. Every one of the speakers is also a transmitter and leads back to only your headphone jack. I wired it in such a way that it's undetectable, and this plane has been gone over by Global Community's best bug finders. If it's ever detected, I'll just tell them I thought that was what they wanted."

Rayford came hustling out of the cockpit. "Earl, you're a genius! I'm not sure what I'll hear, but it has to be an advantage to know what's going on out here."

Buck was boxing up all the pages from Bruce's printout when he heard the Range Rover in the parking lot. By the time Chloe reached the office, he had packaged pages and Bruce's computer into one huge carton. As he lugged it out, he told Chloe, "Drop me off at the Chicago bureau office, and then you'd better check with The Drake and be sure our stuff is still there. We'll want to keep that room until we find a place to live closer to here."

"I was hoping you'd say that," Chloe said. "Loretta is devastated. She's going to need a lot of help here. What are we going to do about a funeral?"

"You're going to have to help handle that, Chlo'. You'll want to check with the coroner's office, have the body delivered to a funeral home nearby here, and all that. With so many casualties, it's going to be a mess, so they'll probably be glad to know that at least one body has been claimed. We're each going to need a vehicle. I have no idea where I'll be expected to go. I can work out of the Chicago office in light of the fact that no one will be going to New York for a long time, but I can't promise I'll be around here all the time."

"Loretta, bless her heart, thought of the same thing in spite of all she's going through. She reminded me that there's a fleet of extra cars among the congregation and has been ever since the Rapture. They lend these out for just such crises as this one."

"Good," Buck said. "Let's get you fixed up with one of those. And remember, we're going to need to get this material reproduced for members of the congregation."

"You're not going to have time to go through all that, are you, Buck?"

"No, but I'm confident that anything in here will be profitable for all."

"Buck, wait a minute. There's no way we can reproduce that until someone has read all of it. There's got to be private, personal stuff in there. And you know there will be direct references to Carpathia and to the Tribulation Force. We can't risk being exposed like that."

Buck had an ego crisis. He loved this woman, but she was ten years his junior and he hated when it seemed as if she was telling him what to do, especially when she was right. As he lay the heavy box of pages and the computer in the back of the Range Rover, Chloe said, "Just entrust it to me, hon. I'll spend every day between now and Sunday poring over it line by line. By then we'll have something to share with the rest of New Hope, and we can even announce that we might have something in copied form for them within a week or so."

"When you're right, you're right. But where will you do this?"

"Loretta has offered to let us stay with her. She's got that big old house, you know."

"That would be perfect, but I hate to impose."

"Buck, we would hardly be imposing. She'll hardly know we're there. Anyway, I sense she's so lonely and beside herself with grief that she really needs us."

"You know it's unlikely I'll be there much," Buck said.

"I'm a big girl. I can take care of myself."

They were in the Range Rover now. "Then what do you need me for?" Buck said.

"I keep you around because you're cute."

"But seriously, Chloe, I'll never forgive myself if I'm in some other city or country and the war comes right here to Mt. Prospect."

"You've forgotten the shelter under the church."

"I haven't forgotten it, Chloe. I'm just praying it'll never come to that. Does anybody else know about that place except the Tribulation Force?"

"No. Not even Loretta. It's an awfully small place. If Daddy and Amanda and you and I had to stay there for any length of time, it wouldn't be much fun."

Half an hour later, Buck pulled into the Chicago area office of *Global Community Weekly* magazine. "I'm going to get us a couple of cell phones," Chloe said. "I'll call The Drake and then get down there and get our stuff. I'll also talk with Loretta about a second vehicle."

"Get five of those cell phones, Chloe, and don't scrimp."

"Five?" she said. "I don't know if Loretta would even know how to use one."

"I'm not thinking of Loretta. I just want to make sure we have a spare."

The Condor 216 was outfitted even more lavishly than *Global Community One* had been, if that was possible. No detail had been missed, and the latest communications devices had been installed. Rayford had bidden farewell to Earl Halliday, urging Earl to let him know

that his home was intact and his wife was safe, as soon
as he knew. "You're not going to like what's happened
to our airport," Rayford had told him. "You won't be
landing at O'Hare."

Rayford and his temporary copilot had irritated
Carpathia by making a trial takeoff and fly-around
before letting the others board the plane. Rayford was
glad he had. While it was true that everything in the
cockpit was identical to a 757, the bigger, heavier plane
behaved more like a 747, and it took some getting used
to. Now that the loaded and airborne Condor 216 was
streaking toward San Francisco at thirty-three thousand
feet and at more than seven hundred miles per hour,
Rayford put the craft on autopilot and urged his first
officer to stay alert.

"What are you going be doing, sir?" the younger man
asked.

"Just sitting here," Rayford said. "Thinking. Reading."

Rayford had cleared his flight path with an Oklahoma
tower and now pushed the button to communicate with
his passengers. "Potentate Carpathia and guests, this is
Captain Steele. Our estimated time of arrival in San
Francisco is 5:00 P.M., Pacific Standard Time. We expect
clear skies and smooth flying."

Rayford sat back and pulled his earphone band
toward the back of his head, as if pulling the phones off.
However, they were still close enough to his ears so that
he could hear and his copilot, because his own earphones
were on, could not. Rayford pulled from his flight bag a

book and opened it, resting it on the controls before him. He would have to remember to turn a page occasionally. He would not really be reading. He would be listening. He slipped his left hand under the seat and quietly depressed the hidden button.

The first voice he heard, clear as if she were talking to him on the phone, was Amanda's. "Yes, sir, I understand. You need not worry about me, no sir."

Now Carpathia spoke: "I trust everyone got enough to eat in Dallas. We will have an entire flight crew joining us in San Francisco, and we will be well taken care of throughout our flight to Baghdad and then on to New Babylon."

Another voice: "Baghdad?"

"Yes," Carpathia said. "I have taken the liberty of flying into Baghdad the remaining three loyal ambassadors. Our enemies might have assumed we would fly them directly into New Babylon. We will pick them up and begin our meetings on the short hop from Baghdad to New Babylon.

"Mrs. Steele, if you would excuse us—"

"Certainly," Amanda said.

"Gentlemen," Carpathia spoke more quietly now, but still clearly enough that Rayford could understand every word. Someday he would have to thank Earl Halliday on behalf of the kingdom of Christ. Earl had no interest in serving God, at least not yet, but whatever motivated him to do Rayford a favor like that, it was certainly going to benefit the enemies of the Antichrist.

Carpathia was saying: "Mr. Fortunato remained in

Dallas briefly to arrange my next radio broadcast from there. I will do it from here; however, it will be patched to Dallas and broadcast, again to throw off any enemies of the Global Community. I do need him in on our talks in the night, so we will wait on the ground in San Francisco until he is able to join us. As soon as we leave the ground out of San Francisco, we will trigger both L.A. and the Bay Area."

"The Bay Area?" came a heavily accented voice.

"Yes, that is San Francisco and the Oakland area."

"What do you mean by 'trigger'?"

Carpathia's tone became grave. "'Trigger' means just what it sounds like it means," he said. "By the time we land in Baghdad, more than Washington, New York, and Chicago will have been decimated. Those are just three of the North American cities that will suffer the most. So far, only the airport and one suburb have suffered in Chicago. That will change within the hour. You already know about London. Do you gentlemen understand the significance of a one-hundred-megaton bomb?"

There was silence. Carpathia continued. "To put it in perspective, history books tell us that a twenty-megaton bomb carries more power than all those dropped in World War II, including the two that fell on Japan."

"The United States of Great Britain had to be taught," came the accented voice again.

"Indeed they did," Carpathia said. "And in North America alone, Montreal, Toronto, Mexico City, Dallas, Washington, D.C., New York, Chicago, San Francisco, and Los Angeles will become object lessons to those who would oppose us."

Rayford whipped off his earphones and unbuckled himself. He stepped through the cockpit door and made eye contact with Amanda. He motioned for her to come to him. Carpathia looked up and smiled. "Captain Steele," he greeted him, "is everything well?"

"Our flight is uneventful, sir, if that's what you're asking. That's the best kind of flight. I can't say much for what's happening on the ground, however."

"True enough," Carpathia said, suddenly sober. "I will soon address the global community with my condolences."

Rayford pulled Amanda into the galley way. "Were Buck and Chloe going to stay at The Drake again tonight?"

"There wasn't time to talk about it, Ray," she said. "I can't imagine what other choice they'd have. It sounds like they may never get back to New York."

"I'm afraid Chicago is a certain someone's next target," Rayford said.

"Oh, I can't imagine," Amanda said.

"I have to warn them."

"Do you want to risk a phone call that could be traced?" she asked.

"Saving their lives would be worth any risk."

Amanda embraced him and went back to her seat.

Rayford used his own cell phone after making sure his first officer had his own earphones on and was otherwise engaged. Reaching The Drake Hotel in Chicago, Rayford asked for the Williamses. "We have three guests named Williams," he was told. "None with the first name of Cameron or Buck or Chloe."

Rayford racked his brain. "Uh, just put me through to Mr. Katz then," he said.

"Herbert Katz?" the operator said.

"That's the one."

After a minute: "No answer, sir. Would you like to leave a message on their voice mail?"

"I would," Rayford said, "but I would also like to be sure that the message light is lit and that they are flagged down for an urgent message should they visit the front desk."

"We'll certainly do that, sir. Thank you for calling The Drake."

When the voice mail tone came on, Rayford spoke quickly. "Kids, you know who this is. Don't take the time to do anything. Get as far away from downtown Chicago as you can. Please trust me on this."

Buck had had innumerable run-ins with Verna Zee in the Chicago office. Once he felt she had overstepped her bounds and had moved too quickly into her former boss's office after Lucinda Washington disappeared in the Rapture. Then, when Buck himself was demoted for ostensibly missing the most important assignment of his life, Verna did become Chicago bureau chief and lorded it over him. Now that he was the publisher, he had been tempted to fire her. But he had let her remain, provided she did the job and kept her nose clean.

Even feisty Verna seemed shell-shocked when Buck swept into the office late that afternoon. As usual in times of international crisis, the staff was huddled around the TV. A couple of employees looked up when Buck came in. "What do you think of this, chief?" one said, and several others noticed him. Verna Zee made a beeline for Buck.

"You have several urgent messages," she said. "Carpathia himself has been trying to reach you all day. There's also an urgent message from a Rayford Steele."

Now there was a choice for all time. Whom should Buck call? He could only guess what spin Carpathia wanted to put on World War III. He had no idea what Rayford might want. "Did Mr. Steele leave a number?"

"You're returning *his* call first?"

"Excuse me?" he said. "I believe I asked you a question."

"His message was simply that you should call your hotel room."

"Call my hotel room?"

"I would have done it for you myself, boss, but I didn't know where you were staying. Where *are* you staying?"

"None of your business, Verna."

"Well, pardon me!" she said and marched away, which was Buck's hope.

"I'll be borrowing your office temporarily," Buck called after her.

She stopped and spun around. "For how long?"

"For as long as I need it," he said. She scowled.

Buck rushed in and shut the door. He dialed The Drake and asked for his own room. Hearing the fear in Rayford's voice, not to mention the message itself, made the color drain from his face. Buck called information for the number of the Land Rover dealership in Arlington Heights. He asked for the sales manager and said it was an emergency.

Within a minute, the man was on the line. As soon as Buck identified himself, the man said, "Everything all right with the—"

"The car is fine, sir. But I need to reach my wife, and she's driving it right now. I need the phone number on that built-in phone."

"That would take a little digging."

"I can't tell you how urgent this is, sir. Let me just say that it's worth my developing a quick case of buyer's remorse and returning the vehicle if I can't get that number right now."

"One moment."

A couple of minutes later Buck dialed the number. It rang four times. "The mobile customer you have dialed is either away from the vehicle or out of the calling zone. Please try your call—"

Buck slammed down the phone, picked it up, and hit the redial button. While listening to the ring, he was startled when the door burst open and Verna Zee mouthed, "Carpathia on the line for you."

"I'm gonna have to call him back!" Buck said.

"You're what?!"

"Take a number!"

"Dial 1-800-FIRED," she said.

———————

Rayford was frantic. He forgot any pretense of doing anything but sitting there, and he stared straight ahead into the late afternoon sky, earphones firmly engaged and his left hand pressing the hidden button hard. He heard Carpathia's aide: "Well, of all the—"

"What?" Carpathia said.

"I'm trying to get this Williams character on the line for you, and he's told his girl there to take a number."

It was all Rayford could do to keep from calling Buck again himself, knowing for sure now that he was at the Chicago office. But if someone told Carpathia Buck couldn't talk to him because he was on with Rayford Steele, that would be disastrous. He heard Carpathia's reassuring voice again. "Just give him the number, my friend. I trust this young man. He is a brilliant journalist and would not keep me waiting without good reason. Of course, he is trying to cover the story of a lifetime, would you not agree?"

———————

Buck ordered Verna Zee to shut the door on her way out and to leave him alone until he was off the phone. She sighed heavily and shook her head, slamming the door.

Buck continued to hit the redial button, hating the sound of that recorded announcement more than anything he had ever heard in his life.

Suddenly the intercom came alive. "I'm sorry to bother you," Verna said in a sickly sweet, singsong voice, "but you have yet another urgent phone call. Chaim Rosenzweig from Israel."

Buck punched the intercom button. "I'm afraid I'm gonna have to call him back, too. Tell him I'm very sorry."

"You should tell *me* you're very sorry," Verna said. "I'm tempted to patch him through anyway."

"I'm very sorry, Verna," Buck said with sarcasm. "Now leave me alone, please!"

The car phone kept ringing. Buck hung up on the recorded message several times. Verna punched back in. "Dr. Rosenzweig says it's a matter of life and death, Cameron."

Buck quickly punched into the blinking line. "Chaim, I'm very sorry, but I'm in the middle of an urgent matter here myself. Can't I call you back?"

"Cameron! Please don't hang up on me! Israel has been spared the terrible bombings that your country has suffered, but Rabbi Ben-Judah's family was abducted and slaughtered! His house has burned to the ground. I pray he is safe, but no one knows where he is!"

Buck was speechless. He hung his head. "His family is gone? Are you sure?"

"It was a public spectacle, Cameron. I was afraid it would come sooner or later. Why, oh why did he have to go public with his views about Messiah? It's one thing to disagree with him, as I do, a respected and trusted friend. But the religious zealots in this country hate a person who believes that Jesus is Messiah. Cameron, he needs our help. What can we do? I have not been able to get through to Nicolae."

"Chaim, do me one huge favor and leave Nicolae out of this, please!"

"Cameron! Nicolae is the most powerful man in the world, and he has pledged to help me and to help Israel and to protect us. Surely, he will step in and preserve the life of a friend of mine!"

"Chaim, I'm begging you to trust me on this. Leave Nicolae out of it. Now I must call you back. I have family members in trouble myself!"

"Forgive me, Cameron! Get back to me as soon as you can."

Buck punched in on his original line and hit redial again. As the numbers sounded in his ear, Verna came on the intercom. "Someone's on the line for you, but since you don't want to be bothered—"

Chloe's car phone was busy! Buck slammed the phone down and punched in on the intercom. "Who is it?"

"I thought you didn't want to be bothered."

"Verna, I have no time for this!"

"If you must know, it was your wife."

"Which line?"

"Line two, but I told her you were probably on the phone with Carpathia or Rosenzweig."

"Where was she calling from?"

"I don't know. She said she would wait for your call."

"Did she leave a number?"

"Yes. It's—"

When Buck heard the first two numbers, he knew it was the car phone. He turned off the intercom and hit the redial button. Verna poked her head in the door and said, "I'm not a secretary, you know, and I'm certainly not *your* secretary!"

Buck had never been angrier with anyone. He stared at Verna. "I'm coming across this desk to kick that door shut. You had better not be in the way."

The car phone was ringing. Verna still stood there. Buck rose from his chair, phone still to his ear, and stepped up onto the desk and across Verna's mess of papers. Her eyes grew wide as he lifted his leg, and she ducked out of the way as he kicked the door shut with all his might. It sounded like a bomb and nearly toppled the wall partitions. Verna screamed. Buck almost wished she'd been in the doorway.

"Buck!" came Chloe's voice from the phone.

"Chloe! Where are you?"

"I'm on my way out of Chicago," she said. "I got the phones and went to The Drake, but there was a message for me at the desk."

"I know."

"Buck, something in Daddy's voice made me not even take the time to get anything from our room."

"Good!"

"But your laptop and all your clothes and all your toiletries and everything I brought from New York—"

"But your dad sounded serious, didn't he?"

"Yes. Oh, Buck, I'm being pulled over by the police! I made a U-turn and I was speeding, and I went through a light, and I was even on the sidewalk for a while."

"Chloe, listen! You know the old saying about how it's easier to ask forgiveness than permission?"

"You want me to try to outrun him?"

"You'll probably be saving his life! There's only one reason your father would want us out of Chicago as far and as fast as possible!"

"OK, Buck, pray for me! Here goes nothing!"

"I'll stay on the line with you, Chloe."

"I need both hands to drive!"

"Hit the speaker button and hang that phone up!" Buck said.

But then he heard an explosion, tires squealing, a scream, and silence. Within seconds the electricity went off in the *Global Community Weekly* office. Buck felt his way out into the hall where battery-operated emergency lights near the ceiling illuminated the doors. "Look at that!" someone shouted, and the staff pushed its way through the front doors and began climbing atop their own cars to watch a huge aerial attack on the city of Chicago.

Rayford clandestinely listened in horror as Carpathia announced to his compatriots, "Chicago should be under retaliatory attack, even as we speak. Thank you for your

part in this, and for the strategic nonuse of radioactive
fallout. I have many loyal employees in that area, and
though I expect to lose some in the initial attack, I need
not lose any to radiation to make my point."

Someone else spoke up. "Shall we watch the news?"

"Good idea," Carpathia said.

Rayford could remain seated no longer. He didn't
know what he would say or do, if anything, but he
simply could not stay in that cockpit, not knowing
whether his loved ones were safe. He entered the cabin
as the television was coming on, showing the first images
from Chicago. Amanda gasped. Rayford went and sat
with her to watch. "Would you go to Chicago for me?"
Rayford whispered.

"If you think I would be safe."

"There's no radiation."

"How do you know that?"

"I'll tell you later. Just tell me you'll go if I can get
permission from Carpathia to have you fly out of
San Francisco."

"I'll do anything for you, Rayford. You know that."

"Listen to me, sweetheart. If you can't get an immediate flight, and I mean before this plane leaves the ground
again, you must reboard the Condor. Do you understand?"

"I understand, but why?"

"I can't tell you now. Just get an immediate flight to
Milwaukee if I can get it cleared. If the plane is not airborne before we are—"

"What?"

"Just be sure, Amanda. I couldn't bear losing you."

Following the news from Chicago, the cable news channel broke for a commercial, and Rayford approached Carpathia. "Sir, may I have a moment?"

"Certainly, Captain. Awful news out of Chicago, is it not?"

"Yes, sir, it is. In fact, that's what I wanted to talk to you about. You know I have family in that area."

"Yes, and I hope they are all safe," Carpathia said.

Rayford wanted to kill him where he sat. He knew full well the man was the Antichrist, and he also knew that this very person would be assassinated one day and be resurrected from the dead by Satan himself. Rayford had never dreamed he might be an agent in that assassination, but at that instant he would have applied for the job. He fought for composure. Whoever killed this man would be merely a pawn in a huge cosmic game. The assassination and resurrection would only make Carpathia more powerful and satanic than ever.

"Sir," Rayford continued, "I was wondering if it would be possible for my wife to deplane in San Francisco and head back to Chicago to check on my people."

"I would be happy to have my staff check on them," Carpathia said, "if you will simply give me their addresses."

"I would really feel a lot better if she could be there with them to help as needed."

"As you wish," Carpathia said, and it was all Rayford could do not to breathe a huge sigh of relief in the man's face.

———————

"Who's got a cell phone I can borrow?" Buck shouted over the din in the parking lot of *Global Community Weekly*.

A woman next to him thrust one into his hands, and he was shocked to realize she was Verna Zee. "I need to make some long-distance calls," he said quickly. "Can I skip all the codes and just pay you back?"

"Don't worry about it, Cameron. Our little feud just got insignificant."

"I need to borrow a car!" Buck shouted. But it quickly became clear that everyone was heading to their own places to check on loved ones and assess the damage. "How about a ride to Mt. Prospect?"

"I'll take you," Verna muttered. "I don't even want to see what's happening in the other direction."

"You live in the city, don't you?" Buck said.

"I did until about five minutes ago," Verna said.

"Maybe you got lucky."

"Cameron, if that big blast was nuclear, none of us will last the week."

"I might know a place you can stay in Mt. Prospect," Buck said.

"I'd be grateful," she said.

Verna went back inside to gather up her stuff. Buck waited in her car, making his phone calls. He started with his own father out west. "I'm so glad you called," his father said. "I tried calling New York for hours."

"Dad, it's a mess here. I'm left with the clothes on my back, and I don't have much time to talk. I just called to make sure everybody was all right."

"Your brother and I are doing all right here," Buck's dad said. "He's still grieving the loss of his family, of course, but we're all right."

"Dad, the wheels are coming off of this country. You're not gonna really be all right until—"

"Cameron, let's not get into this again, OK? I know what you believe, and if it gives you comfort—"

"Dad! It gives me little comfort right now. It kills me that I was so late coming to the truth. I've already lost too many loved ones. I don't want to lose you too."

His father chuckled, maddening Buck. "You're not going to lose me, big boy. Nobody seems to want to even attack us out here. We feel a little neglected."

"Dad! Millions are dying. Don't be glib about this."

"So, how's that new wife of yours? Are we ever gonna get to meet her?"

"I don't know, Dad. I don't know exactly where she is right now, and I don't know whether you'll ever get the chance to meet her."

"You ashamed of your own father?"

"It's not that at all, Dad. I need to make sure she's all right, and we're going to have to try to get out that way somehow. Find a good church there, Dad. Find somebody who can explain to you what's going on."

"I can't think of anybody more qualified than you, Cameron. And you're just gonna have to let me ruminate on this myself."

FOUR

RAYFORD heard Carpathia's people setting up for his broadcast. "Is there any way anyone will be able to tell we are airborne?" Carpathia asked.

"None," he was assured. Rayford wasn't so sure, but certainly, unless Carpathia made some colossal error, no one would have a clue precisely where in the air he was.

At the sound of a knock on the cockpit door, Rayford shut off the hidden button and turned expectantly. It was a Carpathia aide. "Do whatever you have to do to shut down all interference and patch us back through to Dallas. We go live on satellite in about three minutes, and the potentate should be able to be heard everywhere in the world."

Yippee, Rayford thought.

———————

Buck was on the phone with Loretta when Verna Zee slipped behind the wheel. She slung her oversized bag onto the seat behind her, then had trouble fastening her seat belt, she was shaking so. Buck shut off the phone. "Verna, are you all right? I just talked with a woman from our church who has a room and private bath for you."

A mini traffic jam dissipated as Verna and Buck's coworkers wended their way out of the small parking lot. Headlights provided the only illumination in the area.

"Cameron, why are you doing this for me?"

"Why not? You lent me your phone."

"But I've been so awful to you."

"And I've responded in kind. I'm sorry, Verna. This is the last time in the world we should care so much about getting our own way."

Verna started the car but sat with her face in her hands. "You want me to drive?" Buck asked.

"No, just give me a minute."

Buck told her of his urgency to locate a vehicle and try to find Chloe.

"Cameron! You must be frantic!"

"Frankly, I am."

She unlatched her seat belt and reached for the door handle. "Take my car, Cameron. Do whatever you have to do."

"No," Buck said. "I'll let you lend me your car, but let's get you settled first."

"You may not have a minute to spare."

"All I can do is trust God at this point," Buck said.

He pointed Verna in the right direction. She sped to the edge of Mt. Prospect and slid up to the curb in front of Loretta's beautiful, rambling, old home. Verna did not allow Buck to even take the time to make introductions. She said, "We all know who each other is, so let's let Cameron get going."

"I arranged for a car for you," Loretta said. "It should be here in a few minutes."

"I'll take Verna's for now, but I sure appreciate it."

"Keep the phone as long as you need it," Verna said, as Loretta welcomed her.

Buck pushed the driver's seat all the way back and adjusted the mirror. He punched in the number he'd been given for Nicolae Carpathia and tried to return that call. The phone was answered by an aide. "I'll tell him you returned his call, Mr. Williams, but he's conducting an international broadcast just now. You might want to tune it in."

Buck whipped on the radio while racing toward the only route he could imagine Chloe taking to escape Chicago.

———

"Ladies and gentlemen, from an unknown location, we bring you, live, Global Community Potentate Nicolae Carpathia."

Rayford swung around in his chair and propped open the cockpit door. The plane was on autopilot, and both he and his first officer sat watching as Carpathia addressed the world. The potentate looked amused as he was being introduced and winked at a couple of his ambassadors. He pretended to lick his finger and smooth his eyebrows, as if primping for his audience. The others stifled chuckles. Rayford wished he had a weapon.

On cue, Carpathia mustered his most emotional voice. "Brothers and sisters of the Global Community, I am speaking to you with the greatest heaviness of heart I have ever known. I am a man of peace who has been forced to retaliate with arms against international terrorists who would jeopardize the cause of harmony and fraternity. You may rest assured that I grieve with you over the loss of loved ones, of friends, of acquaintances. The horrible toll of civilian lives should haunt these enemies of peace for the rest of their days.

"As you know, most of the ten world regions that comprise the Global Community destroyed 90 percent of their weapon hardware. We have spent nearly the last two years breaking down, packaging, shipping, receiving, and reassembling this hardware in New Babylon. My humble prayer was that we would never have had to use it.

"However, wise counselors persuaded me to stockpile storehouses of technologically superior weapons in strategic locations around the globe. I confess I did this against my will, and my optimistic and overly positive view of the goodness of mankind has proven faulty.

"I am grateful that somehow I allowed myself to be persuaded to keep these weapons at the ready. In my wildest dreams, I never would have imagined that I would have to make the difficult decision to turn this power against enemies on a broad scale. By now you must know that two former members of the exclusive Global Community executive council have viciously and wantonly conspired to revolt against my administration, and another carelessly allowed militia forces in his region to do the same. These forces were led by the now late president of the United States of North America Gerald Fitzhugh, trained by the American militia, and supported also by secretly stored weapons from the United States of Great Britain and the formerly sovereign country of Egypt.

"While I should never have to defend my reputation as an antiwar activist, I am pleased to inform you that we have retaliated severely and with dispatch. Anywhere that Global Community weaponry was employed, it was aimed specifically at rebel military locations. I assure you that all civilian casualties and the destruction of great populated cities in North America and around the world was the work of the rebellion.

"There are no more plans for counterattacks by Global Community forces. We will respond only as necessary and pray that our enemies understand that they have no future. They cannot succeed. They will be utterly destroyed.

"I know that in a time of global war such as this, most of us live in fear and grief. I can assure you that I am with you in your grief but that my fear has been overcome by confidence that the majority of the global community is together, heart and soul, against the enemies of peace.

"As soon as I am convinced of security and safety, I will address you via satellite television and the Internet. I will communicate frequently so you know exactly what is going on and will see that we are making enormous strides toward rebuilding our world. You may rest assured that as we reconstruct and reorganize, we will enjoy the greatest prosperity and the most wonderful home this earth can afford. May we all work together for the common goal."

While Carpathia's aides and ambassadors nodded and clapped him on the back, Rayford caught Amanda's eye and resolutely shut the cockpit door.

Verna Zee's car was a junky old import. It was rattly and drafty, a four-cylinder automatic. In short, it was a dog. Buck decided to test its limits and reimburse Verna later, if necessary. He sped to the Kennedy and headed toward the Edens junction, trying to guess how far Chloe might have gotten from The Drake in heavy traffic that would now be impassable.

What he didn't know was whether she would take Lake Shore Drive (which locals referred to as the LSD) or the Kennedy. This was more her bailiwick than his, but his question soon became moot. Chicago was in flames, and most of the drivers of cars that clogged the Kennedy in both directions stood on the pavement gaping at the holocaust. Buck would have given anything to have had the Range Rover at that moment.

When he whipped Verna's little pile of junk onto the shoulder, he found he wasn't alone. Traffic laws and civility went out the window at a time like this, and there was almost as much traffic off the road as on. He had no choice. Buck had no idea whether he was destined to survive the entire seven years of the Tribulation anyway, and he could think of only one better reason to die than trying to rescue the love of his life.

Ever since he had become a believer, Buck had considered the privilege of giving his life in the service of God. In his mind, regardless of what really killed Bruce, he believed Bruce was a martyr to the cause. Risking his life in traffic may not have been as altruistic as that, but one thing he was sure of: Chloe would not have hesitated had the shoe been on the other foot.

The biggest jam-ups came at the bridge overpasses where the shoulders ended and those fighting to go around stalled traffic had to take turns picking their way through. Angry motorists rightfully tried to block their paths. Buck couldn't blame them. He would have done the same in their places.

He had stored the number of the phone in the Range Rover and continued to redial every chance he got. Every time he first heard a hint of the message "The mobile customer you have called—", he disconnected and tried again.

Just before the initial descent into San Francisco, Rayford huddled with Amanda. "I'm gonna get that door open and get you off this plane as soon as possible," he said. "I'm not going to wait for the postflight checklist or anything. Don't forget, it's imperative that whatever flight you find is off the ground before we are."

"But why, Ray?"

"Just trust me, Amanda. You know I have your best interests in mind. As soon as you can, call me on my universal cell phone and let me know Chloe and Buck are all right."

Buck left the expressway and picked his way through side streets for more than an hour until reaching Evanston. By the time he got to Sheridan Road along the lake, he found it barricaded but not guarded. Apparently every law enforcement officer and emergency medical technician was busy. He thought about ramming one of the construction horses, but didn't want to do that to Verna's car. He stepped out and moved the horse enough to drive through. He was going to leave the opening there, but someone hollered from an apartment, "Hey! What are you doing?"

Buck looked up and waved in the direction of the voice. "Press!" he shouted.

"All right, then! Carry on!"

To make himself look more legitimate, Buck took the time to get out of the car and replace the barrier before driving on. He saw the occasional police car with lights flashing and some uniformed men standing at side streets. Buck merely put on his emergency flashers and kept going. No one stood in his way. No one drew down on him. No one so much as shined a light at him. To Buck it seemed as if they assumed that if he had gone to the trouble of getting so deep into a prohibited area and was now proceeding with such confidence, he must be all right. He could hardly believe how clear the sailing was with all the arteries leading into Sheridan Road blocked off. The question now was what he would find on Lake Shore Drive.

Frustrated was too mild a word for the way Rayford felt as he landed the Condor 216 in San Francisco and taxied to a private jetway. There he sat with the unenviable task of carrying Antichrist himself wherever he wanted to go. Carpathia had just told bald-faced lies to the largest audience that had ever listened to a single radio broadcast. Rayford knew beyond doubt that shortly after takeoff toward New Babylon, San Francisco would be devastated from the air the same way Chicago had been. People would die. Business and industry would crumble. Transportation centers would be destroyed, including that very airport. Rayford's first order of business was to get Amanda off that plane and out of that airport and into the Chicago area. He didn't even want to wait for the jetway to be maneuvered out to the plane. He opened the door himself and lowered the telescoping stairs to the runway. He motioned for Amanda to hurry. Carpathia made some farewell small talk as she hurried past, and Rayford was grateful that she merely thanked the man and kept moving. Ground personnel waved at Rayford and tried to get him to pull the stairs back up. He shouted, "We have one passenger who needs to make a connection!"

Rayford embraced Amanda and whispered, "I checked with the tower. There's a flight to Milwaukee leaving from a gate at the end of this corridor in less than twenty minutes. Make sure you're on it." Rayford kissed Amanda and she hurried down the steps.

He saw the ground crew waiting for him to pull the stairs back up so they could get the jetway into position. He could think of no legitimate reason to stall, so he simply ignored them, walked back into the cockpit, and began postflight checks.

"What's going on?" his copilot asked. "I want to switch places with your guy as soon as I can."

If you only knew what you were walking into, Rayford thought. "Where are you headed tonight?"

"What possible business is that of yours?" the young man said.

Rayford shrugged. He felt like the little Dutch boy with his thumb in the dike. He couldn't save everyone. Could he save *anyone?* A Carpathia aide poked his head into the cockpit. "Captain Steele, you're being summoned by the ground crew."

"I'll handle it, sir. They'll have to wait for our postflight check. You realize that with a new plane there's a lot we need to be sure of before we attempt a trans-Pacific flight."

"Well, we've got McCullum waiting to board, and we've got a full flight crew waiting besides. We'd kind of like to have some service."

Rayford tried to sound cheery. "Safety first."

"Well, hurry it up!"

While the first officer double-checked items on his clipboard, Rayford checked with the tower on the status of the outbound flight to Milwaukee. "Behind schedule about twelve minutes, Condor 216. It shouldn't affect you."

But it will, Rayford thought.

Rayford stepped into the cabin. "Excuse me, sir, but isn't Mr. Fortunato joining us for the next leg of the flight?"

"Yes," an aide said. "He left Dallas half an hour after we did, so he shouldn't be long."

He will be if I can help it.

Buck finally hit the brick wall he knew would be inevitable. He had bounced over a couple of curbs and couldn't avoid smashing one traffic barrier where Sheridan Road jogged to meet Lake Shore Drive. All along the Drive he saw cars off the road, emergency vehicles with lights flashing, and disaster relief specialists trying to flag him down. He floored Verna Zee's little car, and no one dared step in front of him. He had most of the lanes open all the way down the Drive, but he heard people shouting, "Stop! Road closed!"

The radio told him that gridlock within the city proper had ground all fleeing traffic to a halt. One report said it had been that way since the moment of the first blast. Buck wished he had time to scan the exits that led to the beach. There were plenty of places where a Range Rover might have left the road, crashed, or been hidden. If it became clear to Chloe that she could not have made any decent time by heading to the Kennedy or the Eisenhower from The Drake, she might have tried the LSD. But as Buck got to the Michigan Avenue exit that would have taken him within sight of The Drake, he would have had to kill someone or go airborne to go any farther. The barricade that shut down Lake Shore Drive and the exit looked like something from the set of *Les Misérables*. Squad cars, ambulances, fire trucks, construction and traffic horses, caution lights, you name it, were stretched across the entire area, manned by a busy force of emergency workers. Buck came to a screeching halt, swerving and sliding about fifty feet before his right front tire blew. The car spun as emergency workers danced out of the way.

Several swore at him, and a woman police officer advanced, gun drawn. Buck started to get out, but she said, "Stay right where you are, pal!" Buck lowered the window with one hand and reached for his press credentials with the other. The policewoman would have none of that. She thrust her weapon through the window and pressed it to his temple. "Both hands where I can see 'em, scumbag!" She opened the door, and Buck executed the difficult procedure of getting out of a small car without the use of his hands. She made him lie flat on the pavement, spread-eagle.

Two other officers joined the first and roughly frisked Buck.

"Any guns, knives, needles?"

Buck went on the offensive. "Nope, just two sets of IDs."

The cops pulled a wallet out of each of his back pockets, one containing his own papers, the other the documents of the fictitious Herb Katz.

"So, which one are you, and what's the deal?"

"I'm Cameron Williams, publisher of *Global Community Weekly*. I report directly to the potentate. The phony ID is to help me get into unsympathetic countries."

A young, slender cop pulled Buck's real ID wallet from the hands of the woman officer. "Let me just have a look at this," he said with sarcasm. "If you really report to Nicolae Carpathia, you'd have level 2-A clearance, and I don't see—oops, I guess I do see level 2-A security clearance here."

The three officers huddled to peer at the unusual identification card. "You know, carrying phony 2-A security clearance is punishable by death—"

"Yes, I do."

"We aren't even going to be able to run your license plate, with the computers so jammed."

"I can tell you right now," Buck said, "that I borrowed

this car from a friend named Zee. You can check that for sure before you have it junked."

"You can't leave this car here!"

"What am I gonna do with it?" Buck said. "It's worthless, it's got a flat tire, and there's no way we're gonna find help for that tonight."

"Or for the next two weeks, most likely," one of the cops said. "So, where were you goin' in such an all-fired hurry?"

"The Drake."

"Where have you been, pal? Don't you listen to the news? Most of Michigan Avenue is toast."

"Including The Drake?"

"I don't know about that, but it can't be in too good a shape by now."

"If I walk up over that rise and get onto Michigan Avenue on foot, am I gonna die of radiation poisoning?"

"Civil Defense guys tell us there's no fallout readings. That means this must have been done by the militia, trying to spare as much human life as possible. Anyway, if those bombs had been nuclear, the radiation would have traveled a lot farther than this already."

"True enough," Buck said. "Am I free to go?"

"No guarantees you'll get past the guards on Michigan Avenue."

"I'll take my chances."

"Your best bet is with that clearance card. I sure hope it's legit, for your sake."

Rayford couldn't stall the ground crew any longer, at least by merely ignoring them. He pulled the stairs in as if to receive the jetway, but did not fully move them out of the way, knowing that the jetway would never connect. Rather than stay and watch, he returned to the cockpit and busied himself. *I don't even want fuel before Amanda's plane is off the ground.*

It was a full fifteen minutes before Rayford's usual copilot switched places with his temporary one, and a full flight service crew entered the plane. Every time the ground crew radioed Rayford that they were ready to begin refueling, he told them he wasn't ready. Finally, an exasperated laborer barked into his radio, "What's the holdup up there, chief? I was told this was a VIP plane that needed fast service."

"You were told wrong. This is a cargo plane, and it's a new one. We've got a learning curve in the cockpit, plus we're switching crews. Just hold tight. Don't call us, we'll call you."

Rayford breathed a sigh of relief twenty minutes later when he discovered that Amanda's plane was en route to Milwaukee. Now he could refuel, play it by the book, and settle in for the long flight over the Pacific.

"Some plane, huh?" McCullum said as he checked out the cockpit.

"Some plane," Rayford agreed. "It's been a long day for me, Mac. I'd appreciate a good, long snooze once we get her on course."

"My pleasure, Cap. You can sleep the night away for

all I care. You want me to come in and wake you for initial descent?"

"I'm not quite confident enough to leave the cockpit," Rayford said. "I'll be right here if you need me."

It suddenly hit Buck that he had taken a huge risk. It wouldn't be long before Verna Zee learned that he had, at least at one time, been a full-fledged member of New Hope Village Church. He had been so careful about not taking a leadership role there, not speaking in public, not being known to very many people. Now, one of his own employees—and a long-standing enemy at that—would have knowledge that could ruin him, even cost him his life.

He called Loretta's home on Verna's phone. "Loretta," he said, "I need to speak with Verna."

"She's quite distraught just now," Loretta said. "I hope you're prayin' for this girl."

"I certainly will," Buck said. "How are you two getting along?"

"As well as can be expected for two complete strangers," Loretta said. "I'm just tellin' her my story, as I assumed you wanted me to."

Buck was silent. Finally, he said, "Put her on, would you, Loretta?"

She did, and Buck got straight to the point. "Verna, you need a new car."

"Oh no! Cameron, what happened?"

"It's only a flat tire, Verna, but it's going to be impossible to get fixed for several days, and I don't think your car is worth worrying about."

"Well, thanks a lot!"

"How 'bout I replace it with a better car?"

"I can't argue with that," she muttered.

"I promise. Now, Verna, I'm going to abandon this vehicle. Is there anything you need out of it?"

"Nothing I can think of. There is a hairbrush I really like in the glove box."

"Verna!"

"That does seem a little trivial in light of everything."

"No documents, personal belongings, hidden money, anything like that?"

"No. Just do what you gotta do. It would be nice if I didn't get in trouble for this."

"I'll leave word with the authorities that when they get around to it they can tow this car to any junkyard and trade whatever the yard gives them for it for the towing fee."

"Cameron," Verna whispered, "this woman is one strange, old bird."

"I don't have time to discuss that with you now, Verna. But give her a chance. She's sweet. And she *is* providing shelter."

"No, you misunderstand. I'm not saying she isn't wonderful. I'm just saying she's got some really strange ideas."

As Buck scrambled over an embankment to bring Michigan Avenue into view, he fulfilled his promise to

Loretta that he would pray for Verna. Exactly how to pray, he didn't know. *Either she becomes a believer, or I'm dead.*

All Buck could think of as he came into sight of the dozens of bombed-out buildings along Michigan Avenue and knew that they continued almost the entire length of the Magnificent Mile, was his experience in Israel when Russia had attacked. He could imagine the sound of the bombs and the searing heat of the flames, but in that instance the Holy Land had been miraculously delivered from damage. There was no such intervention here. He hit the redial button on Verna's phone, forgetting that he had last called Loretta, not the cell phone in the Range Rover.

When he did not get the usual recording about the "mobile customer you have called," he stood still and prayed Chloe would answer. When it was Loretta, he was speechless at first.

"Hello? Is anyone there?"

"I'm sorry, Loretta," he said. "Wrong number."

"I'm glad you called, Buck. Verna was about to call you."

"About what?"

"I'll let her tell you."

"Cameron, I called the office. A few people are still there, monitoring things and promising to lock up when they're finished. Anyway, there were a couple of phone messages for you."

"From Chloe?"

"No, I'm sorry. There was one from Dr. Rosenzweig

in Israel. Another was from a man claiming to be your father-in-law. And another from a Miss White, who says she needs to be picked up at Mitchell Field in Milwaukee at midnight."

Miss White? Buck thought. *Crafty of Amanda to keep hidden how connected our little family has become.*

"Thanks, Verna. Got it."

"Cameron, how are you going to pick anyone up in Milwaukee without a vehicle?"

"I've still got a few hours to figure that out. Right now that much time seems like a luxury."

"Loretta has offered her car, provided I'm willing to drive," Verna said.

"I hope that won't be necessary," Buck said. "But I appreciate it. I'll let you know."

Buck didn't feel much like a journalist, standing in the midst of the chaos. He should have been drinking it all in, impressing it upon his brain, asking questions of people who seemed to be in charge. But no one seemed in charge. Everyone was working. And Buck didn't care whether he could translate this into a story or not. His magazine, along with every other major media outlet, was controlled, if not owned, by Nicolae Carpathia. As much as he strived to keep things objective, everything seemed to come out with the spin of the master deceiver. The worst part was, Nicolae was good at it. Of course, he had to be. It was his very nature. Buck just hated the idea that he himself was being used to spread propaganda and lies that people were eating like ice cream.

Most of all though, right now, right here, he cared

about nothing but Chloe. He had allowed the thought to invade his mind that he might have lost her. He knew he would see her again at the end of the Tribulation, but would he have the will to go on without her? She had become the center of his life, around which everything else revolved. During the short time they had been together, she had proved more than he ever could have hoped for in a wife. It was true they were bound in a common cause that made them look past the insignificant and the petty, which seemed to get in so many other couples' way. But he sensed she would never have been catty or a nag anyway. She was selfless and loving. She trusted him and supported him completely. He would not stop until he found her. And until he knew for sure, he would never believe her dead.

Buck dialed the number in the Range Rover. How many dozens of times had he done this now? He knew the routine by heart. When he got a busy signal, his knees nearly buckled. Had he dialed the right number? He'd had to punch it in anew because redial would have given him Loretta's home again. He stopped dead on the sidewalk, mayhem all around him, and with fingers shaking, carefully and resolutely punched in the numbers. He pressed the phone to his ear. "The mobile customer you have called—" Buck swore and gripped Verna's phone so tightly he thought it might break. He took a step and pulled his arm back as if to fire the blasted machine into the side of a building. He followed through but hung onto the phone, realizing it would be the stupidest thing he had ever done. He shook his head at the word that had burst from his lips when that cursed recording had come on. *So, the old nature is still just under the surface.*

He was mad at himself. How, in such dire circumstances, could he have dialed the wrong number?

Though he knew he would hear that recording again and that he would hate it as never before, he couldn't keep himself from hitting the redial button yet again. Now the line was busy! Was it a malfunction? Some cruel cosmic joke? Or was somebody, somewhere, trying to use that phone?

There was no guarantee it was Chloe. It could be anyone. It could be a cop. It could be an emergency worker. It could be someone who found her wrecked Range Rover.

No, he would not allow himself to believe that. Chloe was alive. Chloe was trying to call him. But where would she call? No one was at the church. For all he knew, no one was still at the *Global Community Weekly* office. Did Chloe know Loretta's number? It would be easy enough to get. The question was whether he should try calling the places she might have called, or just keep redialing her number in hopes of catching her between calls.

The senior flight attendant of a crew that was two-thirds as many people as the entire passenger list rapped on the cockpit door and opened it as Rayford taxied slowly down the runway. "Captain," she said as he lifted the headphone from his right ear, "not everyone is seated and buckled in."

"Well, I'm not going to stop," he said. "Can't you handle it?"

"The offending party, sir, is Mr. Carpathia himself."

"I don't have jurisdiction over him," Rayford said. "And neither do you."

"Federal Aviation Administration rules require that—"

"In case you haven't noticed, 'federal anything' means nothing anymore. Everything is global. And Carpathia is above global. If he doesn't want to sit down, he can stand. I've made my announcement, and you have given your instructions, right?"

"Right."

"Then you go get strapped in and let the potentate worry about himself."

"If you say so, Captain. But if this plane is as powerful as a 757, I wouldn't want to be standing when you accelerate—"

But Rayford had replaced his earphones and was getting the plane into position for takeoff. As he awaited instructions from the tower, Rayford surreptitiously slipped his left hand beneath the seat and depressed the intercom button. Someone was asking Carpathia if he didn't want to sit down. Rayford was aware of McCullum looking at him expectantly, as if he had heard something through his earphones that Rayford had not. Rayford quickly released the intercom button and heard McCullum say, "We have clearance, Cap.

We can roll." Rayford could have begun gradually and slowly picked up enough speed to go airborne. But everybody enjoyed a powerful takeoff once in a while, right? He throttled up and took off down the runway with such speed and power that he and McCullum were driven back into their seats.

"Yeehah!" McCullum cried. "Ride 'em cowboy!"

Rayford had a lot to think about, and taking off for only the second time in a new aircraft, he should have remained focused on the task at hand. But he couldn't resist pressing that intercom button again and hearing what he might have done to Carpathia. In his mind's eye he pictured the man somersaulting all the way to the back of the plane, and he only wished there was a back door he could open from the cockpit.

"Oh, my goodness!" he heard over the intercom. "Potentate, are you all right?"

Rayford heard movement, as if others were trying to unstrap themselves to help Carpathia, but with the plane still hurtling down the runway, those people would be pinned in their seats by centrifugal force.

"I am all right," Carpathia insisted. "It is my own fault. I will be fine."

Rayford turned off the intercom and concentrated on his takeoff. Secretly, he hoped Carpathia had been leaning against one of the seats at the time of the initial thrust. That would have spun him around and nearly flipped him over. *Probably my last chance to inflict any justice.*

No one paid attention to Buck anyway, but still, he didn't want to be conspicuous. He ducked around a corner and stood in the shadows, punching the redial button over and over, not wanting a second to pass between calls if Chloe was using her phone. Somehow, in the brief moment it took between hearing that busy signal and hanging up and punching redial again, his own phone rang. Buck shouted, "Hello! Chloe?" before he had even hit the receive button. His fingers were shaking so badly he nearly dropped the phone. He pushed the button and shouted, "Chloe?"

"No, Cameron, it's Verna. But I just heard from the office that Chloe tried to reach you there."

"Did somebody give her the number of this phone?"

"No. They didn't know you had my phone."

"I'm trying to call her now, Verna. The line is busy."

"Keep trying, Cameron. She didn't say where she was or how she was, but at least you know she's alive."

"Thank God for that!"

FIVE

BUCK wanted to jump or shout or run somewhere, but he didn't know where to go. Knowing Chloe was alive was the best news he'd ever had, but now he wanted to act on it. He kept pushing the redial button and getting that busy signal.

Suddenly his phone rang again.

"Chloe!"

"No, sorry, Cameron, it's Verna again."

"Verna, please! I'm trying to reach Chloe!"

"Calm down, big boy. She got through to the *Weekly* office again. Now, listen up. Where are you now and where have you been?"

"I'm on Michigan Avenue near Water Tower Place, or what used to be Water Tower Place."

"How did you get there?"

"Sheridan to Lake Shore Drive."

"OK," Verna said. "Chloe told somebody in our office that she's the other way on Lake Shore Drive."

"The other way?"

"That's all I know, Cameron. You're gonna need to look off the road, lakeside, the other way from where you might expect on Lake Shore Drive."

Buck was already moving that way as he spoke. "I don't see how she could have gotten onto the lakeside if she was heading south on the Drive."

"I don't know either," Verna said. "Maybe she was hoping to go around everything by heading that way, saw that she couldn't, and popped a U-turn."

"Tell anybody who hears from her that she should stay off the phone until I can connect. She's gonna have to direct me right to her, if possible."

Any remaining doubts Rayford Steele had about the incredible and instant evil power that Nicolae Carpathia wielded were eradicated a few minutes after the Condor 216 left the ground at San Francisco International. Through the privately bugged intercom he heard one of Carpathia's aides ask, "Now, sir, on San Francisco?"

"Trigger," came the whispered reply.

The aide, obviously speaking into a phone, said simply, "It's a go."

"Look out the window on that side," Carpathia said, the excitement obvious in his voice. "Look at that!"

Rayford was tempted to turn the plane so he could see

too, but this was something he would rather try to forget than have visually burned into his memory. He and McCullum looked at each other as their earphones came alive with startled cries from the control tower. "Mayday! Mayday! We're being attacked from the air!" The concussions knocked out communications, but Rayford knew the bombs themselves would easily take out that whole tower, not to mention the rest of the airport and who knew what portion of the surrounding area.

Rayford didn't know how much longer he could take being the devil's own pilot.

Buck was in reasonably good shape for a man in his early thirties, but now his joints ached and his lungs pleaded for air as he sprinted to Chicago Avenue and headed east toward the lake. How far south might Chloe have gotten before turning around? She had to turn around. Otherwise, how could she have gone off the road and wound up on that side?

When he finally got to the Drive, he found it empty. He knew it was barricaded from the north at the Michigan Avenue exit. It had to have been blocked from the far south end too. Gasping, he hurdled the guardrail, jogged to the middle, heard the clicking of meaningless traffic lights, and raced across to the other side. He jogged south, knowing Chloe was alive but not knowing what he might find. The biggest question now, assuming Chloe didn't have some life-threatening injury, was whether those printouts of Bruce's personal commentaries—or worse, the computer itself—might have fallen into the wrong hands. Surely, parts of that narrative were quite clear about Bruce's belief that Nicolae Carpathia was Antichrist.

Buck didn't know how he was able to put one foot in front of the other, but on he ran, pushing redial and holding the phone to his ear as he went. When he could go no further, he slumped into the sand and leaned back against the outside of the guardrail, gasping. Finally, Chloe answered her phone.

Having not planned what to say, Buck found himself majoring on the majors. "Are you all right? Are you hurt? Where are you?" He hadn't told her he loved her or that he was scared to death about her or that he was glad she was alive. He would assume she knew that until he could tell her later.

She sounded weak. "Buck," she said, "where are you?"

"I'm heading south on Lake Shore Drive, south of Chicago Avenue."

"Thank God," she said. "I'm guessing you've got about another mile to go."

"Are you hurt?"

"I'm afraid I am, Buck," she said. "I don't know how long I was unconscious. I'm not even sure how I got where I am."

"Which is where, exactly?"

Buck had risen and was walking quickly. There was no running left in him, despite his fear that she might be bleeding or in shock.

"I'm in the strangest place," she said, and he sensed her fading. He knew she had to still be in the vehicle because that phone was not removable. "The airbag deployed," she added.

"Is the Rover still driveable?"

"I have no idea, Buck."

"Chloe, you're gonna have to tell me what I'm looking for. Are you out in the open? Did you elude that cop?"

"Buck, the Range Rover seems to be stuck between a tree and a concrete abutment."

"What?"

"I was doing about sixty," she said, "when I thought I saw an exit ramp. I took it, and that's when I heard the bomb go off."

"The bomb?"

"Yes, Buck, surely you know a bomb exploded in Chicago."

One bomb? Buck thought. *Maybe it was merciful she was out for all the bombs that followed.*

"Anyway, I saw the squad car pass me. Maybe he wasn't after me after all. All the traffic on Lake Shore Drive stopped when they saw and heard the bomb, and the cop slammed into someone. I hope he's all right. I hope he doesn't die. I'll feel responsible."

"So, where did you wind up then, Chloe?"

"Well, I guess what I thought was an exit wasn't really an exit. I never hit the brake, but I did take my foot off the gas. The Range Rover was in the air for a few seconds. I felt like I was floating for a hundred feet or so.

There's some sort of a dropoff next to me, and I landed on the tops of some trees and turned sideways. The next thing I knew, I woke up and I was alone here."

"Where?" Buck was exasperated, but he certainly couldn't blame Chloe for not being more specific.

"Nobody saw me, Buck," she said dreamily. "Something must have turned my lights off. I'm stuck in the front seat, kind of hanging here by the seat belt. I can reach the rearview mirror, and all I saw was traffic all racing away and then no more traffic. No more emergency lights, no nothing."

"There's nobody around you?"

"Nobody. I had to turn the car off and then back on to get the phone to turn on. I was just praying you'd come looking for me, Buck."

She sounded as if she were about to fall asleep. "Just stay on the line with me, Chloe. Don't talk, just keep the line open so I can be sure I don't miss you."

The only lights Buck saw were emergency flashers far in the distance toward the inner city, fires still blazing here and there, and a few tiny lights from the boats on the lake. Lake Shore Drive was dark as midnight. All the streetlights were out north of where he had seen the traffic light flashing. He came around a long bend and squinted into the distance. From the faint light of the moon he thought he saw a torn up stretch of guardrail, some trees, and a concrete abutment, one of those that formed an underpass to get to the beach. He moved slowly forward and then stopped to stare. He guessed he was two hundred yards from the spot. "Chloe?" he said into the phone.

No response.

"Chloe? Are you there?"

He heard a sigh. "I'm here, Buck. But I don't feel so good."

"Can you reach your lights?"

"I can try."

"Do. Just don't hurt yourself."

"I'll try to pull myself up that way by the steering wheel."

Buck heard her groan painfully. Suddenly in the distance, he saw the crazy, vertical angle of headlights shining out onto the sand.

"I see you, Chloe. Hang on."

Rayford assumed that McCullum assumed that Rayford was sleeping. He was slouched in his pilot's chair, chin to his chest, breathing evenly. But his headphones were on, and his left hand had depressed the intercom receiver. Carpathia was talking in low tones, thinking he was keeping his secrets from the flight crew.

"I was so excited and so full of ideas," the potentate said, "that I could not stay seated. I hope I do not have a bruise to show for it." His lackeys all roared with laughter.

Nothing funnier than the boss's joke, Rayford thought.

"We have so much to talk about, so much to do,"

Carpathia continued. "When our compatriots join us in Baghdad, we will get right to work."

The destruction of the San Francisco airport and much of the Bay Area had already made the news. Rayford saw the fear in McCullum's eyes. Maybe the man would have felt more confident had he known that his ultimate boss, Nicolae Carpathia, had most everything under control for the next few years.

Suddenly Rayford heard the unmistakable voice of Leon Fortunato. "Potentate," he whispered, "we'll need replacements for Hernandez, Halliday, and your fiancée, will we not?"

Rayford sat up. Was it possible? Had they already eliminated those three, and why Hattie Durham? He felt responsible that his former senior flight attendant was now not only in Carpathia's employ, but was also his lover and the soon-to-be mother of his child. So, was he not going to marry her? Did he not want a child? He had put on such a good front before Rayford and Amanda when Hattie had announced the news.

Carpathia chuckled. "Please do not put Ms. Durham in the same category as our late friends. Hernandez was expendable. Halliday was a temporary necessity. Let us replace Hernandez and not worry about replacing Halliday. He served a purpose. The only reason I asked you to replace Hattie is that the job has passed her by. I knew that her clerical skills were suspect when I brought her on. I needed an assistant, and of course I wanted her. But I will use the excuse of her pregnancy to get her out of the office."

"Did you want me to handle that for you?" Fortunato said.

"I will tell her myself, if that is what you mean," Carpathia said. "I would like you to handle finding new secretarial personnel."

Rayford fought for composure. He did not want to give anything away to McCullum. No one could ever know Rayford could hear those conversations. But now he was hearing things he never wanted to hear. Maybe there was some advantage to knowing this stuff, and perhaps it might be useful to the Tribulation Force. But life had become so cheap that in a matter of hours he had lost a new acquaintance, Hernandez, and a dear old mentor and friend, Earl Halliday. He had promised Earl he would communicate with Earl's wife should anything happen. He did not look forward to that.

Rayford shut off the intercom. He flipped the switch that allowed him to speak to his first officer through the headphones. "I think I *will* take a break in my quarters," he said. McCullum nodded, and Rayford made his way out of the cockpit and into his chamber, which was even more lavishly appointed than his area on the now-destroyed *Global Community One.* Rayford removed his shoes and stretched out on his back. He thought about Earl. He thought about Amanda. He thought about Chloe and Buck. And he worried. And it all started with the loss of Bruce. Rayford turned on his side and buried his face in his hands and wept. How many close to him might he lose today alone?

The Range Rover was lodged between the trunk and lower branches of a large tree and the concrete abutment. "Turn those lights off, hon!" Buck called out. "Let's not draw attention to ourselves now."

The wheels of the vehicle pressed almost flat against the wall, and Buck was amazed that the tree could sustain the weight. Buck had to climb into the tree to look down through the driver's-side window. "Can you reach the ignition?" he asked.

"Yes, I had to turn the car off because the wheels were spinning against the wall."

"Just turn the key halfway and lower the window so I can help you."

Chloe seemed to be dangling from the seat belt. "I'm not sure I can reach the window button on that side."

"Can you unlatch your seat belt without hurting yourself?"

"I'll try, Buck, but I hurt all over. I'm not sure what's broken and what isn't."

"Try to brace yourself somehow and get loose of that thing. Then you can stand on the passenger's-side window and lower this one." But Chloe was so hopelessly entangled in the strap that it was all she could do to swing her body around and turn the ignition switch halfway. She pulled herself up with her right hand to reach the window button. When the window was open, Buck reached down with both hands to try to support her. "I was so worried about you," he said.

"I was worried about me too," Chloe said. "I think

I took all the damage to my left side. I think my ankle's broken, my wrist is sprained, and I feel pain in my left knee and shoulder."

"Makes sense, from the looks of things," Buck said. "Does it hurt if I hold you this way so you can put your good foot down on the passenger's-side window?"

Buck lay across the side of the nearly upended Range Rover and reached way down in to put one forearm under Chloe's right arm and grab her waistband at the back with the other. He lifted as she pushed the seat belt button. She was petite, but with no foundation or way to brace himself it was all Buck could do to keep from dropping her. She moved her feet out from under the dashboard and stood gingerly. Her feet were on the passenger's-side door, and her head now was near the steering wheel.

"You're not bleeding anywhere?"

"I don't think so."

"I hope you're not bleeding internally."

"Buck, I'm sure I'd be long gone by now if I were bleeding internally."

"So you're basically all right if I can get you out of there?"

"I really want out of here in a bad way, Buck. Can we get that door open, and can you help me climb?"

"I just have one question for you first. Is this how our married life is going to be? I'm going to buy you expensive cars, and you're going to ruin them the first day?"

"Normally that would be funny—"

"Sorry."

Buck directed Chloe to use her good foot as a base and her good arm to push as he pulled open the door. The bottom of the door scraped on the abutment, and Buck was struck with how relatively little other damage there was to the vehicle, from what he could see in the dim light. "There should be a flashlight in the glove box," he said. Chloe handed it up to him. He looked all around the vehicle. The tires were still good. There was some damage to the front grille, but nothing substantial. He turned off the flashlight and slid it into his pocket. With much groaning and whimpering, Chloe came climbing out of the car, with Buck's help.

As they both sat on the upturned driver's side, Buck felt the heavy machine moving in its precarious position.

"We have to get you down from here," he said.

"Let me see that flashlight for a second," Chloe said. She shined it above her. "It would be easier to go two feet up to the top of the abutment," she said.

"You're right," he said. "Can you make it?"

"I think I can," she said. "I'm the little engine who could."

"Tell me about it."

Chloe hopped to where she could reach the top of the wall with her good hand, and she asked Buck to push until she had most of her weight atop the wall. When she made the last thrust with her good leg, the Range Rover shifted just enough to loosen itself from the wickedly bent tree branches. The tree and the Range Rover shuddered and began to move. "Buck! Get out of there! You're going to be crushed!"

Buck was spread-eagled on the side of the Range
Rover that had been facing up. Now it was shifting
toward the abutment, the tires scraping and leaving huge
marks on the concrete. The more Buck tried to move, the
faster the vehicle shifted, and he realized he had to stay
clear of that wall to survive. He grabbed the luggage rack
as it moved toward him and pulled himself to the actual
top of the Range Rover. Branches snapped free from
under the vehicle and smacked him in the head, scraping
across his ear. The more the car moved, the more it
seemed to want to move, and to Buck that was good
news—provided he could keep from falling. First the
car moved, then the tree moved, then both seemed to
readjust themselves at once. Buck guessed that the Range
Rover, once free of the pressure from the branches, had
about three feet to drop to the ground. He only hoped it
would land flat. It didn't.

The heavy vehicle, left tires pressed against the concrete and several deeply bowed branches pushing it from
the right side, began slipping to the right. Buck buried
his head in his hands to avoid the springing out of those
branches as the Range Rover fell clear of them. They
nearly knocked him into the wall again. Once the Range
Rover was free of the pressure of the branches, it lurched
down onto its right side tires and nearly toppled. Had it
rolled that way, it would have crushed him into the tree.
But as soon as those tires hit the ground, the whole thing
bounced and lurched, and the left tires landed just free
of the concrete. The momentum made the left side of the
vehicle smash into the concrete, and finally it came to rest.

Less than an inch separated the vehicle from the wall
now, but there the thing sat on uneven ground. Damaged
branches hung above it. Buck used the flashlight to illu-
minate the violated car. Except for the damage to the
front grille and the scrapes on both sides, one from
concrete and one from tree branches, the car looked little
the worse for wear.

Buck had no idea how to reset an airbag, so he
decided to cut it off and worry about that later if he
could get the Range Rover to run. His side ached, and
he was certain he had cracked a rib when the Rover had
finally hit bottom. He gingerly climbed down and stood
under the tree, the branches now blocking his view of
Chloe.

"Buck? Are you all right?"

"Stay right where you are, Chloe. I'm gonna try something."

Buck climbed in the passenger side, strapped himself
behind the wheel, and started the engine. It sounded
perfect. He carefully watched the gauges to make sure
nothing was empty, dry, or overheated. The Rover was
in automatic and four-wheel drive. When he tried to go
forward it seemed he was in a rut. He quickly switched
to stick shift and all-wheel drive, gunned the engine, and
popped the clutch. Within seconds he was free of the tree
and out onto the sand. He took a sharp right and moved
back up next to the guardrail that separated the sand
from Lake Shore Drive. He drove about a quarter of a
mile until he found a spot he could slip through the
guardrail and turn around. He headed back up toward

the overpass where Chloe stood, favoring one foot and holding her left wrist in her other hand. To Buck she had never looked better.

He pulled up next to her and ran around to help her into the car. He fastened her seat belt and was on the phone before he got back into the car. "Loretta? Chloe is safe. She's banged up a little, and I'd like to get her checked out as soon as possible. If you could call around and find any doctor in the church who has not been pressed into service, I'd sure appreciate it."

Buck tried to drive carefully so as not to exacerbate Chloe's pain. However, he knew the shortest way home. When he got to the huge barrier at Michigan Avenue on the LSD, he swung left and went up over the embankment he had previously walked. He saw Verna's now deceased automobile and ignored the waves and warnings of the cops he had talked to not so long ago. He sped up Lake Shore Drive, went around the barriers at Sheridan, followed Chloe's directions to Dempster, and was soon back into the northwest suburbs.

Loretta and Verna were watching from the window as he pulled into the drive. Only then did he smack himself in the head and remember. He jumped out of the car and raced around to the back. Fumbling with the keys, he opened the back latch and found, strewn all over, Bruce's pages. The computer was there too, along with the phones Chloe had bought. "Chloe," he said, and she turned gingerly. "As soon as we get you inside, I'd better get back to Carpathia."

———————

Rayford was back in the cockpit. As the night wore on, the cabin grew more and more quiet. The conversation deteriorated into small talk. The dignitaries were well fed by the crew, and Rayford got the impression they were settling in for the long haul.

Rayford awakened with a start and realized his finger had slipped off the intercom button. He pressed it again and still heard nothing. He had heard more than he wanted to hear already anyway. He decided to stretch his legs.

As he walked back through the main cabin to watch one of the televisions in the back of the plane, everyone except Carpathia ignored him. Some dozed and some were being attended to by the flight crew, who were clearing trays and finding blankets and pillows.

Carpathia nodded and smiled and waved to Rayford.

How can he do that? Rayford wondered. *Bruce said the Antichrist would not be indwelt by Satan himself until halfway into the Tribulation, but surely this man is the embodiment of evil.*

Rayford could not let on that he knew the truth, despite the fact that Carpathia was well aware of his Christian beliefs. Rayford merely nodded and walked on. On television he saw live reports from around the world. Scripture had come to life. This was the Red Horse of the Apocalypse. Next would come more death by famine and plagues until a quarter of the population of the earth that remained after the Rapture was wiped out. His universal cell phone vibrated in his pocket. Few people not on that plane knew his number. *Thank God for technology,* he thought. He didn't want anyone to hear him. He slipped deeper into the back of the plane and stood near a window. The night was as black as Carpathia's soul.

"This is Rayford Steele," he said.

"Daddy?"

"Chloe! Thank God! Chloe, are you all right?"

"I had a little car accident, Dad. I just wanted you to know that you saved my life again."

"What do you mean?"

"I got that message you left at The Drake," she said. "If I had taken the time to go to our room, I probably wouldn't be here."

"And Buck's OK?"

"He's fine. He's late returning a call to you-know-who, so he's trying to do that right now."

"Let me excuse myself, then," Rayford said. "I'll get back to you."

Rayford strode back to the cockpit, trying not to appear in a hurry. As he passed Fortunato, Leon was handing a phone to Carpathia. "Williams from Chicago," he said. "It's about time."

Carpathia made a face as if he felt Leon was overreacting. As Rayford reached the cockpit, he heard Carpathia exalt, "Cameron, my friend! I have been worried about you."

Rayford quickly settled in and set his earphones. McCullum looked at him expectantly, but Rayford ignored him and closed his eyes, pressing the secret button.

"I am curious about coverage," Carpathia was saying. "What is happening there in Chicago? Yes—yes—devastation, I understand—yes. Yes, a tragedy—"

Sickening, Rayford thought.

"Cameron," Carpathia said, "would it be possible for you to get to New Babylon within the next few days? Ah, I see—Israel? Yes, I see the wisdom of that. The so-called holy lands were spared again, were they not? I would like pooled coverage of high-level meetings in Baghdad and New Babylon. I would like to have your pen on it, but Steve Plank, your old friend, can run the point. You and he can work together to see that the appropriate coverage is carried in all our print media. . . ."

Rayford would be eager to talk to Buck. He admired his son-in-law's moxie and ability to set his own agenda and even gracefully decline suggested directives from Carpathia. Rayford wondered how long Carpathia would stand for that. For now, he apparently respected Buck enough and was, Rayford hoped, still unaware of Buck's true loyalties.

"Well," Carpathia was saying, "of course I am grieving. You will keep in touch then, and I will hear from you from Israel."

SIX

Buck sat bleary-eyed at the breakfast table, his ear sting-
ing and his rib cage tender. Only he and Loretta were up.
She was heading to the church office after having been
assured she would not have to handle the arrangements
for Bruce's body or for the memorial service, which
would be part of Sunday morning's agenda. Verna Zee
was asleep in a small bedroom in the finished basement.
"It feels so good to have people in this place again,"
Loretta said. "Y'all can stay as long as you need to or
want to."

"We're grateful," Buck said. "Amanda may sleep till
noon, but then she'll get right on those arrangements
with the coroner's office. Chloe didn't sleep much with
that ankle cast. She's dead to the world now, though, so
I expect her to sleep a long time."

Buck had used the dining-room table to put back in

order all the pages from Bruce's transcripts that had been strewn throughout the back of the Range Rover. He had a huge job ahead of him, checking the text and determining what would be best for reproduction and distribution. He set the stacks to one side and laid out the five deluxe universal cell phones Chloe had bought. Fortunately, they had been packed in spongy foam and had survived her accident.

He had told her not to scrimp, and she certainly hadn't. He didn't even want to guess the total price, but these phones had everything, including the ability to take calls anywhere in the world, due to a built-in satellite chip.

After Loretta left for the church, Buck rummaged for batteries, then quickly taught himself the basics from the instruction manual and tried his first phone call. For once, he was glad he had always been manic about hanging onto old phone numbers. Deep in his wallet was just the one he needed. Ken Ritz, a former commercial pilot and now owner of his own jet charter service, had bailed out Buck before. He was the one who had flown Buck from a tiny airstrip in Waukegan, Illinois, to New York the day after the vanishings. "I know you're busy, Mr. Ritz, and probably don't need my business," Buck said, "but you also know I'm on a big, fat expense account and can pay more than anyone else."

"I'm down to one jet," Ritz said. "It's at Palwaukee, and right now both it and I are available. I'm charging two bucks a mile and a thousand dollars a day for down time. Where do you want to go?"

"Israel," Buck said. "And I have to be back here by Saturday night at the latest."

"Jet lag city," Ritz said. "It's best to fly that way early evening and land there the next day. Meet me at Palwaukee at seven, and we've got a deal."

Rayford had finally fallen off to sleep for real, snoring, according to McCullum, for several hours.

About an hour outside Baghdad, Leon Fortunato entered the cockpit and knelt next to Rayford. "We're not entirely sure of security in New Babylon," he said. "No one expects us to land in Baghdad. Let's keep maintaining with the New Babylon tower that we're on our way directly there. When we pick up our other three ambassadors, we may just stay on the ground for a few hours until our security forces have had a chance to clear New Babylon."

"Will that affect your meetings?" Rayford said, trying to sound casual.

"I don't see how it concerns you one way or the other. We can easily meet on the plane while it is being refueled. You can keep the air-conditioning on, right?"

"Sure," Rayford said, trying to think quickly, "there is still a lot I'd like to teach myself about this craft. I'll stay in the cockpit or in my quarters and keep out of your way."

"See that you do."

———————

Buck checked in with Donny Moore, who said he had found some incredible deals on individual components and was putting together the five mega-laptops himself. "That'll save you a little money," he said. "Just a little over twenty thousand apiece, I figure."

"And I can have these when I get back from a trip, on Sunday?"

"Guaranteed, sir."

Buck told key people at *Global Community Weekly* his new universal cell phone number and asked that they keep it confidential except from Carpathia, Plank, and Rosenzweig. Buck carefully packed his one big, leather shoulder bag and spent the rest of the day working on Bruce's transcripts and trying to reach Rosenzweig. The old man had seemed to be trying to tell him, not in so many words, that he knew Dr. Ben-Judah was alive and safe somewhere. He just hoped Rosenzweig had followed his advice and was keeping Carpathia out of the picture. Buck had no idea where Tsion Ben-Judah might be hiding out. But if Rosenzweig knew, Buck wanted to talk with him before he and Ken Ritz hit the ground at Ben Gurion Airport.

How long, he wondered, before he and his loved ones would be hiding out in the shelter under the church?

Security was tight at Baghdad. Rayford had been
instructed not to communicate with the tower there so
as not to allow enemy aircraft to know where they were.
Rayford was convinced that the retaliatory strikes by
Global Community forces in London and Cairo, not to
mention North America, would have kept all but the
suicidal out of Iraq. However, he did what he was told.

Leon Fortunato communicated by phone with both
Baghdad and New Babylon towers. Rayford phoned
ahead to be sure there was a place he and McCullum
could stretch their legs and relax inside the terminal.
Despite his years of flying, there came certain points even
for him when he became claustrophobic aboard a plane.

A ring of heavily armed GC soldiers surrounded the
plane as it slowly rolled to a stop at the most secure end
of the Baghdad terminal. The six-member crew of stew-
ards and flight attendants were the first to get off.
Fortunato waited until Rayford and McCullum had run
through their postflight checklist. He got off with them.
"Captain Steele," he said, "I will be bringing the three
other ambassadors back on board within the hour."

"And when would you like to leave for New Babylon?"

"Probably not for another four hours or so."

"International aviation rules prohibit me from flying
again for twenty-four hours."

"Nonsense," Fortunato said. "How do you feel?"

"Exhausted."

"Nevertheless, you're the only one qualified to fly this

plane, and you'll be flying it when we say you'll be flying it."

"So international aviation rules go out the window?"

"Steele, you know that international rules on everything are embodied in the man sitting on that plane. When he wants to go to New Babylon, you'll fly him to New Babylon. Understood?"

"And if I refuse?"

"Don't be silly."

"Let me remind you, Leon, that once I've gotten a break, I'll want to be on that plane, familiarizing myself with all its details."

"Yeah, yeah, I know. Just stay out of our way. And I would appreciate it if you would refer to me as Mr. Fortunato."

"That means a lot to you, does it, Leon?"

"Don't push me, Steele."

As they entered the terminal, Rayford said, "As I am the only one who can fly that plane, I would appreciate it if you would call me Captain Steele."

Late in the afternoon, Chicago time, Buck broke from the fascinating reading of Bruce Barnes's writing and finally got through to Chaim Rosenzweig.

"Cameron! I have finally talked live with our mutual friend. Let us not mention his name on the phone. He did not speak to me long, but he sounded so empty and hollow that it moved me to my very soul. It was a strange message, Cameron. He simply said that you would know whom to talk with about his whereabouts."

"That *I* would know?"

"That's what he said, Cameron. That you would know. Do you suppose he means NC?"

"No! No! Chaim, I'm still praying you're keeping him out of this."

"I am, Cameron, but it is not easy! Who else can intercede for the life of my friend? I am frantic that the worst will happen, and I will feel responsible."

"I'm coming there. Can you arrange a car for me?"

"Our mutual friend's car and driver are available, but dare I trust him?"

"Do you think he had anything to do with the trouble?"

"I should think he had more to do with getting our friend to safety."

"Then he is probably in danger," Buck said.

"Oh, I hope not," Rosenzweig said. "Anyway, I will meet you at the airport myself. Somehow we will get you where you need to go. Can I arrange a room for you somewhere?"

"You know where I've always stayed," Buck said, "but I think I'd better stay somewhere else this time."

"Very well, Cameron. There's a nice hotel within driving distance of your usual, and I am known there."

Rayford stretched and stood watching the Cable News Network/Global Community Network television broadcast originating in Atlanta and beamed throughout the world. It was clear Carpathia had completely effected his will and spin onto the news directors at every venue. While the stories carried the horrifying pictures of war, bloodshed, injury, and death, each also spoke glowingly of the swift and decisive action of the potentate in responding to the crisis and crushing the rebellion. Water supplies had been contaminated, power was out in many areas, millions were instantly homeless.

Rayford noticed activity outside the terminal. A dolly carrying television equipment, including a camera, were wheeled toward the Condor 216. Soon enough, CNN/GCN announced the impending live television broadcast from Potentate Carpathia at an unknown location. Rayford shook his head and went to a desk in the corner, where he found stationery from a Middle Eastern airline and began composing a letter to Earl Halliday's wife.

Logic told Rayford he should not feel responsible. Apparently Halliday had been cooperating with Carpathia and his people on the Condor 216 long before Rayford was even aware of it. However, there would be no way Mrs. Halliday would know or understand anything except that it appeared Rayford had led his old friend and boss directly to his death. Rayford didn't even know yet how Earl had been killed. Perhaps everyone on his flight to Glenview had perished. All he knew was that the deed had been done, and Earl Halliday was no more. As he sat trying to compose a letter with words that could never be right, he felt a huge, dark cloud of depression begin to settle on him. He missed his wife. He missed his daughter. He grieved over his pastor. He mourned the loss of friends and acquaintances, new and old. How had it come to this?

Rayford knew he was not responsible for what Nicolae Carpathia meted out against his enemies. The terrible, dark judgment on the earth rendered by this evil man would not stop if Rayford merely quit his job. Hundreds of pilots could fly this plane. He himself had learned in half an hour. He didn't need the job, didn't want the job, didn't ask for the job. Somehow, he knew God had placed him there. For what? Was this surprising bugging of the intercom system by Earl Halliday a gift directly from God that allowed Rayford to somehow protect a few from the wrath of Carpathia?

Already he believed it had saved his daughter and son-in-law from certain death in the Chicago bombings, and now, as he looked at television reports from America's West Coast, he wished there had been something he could have done to have warned people in San Francisco and Los Angeles of their impending doom. He was fighting an uphill battle, and in himself he didn't have the strength to carry on.

He finished the brief note of condolence and regret to Mrs. Halliday, lowered his head to his arms on the desk, felt a lump in his throat, but was unable to produce tears. He knew he could cry twenty-four hours a day from now until the end of the Tribulation, when his pastor had promised that Christ would return yet again in what Bruce had called "the Glorious Appearing." How he longed for that day! Would he or his loved ones survive to see it, or would they be "tribulation martyrs," as Bruce had been? At times like this Rayford wished for some quick, painless death that would take him directly to heaven to be with Christ. It was selfish, he knew. He wouldn't really want to leave those he loved and who loved him, but the prospect of five more years of this was nearly unbearable.

And now came a brief address from Global Community Potentate Nicolae Carpathia. Rayford knew he was sitting within two hundred feet of the man, and yet he watched it on television, as did millions of others across the globe.

———————

It was nearly time for Buck to head for Palwaukee Airport. Verna Zee was back at the *Global Community Weekly* office with the new (to her) used car Buck had promised to buy her from the fleet of leftovers from New Hope. Loretta was at the church office fielding the constant phone calls about Sunday's memorial service. Chloe hobbled around on a cane, needing crutches but unable to manage them with her sprained wrist in a sling. That left Amanda to take Buck to the airport.

"I want to ride along," Chloe said.

"Are you sure you're up to it, hon?" Buck said.

Chloe's voice was quavery. "Buck, I hate to say it, but in this day and age we never know when we might or might not ever see each other again."

"You're being a little maudlin, aren't you?" he said.

"Buck!" Amanda said in a scolding tone. "You cater to her feelings now. I had to kiss my husband good-bye in front of the Antichrist. You think that gives me confidence about whether I'll ever see *him* again?"

Buck was properly chastised. "Let's go," he said. He jogged out to the Range Rover and swung his bag into the back, returning quickly to help Chloe to the car. Amanda sat in the backseat and would drive Chloe home later.

Buck was amazed that the built-in TV had survived Chloe's crash. He was not in a position to see it, but he listened as Amanda and Chloe watched. Nicolae Carpathia, in his usual overly humble manner, was holding forth:

"Make no mistake, my brothers and sisters, there will be many dark days ahead. It will take tremendous resources to begin the rebuilding process, but because of the generosity of the seven loyal global regions and with the support of those citizens in the other three areas who were loyal to the Global Community and not to the insurrectionists, we are amassing the largest relief fund in the history of mankind. This will be administered to needy nations from New Babylon and the Global Community headquarters under my personal supervision. With the chaos that has resulted from this most sinister and unwise rebellion, local efforts to rebuild and care for the displaced will likely be thwarted by opportunists and looters. The relief effort carried out under the auspices of the Global Community will be handled in a swift and generous way that will allow as many loyal

members of the Global Community as possible to return
to their prosperous standard of living.

"Continue to resist naysayers and insurrectionists.
Continue to support the Global Community. And
remember that though I did not seek this position,
I accept it with gravity and with resolve to pour out
my life in service to the brotherhood and sisterhood of
mankind. I appreciate your support as we set about to
sacrificially stand by each other and pull ourselves out
of this morass and to a higher plane than any of us could
reach without the help of the other."

Buck shook his head. "He sure tells 'em what they
wanna hear, doesn't he?"

Chloe and Amanda were silent.

———————

Rayford told First Officer McCullum to hang loose and
be ready to depart for New Babylon whenever they were
asked. He guessed it would be several hours yet. "But, at
least stay available," Rayford told him.

When Rayford boarded the plane, ostensibly to famil-
iarize himself better with all the new whistles and bells, he
went first to the pilot's quarters, noticing that Carpathia
and his aides were merely greeting and small-talking with
the seven loyal ambassadors to the Global Community.

When Rayford moved from his quarters into the
cockpit, he noticed Fortunato look up. He whispered
something to Carpathia. Carpathia agreed, and the
entire meeting was moved back one compartment in the

middle of the aircraft. "This will be more comfortable anyway," Carpathia was saying. "There is a nice conference table in here."

Rayford shut the cockpit door and locked it. He pulled out pre- and postflight checklists and put them on a clipboard with other blank sheets, just to make it look good in case someone knocked. He sat in his chair, applied his headphones, and hit the intercom button.

The Middle Eastern ambassador was speaking. "Dr. Rosenzweig sends his most heartfelt and loyal greetings to you, Potentate. There is an urgent personal matter he wants me to share with you."

"Is it confidential?" Carpathia said.

"I don't believe so, sir. It concerns Rabbi Tsion Ben-Judah."

"The scholar who has been creating such a furor with his controversial message?"

"One and the same," the Middle Eastern ambassador said. "Apparently his wife and two stepchildren have been murdered by zealots, and Dr. Ben-Judah himself is in hiding somewhere."

"He should have expected no better," Nicolae said.

Rayford shuddered as he always did when Carpathia's voice waxed grave.

"I couldn't agree with you more, Potentate," the ambassador said. "I can't believe those zealots let him slip through their fingers."

"So, what does Rosenzweig want from me?"

"He wants you to intercede on Ben-Judah's behalf."

"With whom?"

"I suppose with the zealots," the ambassador said, bursting into laughter.

Rayford recognized Carpathia's laughter as well, and soon the others joined in.

"OK, gentlemen, calm down," Carpathia said. "Perhaps what I should do is accede to Dr. Rosenzweig's request and speak directly with the head of the zealot faction. I would give him my full blessing and support and perhaps even supply some technology that would help him find his prey and eliminate him with dispatch."

The ambassador responded, "Seriously, Potentate, how shall I respond to Dr. Rosenzweig?"

"Stall him for a while. Be hard to reach. Then tell him that you have not found the proper moment to raise the issue with me. After an appropriate lapse, tell him I have been too busy to pursue it. Finally, you can tell him that I have chosen to remain neutral on the subject."

"Very good, sir."

But Carpathia was not neutral. He had just begun to warm to the subject. Rayford heard the squeak of a leather seat and imagined Carpathia leaning forward to speak earnestly to his cadre of international henchmen. "But let me tell you this, gentlemen. A person such as Dr. Ben-Judah is much more dangerous to our cause than an old fool like Rosenzweig. Rosenzweig is a brilliant scientist, but he is not wise in the ways of the world. Ben-Judah is more than a brilliant scholar. He has the ability to sway people, which would not be a bad thing if he served our cause. But he wants to fill his countrymen's minds with this blather about the Messiah having already returned. How anyone can still insist on taking the Bible literally and interpreting its prophecies in that light is beyond me, but tens of thousands of converts and devotees have sprung up in Israel and around the world due to his preaching at Teddy Kollek Stadium and in other huge venues. People will believe anything. And when they do, they are dangerous. Ben-Judah's time is short, and I will not stand in the way of his demise. Now, let us get down to business."

Rayford pulled up the top two sheets on his clipboard and began to take notes, as Carpathia outlined immediate plans.

"We must act swiftly," he was saying, "while the people are most vulnerable and open. They will look to the Global Community for help and aid, and we will give it to them. However, they will give it to us first. We had an enormous storehouse of income before the rebuilding of Babylon. We will need much more to effect our plan of raising the level of Third World countries so that the entire globe is on equal footing. I tell you, gentlemen, I was so excited and full of ideas last night that I could not sit down for our takeoff out of San Francisco. I was nearly thrown into this room from the forward cabin when we started down the runway. Here is what I was thinking about:

"You all have been doing a wonderful job of moving to the one-world currency. We are close to a cashless society, which can only help the Global Community administration. Upon your return to your respective areas, I would like you to announce, simultaneously, the initiation of a

ten-cent tax on all electronic money transfers. When we
get to the totally cashless system, you can imagine that
every transaction will be electronic. I estimate that this
will generate more than one and a half trillion dollars
annually.

"I am also initiating a one-dollar-per-barrel tax on oil
at the well, plus a ten-cents-per-gallon tax at the pump on
gasoline. My economic advisers tell me this could net us
more than half a trillion dollars every year. You knew the
time would come for a tax to the Global Community on
each area's Gross National Product. That time has come.
While the insurrectionists from Egypt, Great Britain, and
North America have been devastated militarily, they must
also be disciplined with a 50 percent tax on their GNP.
The rest of you will pay 30 percent.

"Now do not give me those looks, gentlemen. You
understand that everything you pay in will be returned to
you in multiplied benefits. We are building a new global
community. Pain is part of the process. The devastation
and death of this war will blossom into a utopia unlike
any the world has ever seen. And you will be in the fore-
front of it. Your countries and regions will benefit, and
you personally most of all.

"Here is what else I have in mind. As you know, our
intelligence sources quickly became convinced that the
attack on New York had been planned by American
militia under the clandestine leadership of President
Fitzhugh. This only confirmed my earlier decision to
virtually strip him of executive power. We now know
that he was killed in our retaliatory attack on Washing-

ton, D.C., which we have been able to effectively lay at the feet of the insurrectionists. Those limited few who remain loyal to him will likely turn against the rebels and see that they were bumbling fools.

"As you know, the second largest pool of oil, second only to the one in Saudi Arabia, was discovered above the Prudhoe Bay in Alaska. During the state of this leadership vacuum in North America, the Global Community will appropriate the vast oil fields in Alaska, including that huge pool. Years ago it was capped off to satisfy environmentalists; however, I have ordered teams of laborers into the region to install a series of sixteen-inch pipelines that would route that oil through Canada and to waterways where it could be barged to international trade centers. We already own the rights to oil in Saudi Arabia, Kuwait, Iraq, Iran, and the rest of the Middle East. That gives us control of two-thirds of the world's oil supply.

"We will gradually but steadily raise the price of oil, which will further finance our plans to inject social services into underprivileged countries and make the world playing field equal for everyone. From oil alone, we should be able to profit at a rate of about one trillion dollars per year.

"I will soon be appointing leaders to replace the three ambassadors of the regions that turned against us. That will bring the Global Community administration back to its full complement of ten regions. While you are now known as ambassadors to the Global Community, forthwith I will begin referring to you as sovereign heads of your own kingdoms. You will each continue to report directly to me. I will approve your budgets, receive your taxes, and give you bloc grants. Some will criticize this as making it appear that all nations and regions are dependent upon the Global Community for their income and thus assuring our control over the destiny of your people. You know better. You know that your loyalty will be rewarded, that the world will be a better place in which to live, and that our destiny is a utopian society based on peace and brotherhood.

"I am sure you all agree that the world has had enough of an antagonistic press. Even I, who have no designs on personal gain and certainly only altruistic motives for humbly and unwillingly accepting the heavy mantle of responsibility for world leadership, have been attacked and criticized by editorialists. The Global Community's ability to purchase all the major media outlets has virtually eliminated that. While we may have been criticized for threatening freedom of speech or freedom of the press, I believe the world can see that those unchecked freedoms led to excesses that stifled the ability and creativity of any leader. While they may once have been necessary to keep evil dictators from taking over, when there is nothing to criticize, such oppositional editorialists are anachronistic."

Rayford felt a tingle up his spine and nearly turned, convinced someone was standing right outside the cockpit door. Finally the feeling became so foreboding and pervasive that he whipped off his headphones and stood, leaning to peek through the fish-eye peephole. No one was there. Was God trying to tell him something? He was reminded of the same sense of fear that had overcome him when Buck had told his terrifying story of sitting through a meeting where Carpathia had single-handedly hypnotized and brainwashed everyone in the room except Buck.

Rayford sat back in his seat and put the headphones on. When he depressed the intercom button, it was as if he were hearing a new Carpathia. Nicolae spoke very softly, very earnestly, in a monotone. None of the flourishes and inflections that usually characterized his speech were evident. "I want to tell you all something, and I want you to listen very carefully and understand fully. This same control that we now have over all media, we also need over industry and commerce. It is not necessary for us to buy or own all of it. That would be too obvious and too easily opposed. Ownership is not the issue. Control is. Within the next few months we shall all announce unanimous decisions allowing us to control business, education, health care, and even the way your individual kingdoms choose their leaders. The fact is, democracy and voting will be suspended. They are inefficient and not in the best interests of the people. Because of what we will provide people, they will quickly understand that this is correct. Each of you can go back to your subjects and honestly tell them that this was your idea, you raised it, you sought support of your colleagues and me for it, and you prevailed. I will publicly reluctantly accede to your wishes, and we will all win."

Rayford listened to a long silence, wondering if his bugging device was malfunctioning. He released and depressed it several times, finally deciding that no one was saying anything in the conference area. So this was the mind control Buck had witnessed firsthand. Finally, Leon Fortunato spoke up. "Potentate Carpathia," he began deferentially, "I know I am merely your aide and not a member of this august body. However, may I make a suggestion?"

"Why, yes, Leon," Carpathia said, seeming pleasantly surprised. "You are in a significant position of trust and confidence, and we all value your input."

"I was just thinking, sir," Fortunato said, "that you and your colleagues here might consider suspending popular voting as inefficient and not in the best interests of the people, at least temporarily."

"Oh, Mr. Fortunato," Carpathia said, "I do not know. How do you feel people would respond to such a controversial proposal?"

The others seemed unable to keep from talking over each other. Rayford heard them all agreeing with Fortunato and urging Carpathia to consider this. One repeated Carpathia's statement about how much healthier the press was now that the Global Community owned it and added that ownership of industry and commerce was not as necessary as ownership of the press, as long as it was Carpathia controlled and Global Community led.

"Thank you very much for your input, gentlemen. It has been most stimulating and inspiring. I will take all these matters to heart and let you know soon of their disposition and implementation."

The meeting lasted another couple of hours and consisted mostly of Carpathia's so-called kings parroting back to him everything he had assured them that they would find brilliant when they thought about it. Each seemed to raise these as new and fresh ideas. Not only had Carpathia just mentioned them, but often the ambassadors would repeat each other as if not having heard.

"Now, gentlemen," Carpathia concluded, "in a few hours we will be in New Babylon, and I will soon appoint the three new ambassador rulers. I want you to be aware of the inevitable. We cannot pretend that the world as we know it has not been almost destroyed by this outbreak of global war. It is not over yet. There will be more skirmishes. There will be more surreptitious attacks. We will have to reluctantly access our power base of weaponry, which you all know I am loath to do, and many more thousands of lives will be lost in addition to the hundreds of thousands already taken. In spite of all of our best efforts and the wonderful ideas you have shared with me today, we must face the fact that for a long time we will be fighting an uphill battle.

"Opportunists always come to the fore at a time such as this. Those who would oppose us will take advantage of the impossibility of our peacekeeping forces to be everywhere at once, and this will result in famine, poverty, and disease. In one way, there is a positive side to this. Due to the incredible cost of rebuilding, the fewer people we must feed and whose standard of living we must raise, the more quickly and economically we can do this. As the population level decreases and then stabilizes, it will be important for us to be sure that it does not then explode again too quickly. With proper legislation regarding abortion, assisted suicide, and the reduction of expensive care for the defective and handicapped, we should be able to get a handle on worldwide population control."

All Rayford could do was pray. "Lord," he said silently, "I wish I was a more willing servant. Is there no other role for me? Could I not be used in some sort of active opposition or judgment against this evil one? I can only trust in your purpose. Keep my loved ones safe until we see you in all your glory. I know you have long since forgiven me for my years of disbelief and indifference, but still it weighs heavily on me. Thank you for helping me find the truth. Thank you for Bruce Barnes. And thank you for being with us as we fight this ultimate battle."

SEVEN

Buck had always had the ability to sleep well, even when he couldn't sleep long. He could have used a dozen or more hours the night before, after the day he had had. However, seven-plus hours had been just enough because when he was out, he was out. He knew Chloe had slept fitfully only because she told him in the morning. Her tossing and turning and winces of pain had not affected his slumber.

Now, as Ken Ritz landed the Learjet in Easton, Pennsylvania, "just to top off the tank before headin' to Tel Aviv," Buck was alert. He and the lanky, weathered, veteran pilot in his late fifties seemed to have picked up where they left off the last time he had employed this freelance charter service. Ritz was a talker, a raconteur, opinionated, interesting, and interested. He was as eager to know Buck's latest thoughts on the vanishings and the global war as he was in sharing his own views.

"So, what's new with the jet-setting young magazine writer since I saw you last, what, almost two years ago?" Ritz had begun.

Buck told him. He recalled that Ritz had been forthright and outspoken when they first met, admitting that he had no more idea than anyone else what might have caused the vanishings but coming down on the side of aliens from outer space. It had hit Buck as a wild idea for a buttoned-down pilot, but Buck hadn't come to any conclusions at that time either. One theory was as good as the next. Ritz had told him of many strange encounters in the air that made it plausible that an airman might believe in such things.

That gave Buck the confidence to tell his own story without apology. It didn't seem to faze Ritz, at least negatively. He listened quietly, and when Buck was through, Ritz simply nodded.

"So," Buck said, "do I seem as weird to you now as you did to me when you were propounding the space aliens theory?"

"Not really," Ritz said. "You'd be amazed at the number of people just like you that I've run into since the last time we talked. I don't know what it all means, but I'm beginning to believe there are more people who agree with you than agree with me."

"I'll tell you one thing," Buck said, "if I'm right, I'm still in big trouble. We are all gonna go through some real horror. But people who don't believe are going to be in worse trouble than they could ever imagine."

"I can't imagine worse trouble than we're in right now."

"I know what you mean," Buck said. "I used to apologize and try to make sure I wasn't coming on too strong or being obnoxious, but let me just urge you to investigate what I've said. And don't assume you've got a lot of time to do it."

"That's all part of the belief system, isn't it?" Ritz said. "If what you say is true, the end isn't that far off. Just a few years."

"Exactly."

"Then, if a fella was gonna check it out, he better get to it."

"I couldn't have said it better myself," Buck said.

After refueling in Easton, Ritz spent the hours over the Atlantic asking "what if" questions. Buck had to keep assuring him he was not a student or a scholar, but he amazed even himself at what he remembered from Bruce's teaching.

"It must have hurt like everything to lose a friend like that," Ritz said.

"You can't imagine."

———

Leon Fortunato instructed everyone on the plane when to get off and where to stand for the cameras when they finally reached New Babylon.

"Mr. Fortunato," Rayford said, careful to follow Leon's wishes, at least in front of others, "McCullum and I don't really need to be in the photograph, do we?"

"Not unless you'd like to go against the wishes of the potentate himself," Fortunato said. "Please just do what you're told."

The plane was on the ground and secure in New Babylon for several minutes before the doors were opened and the Carpathia-controlled press was assembled. Rayford sat in the cockpit, still listening over the two-way intercom. "Remember," Carpathia said, "no smiles. This is a grave, sad day. Appropriate expressions, please."

Rayford wondered why anyone would have to be reminded not to smile on a day like this.

Next came Fortunato's voice: "Potentate, apparently there's a surprise waiting for you."

"You know I do not like surprises," Carpathia said.

"It seems your fiancée is waiting with the crowd."

"That is totally inappropriate."

"Would you like me to have her removed?"

"No, I am not sure how she might react. We certainly would not like a scene. I just hope she knows how to act. This is not her strength, as you know."

Rayford thought Fortunato was diplomatic to not respond to that.

There was a rap at the cockpit door. "Pilot and copilot first," Fortunato called out. "Let's go!"

Rayford buttoned his dress uniform jacket and put his hat on as he stepped out of the cockpit. He and

McCullum trotted down the steps and began the right side of a V of people who would flank the potentate, the last to disembark.

Next came the flight service crew, who seemed awkward and nervous. They knew enough not to giggle, but simply looked down and walked directly to their spots. Fortunato and two other Carpathia aides led the seven ambassadors down the steps. Rayford turned to watch Carpathia appear in the opening at the top of the stairs.

The potentate always seemed taller than he really was in these situations, Rayford thought. He appeared to have just shaved and washed his hair, though Rayford had not been aware he had the time for that. His suit, shirt, and tie were exquisite, and he was understatedly elegant in his accessories. He waited ever so briefly, one hand in his right suit pocket, the other carrying a thin, glove-leather portfolio. *Always looking as if he's busily at the task at hand,* Rayford thought.

Rayford was amazed at Carpathia's ability to strike just the right pose and expression. He appeared concerned, grave, and yet somehow purposeful and confident. As lights flashed all around him and cameras whirred, he resolutely descended the steps and approached a bank of microphones. Every network insignia on each microphone had been redesigned to include the letters "GCN," the Global Community Network.

The only person he couldn't fully control chose that moment to burst Carpathia's bubble of propriety. Hattie Durham broke from the crowd and ran directly for him.

Security guards who stepped in her way quickly realized who she was and let her through. She did everything, Rayford thought, except squeal in delight. Carpathia looked embarrassed and awkward for the first time in Rayford's memory. It was as if he had to decide which would be worse: to brush her off or to welcome her to his side.

He chose the latter, but it was clear he was holding her at bay. She leaned in to kiss him and he bent to brush her cheek with his lips. When she turned to plant an open-mouthed kiss on his lips, he pulled her ear to his mouth and whispered sternly. Hattie looked stricken. Near tears, she began to pull away from him, but he grabbed her wrist and kept her standing next to him there at the microphones.

"It is so good to be back where I belong," he said. "It is wonderful to reunite with loved ones. My fiancée is overcome with grief, as I am, at the horrible events that began so relatively few hours ago. This is a difficult time in which we live, and yet our horizons have never been wider, our challenges so great, our future so potentially bright.

"That may seem an incongruous statement in light of the tragedy and devastation we have all suffered, but we are all destined for prosperity if we commit to standing together. We will stand against any enemy of peace and embrace any friend of the Global Community."

The crowd, including the press, applauded with just the right solemnity. Rayford was sick to his stomach, eager to get to his own apartment, and desperate to phone his wife as soon as he was sure it was daytime in the States.

———

"Don't worry about me, buddy boy," Ken Ritz told Buck as he helped him off the Learjet. "I'll hangar this baby and find a place to crash for a few days. I've always wanted to tour this country, and it's nice to be in a place that hasn't been blown to bits. You know how to reach me. When you're ready to head back, just leave a message here at the airport. I'll be checking in frequently."

Buck thanked him and grabbed his bag, slinging it over his shoulder. He headed toward the terminal. There, beyond the plate-glass window, he saw the enthusiastic wave of the wispy little old man with the flyaway hair, Chaim Rosenzweig. How he wanted this man to become a believer! Buck had come to love Chaim. That was not an expression he would have used about the other man back when he first met the scientist. It had been only a few years, but it seemed so long ago. Buck had been the youngest senior writer in the history of *Global Weekly*— in fact, in the history of international journalism. He had unabashedly campaigned for the job of profiling Dr. Rosenzweig as the *Weekly's* "Man of the Year."

Buck had first met the man a little more than a year before that assignment, after Rosenzweig had won a huge international prize for his invention (Chaim himself always called it more of a discovery) of a botanic formula.

Rosenzweig's concoction, some said without much exaggeration, allowed flora to grow anywhere—even on concrete.

The latter had never been proven; however, the desert sands of Israel soon began to blossom like a greenhouse. Flowers, corn, beans, you name it, every spare inch of the tiny nation was quickly cleared for agriculture. Overnight, Israel had become the richest nation in the world.

Other nations had been jealous to get hold of the formula. Clearly, this was the answer to any economic woes. Israel had gone from vulnerable, geographically defenseless country to a world power—respected, feared, envied.

Rosenzweig had become the man of the hour and, according to *Global Weekly,* "Man of the Year."

Buck had enjoyed meeting him more than any powerful politician he had ever interviewed. Here was a brilliant man of science, humble and self-effacing, naïve to the point of childlikeness, warm, personable, and unforgettable. He treated Buck like a son.

Other nations wanted Rosenzweig's formula so badly that they assigned high-level diplomats and politicians to court him. He acceded to audiences from so many dignitaries that his life's work had to be set aside. He was past retirement age anyway, but clearly here was a man more comfortable in a laboratory or a classroom than in a diplomatic setting. The darling of Israel had become the icon of world governments, and they all came calling.

Chaim had told Buck at one point that each suitor had his own not-so-hidden agenda. "I did my best to remain calm and diplomatic," he told Buck, "but only because I was representing my mother country. I grew almost physically ill," he added with his charming Hebrew-accented dialect, "when each began trying to persuade me that I would personally become the wealthiest man in the world if I would condescend to rent them my formula."

The Israeli government was even more protective of the formula. They made it so clear that the formula was not for sale or rent that other countries threatened war over it, and Russia actually attacked. Buck had been in Haifa the night the warplanes came screaming in. The miraculous delivery of that country from any damage, injury, or death—despite the incredible aerial assault—made Buck a believer in God, though not yet in Christ. There was no other explanation for bombs, missiles, and warships crashing and burning all over the nation, yet every citizen and building escaping unscathed.

That had sent Buck, who had feared for his life that night, on a quest for truth that was satisfied only after the vanishings and his meeting Rayford and Chloe Steele.

It had been Chaim Rosenzweig who had first mentioned the name Nicolae Carpathia to Buck. Buck had asked the old man if any of those who had been sent to court him about the formula had impressed him. Only one, Rosenzweig had told him; a young midlevel politician from the little country of Romania. Chaim had been taken with Carpathia's pacifist views, his selfless demeanor, and his insistence that the formula had the potential to change the world and save lives. It still rang in Buck's ears that Chaim Rosenzweig had once told him, "You and Carpathia must meet one day. You would like each other."

Buck could hardly remember when he had not been aware of Nicolae Carpathia, though his first exposure even to the name had been in that interview with Rosenzweig. Within days after the vanishings, the man who had seemingly overnight become president of Romania was a guest speaker at the United Nations. His brief address was so powerful, so magnetic, so impressive, that he had drawn a standing ovation even from the press—even from Buck. Of course, the world was in shock, terrified by the disappearances, and the time had been perfect for someone to step to the fore and offer a new international agenda for peace, harmony, and brotherhood.

Carpathia was thrust, ostensibly against his will, into power. He displaced the former secretary-general of the United Nations, reorganized it to include ten international mega-territories, renamed it the Global Community, moved it to Babylon (which was rebuilt and renamed New Babylon), and then set about disarming the entire globe.

It had taken more than Carpathia's charismatic personality to effect all this. He had a trump card. He had gotten to Rosenzweig. He had convinced the old man and his government that the key to the new world was Carpathia's and Global Community's ability to broker Rosenzweig's formula in exchange for compliance with international rules for disarmament. In exchange for a Carpathia-signed guarantee of at least seven years of protection from her enemies, Israel licensed to him the formula that allowed him to extract any promise he needed from any country in the world. With the formula, Russia could grow grain in the frozen tundra of Siberia. Destitute African nations became hothouses of domestic food sources and agricultural exports.

The power the formula allowed Carpathia to wield made it possible for him to bring the rest of the world willingly to its knees. Under the guise of his peacenik philosophies, member nations of the Global Community were required to destroy 90 percent of their weaponry and to donate the other 10 percent to Global Community headquarters. Before anyone realized what had happened, Nicolae Carpathia, now called the grand potentate of the Global Community, had quietly become the most militarily powerful pacifist in the history of the globe. Only those few nations that were suspicious of him kept back any firepower. Egypt, the new United States of Great Britain, and a surprisingly organized underground group of American militia forces had stockpiled just enough firepower to become a nuisance, an irritant, a trigger for Carpathia's angry retaliation. In short, their insurrection and his incredible overreaction had been the recipe for World War III, which the Bible had symbolically foretold as the Red Horse of the Apocalypse.

The irony of all this was that the sweet-spirited and innocent Chaim Rosenzweig, who always seemed to have everyone else's interests at heart, became an unabashed

devotee of Nicolae Carpathia. The man whom Buck
and his loved ones in the Tribulation Force had come to
believe was Antichrist himself played the gentle botanist
like a violin. Carpathia included Rosenzweig in many
visible diplomatic situations and even pretended Chaim
was part of his elite inner circle. It was clear to everyone
else that Rosenzweig was merely tolerated and humored.
Carpathia did what he wanted. Still, Rosenzweig nearly
worshiped the man, once intimating to Buck that if anyone embodied the qualities of the long-sought Jewish
Messiah, it was Nicolae himself.

That had been before one of Rosenzweig's younger
protégés, Rabbi Tsion Ben-Judah, had broadcast to the
world the findings of his government-sanctioned quest
for what Israel should look for in the Messiah.

Rabbi Ben-Judah, who had conducted a thorough
study of ancient manuscripts, including the Old and New
Testaments, had come to the conclusion that only Jesus
Christ had fulfilled all the prophecies necessary to qualify
for the role. To his regret, Rabbi Ben-Judah had come
just short of receiving Christ and committing his life to
him when the Rapture occurred. That sealed for sure his
view that Jesus was Messiah and had come for his own.
The Rabbi, in his mid-forties, had been left behind with a
wife of six years and two teenage stepchildren, a boy and
a girl. He had shocked the world, and especially his own
nation, when he withheld the conclusion of his three-
year study until a live international television broadcast.
Once he had clearly stated his belief, he became a
marked man.

Though Ben-Judah had been a student, protégé, and eventually a colleague of Dr. Rosenzweig, the latter still considered himself a nonreligious, nonpracticing Jew. In short, he did not agree with Ben-Judah's conclusion about Jesus, but mostly it was simply something he didn't want to talk about.

That, however, made him no less a friend of Ben-Judah's and no less an advocate. When Ben-Judah, with the encouragement and support of the two strange, other-worldly preachers at the Wailing Wall, began sharing his message, first at Teddy Kollek Stadium and then in other similar venues around the world, everyone knew it was just a matter of time before he would suffer for it.

Buck knew that one reason Rabbi Tsion Ben-Judah was still alive was that any attempt on his life was treated by the two preachers, Moishe and Eli, as attempts on their own. Many had died mysterious and fiery deaths trying to attack those two. Most everyone knew that Ben-Judah was "their guy," and thus he had so far eluded mortal harm.

That safety seemed at an end now, and that was why Buck was in Israel. Buck was convinced that Carpathia himself was behind the horror and tragedy that had come to Ben-Judah's family. News reports said black-hooded thugs pulled up to Ben-Judah's home in the middle of a sunny afternoon when the teenagers had just returned from Hebrew school. Two armed guards were shot to death, and Mrs. Ben-Judah and her son and daughter were dragged out into the street, decapitated, and left in pools of their own blood.

The murderers had driven away in a nondescript and unmarked van. Ben-Judah's driver had raced to the rabbi's university office as soon as he heard the news, and he had reportedly driven Ben-Judah to safety. Where, no one knew. Upon his return, the driver denied knowledge of Ben-Judah's whereabouts to the authorities and the press, claiming he had not seen him since before the murders and that he merely hoped to hear from him at some point.

EIGHT

RAYFORD thought he had had enough sleep, catching catnaps on his long journey. He had not figured the toll that tension and terror and disgust would exact on his mind and body. In his and Amanda's own apartment, as comfortable as air-conditioning could make a place in Iraq, Rayford disrobed to his boxers and sat on the end of his bed. Shoulders slumped, elbows on knees, he exhaled loudly and realized how exhausted he truly was. He had finally heard from home. He knew Amanda was safe, Chloe was on the mend, and Buck—as usual—was on the move. He didn't know what he thought about this Verna Zee threatening the security of the Tribulation Force's new safe house (Loretta's). But he would trust Buck, and God, in that.

Rayford stretched out on his back atop the bedcovers. He put his hands behind his head and stared at the ceiling. How he'd love to get a peek at the treasure trove of Bruce's computer archives. But as he drifted off to a sound sleep, he was trying to figure a way to get back to Chicago by Sunday. Surely there had to be some way he could make it to Bruce's memorial service. He was pleading his case with God as sleep enveloped him.

————————

Buck had often been warmed by Chaim Rosenzweig's ancient-faced smile of greeting. There was no hint of that now. As Buck strode toward the old man, Rosenzweig merely opened his arms for an embrace and said hoarsely, "Cameron! Cameron!"

Buck bent to hug his tiny friend, and Rosenzweig clasped his hands behind Buck and squeezed tightly as a child. He buried his face in Buck's neck and wept bitterly. Buck nearly lost his balance, the weight of his bag pulling him one way and Chaim Rosenzweig's vice-grip pulling him forward. He felt as if he might stumble and fall atop his friend. He fought to stay upright, holding Chaim and letting him cry.

Finally Rosenzweig released his grip and pulled Buck toward a row of chairs. Buck became aware of Rosenzweig's tall, dark-complected driver standing about ten feet away with his hands clasped before him. He appeared concerned for his employer, and embarrassed.

Chaim nodded toward him. "You remember Andre," Rosenzweig said.

"Yeah," Buck said, nodding, "how ya doin'?"

Andre responded in Hebrew. He neither spoke nor understood English. Buck knew no Hebrew.

Rosenzweig spoke to Andre and he hurried away. "He'll bring the car around," Chaim said.

"I have only a few days here," Buck said. "What can you tell me? Do you know where Tsion is?"

"No! Cameron, it's so terrible! What a hideous, horrible defiling of a man's family and of his name!"

"But you heard from him—"

"One phone call. He said you would know where to begin looking for him. But, Cameron, have you not heard the latest?"

"I can't imagine."

"The authorities are trying to implicate him in the murders of his own family."

"Oh, come on! No one is going to buy that! Nothing even points in that direction. Why would he do that?"

"Of course, you and I know he would never do such a thing, Cameron, but when evil elements are out to get you, they stop at nothing. You heard, of course, about his driver."

"No."

Rosenzweig shook his head and lowered his chin to his chest.

"What?" Buck asked. "Not him too?"

"I'm afraid so. A car bombing. His body was barely recognizable."

"Chaim! Are you sure you're safe? Does your driver know how to—"

"Drive defensively? Check for car bombs? Defend himself or me? Yes to all of those. Andre is quite skilled. It makes me no less terrified, I admit, but I feel I am protected the best I can be."

"But you are associated with Dr. Ben-Judah. Those looking for him will try to follow you to him."

"Which means you should not be seen with me either," Rosenzweig said.

"It's too late for that," Buck said.

"Don't be too sure. Andre assured me we were not followed here. It wouldn't surprise me if someone picked us up at this point and followed us, but for the instant, I believe we are here undetected."

"Good! I cleared customs with my phony passport. Did you use my name when booking me a room?"

"Unfortunately I did, Cameron. I'm sorry. I even used my own name to secure it."

Buck had to suppress a smile at the man's sweet naïveté. "Well, friend, we'll just use that to keep them off our trail, hm?"

"Cameron, I'm afraid I'm not too good at all this."

"Why don't you have Andre drive you directly to that hotel. Tell them my plans have changed and that I will not be in until Sunday."

"Cameron! How do you think of such things so quickly?"

"Hurry now. And we must not be seen together anymore. I will leave here no later than Saturday night. You can reach me at this number."

"Is it secure?"

"It's a satellite phone, the latest technology. No one can tap into it. Just don't put my name next to that number, and don't give that number to anyone else."

"Cameron, where will you begin looking for Tsion?"

"I have a couple of ideas," Buck said. "And you must know, if I can get him out of this country, I'll do it."

"Excellent! If I were a praying man, I'd pray for you."

"Chaim, one of these days soon, you *need* to become a praying man."

Chaim changed the subject. "One more thing, Cameron. I have placed a call to Carpathia for his assistance in this."

"I wish you hadn't done that, Chaim. I don't trust him the way you do."

"I've sensed that, Buck," Rosenzweig said, "but you need to get to know the man better."

If you only knew, Buck thought. "Chaim, I'll try to communicate with you as soon as I know anything. Call me only if you need to."

Rosenzweig embraced him fiercely again and hurried off. Buck used a pay phone to call the King David Hotel. He booked a room for two weeks under the name of Herb Katz. "Representing what company?" the clerk said.

Buck thought a moment. "International Harvester," he said, deciding that that would have been a great description of both Bruce Barnes and Tsion Ben-Judah.

Rayford's eyes popped open. He had not moved a muscle. He had no idea how long he had slept, but something had interrupted his reverie. The jangling phone on the bedside table made him jump. Reaching for it, he realized his arm was asleep. It didn't want to go where he wanted it to. Somehow he forced himself to grasp the receiver. "Steele here," he gargled.

"Captain Steele? Are you all right?" It was Hattie Durham.

Rayford rolled onto his side and tucked the receiver under his chin. Leaning on his elbow, he said, "I'm all right, Hattie. How are you?"

"Not so good. I'd like to see you if I could."

Despite the closed curtains, the brilliant afternoon sun forced its way into the room. "When?" Rayford said.

"Dinner tonight?" she said. "About six?"

Rayford's mind was reeling. Had she already been told of her lessened role in the Carpathia administration? Did he want to be seen in public with her while Amanda was away? "Is there a rush, Hattie? Amanda's in the States, but she'll be back in a week or so—"

"No, Rayford, I really need to talk to you. Nicolae has meetings from now until midnight, and their dinner is being catered. He said he didn't have a problem with my talking with you. I know you want to be appropriate and all that. It's not a date. Let's just have dinner somewhere where it will be obvious that we're just old friends talking. Please?"

"I guess," Rayford said, curious.

"My driver will pick you up at six then, Rayford."

"Hattie, do me a favor. If you agree this shouldn't look like a date, don't dress up."

"Captain Steele," she said, suddenly formal, "stepping out is the last thing on my mind."

———

Buck settled into his room on the third floor of the King David Hotel. On a hunch he called the offices of the *Global Community East Coast Daily Times* in Boston and asked for his old friend, Steve Plank. Plank had been his boss at *Global Weekly* what seemed eons ago. He had abruptly left there to become Carpathia's press secretary when Nicolae became secretary-general of the United Nations. It wasn't long before Steve was tabbed for the lucrative position he now held.

It was no surprise to Buck to find that Plank was not in the office. He was in New Babylon at the behest of Nicolae Carpathia and no doubt feeling very special about it.

Buck showered and took a nap.

———

Rayford felt as if he could use another several hours' sleep. He certainly didn't intend to stay out long with Hattie Durham. He dressed casually, just barely presentable enough for a place like Global Bistro, where Hattie and Nicolae were often seen.

Of course, Rayford would not be able to let on that he had known about Hattie's demotion before she did. He would have to let her play the story out with all her characteristic emotion and angst. He didn't mind. He owed her that much. He still felt guilty about where she was, both geographically and in her life. It didn't seem that long ago that she had been the object of his lust.

Rayford had never acted on it, of course, but it was Hattie whom he was thinking of the night of the Rapture. How could he have been so deaf, so blind, so out of touch with reality? A successful professional man, married more than twenty years with a college-age daughter and a twelve-year-old son, daydreaming about his senior flight attendant and justifying it because his wife had been on a religious kick! He shook his head. Irene, the lovely little woman he had for so long taken for granted, the one with the name of an aunt many years her senior, had known real truth with a capital T long before any of them.

Rayford had always been a churchgoer and would have called himself a Christian. But to him church was a place to see and be seen, to network, to look respectable. When preachers got too judgmental or too literal, it made him nervous. And when Irene had found a new, smaller congregation that seemed much more aggressive in their faith, he had begun finding reasons not to go with her. When she started talking about the salvation of souls, the blood of Christ, and the return of Christ, he became convinced she was off her nut. How long before she had him traipsing along behind her, passing out literature door-to-door?

That was how he had justified the dalliance, only in his mind, with Hattie Durham. Hattie was fifteen years his junior, and she was a knockout. Though they had enjoyed dinner together a few times and drinks several times, and despite the silent language of the body and the eyes, Rayford had never so much as touched her. It had not been beyond Hattie to grab his arm as she brushed past him or even to put her hands on his shoulders when speaking to him in the cockpit, but Rayford had somehow kept from letting things go further. That night over the Atlantic, with a fully loaded 747 on autopilot, he had finally worked up the courage to suggest something concrete to her. Ashamed as he was now to admit it even to himself, he had been ready to take the next, bold, decisive step toward a physical relationship.

But he had never gotten the words out of his mouth. When he left the cockpit to find her, she had nearly bowled him over with the news that about a quarter of his passengers had disappeared, leaving everything material behind. The cabin, which was normally a black, humming, sleep chamber at four o'clock in the morning, quickly became a beehive of panic as people realized what was happening. That was the night Rayford told Hattie he didn't know what was happening any more than she did. The truth was that he knew all too well. Irene had been right. Christ had returned to rapture his church, and Rayford, Hattie, and three-fourths of their passengers had been left behind.

Rayford had not known Buck Williams at that time, didn't know Buck was a first class passenger on that very flight. He couldn't know that Buck and Hattie had chatted, that Buck had used his computer and the Internet to try to reach her people to see if they were OK. Only later would he discover that Buck had introduced Hattie to the new, sparkling international celebrity leader, Nicolae Carpathia. Rayford had met Buck in New York. Rayford was there to apologize to Hattie for his inappropriate actions toward her in the past and to try to convince her of the truth about the vanishings. Buck was there to introduce her to Carpathia, to interview Carpathia, and to interview Rayford—Hattie's captain. Buck was merely trying to put a story together about various views of the disappearances.

Rayford had been earnest and focused in his attempts to persuade Buck that he had found the real truth too. That was the night Buck met Chloe. So much had happened in so short a time. Less than two years later, Hattie was the personal assistant and lover of Nicolae Carpathia, the Antichrist. Rayford, Buck, and Chloe were believers in Christ. And all three of them agonized over the plight of Hattie Durham.

Maybe tonight, Rayford thought, he could finally have some positive influence on Hattie.

Buck had always been able to awaken himself whenever he wanted. The gift had failed him very infrequently. He had told himself he wanted to be up and moving by 6:00 P.M. He awoke on time, less refreshed than he had hoped, but eager to get going. He told his cabbie, "The Wailing Wall, please."

Moments later, Buck disembarked. There, not far from the Wailing Wall, behind a wrought-iron fence, stood the men Buck had come to know as the two witnesses prophesied in Scripture.

They called themselves Moishe and Eli, and truly they seemed to have come from another time and another place. They wore ragged, burlap-like robes. They were barefoot with leathery, dark skin. Both had long, dark gray hair and unkempt beards. They were sinewy with bony joints and long muscled arms and legs. Anyone who dared get close to them smelled smoke. Those who dared attack them had been killed. It was as simple as that. Several had rushed them with automatic weapons, only to seem to hit an invisible wall and drop dead on the spot. Others had been incinerated where they stood, by fire that had come from the witnesses' mouths.

They preached nearly constantly in the language and cadence of the Bible, and what they said was blasphemous to the ears of devout Jews. They preached Christ and him crucified, proclaiming him the Messiah, the Son of God.

The only time they had been seen apart from the Wailing Wall was at Teddy Kollek Stadium, when they appeared on the platform with Rabbi Tsion Ben-Judah, a recent convert to Christ. News coverage broadcast around the world showed these two strange men, speaking in unison, not using microphones and yet being heard distinctly in the back rows. "Come nigh and listen," they had shouted, "to the chosen servant of the most high God! He is among the first of the 144,000 who shall go forth from this and many nations to proclaim the gospel of Christ throughout the world! Those who come against him, just as those who have come against us before the due time, shall surely die!"

The witnesses had not stayed on the platform or even in the stadium for that first big evangelistic rally at Kollek Stadium. They slipped away and were back at the Wailing Wall by the time the meeting was over. Thatcoming together in a huge stadium was reproduced dozens of times in almost every country of the world over the next year and a half, resulting in tens of thousands of converts.

Enemies of Rabbi Ben-Judah did try to "come against" him during those eighteen months, as the witnesses had warned. It seemed others had gotten the point and had repented of their intentions. A lull of three to four weeks since any threats on his life had been a pleasant respite for the indefatigable Ben-Judah. But now he was in hiding, and his family and his driver had been slaughtered.

Ironically, the last time Buck had been at the Wailing Wall to watch and hear the two witnesses, he had been with Rabbi Ben-Judah. They had come back later the same night and dared approach the fence and speak to the men who had killed all others who had gotten that close. Buck had been able to understand them in his own language, though his tape recording of the incident later proved they had been speaking in Hebrew. Rabbi Ben-Judah had begun reciting the words of Nicodemus from the famous meeting of Jesus by night, and the witnesses had responded the way Jesus had. It had been the most chilling night of Buck's life.

Now, here he was, alone. He was looking for Ben-Judah, who had told Chaim Rosenzweig that Buck would know where to start looking. He could think of no better place.

As usual, a huge crowd had gathered before the witnesses, though people knew well enough to keep their distance. Even the rage and hatred of Nicolae Carpathia had not yet affected Moishe and Eli. More than once, even in public, Carpathia had asked if there was not someone who could do away with those two nuisances. He had been informed apologetically by military leaders that no weapons seemed capable of harming them. The witnesses themselves continually referred to the folly of trying to harm them "before the due time."

Bruce Barnes had explained to the Tribulation Force that, indeed, in due time God would allow the witnesses to become vulnerable, and they would be attacked. That incident was still more than a year and a half away, Buck believed, but even the thought of it was a nightmare to his soul.

This evening the witnesses were doing as they had done every day since the signing of the treaty between Israel and Carpathia: They were proclaiming the terrible day of the Lord. And they were acknowledging Jesus Christ as "the Mighty God, the Everlasting Father, and the Prince of Peace. Let no other man anywhere call himself the ruler of this world! Any man who makes such a claim is not the Christ but the Antichrist, and he shall surely die! Woe unto anyone who preaches another gospel! Jesus is the only true God, maker of heaven and earth!"

Buck was always thrilled and moved by the preaching of the witnesses. He looked around the crowd and saw people from various races and cultures. He knew from experience that many of them understood no Hebrew. They were understanding the witnesses in their own tongues, just as he was.

Buck edged a quarter of the way into the crowd of about three hundred. He stood on tiptoes to see the witnesses. Suddenly both stopped preaching and moved forward toward the fence. The crowd seemed to step back as one, fearing for its life. The witnesses now stood inches from the fence, the crowd keeping about a fifty-foot distance with Buck near the back.

To Buck it seemed clear the witnesses had noticed him. Both stared directly into his eyes, and he could not move. Without gesturing or moving, Eli began to preach. "He who has ears to hear, let him hear! Do not be afraid, for I know that you seek Jesus who was crucified. He is not here; for He is risen, as He said."

Believers in the crowd mumbled their amens and their agreement. Buck was riveted. Moishe stepped forward and seemed to speak directly to him. "Do not be afraid, for I know whom you seek. He is not here."

Eli again: "Go quickly and tell His disciples that Christ is risen from the dead!"

Moishe, still staring at Buck: "Indeed He is going

before you into Galilee. There you will see Him. Behold, I have told you."

The witnesses stood and stared silently for so long, unmoving, it was as if they had turned to stone. The crowd grew nervous and began to dissipate. Some waited to see if the witnesses would speak again, but they did not. Soon only Buck stood where he had stood for the last several minutes. He couldn't take his eyes off the eyes of Moishe. The two merely stood at the fence and stared at him. Buck began to advance on them, coming to within about twenty feet. The witnesses didn't move. They seemed not even to be breathing. Buck noticed no blink, no twitch. In the fading twilight, he carefully watched their faces. Neither opened his mouth, and yet Buck heard, plain as day in his own language, "He who has ears to hear, let him hear."

NINE

THE intercom summoned Rayford to the front door of his condominium, where Hattie's driver waited. He led Rayford to the white stretch Mercedes and opened the back door. There was room on the seat next to Hattie, but Rayford chose to sit across from her. She had honored his request not to dress up, but even casually attired, she looked lovely. He decided not to say so.

Trouble was etched on her face. "I really appreciate your agreeing to see me."

"Sure. What's up?"

Hattie glanced toward the driver. "Let's talk at dinner," she said. "The Bistro OK?"

Buck stood riveted before the witnesses as the sun went down. He looked around to be sure it was still just him and them. "That's all I get? He's in Galilee?"

Again, without moving their lips, the witnesses spoke: "He who has ears to hear, let him hear."

Galilee? Did it even exist anymore? Where would Buck start, and when would he start? Surely he didn't want to be poking around there in the night. He had to know where he was going, have some sort of bearing. He spun on his heel to see if any taxis were in the area. He saw a few. He turned back to the witnesses. "If I came back here later tonight, might I learn more?"

Moishe backed away from the fence and sat on the pavement, leaning against a wall. Eli gestured and spoke aloud, "Birds of the air have nests," he said, "but the Son of Man has nowhere to lay his head."

"I don't understand," Buck said. "Tell me more."

"He who has ears—"

Buck was frustrated. "I'll come back at midnight. I'm pleading for your help."

Eli was now backing away too. "Lo, I am with you always, even to the end of the age."

Buck left, still planning to come back, but also strangely warmed by that last mysterious promise. Those were the words of Christ. Was Jesus speaking directly to him through the mouths of these witnesses? What an unspeakable privilege! He took a cab back to the King David, confident that he would, before long, be reunited with Tsion Ben-Judah.

Rayford and Hattie were welcomed expansively by the maître d' of the Global Bistro. The man recognized her, of course, but not Rayford. "Your usual table, ma'am?"

"No, thank you, Jeoffrey, but neither would we like to be hidden."

They were led to a table set for four. But even though two busboys hurried out to clear away two sets of dinnerware, and the waiter pulled out a chair for Hattie while pointing Rayford to one next to her, Rayford was still thinking of appearances. He sat directly across from Hattie, knowing they would nearly have to shout to hear each other in the noisy place. The waiter hesitated, looking irritated, and finally moved Rayford's tableware back to in front of him. That was something Hattie and Rayford might have chuckled over in their past, which included a half-dozen clandestine dinners where each seemed to be wondering what the other was thinking about their future. Hattie had been more flirtatious than Rayford, though he had never discouraged her.

Televisions throughout the Bistro carried the continuing news of war around the world. Hattie signaled for the maître d', who came running. "I doubt the potentate would appreciate this news depressing patrons who came in here for a little relaxation."

"I'm afraid it's on every station, ma'am."

"There's not even a music station of some kind?"

"I'll check."

Within moments, all the television sets in the Global

Bistro showed music videos. Several applauded this, but
Rayford sensed Hattie barely noticed.

In the past, when they were playing around the edges
of an affair of the mind, Rayford had to remind Hattie to
order and then encourage her to eat. Her attention had
been riveted on him, and he had found that flattering
and alluring. Now the opposite seemed the case.

Hattie studied her menu as if she faced a final exam
on it in the morning. She was as beautiful as ever, now
twenty-nine and pregnant for the first time. She was
early enough along that no one would know unless she
told them. She had told Rayford and Amanda the last
time they were together. At that time she seemed thrilled,
proud of her new diamond, and eager to talk about her
pending marriage. She had told Amanda that Nicolae
was "going to make an honest woman of me yet."

Hattie was wearing her ostentatious engagement ring;
however, the diamond was turned in toward her palm
so only the band was visible. Hattie was clearly not
a happy woman, and Rayford wondered if this all
stemmed from her getting the cold shoulder from
Nicolae at the airport. He wanted to ask her, but this
meeting was her idea. She would say what she wanted
to say soon enough.

Though the Global Bistro had a French-sounding
name, Hattie herself had helped conceive it, and the
menu carried international cuisine, mostly American.
She ordered an unusually large meal. Rayford had just a
sandwich. Hattie small-talked until she had finished her
food, including dessert. Rayford knew all the clichés,

such as that she was now eating for two, but he believed she was eating out of nervousness and in an attempt to put off what she really wanted to talk about.

"Can you believe it's been nearly two years since you last served as my senior flight attendant?" he said, trying to get the ball rolling.

Hattie sat up straight in her chair, folded her hands in her lap, and leaned forward. "Rayford, this has been the most incredible two years of my life."

He looked at her expectantly, wondering if she meant that was good or bad. "You've expanded your horizons," he said.

"Think about it, Rayford. All I ever wanted to be was a flight attendant. The entire cheerleading squad at Maine East High School wanted to be flight attendants. We all applied, but I was the only one who made it. I was so proud, but flying quickly lost its appeal. Half the time I had to remind myself where we were going and when we would get there and when we would get back. But I loved the people, I loved the freedom of traveling, and I loved visiting all those places. You know I had a couple of serious boyfriends here and there, but nothing ever worked out. When I finally worked my way up to the planes and routes that only seniority could bring, I had a huge crush on one of my pilots, but that never worked either."

"Hattie, I wish you wouldn't dredge that up. You know how I feel about that period."

"I know, and I'm sorry. Nothing ever came of it, though I could have hoped for more. I've accepted your explanation and your apology, and that's not what this is about at all."

"That's good, because as you know, I am again happily married."

"I envy you, Rayford."

"I thought you and Nicolae were going to get married."

"So did I. Now I'm not so sure. And I'm not so sure I want to either."

"If you want to talk about it, I'm happy to listen. I'm no expert in matters of the heart, so I probably won't have any advice, but I'm an ear if that's what you want."

Hattie waited until the dishes were cleared, then told the waiter, "We'll be here awhile."

"I'll apply this to your tab," the waiter said. "I doubt anyone will be giving *you* the bum's rush." He smiled at Rayford, seeming to appreciate his own humor. Rayford forced a smile.

When the waiter was gone, Hattie seemed to feel the freedom to continue. "Rayford, you may not know this, but I actually had a thing for Buck Williams once. You remember he was on your plane that night."

"Of course."

"I didn't look at him romantically then, of course, because I was still enamored with you. But he was sweet. And he was cute. And he had that big, important job. He and I are closer in age, too."

"And . . . ?"

"Well, to tell you the truth, when you dumped me—"

"Hattie, I never dumped you. There was nothing to dump. We were not an item."

"Yet."

"OK, yet," he said. "That's fair. But you have to admit there had been no commitment or even an expression of a commitment."

"There had been plenty of signals, Rayford."

"I have to acknowledge that. Still, it's unfair to say I dumped you."

"Call it whatever you want so you can deal with it, but I felt dumped, OK? Anyway, all of sudden Buck Williams looked more attractive to me than ever. I'm sure he thought I was using him to meet a celebrity, which also happened. I was so grateful for Buck's introducing me to Nicolae."

"Forgive me, Hattie, but this is old news."

"I know, but I'm getting somewhere. Bear with me. As soon as I met Nicolae, I was stricken. He was only about as much older than Buck as Buck was older than I. But he seemed so much older. He was a world traveler, an international politician, a leader. He was already the most famous man in the world. I knew he was going places. I felt like a giggling schoolgirl and couldn't imagine I had impressed him in the least. When he began to show interest, I thought it was merely physical. And, I admit, I would have probably slept with him in a minute and not regretted it. We had an affair, and I fell in love, but as God is my witness—oh, Rayford, I'm sorry. I shouldn't use those kind of references around you—I never expected him to be truly interested in me. I knew the whole thing was temporary, and I was determined to just enjoy it while it lasted.

"It got to the point where I dreaded his being away. I kept telling myself to maintain a level head. The end would have to come soon, and I really believe I was prepared for it. But then he shocked me. He made me his personal assistant. I had no experience, no skills. I knew it was just a way to keep me available to him after hours. That was all right with me, though I was afraid of what my life might become when he became even busier. Well, my worst fears were realized. He's still charming and smooth and dynamic and powerful and the most incredible person I've ever met. But I mean exactly to him what I always feared I did. You know the man usually works at least eighteen hours a day and sometimes twenty? I mean nothing to him, and I know it.

"I used to be involved in some discussions. He used to bounce an idea or two off me. But what do I know about international politics? I would make some silly statement based on my limited knowledge, and he would either laugh at me or ignore me. Then he came to where he never sought my opinions anymore. I was allowed little playthings, like helping develop this restaurant and being available to greet groups touring the new Global Community headquarters. But I'm merely window-dressing now, Rayford. He didn't give me a ring until after I was pregnant, and he still hasn't asked me if I would marry him. I guess that's supposed to be understood."

"By accepting his ring, did you not imply that you would marry him?"

"Oh, Rayford, it wasn't nearly that romantic. He merely asked me to close my eyes and stick out my hand. Then he put the ring on my finger. I didn't know what to say. He just smiled."

"You're saying you don't feel committed?"

"I don't feel anything anymore. And I don't think he ever felt anything for me except physical attraction."

"And all the trappings? The wealth? Your own car and driver? I assume you have an expense account—"

"I have all that, yes." Hattie seemed tired. She continued. "To tell you the truth, all that stuff is a lot like what flying was to me. You quickly get tired of the routine. I was drunk with the power and the glitter and the glamour of it for a while, sure. But it's not who I am. I know no one here. People treat me with deference and respect only because of who I live with. But they don't really know him either. Neither do I. I'd rather he be mad at me than ignore me. I asked him the other day if I could go back to the States for a while and visit my friends and family. He was irritated. He said I didn't even have to ask. He said, 'Just let me know and go ahead and arrange it. I've got more to do than worry about your little schedule.' I'm just a piece of furniture to him, Rayford."

Rayford was biding his time. There was so much he wanted to tell her. "How much do you talk?"

"What do you mean? We don't talk. We just coexist now."

Rayford spoke carefully, "I'm just curious about how much he knows about Chloe and Buck."

"Oh, you don't have to worry about that. Smart as he is and well connected as he is, and for as many 'eyes' as he has out there surveilling everything and everybody, I don't think he has any idea of a connection between you and Buck. I have never mentioned that Buck married your daughter. And I never would."

"Why?"

"I don't think he needs to know, that's all. For some reason, Rayford, he trusts you implicitly on some things and not at all on others."

"I've noticed."

"What have you noticed?" she asked.

"Being left out of the plans for the Condor 216, for one," Rayford said.

"Yeah," she said, "and wasn't that creative of him to use his office suite number as part of the name of the plane?"

"It just seemed bizarre to be his pilot and to be surprised by new equipment."

"If you lived with him, that would not surprise you. I've been out of the loop for months. Rayford, do you realize that I was not contacted by anyone when the war broke out?"

"He didn't call you?"

"I didn't know whether he was dead or alive. I heard him on the news, just like everyone else. He didn't even call after that. No aide let me know. No assistant so much as sent me a memo. I called everywhere. I talked to every person in the organization I knew. I even got as far as Leon Fortunato. He told me he would tell Nicolae that I called. Can you imagine? He would tell him I called!"

"So when you saw him at the airstrip . . . ?"

"I was testing him. I won't deny it. I wasn't as eager to see him as I let on, but I was giving him one more chance. Wasn't it obvious I spoiled his big appearance?"

"That's the impression I had," Rayford said, wondering if he was wise in surrendering his neutral role.

"When I tried to kiss him, he told me it was inappropriate and to act like an adult. At least in his remarks he referred to me as his fiancée. He said I was overcome with grief, as he was. I know him well enough to know there was no grief. I could see it written all over him. He loves this stuff. And regardless of what he says, he's right in the middle of it. He talks like a pacifist, but he hopes people will attack him so he can justify retaliating. I was so horrified and sad, hearing about all the death and destruction, but he comes back here to his self-made palace, pretending to grieve with all the heartbroken people around the world. But in private it's like he's celebrating. He can't get enough of this. He's rubbing his hands, making plans, devising strategies. He's putting together his new team. They're meeting right now. Who knows what they'll dream up!"

"What are you gonna do, Hattie? This is no kind of life for you."

"He doesn't even want me in the office anymore."

Rayford knew that but couldn't let on. "What do you mean?"

"I was actually fired today, by my own fiancé. He asked if he could meet me in my quarters."

"Your quarters?"

"We don't really live together anymore. I'm just down the hall, and he visits once in a great while in the middle of the night—between meetings, I guess. But I've been a fairly high-maintenance girl-next-door for a long time."

"So what did he want?"

"I thought I knew. I thought he'd been away long enough that he just wanted the usual. But he just told me he was replacing me."

"You mean you're out?"

"No. He still wants me around. Still wants me to bear his child. He just thinks the job has passed me by. I told him, 'Nicolae, that job passed me by the day before I took it. I've never been cut out to be a secretary. I was OK with the public relations and the people contacts, but making me your personal assistant was a mistake.'"

"I always thought you looked the part."

"Well, thanks for that, Rayford. But losing that job was a relief in a way."

"Only in a way?"

"Yes. Where does this leave me? I asked him what the future was for us. He had the audacity to say, 'Us?' I said, 'Yes! Us! I'm wearing your ring and carrying your child. When do we make this permanent?'"

Buck woke with a start. He had been dreaming. It was dark. He turned on a small lamp and squinted at his watch. He still had several hours before his appointment with Moishe and Eli at midnight. But what had that dream been all about? Buck had dreamed that he was Joseph, Mary's husband. He had heard an angel of the Lord saying, "Arise, flee to Egypt, and stay there until I bring you word."

Buck was confused. He had never been communicated to in a dream, by God or anyone else. He had always considered dreams just aberrations based on daily life. Here he was in the Holy Land, thinking about God, thinking about Jesus, communicating with the two witnesses, trying to steer clear of the Antichrist and his cohorts. It made sense he might have a dream related to biblical stories. Or was God trying to tell him that he would find Tsion Ben-Judah in Egypt, rather than wherever it seemed the witnesses were sending him? They always spoke so circumspectly. He would have to simply ask them. How could he be expected to understand biblical references when he was so new at all this? He wanted to sleep until eleven-thirty before taking a cab to the Wailing Wall, but he found it difficult to fall back to sleep with the weird dream playing itself over and over in his mind. One thing he didn't want to do, especially with the news of war coming out of Cairo, was to go anywhere near Egypt. He wasn't much more than two hundred miles from Cairo as the crow flew anyway. That was plenty close enough, even if Carpathia had not used nuclear weapons on the Egyptian capital.

Buck lay back in the darkness, wondering.

Rayford was torn. What could he tell his old friend? She was clearly in pain, clearly at a loss. He couldn't blurt that her lover was the Antichrist and that Rayford and his friends knew it. What he really wanted was to plead with her, to beg her to receive Christ. But hadn't he already done that once? Hadn't he spelled out to her everything he had learned following the vanishings, which he now knew as the Rapture?

She knew the truth. At least she knew what he believed was the truth. He had spilled his guts to her, Chloe, and Buck at a restaurant in New York, and he felt he had alienated Hattie by repeating what he had said to her earlier that day in private. He had been certain his daughter was embarrassed to death. And he had been convinced that the erudite Buck Williams was merely tolerating him. It had been a shock to find that Chloe took a huge step closer to her own personal decision to follow Christ after seeing his passion that night. That meeting had also been a huge influence on Buck.

Now he tried a new tack. "Let me tell you something, Hattie. You need to know that Buck and Chloe and I all care very deeply about you."

"I know, Rayford, but—"

"I don't think you do know," Rayford said. "We have all wondered if this was the best thing for you, and each of us feels somehow responsible for your having left your job and loved ones and gone first to New York and now to New Babylon. And for what?"

Hattie stared at him. "But I hardly heard from any of you."

"We didn't feel we had a right to say anything. You're an adult. It's your life. I felt my antics had pushed you away from the aviation industry. Buck feels guilty for having introduced you to Nicolae in the first place. Chloe often wonders if she couldn't have said or done something that might have changed your mind."

"But why?" Hattie said. "How did any of you know I was not happy here?"

Now Rayford was stuck. How, indeed, did they know? "We just sensed the odds were against you," he said.

"And I don't suppose I gave you any indication that you were right, always trying to impress you whenever I saw you or Buck with Nicolae."

"There was that, yes."

"Well, Rayford, it may also come as a shock to you to know that I had never foreseen becoming pregnant out of wedlock either."

"Why should that surprise me?"

"Because I can't say my morals were exactly pristine. I mean, I was close to an affair with you. I'm just saying I wasn't raised that way, and I certainly wouldn't have planned to have a baby without being married."

"And now?"

"The same is true now, Rayford." Hattie's voice had flattened. It was clear she was tired, but now she sounded defeated, almost dead. "I am not going to use this pregnancy to force Nicolae Carpathia to marry me.

He wouldn't anyway. He's not forced by anyone to do anything. If I pushed him, he'd probably tell me to have an abortion."

"Oh no!" Rayford said. "You'd never consider that, would you?"

"Wouldn't consider it? I think about it every day."

Rayford winced and rubbed his forehead. Why did he expect Hattie to live like a believer when she was not? It wasn't fair to assume she agreed with him on these issues. "Hattie, do me a big favor, will you?"

"Maybe."

"Would you think about that very carefully before you take any action? Would you seek counsel from your family, from your friends?"

"Rayford, I hardly have any friends anymore."

"Chloe and Buck and I still consider you our friend. And I believe Amanda could become your friend if she got to know you."

Hattie snorted. "I have a feeling that the more Amanda got to know me, the less she'd like me."

"That just proves you don't know her," Rayford said. "She's the type who doesn't even have to like you to love you, if you know what I mean."

Hattie raised her eyebrows. "What an interesting way to say that," she said. "I guess that's the way parents feel about their kids sometimes. My dad once told me that, when I was a rebellious teenager. He said, 'Hattie, it's a good thing I love you so much, because I don't like you at all.' That brought me up short, Rayford. You know what I mean?"

"Sure," he said. "You really ought to get to know Amanda. She'd be like another mother-figure to you."

"One is more than enough," Hattie said. "Don't forget, my mother's the one that gave me this crazy name that belongs to someone two generations older than me."

Rayford smiled. He had always wondered about that. "Anyway, you said Nicolae didn't mind if you took a trip back to the States?"

"Yeah, but that was before the war broke out."

"Hattie, several airports are still taking incoming flights. And as far as I know, no nuclear-equipped warheads landed on any major cities. The only nuclear radiation fallout was in London. You'd want to stay out of there for at least a year, I should think. But even the devastation in Cairo didn't have radiation associated with it."

"You think he'd still let me go back to the States soon then?"

"I wouldn't know, but I'm trying to get back there by Sunday to check on Amanda and to attend a memorial service."

"How are you getting there, Rayford?"

"Commercial. Personally, I think carting around even a dozen or fewer dignitaries is extravagant for the Condor 216. Anyway, the potentate—"

"Oh, please, Rayford, don't call him that."

"Does that sound as ridiculous to you as it does to me?"

"It always has. For such a brilliant, powerful man, that stupid title makes him sound like a buffoon."

"Well, I don't really know him well enough to call him Nicolae, and that last name is a mouthful."

"Don't most of you church types consider him the Antichrist?"

Rayford flinched. He never would have expected that out of her mouth. Was she serious? He decided it was too soon to come clean. "The Antichrist?"

"I can read," she said. "In fact, I like Buck's writing. I've read his pieces in the *Weekly*. When he covers all the various theories and talks about what people think, it comes out that there's a big faction who believes that Nicolae might be the Antichrist."

"I've heard that," Rayford said.

"So you could call him Antichrist, or A.C. for short," she said.

"That's not funny," he said.

"I know," she said. "I'm sorry. I don't go in for all that cosmic war between good and evil stuff anyway. I wouldn't know if a person was the Antichrist if he was staring me in the face."

He's probably stared you in the face more than anyone else over the last couple of years, Rayford thought.

"Anyway, Hattie, I think you should ask—for lack of a better title—Global Community Grand Potentate Nicolae Carpathia if it's still all right that you take a brief trip home. I'm taking a Saturday morning flight that will arrive nonstop in Milwaukee at about noon Chicago time the same day. From what I understand, there's room in the big house of a woman from our church. You could stay with us."

"I couldn't do that, Rayford. My mother is in Denver. They haven't suffered any damage yet, have they?"

"Not as far as I know. I'm sure we could book you through to Denver." Rayford was disappointed. Here was a chance to have some influence on Hattie, but there would be no getting her to the Chicago area.

"I'm not going to ask Nicolae," she said.

"You don't want to go?"

"Oh, I want to go. And I will go. I'm just going to leave word that I'm gone. That's what he said last time I checked with him. He told me I was an adult and should make these decisions for myself. He's got more important things on his mind. Maybe I'll see you on the flight to Milwaukee. In fact, unless you hear otherwise from me, why don't you assume my driver will pick you up Saturday morning. You think it would be all right with Amanda if we sat together?"

"I hope you're not being facetious," Rayford said, "because if you really wanted to talk, I'd let her know in advance."

"Wow, I don't remember your first wife being so possessive."

"She would have been if she'd known what kind of a man I was."

"Or what kind of a woman *I* was."

"Well, maybe—"

"You go ahead and check with your wife, Rayford. If I have to sit by myself, I'll understand. Who knows? Maybe we can sit across the aisle from each other."

Rayford smiled tolerantly. He hoped for at least that.

TEN

BUCK followed a strong urge to take his bag when he left the King David that night. In it was his small dictation machine, his sub-notebook computer (which would soon be replaced by the mother of all computers), his camera, that great cell phone, his toiletries, and two changes of clothing.

He left his key at the front desk and took a cab to the Wailing Wall, asking the cabbie if he spoke English. The driver held up his thumb and forefinger an inch apart and smiled apologetically.

"How far to Galilee?" Buck said.

The cabbie took his foot off the accelerator. "You go to Galilee? Wailing Wall in Jerusalem."

Buck waved him on. "I know. Wailing Wall now. Galilee later."

The cabbie headed for the Wailing Wall. "Galilee now Lake Tiberius," he said. "About 120 kilometers."

Hardly anyone was at the Wailing Wall or even in the entire temple mount area at this time of the night. The newly rebuilt temple was illuminated magnificently and looked like something in a three-dimensional picture show. It seemed to hover on the horizon. Bruce had taught Buck that one day Carpathia would sit in that new temple and proclaim himself God. The journalist in Buck wanted to be there when that happened.

Buck did not at first see the two witnesses. A small group of sailors strolled past the wrought-iron fence at the end of the Wall where the witnesses usually stood and preached. The sailors chatted in English and one pointed. "I think that's them, right over there," he said. The others turned and stared. Buck followed their gaze past the fence and to a stone building. The two mysterious figures sat with their backs against it, feet tucked under them, chins resting on their knees. They were motionless, appearing to sleep. The sailors gawked and tiptoed closer. They never got within a hundred feet of the fence, apparently having heard enough stories. They weren't going to rouse the two, the way they might do to animals at the zoo for sport. These were more than animals. These were dangerous beings who had been known to toast people who trifled with them. Buck did not want to draw attention to himself by boldly approaching the fence. He waited until the sailors got bored and moved on.

As soon as the young men were out of the area, Eli and Moishe raised their heads and looked directly at Buck. He was drawn to them. He walked directly to the fence. The witnesses rose and stood about twenty feet from Buck. "I need clarification," Buck whispered. "Can I know more about my friend's location?"

"He who has ears—"

"I know that," Buck said, "but I—"

"You would dare interrupt the servants of the Most High God?" Eli said.

"Forgive me," Buck said. He wanted to explain himself but decided to remain silent.

Moishe spoke. "You must first communicate with one who loves you."

Buck waited for more. The witnesses stood there, silent. He held out both hands in puzzlement. He felt a vibration in his shoulder bag and realized his cell phone was buzzing. Now what was he supposed to do? If he wasn't to interrupt the servants of the Most High God, did he dare take a call while conversing with them? He felt a fool. He moved away from the fence and grabbed the phone, clicked it open, and said, "This is Buck."

"Buck! It's Chloe! It's about midnight there, right?"

"Right, Chloe, but right now I'm—"

"Buck, were you sleeping?"

"No, I'm up and I'm—"

"Buck, just tell me you're not at the King David."

"Well, I'm staying there, but—"

"But you're not there right now, right?"

"No, I'm at—"

"Honey, I don't know how to tell you this, but I just have this feeling that you should not be in that hotel tonight. In fact, I just have a premonition that you

shouldn't be in Jerusalem overnight. I don't know about
tomorrow, and I don't know about premonitions and all
that, but the feeling is so strong—"

"Chloe, I'm gonna need to call you back, OK?"

Chloe hesitated. "Well, OK, but you can't take the
time to talk to me for a moment when—"

"Chloe, I won't stay at the King David tonight, and
I won't stay in Jerusalem overnight, OK?"

"That makes me feel better, Buck, but I'd still like to
talk—"

"I'll call you back, hon, OK?"

Buck didn't know what he thought about this new
level of what Bruce had referred to as "walking in the
spirit." The witnesses had implied he would find who
he was looking for in Galilee, which didn't really exist
anymore. The Sea of Galilee was now Lake Tiberius.
His dream, if he could put any stock in that, implied he
should go to Egypt for some reason. Now the witnesses
wanted him to use his ears to understand. He was sorry
he was not "John the Revelator," but he was going to
have to ask for more information. And how had they
known he had to talk to Chloe first? He had been
around the two witnesses enough to know that they
were never too far from the miraculous. He just wished
they didn't have to be so cryptic. He was here on a dangerous mission. If they could help him, he wanted their
help.

Buck set his bag down and straddled it, trying to indicate that he was willing to stop anything else he was
doing and simply listen. Moishe and Eli huddled and

seemed to be whispering. They approached the fence. Buck began to move toward them, as he had done the last time he visited with Rabbi Tsion Ben-Judah, but both witnesses held up a hand and he stopped a few feet from his bag and several feet short of the fence. Suddenly the two began to shout at the top of their lungs. Buck was at first startled and backed up, tripping over his own bag. He righted himself. Eli and Moishe traded off quoting verses Buck recognized from Acts and Bruce's teaching.

They shouted: "And it shall come to pass in the last days, says God, that I will pour out of My Spirit on all flesh; your sons and your daughters shall prophesy, your young men shall see visions, your old men shall dream dreams."

Buck knew there was more to the passage, but the witnesses stopped and stared at him. Was he an old man already, having just turned thirty-two? Was he one of the old men who dreamed a dream? Did they know that? Were they telling him his dream was valid?

They continued: "And on My menservants and on My maidservants I will pour out My Spirit in those days; and they shall prophesy. I will show wonders in heaven above and signs in the earth beneath: blood and fire and vapor of smoke. The sun shall be turned into darkness, and the moon into blood, before the coming of the great and awesome day of the Lord. And it shall come to pass that whoever calls on the name of the Lord shall be saved."

Buck was inspired, moved, excited to get on about his

task. But where should he start? And why couldn't the witnesses just tell him? He was surprised to realize he was no longer alone. The shouting of Scripture by the witnesses had produced another small crowd. Buck didn't want to wait any longer. He picked up his bag and moved toward the fence. People warned him not to advance. He heard warnings in other languages, and a few in English. "You'll regret that, son!"

Buck came within a few feet of the witnesses. No one else dared come close. He whispered, "By 'Galilee' I can only assume you mean Lake Tiberius," he said. How was one supposed to tell people who seemed to have come back from Bible times that their geography was out of date? "Will I find my friend in Galilee, or on the Sea of Galilee, or where?"

"He who has ears to hear . . ."

Buck knew better than to interrupt and show his frustration. "How do I get there?" he asked.

Eli spoke softly. "It will go well with you if you return to the multitude," he said.

Return to the multitude? Buck thought. He backed up and rejoined the crowd.

"Are you all right, son?" someone said. "Did they hurt you?" Buck shook his head.

Moishe began to preach in a loud voice: "Now after John was put in prison, Jesus came to Galilee, preaching the gospel of the kingdom of God, and saying 'The time is fulfilled, and the kingdom of God is at hand. Repent, and believe in the gospel.'

"And as He walked by the Sea of Galilee, He saw

Simon and Andrew his brother casting a net into the sea; for they were fishermen. Then Jesus said to them, 'Follow Me, and I will make you become fishers of men.'

"They immediately left their nets and followed Him."

Buck wasn't sure what to make of all that, but he sensed he had gotten all he was going to get from the witnesses that night. Though they continued to preach, and more people gathered seemingly from nowhere to listen, Buck drifted away. He lugged his bag to a short taxi line and climbed into the back of a small cab.

"Can a fella get a boat ride up the Jordan River into Lake Tiberius at this time of night?" he asked the driver.

"Well, sir, to tell you the truth, it's a lot easier coming the other way. But, yes, there are motorized boats heading north. And some do run in the night. Of course, your touring boats are daytime affairs, but there's always someone who will take you where you want to go for the right price, any time of the day or night."

"I figured that," Buck said. Not long later he was dickering with a boatman named Michael, who refused to give a last name. "In the daytime I can carry twenty tourists on this rig, and four strong young men and I pilot it by arm power, if you know what I mean."

"Oars?"

"Yes sir, just like in the Bible. Boat's made of wood. We cover the twin outboards with wood and burlap, and no one's the wiser. Makes for a pretty long, tiring day. But when we have to go back upriver, we can't do that with the oars."

It was only Michael, the twin outboards, and Buck

heading north after midnight, but Buck felt as if he had paid for twenty tourists and four oarsmen as well.

Buck began the trip standing in the bow and letting the crisp air race through his hair. He soon had to zip his leather jacket to the neck and thrust his hands deep into his pockets. Before long he was back next to Michael, who piloted the long, rustic, wood boat from just ahead of the outboard motors. Few other crafts were on the Jordan that night.

Michael shouted above the wind and the sound of the water. "So, you don't really know who you're looking for or exactly where they'll be?"

They had set out from near Jericho, and Michael had told him they had more than a hundred kilometers to travel against the current. "Could take nearly three hours just to get to the mouth of Lake Tiberius," he had added.

"I don't know much," Buck admitted. "I'm just counting on figuring it out when I get there."

Michael shook his head. "Lake Tiberius is no pond. Your friend or friends could be on either shore or at either end."

Buck nodded and sat, burying his chin in his chest to keep warm, to think, and to pray.

"Lord," he said silently, "you've never spoken to me audibly, and I don't expect you to start now, but I could sure use more direction. I don't know if the dream was from you and I'm supposed to go through Egypt on the way back or what. I don't know if I'm going to find Ben-Judah with some fishermen or whether I'm even on the right track by heading to the old Sea of Galilee. I've always enjoyed being independent and resourceful, but I confess I'm at the end of myself here. A lot of people have to be looking for Ben-Judah, and I desperately want to be the first one to find him."

The small craft had just gone around a bend when the engines sputtered and the lights, fore and aft, went out. *So much for the answer to that prayer,* Buck thought.

"Trouble, Michael?"

Buck was struck by the sudden silence as the boat drifted. It seemed headed toward shore. "No trouble, Mr. Katz. Until your eyes grow accustomed to the darkness, you're not going to be able to see that I've got a high-powered weapon pointed at your head. I would like you to remain seated and answer a few questions."

Buck felt a strange calmness. This was too bizarre, too strange even for his weird life. "I mean you no harm, Michael," he said. "You have nothing to fear from me."

"I'm not the one who should be afraid just now, sir," Michael said. "I have twice within the last forty-eight hours fired this weapon into the heads of people I've believed were enemies of God."

Buck was nearly speechless. "One thing I can assure you of, Michael, is that I am in no way an enemy of God. Are you telling me you are a servant of his?"

"I am. The question is, Mr. Katz, are you? And if you are, how will you prove it?"

"Apparently," Buck said, "we will need to assure each other we are on the same side."

"The responsibility is yours. People coming up this

river looking for someone I don't want them to find wind up dead. If you're the third to go, I'll still sleep like a baby tonight."

"And you justify this homicide how?" Buck said.

"Those were the wrong people looking for the wrong person. What I want from you is your real name, the name of the person you're looking for, why you are looking for that person, and what you plan to do should you find that person."

"But Michael, until I'm sure you are on my side, I could never risk revealing that information."

"Even to the point where you'd be willing to die to protect your friend?"

"I hope it doesn't come to that, but yes."

Buck's eyes were adjusting to the darkness. Michael had carefully pointed the craft in such a way that when the power had been cut it drifted back and gently nudged an outcropping of dirt and rock jutting from the shore.

"I am impressed with that answer," Michael said. "But I will not hesitate to add you to the list of dead enemies if you can't convince me you have the right motives for locating whoever it is you want to locate."

"Test me," Buck said. "What will convince you I'm not bluffing, but at the same time convince me that you have the same person in mind?"

"Excellent," Michael said. "True or false: the person you are looking for is young."

Buck responded quickly. "Compared to you, false."

Michael continued: "The person you are looking for is female."

"False."

"The person you are looking for is a medical doctor."

"False."

"A Gentile?"

"False."

"Uneducated?"

"False."

"Bilingual?"

"False."

Buck heard Michael move the huge weapon in his hands. Buck quickly added, "Bilingual doesn't say enough. Multilingual is more like it." Michael stepped forward and pressed the barrel of the weapon against Buck's throat. Buck grimaced and shut his eyes. "The man you are looking for is a rabbi, Dr. Tsion Ben-Judah." Buck did not respond. The weapon pushed harder against his neck. Michael continued: "If you are seeking to kill him, and I was his compatriot, I would kill you. If you were seeking to rescue him, and I represented his captors, I would kill you."

"But in the latter case," Buck managed, "you would have been lying about serving God."

"True enough. And what would happen to me then?"

"You might kill me, but you will ultimately lose."

"And how do we know that?"

Buck had nothing to lose. "It's all been foretold. God wins."

"If that's true, and I turn out to be your brother, you

can tell me your real name." Buck hesitated. "If it turns out that I am your enemy," Michael continued, "I'll kill you anyway."

Buck couldn't argue with that. "My name is Cameron Williams. I am a friend of Dr. Ben-Judah."

"Would you be the American he talks about?"

"Probably."

"One last test, if you don't mind."

"I seem to have no choice."

"True. Quickly list for me six prophecies of Messiah that were fulfilled in Jesus Christ, according to the witnesses who preach at the Wailing Wall."

Buck breathed a huge sigh of relief and smiled. "Michael, you are my brother in Christ. All the prophecies of the Messiah were fulfilled in Jesus Christ. I can tell you six that have to do with your culture alone. He would be a descendant of Abraham, a descendant of Isaac, a descendant of Jacob, from the tribe of Judah, heir to the throne of David, and born in Bethlehem."

The weapon rattled as Michael lay it on the deck and reached to embrace Buck. He squeezed him with a huge bear hug and was laughing and weeping. "And who told you where you might find Tsion?"

"Moishe and Eli."

"They are my mentors," Michael said. "I am one who became a believer under their preaching and that of Tsion."

"And have you murdered others looking for Dr. Ben-Judah?"

"I do not consider it murder. Their bodies will be

buoyed up and burned by the salt when they reach the Dead Sea. Better their bodies than his."

"Are you, then, an evangelist?"

"In the manner of Paul the apostle, according to Dr. Ben-Judah. He says there are 144,000 of us around the world, all with the same assignment that Moishe and Eli have: to preach Christ as the only everlasting Son of the Father."

"Would you believe you were an almost instant answer to prayer?" Buck said.

"That would not surprise me in the least," Michael said. "You must realize that you are the same."

Buck was spent. He was glad Michael had to go back to the outboards and busy himself with the boat. Buck turned his face away and wept. God was so good. Michael left him alone with his thoughts for a while, but then called out with good news. "You know, we're not going all the way to Lake Tiberius."

"We're not?" Buck said, moving back toward Michael.

"You're doing what you're supposed to do by heading *toward* Galilee," Michael said. "About halfway between Jericho and Lake Tiberius we will put ashore on the east side of the river. We will hike about five kilometers inland to where my compatriots and I have hidden Dr. Ben-Judah."

"How are you able to elude the zealots?"

"An escape plan has been in place since the first time Dr. Ben-Judah spoke at Kollek Stadium. For many months we thought the guarding of his family was unnecessary. It was him the zealots wanted. At the first sign of a threat or an attack, we sent to Tsion's office a car so small it appeared only the driver could fit in it. Tsion lay on the floor of the backseat, curled into a ball and covered with a blanket. He was raced to this very boat, and I took him upriver."

"And these stories about his driver having been in on the slaughter of his family?"

Michael shook his head. "That man was exonerated in a most decisive way, would you not agree?"

"Was he also a believer?"

"Sadly, no. But he was loyal and sympathetic. We believed it was only a matter of time. We were wrong. Dr. Ben-Judah is not aware of the loss of his driver, by the way."

"He, of course, knows about his family?"

"Yes, and you can imagine how awful that is for him. When we loaded him into the boat he remained in that fetal position, covered by the blanket. In a way, that was good. It allowed us to keep him in hiding until we got him to the drop-off point. I could hear his loud sobbing over the sound of the boat throughout the entire voyage. I can still hear it."

"Only God can console him," Buck said.

"I pray so," Michael said. "I confess, the consolation period has not yet begun. He has not been able to speak. He cries and cries."

"What are your plans for him?" Buck said.

"He must leave the country. His life is worthless here. His enemies far outnumber us. He will not be safe any-where, but at least outside Israel he has a chance."

"And where will you and your friends take him?"

"Me and my friends!?"

"Who, then?"

"You, my friend!"

"Me?" Buck said.

"God spoke through the two witnesses. He assured us a deliverer would come. He would know the rabbi. He would know the witnesses. He would know the messianic prophecies. And most of all, he would know the Lord's Christ. That, my friend, is you."

Buck nearly buckled. He had felt God's protection. He had felt the excitement of serving him. But he had never felt so directly and specifically a servant of his. He was humbled to the point of shame. He felt suddenly unworthy, undisciplined, inconsistent. He had been so blessed, and what had he done with his newfound faith? He had tried to be obedient, and he had tried to tell others. But surely he was unworthy to be used in such a way.

"What do you expect me to do with Tsion?"

"We don't know. We assumed you would smuggle him out of the country."

"That will not be easy."

"Face it, Mr. Williams, it was not easy for you to find the rabbi, was it? You very nearly got yourself killed."

"Did you think you were going to have to kill me?"

"I was merely hopeful that I would not. The odds were against your being the agent of delivery, but I was praying."

"Is there an airport anywhere near that can handle a Learjet?"

"There is a strip west of Jericho near Al Birah."

"That's back downriver, right?"

"Yes, which is an easier trip, of course. But you know that is the airport that serves Jerusalem. Most flights in and out of Israel start or end at Ben Gurion Airport in Tel Aviv, but there is also a lot of air traffic near Jerusalem."

"The rabbi has to be one of the most recognizable people in Israel," Buck said. "How in the world will I get him through customs?"

Michael smiled in the darkness. "How else? Supernaturally."

Buck asked for a blanket, which Michael produced from a compartment near the back. Buck wrapped it around his shoulders and pulled it up over his head. "How much farther?" he asked.

"About another twenty minutes," Michael said.

"I need to tell you something you may find strange," Buck said.

"Something stranger than tonight?"

Buck chuckled. "I don't suppose. It's just that I may have been warned in a dream to leave through Egypt rather than Israel."

"You *may* have?"

"I'm not used to this kind of communication from God, so I don't know."

"I wouldn't argue with a dream that seemed to come from God," Michael said.

"But does it make sense?"

"It makes more sense than trying to smuggle a target

of the zealots out of here through an international airport."

"But Cairo has been destroyed. Where are flights in and out of there being rerouted to?"

"Alexandria," Michael said. "But still, you have to get out of Israel somehow."

"Find me a small strip somewhere, and we can avoid customs and go from there."

"What then do you do about going through Egypt?"

"I don't know what to make of it. Maybe the dream simply meant I should take other than a usual route."

"One thing is certain," Michael said. "This will have to be done after dark. If not tonight, then tomorrow night."

"I wouldn't be able to do it tonight if the skies opened and God pointed in my face."

Michael smiled. "My friend, if I had gone through what you've gone through and seen prayer answered the way you have, I would not be challenging God to do something so simple."

"Let's just say then that I am praying God will let me wait one more day. I have to be in touch with my pilot, and we're all going to have to work together at determining the best spot from which to head back to the United States."

"There is one thing you should know," Michael said.

"Just one?"

"No, but something very important. I believe Dr. Ben-Judah will be reluctant to flee."

"What choice does he have?"

"That's just it. He may not want a choice. With his wife and children gone, he may see no reason to go on, let alone to live."

"Nonsense! The world needs him! We must keep his ministry alive."

"You don't need to convince me, Mr. Williams. I'm just telling you, you may have a selling job to get him to flee to the United States. I believe, however, that he will likely be safer there than anywhere, if he can be safe anyplace."

"Your boots will stay driest if you stand in the bow and leap out when you hear the bottom scraping the sand," Michael said. He had turned east and raced toward the shore. In what seemed to Buck the last instant, Michael cut the engines and raised them from the water. He nimbly jogged up next to Buck and peeled his eyes, bracing himself. "Fling your bag as far as you can, jump with me, and make sure you outrun the boat!"

The boat slid along the bottom, and Buck followed orders. But when he leaped, he fell sideways and rolled. The boat barely missed him. He sat up, covered with wet sand.

"Help me, please!" Michael said. He had grabbed the boat and was tugging it onto land. Once they had secured it, Buck brushed himself off, happily found his boots were fairly dry, and began following his new friend. Buck had only his bag. Michael had only his weapon. But he also knew where he was going.

"I must ask you to be very silent now," Michael whispered as they pushed their way through underbrush. "We are secluded, but we take no chances."

Buck had forgotten how long five kilometers could be. The ground was uneven and moist. The overgrowth slapped him in the face. He switched his bag from shoulder to shoulder, never fully comfortable. He was in good shape, but this was hard. This was not jogging or cycling or running on a treadmill. This was working your way through sandy shoreline to who knew where?

He dreaded seeing Dr. Ben-Judah. He wanted to be reunited with his friend and brother in Christ, but what does one say to one who has lost his family? No platitudes, no words would make it better. The man had paid one of the steepest prices anyone could pay, and nothing short of heaven could make it better.

Half an hour later, panting and sore, he and Michael came within sight of the hideout. Michael put a finger to his lips and bent low. He held aside a bundle of dried twigs, and they advanced. Twenty yards farther, in a grove of trees, was an opening to an underground shelter invisible to anyone who hadn't come there on purpose.

ELEVEN

BUCK was struck that there were no real beds and no pillows in the hideout. *So this is what the witnesses meant when they quoted that verse about having nowhere to lay his head,* Buck thought.

Three other gaunt and desperate-looking young men, who could have been Michael's brothers, huddled in the dugout, where there was barely room to stand. Buck noticed a clear view at ground level to the path behind him. That explained why Michael had not had to declare himself or give any signal to approach.

He was introduced all around, but only Michael, of the four, understood English. Buck squinted, looking for Tsion. He could hear him, but he could not see him. Finally, a dim, electric lantern was illuminated. There, sitting in the corner, his back to the wall, was one of the first and surely the most famous of what would become the 144,000 witnesses prophesied of in the Bible.

He sat with his knees pulled up to his chest, arms wrapped around his legs. He wore a white dress shirt with the sleeves rolled up and dark dress pants that rode high on his shins and left a gap between the cuffs and the top of his socks. He wore no shoes.

How young Tsion appeared! Buck knew him to be a youthful middle age anyway, but sitting there rocking and crying he appeared young as a child. He neither looked up nor acknowledged Buck.

Buck whispered that he would like a moment alone with Tsion. Michael and the others climbed through the opening and stood idly in the underbrush, weapons at the ready. Buck crouched next to Dr. Ben-Judah.

"Tsion," Buck said, "God loves you." The words had surprised even Buck. Could it possibly seem to Tsion that God loved him now? And what kind of a platitude was that? Was it now his place to speak for God?

"What do you know for sure?" Buck asked, wondering himself what in the world he was talking about.

Tsion's reply, in his barely understandable Israeli accent, squeaked from a constricted throat: "I know that my Redeemer lives."

"What else do you know?" Buck said, listening as much as speaking.

"I know that He who has begun a good work in me will be faithful to complete it."

Praise God! Buck thought.

Buck slumped to the ground and sat next to Ben-Judah,

his back against the wall. He had come to rescue this man, to minister to him. Now he had been ministered to. Only God could provide such assurance and confidence at a time of such grief.

"Your wife and your children were believers—"

"Today they see God," Tsion finished for him.

Buck had worried, Buck had wondered: Would Tsion Ben-Judah be so devastated at his inequitable loss that his faith would be shaken? Would he be so fragile that it would be impossible for him to go on? He would grieve, make no mistake. He would mourn. *But not as the heathen, who have no hope.*

"Cameron, my friend," Tsion managed, "did you bring your Bible?"

"Not in book form, sir. I have the entire Scripture on my computer."

"I have lost more than my family, Buck."

"Sir?"

"My library. My sacred books. All burned. All gone. The only things I love more in this life were my family."

"You brought nothing from your office?"

"I threw on a ridiculous disguise, the long locks of the Orthodox. Even a phony beard. I carried nothing, so as not to look like a resident scholar."

"Could not someone forward the books from your office?"

"Not without endangering their life. I am the chief suspect in the murder of my family."

"That's nonsense!"

"We both know that, my friend, but a man's perception soon becomes his reality. Anyway, where could someone send my things without leading my enemies to me?"

Buck dug into his bag and produced his laptop. "I'm not sure how much battery life is left," he said. He turned on the back-lit screen.

"This would not happen to have the Old Testament in Hebrew?" Tsion said.

"No, but those programs are widely available."

"At least they are now," Tsion said, a sob still in his throat. "My most recent studies have led me to believe that our religious freedoms will soon become scarce at an alarming pace."

"What would you like to see, sir?"

At first Buck thought Tsion had not heard his question. Then he wondered if Tsion had spoken and he himself had not heard the answer. The computer ground away, bringing up a menu of Old Testament books. Buck stole a glance at his friend. Clearly, he was trying to speak. The words would not come.

"I sometimes find the Psalms comforting," Buck said.

Tsion nodded, now covering his mouth with his hand. The man's chest heaved and he could hold back the sobs no longer. He leaned over onto Buck and collapsed in tears. "The joy of the Lord is my strength," he moaned over and over. "The joy of the Lord is my strength."

Joy, Buck thought. *What a concept in this place, at this time.* The name of the game now was survival. Certainly joy took on a different meaning than ever before in Buck's life. He used to equate joy with happiness. Clearly Tsion Ben-Judah was not implying that he was happy. He might never be happy again. This joy was a deep abiding peace, an assurance that God was sovereign. They didn't have to like what was happening. They merely had to trust that God knew what he was doing.

That made it no easier. Buck knew well that things would get worse before they ever got better. If a man was not rock solid in his faith now, he never would be. Buck sat in that damp, moist, earthen hideout in the middle of nowhere, knowing with more certainty than ever that he had put his faith in the only begotten Son of the Father. With his bent and nearly broken brother sobbing in his lap, Buck felt as close to God as he had the day he trusted Christ.

Tsion composed himself and reached for the computer. He fumbled with the keys for a minute before asking for help. "Just bring up the Psalms," he said. Buck did, and Tsion cursored through them, one hand on the computer mouse and the other covering his mouth as he wept. "Ask the others to join us for prayer," he whispered.

A few minutes later, the six men knelt in a circle. Tsion spoke to them briefly in Hebrew, Michael quietly whispering the interpretation into Buck's ear. "My friends and brothers in Christ, though I am deeply wounded, yet I must pray. I pray to the God of Abraham, Isaac, and Jacob. I praise you because you are the one and only true God, the God above all other gods. You sit high above the heavens. There is none other like you. In you there is no variation or shadow of turning."

With that, Tsion broke down again and asked that the others pray for him.

Buck had never heard people praying together aloud in a foreign language. Hearing the fervency of these witness-evangelists made him fall prostrate. He felt the cold mud on the backs of his hands as he buried his face in his palms. He didn't know about Tsion but felt as if he were being borne along on clouds of peace. Suddenly Tsion's voice could be heard above the rest. Michael bent down and whispered in Buck's ear, "If God is for us, who can be against us?"

Buck did not know how long he lay on the floor. Eventually the prayers became groanings and what sounded like Hebrew versions of *amens* and *hallelujahs*. Buck rose to his knees and felt stiff and sore. Tsion looked at him, his face still wet but seemingly finished crying for now. "I believe I can finally sleep," the rabbi said.

"Then you should. We'll not be going anywhere tonight. I'll make arrangements for after dark tomorrow."

"You should call your friend," Michael said.

"You realize what time it is?" Buck said.

Michael looked at his watch, smiled, shook his head, and said simply, "Oh."

"Alexandria?" Ken Ritz said by phone the next morning. "Sure, I can get there easily enough. It's a big airport. When will you be along?"

Buck, who had bathed and washed out a change of clothes in a tiny tributary off the Jordan, dried himself with a blanket. One of Tsion Ben-Judah's Hebrew-speaking guards was nearby. He had cooked breakfast and now appeared to roast Tsion's socks and underwear over the small fire.

"We'll leave here tonight, as soon as the sky is black," Buck said. "Then, however long it takes a forty-foot wood boat with two outboard motors and six adult men aboard to get to Alexandria—"

Ritz was laughing. "This is my first time over here, as I think I told you," he said, "but one thing I'm pretty sure about: if you think you're coming from where you are to Alexandria without carrying that boat across dry land to the sea, you're kidding yourself."

At midday all six men were out of the dugout. They were confident no one had followed them to this remote location and that as long as they stayed out of sight from the air, they could stretch their legs and breathe a little.

Michael was not as amused at Buck's naïveté as Ken Ritz had been. He found little to smile about and nothing to laugh about these days. Michael leaned back against a tree. "There are some small airports here and there in Israel," he said. "Why are you so determined to fly out of Egypt?"

"Well, that dream—I don't know, this is all new to me. I'm trying to be practical, listen to the witnesses, follow the leadings of God. What am I supposed to do about that dream?"

"I'm a newer believer than you, my friend," Michael said. "But I wouldn't argue with a dream that was so clear."

"Maybe we have some advantage in Egypt we would not have in Israel," Buck suggested.

"I can't imagine what," Michael said. "For you to legally get out of Israel and into Egypt, you still have to go through customs somewhere."

"How realistic is that, considering my guest?"

"You mean your contraband cargo?"

Now there had been an attempt at humor, but still Michael had not smiled when he said it. "I'm just wondering," Buck said, "how carefully customs officers and border guards will be looking for Dr. Ben-Judah."

"You're wondering? I'm not wondering. We either avoid the border crossings or seek yet another supernatural act."

"I'm open to any suggestion," Buck said.

———

Rayford was on the phone with Amanda. She had filled him in on everything. "I miss you more than ever right now," he told her.

"Having me come back here was sure the right idea," she said. "With Buck gone and Chloe still tender, I feel needed here."

"You're needed here too, sweetheart, but I'm counting the days."

Rayford told her about his conversation with Hattie and her plans to fly to the States. "I trust you, Rayford. She sounds like she's hurting. We'll pray for her. What I wouldn't give to get that girl under some sound teaching."

Rayford agreed. "If she could only stop through our area on her way back. Maybe when Bruce is going through some chapter on—" Rayford realized what he had said.

"Oh, Ray—"

"It's still too fresh, I guess," he said. "I just hope God provides some other Bible teacher for us. Well, it won't be another Bruce."

"No," Amanda said, "and it won't likely be soon enough to do Hattie any good, even if she does come here."

———

Late that afternoon, Buck took a call from Ken Ritz. "You still want me to meet you in Alexandria?"

"We're talking about it, Ken. I'll get back to you."

"Can you drive a stick shift, Buck?" Michael asked.

"Sure."

"An ancient one?"

"They're the most fun, aren't they?"

"Not as ancient as this one," Michael said. "I've got an old school bus that smells of fish and paint. I use it for both professions. It's on its last legs, but if we could get you down to the southern mouth of the Jordan, you might be able to use it to find a way across the border into the Sinai. I'd stock you with petrol and water. That thing'll drink more water than it will gasoline any day."

"How big is this bus?"

"Not big. Holds about twenty passengers."

"Four-wheel drive?"

"No, sorry."

"An oil burner?"

"Not as much as water, but yes, I'm afraid so."

"What's in the Sinai?"

"You don't know?"

"I know it's a desert."

"Then you know all you need to know. You'll be jealous of the bus engine and its water needs."

"What are you proposing?"

"I sell you the bus, fair and square. You get all the paperwork. If you get stopped, the tags are traced to me, but I sold the bus."

"Keep talking—"

"You hide Dr. Ben-Judah under the seats in the back. If you can get him across the border and into the Sinai, that bus should get you as far as Al Arish, less than fifty kilometers west of the Gaza Strip and right on the Mediterranean."

"And what, you'll meet us there with your wood boat and ferry us to America?"

Finally, Buck had elicited a resigned smile from Michael. "There is an airstrip there, and it's unlikely the Egyptians will care about a man wanted in Israel. If they even seem to care, they can be bought."

One of the other guards appeared to have understood the name of the seaport city, and Buck guessed he was asking in Hebrew for Michael to explain his strategy. He spoke earnestly to Michael, and Michael turned to Buck. "My comrade is right about the risk. Israel might have already announced a huge ransom for the rabbi. Unless you could beat their price, the Egyptians might lean toward selling him back."

"How will I know the price?"

"You'll just have to guess. Keep bidding until you can beat it."

"What would be your guess?"

"Not less than a million dollars."

"A million dollars? Do you think every American has that kind of money?"

"Don't you?"

"No! And anyone who did wouldn't carry it in cash."

"Would you have half that much?"

Buck shook his head and walked away. He slipped down into the hideout. Tsion followed. "What's troubling you, my friend?" the rabbi said.

"I need to get you out of here," Buck said. "And I have no idea how."

"Have you prayed?"

"Constantly."

"The Lord will make a way somehow."

"It seems impossible right now, sir."

"Yahweh is the God of the impossible," Tsion said.

Night was falling. Buck felt all dressed up with nowhere to go. He borrowed a map from Michael and carefully studied it, looking north and south along the waterways that divided Israel from Jordan. If only there were a clear water route from the Jordan River or Lake Tiberius to the Mediterranean!

Buck resolutely rerolled the map and handed it to

Michael. "You know," he said, thinking, "I have two sets of identification. I'm in the country under the name of Herb Katz, an American businessman. But I have my real ID as well."

"So?"

"So, how 'bout we get me across the border as Herb Katz and the rabbi as Cameron Williams?"

"You forget, Mr. Williams, that even we ancient, dusty countries are now computerized. If you came into Israel as Herb Katz, there is no record that Cameron Williams is here. If he's not here, how can he leave?"

"All right then, let's say *I* leave as Cameron Williams and the rabbi leaves as Herb Katz. Though there is no record of my being here under my own name, I can show them my clearance level and my proximity to Carpathia and tell them not to ask any questions. That often works."

"There's an outside chance, but Tsion Ben-Judah does not speak like an American Jew, does he?"

"No, but—"

"And he does not look in the least like you or your picture."

Buck was frustrated. "We are agreed that we have to get him out of here, aren't we?"

"No question," Michael said.

"Then what do you propose? I am at an end."

Dr. Ben-Judah crawled to them, obviously not wanting even to stand in the low, earthen shelter. "Michael," he said, "I cannot tell you how grateful I am for your sacrifice, for your protection. I appreciate also your sympathy and your prayers. This is very hard for me. In my flesh, I would rather not go on. Part of me very much wants to die and to be with my wife and children. Only the grace of God sustains me. Only he keeps me from wanting to avenge their deaths at any price. I foresee for myself long, lonely days and nights of dark despair. My faith is immovable and unshakable, and for that I can only thank the Lord. I feel called to continue to try to serve him, even in my grief. I do not know why he has allowed this, and I do not know how much longer he will give me to preach and teach the gospel of Christ. But something deep within me tells me that he would not have uniquely prepared me my whole life and then allowed me this second chance and used me to proclaim to the world that Jesus is Messiah unless he had more use for me.

"I am wounded. I feel as if a huge hole has been left in my chest. I cannot imagine it ever being filled. I pray for relief from the pain. I pray for release from hatred and thoughts of vengeance. But mostly I pray for peace and rest so that I may somehow rebuild something from these remaining fragments of my life. I know my life is worthless in this country now. My message has angered all those except the believers, and now with the trumped-up charges against me, I must get out. If Nicolae Carpathia focuses on me, I will be a fugitive everywhere. But it makes no sense for me to stay here. I cannot hide out forever, and I must have some outlet for my ministry."

Michael stood between Tsion and Buck and put his hands on them. "Tsion, my friend, you know that my compatriots and I are risking everything to protect you.

We love you as our spiritual father, and we will die before we see you die. Of course we agree that you must go. Sometimes it seems that short of God sending an angel to whisk you away, no one as recognizable and as much a fugitive as you could slip past Israeli borders. In the midst of your pain and suffering, we dare not ask you for counsel. But if God has told you anything, we need to hear it and we need to hear it now.

"The sky is getting black, and unless we want to wait another twenty-four hours, the time to move is now. What shall we do? Where shall we go? I am willing to lead you through customs at any border crossing with weapons, but we all know the folly of that."

Buck looked to Dr. Ben-Judah, who simply bowed his head and prayed aloud once more. "O God, our help in ages past—"

Buck immediately began to shiver and dropped to his knees. He sensed the Lord impressing upon him that the answer was before them. Echoing in his mind was a phrase he could only assume was of God: "I have spoken. I have provided. Do not hesitate."

Buck felt humbled and emboldened, but still he didn't know what to do. If God had told him to go through Egypt, he was willing. Was that it? What had been provided?

Michael and Tsion were now on their knees with Buck, huddled together, shoulders touching. None of them spoke. Buck felt the presence of the Spirit of God and began to weep. The other two seemed to be shivering as well. Suddenly Michael spoke, "The glory of the Lord shall be your rear guard."

Words filled Buck's mind. Though he could barely pronounce them through his emotion, he blurted, "You give me living water and I thirst no more." What was that? Was God telling him he could travel into the Sinai desert and not die of thirst?

Tsion Ben-Judah prostrated himself on the floor, sobbing and groaning. "Oh God, oh God, oh God—"

Michael lifted his face and said, "Speak Lord, for your servants hear. Heed the words of the Lord. He who has ears to hear, let him hear. . . ."

Tsion again: "The Lord of hosts has sworn, saying, 'Surely as I have thought, so shall it come to pass, and as I have purposed, so it shall stand.'"

It was as if Buck had been steamrollered by the Spirit of God. Suddenly he knew what they must do. The pieces of the puzzle were all there. He, and they, had been waiting for some miraculous intervention. The fact was, if God wanted Tsion Ben-Judah out of Israel, he would make it out. If he did not, then he would not. God had told Buck in a dream to go another way, through Egypt. He had provided transportation through Michael. And now he had promised that his glory would be their rear guard.

"Amen," Buck said, "and amen." He rose and said, "It's time, gentlemen. Let's move."

Dr. Ben-Judah looked surprised. "Has the Lord spoken to you?"

Buck shot him a double take. "Did he not speak to you, Tsion?"

"Yes! I just wanted to make sure we were in agreement."

"If I have a vote," Michael said, "we're unanimous. Let's get going."

Michael's compatriots pulled the boat into position as Buck slung in his bag and Tsion climbed aboard. As Michael fired up the engines and they started back down the Jordan, Buck handed Tsion the identification papers that carried Buck's own name and picture. Tsion looked surprised. "I have felt no leading that I should use these," he said.

"And I have a definite leading that I should not have them on my person," Buck said. "I am in the country as Herb Katz, and I'll leave the country as Herb Katz. I'll ask you for the documents back when we get into the Sinai."

"This is exciting," Tsion said, "is it not? We are talking confidently about getting into the Sinai, and we have no idea how God is going to do it."

Michael left the boat in the hands of one of his friends and sat with Buck and Tsion. "Tsion has a little cash, a few credit cards, and his own papers. If he is found with those, he will be detained and likely put to death. Shall we keep those for him?"

Tsion reached for his wallet and opened it in the moonlight. He removed the cash, folded it once, and stuck it in his pocket. The credit cards he began flipping one by one into the Jordan River. It was as close to amusement as Buck had noticed in the man since he had first seen him in the hideout. Almost everything went into the drink—all forms of identification and the miscellaneous documentation he had gathered over the years. He pulled out a small photo section and gasped. He turned the pictures toward the moon and wept openly. "Michael, I must ask you to someday ship these to me."

"I will do it."

Tsion flipped the old wallet into the water. "And now," Michael said, "I believe you should return Mr. Williams's papers to him."

Tsion reached for them. "Wait a minute," Buck said. "Should we not try to get him some phony ID, if he's not going to use mine?"

"Somehow," Tsion said, "what Michael says seems right. I am a man who has been stripped of everything, even his identity."

Buck took back his ID and began rummaging in his bag for a place to hide it. "No good," Michael said. "There's nowhere on your person or in your bag they will not search and find an extra ID."

"Well," Buck said, "I can't toss mine into the Jordan."

Michael held out a hand. "I will ship it to you along with Tsion's photographs," he said. "It's the safest."

Buck hesitated. "You must not be found with that either," he said.

Michael took it. "My life is destined to be short anyway, brother," he said. "I feel most honored and blessed to be one of the witnesses predicted in the Scriptures. But my assignment is to preach in Israel, where the real

Messiah is hated. My days are limited whether I am caught with your papers or not."

Buck thanked him and shook his head. "I still don't see how we're going to get Tsion across any border without papers, real or phony."

"We already prayed," Tsion said. "I do not know how God is going to do this either. I just know that he is."

Buck's practicality and resourcefulness were at war with his faith. "But don't we at least have to do our part?"

"And what is our part, Cameron?" the rabbi said. "It is when we are out of ideas and options and actions that we can only depend upon God."

Buck pressed his lips together and turned his face away. He wished he had the same faith Tsion had. In many ways, he knew he did. But still it didn't make sense to just plunge ahead, daring border guards to guess who Tsion was.

"I'm sorry for calling now," Chloe said. "But, Daddy, I've been trying to reach Buck on his cell phone."

"I wouldn't worry about Buck, honey. You know he finds ways to stay safe."

"Oh, Dad! Buck finds ways to nearly get himself killed. I know he was at the King David under his phony name, and I'm tempted to call there, but he promised he would stay away from there tonight."

"Then I'd wait on that, Chloe. You know Buck rarely

cares much about what time of the day it is. If the story
or the caper takes him all night, then it takes him all
night."

"You're a big help."

"I'm trying to be."

"Well, I just don't understand why he wouldn't have
his cell phone with him all the time. You keep yours in
your pocket, don't you?"

"Usually. But maybe it's in his bag."

"So if his bag is in the hotel and he's out gallivanting,
I'm out of luck?"

"I guess so, hon."

"I wish he'd take his phone with him, even if he doesn't
take his bag."

"Try not to worry, Chloe. Buck always turns up somewhere."

———————

When Michael docked at the mouth of the Jordan, he and
his fellow guards scanned the horizon and then casually
walked to his tiny car and crammed themselves inside.
Michael drove to his home, which had a tiny lean-to that
served as a garage. That was too small for the bus that
dominated the alley behind his humble place. Lights came
on. A baby cried. Michael's wife padded out in a robe and
embraced him desperately. She spoke urgently to him in
Hebrew. Michael looked apologetically at Buck. "I need
to keep in touch more," he said, shrugging.

Buck patted his pocket, feeling for his phone. It was

not there. He dug in his bag and found it. He should
keep in touch with Chloe more too, but for right now it
was more important that he get ahold of Ken Ritz. While
Buck was on the phone he was aware of all the activity
around him. Silently, Michael and his friends went to
work. Oil and water were dumped into the engine and
radiator of the rickety old school bus. One of the men
filled the gas tank from cans stored at the side of the
house. Michael's wife handed out a stack of blankets and
a basket of clothes for Tsion.

As Buck hung up from talking to Ritz, who had
agreed to meet them at Al Arish in the Sinai, Buck passed
Michael's wife on his way out to the bus. She hesitated
shyly, glancing at him. He slowed, assuming she did
not understand English but also wanting to express his
gratitude.

"English?" he tried. She closed her eyes briefly and
shook her head. "I, uh, just wanted to thank you," he
said. "So, uh, thank you." He spread his hands and then
clasped them together under his chin, hoping she would
know what he meant. She was a tiny, fragile-looking,
dark-eyed thing. Sadness and terror were etched on her
face and in her eyes. It was as if she knew she was on the
right side, but that her time was limited. It couldn't be
long before her husband was found out. He was not only
a convert to the true Messiah, but he had also defended
an enemy of the state. Buck knew Michael's wife must be
wondering how long it would be before she and her children suffered the same fate that Tsion Ben-Judah's family

suffered. And short of that, how long before she lost her husband to the cause, worthy though it was.

It would have been against custom for her to have touched Buck, so he was startled when she approached. She stood just two feet from his face and stared into his eyes. She said something in Hebrew and he recognized only the last two words: *"Y'shua Hamashiach."*

When Buck slipped away in the darkness and arrived at the bus, Tsion was already stretched out under the seats in the back. Food and extra water and oil and gasoline had already been stored.

Michael approached, his three friends behind him. He embraced Buck and kissed him on both cheeks. "Go with God," he said, handing him the ownership documents. Buck reached to shake hands with the other three, who apparently knew he wouldn't understand them anyway, and said nothing.

He stepped onto the bus and shut the door, settling into the creaky chair behind the wheel. Michael signaled him from outside to slide open his driver's-side window. "Feather it," Michael said.

"Feather it?" Buck said.

"The throttle."

Buck put the pedal down and released it, turning the key. The engine roared noisily to life. Michael put up both hands to urge him to be as quiet as possible. Buck slowly let out the clutch, and the old crate shuddered and jumped and lurched. Just to get out of the alleyway and onto the main thoroughfare, Buck felt as if he were riding the clutch. Shifting, clutching, and, yes, feathering the throttle, he was finally free of the tiny neighborhood and out onto the road. Now, if he could just follow Michael's instructions and directions and somehow get to the border, the rest would be up to God. He felt an unusual sense of freedom, simply piloting a vehicle—albeit one like this—on his own. He was on a journey that would lead him somewhere. By dawn, he could be anywhere: detained, imprisoned, in the desert, in the air, or in heaven.

TWELVE

IT didn't take Buck long to learn what Michael meant by "feathering" the throttle. Any time Buck clutched to shift, the engine nearly stalled. When he came to a complete stop, he had to keep his left foot on the clutch, his right heel on the brake, and feather the throttle with the toes of his right foot.

Along with the title to the dilapidated rig, Michael had included a rough map. "There are four different places where you can cross over from Israel into Egypt by auto," Michael had told him. The two most direct were at Rafah on the Gaza Strip. "But these have always been heavily patrolled. You might rather head south directly out of Jerusalem through Hebron to Beersheba. I would advise continuing southeast out of Beersheba, though that is slightly out of your way. About two-thirds of the way between Beersheba and Yeroham is a southern but mostly western cutoff that takes you through the northern edge of the Negev. You're less than fifty kilometers from the border there, and when you come within less than ten kilometers, you can head north and west or continue due west. I couldn't guess which border would be easier to get through. I would recommend the southern, because you can then continue to a northwest route that takes you directly into Al Arish. If you take the northern pass, you must go back up to the main road between Rafah and Al Arish, which is more heavily traveled and more carefully watched."

That had been all Buck needed to hear. He would take the southernmost of the four border crossings and pray he was not stopped until then.

Tsion Ben-Judah stayed on the floor under the seats until Buck had rumbled far enough south of Jerusalem that they both felt safe. Tsion moved up and crouched next to Buck. "Are you tired?" he asked. "Would you like me to take over driving?"

"You're joking."

"It may be many months before I am able to find humor in anything," Tsion said.

"But you're not serious about sitting behind the wheel of this bus, are you? What would we do if we were stopped? Trade places?"

"I was just offering."

"I appreciate it, but it's out of the question. I'm fine, well rested. Anyway, I'm scared to death. That will keep me alert."

Buck downshifted to navigate a curve, and Tsion

swung forward from the momentum. He hung on to the metal pole next to the driver's seat, and he spun around and smacked into Buck, pushing him to the left.

"I told you, Tsion, I'm awake. You need not continually try to rouse me."

He looked at Tsion to see if he had elicited a smile. It appeared Tsion was trying to be polite. He apologized profusely and slid into the seat behind Buck, his head low, his chin resting on his hands, which gripped the bar that separated the driver from the first seat. "Tell me when I need to duck."

"By the time I know that, you'll likely already be seen."

"I do not think I can take riding long on the floorboards," Ben-Judah said. "Let us both just be on the lookout."

It was difficult for Buck to get the old bus to move faster than seventy kilometers per hour. He feared it would take all night to get to the border. Maybe that was OK. The darker and the later the better. As he chugged along, watching the gauges and trying not to do anything that might draw attention to them, he noticed in his rearview mirror that Tsion had slumped in the seat and was trying to rest on his side. Buck thought the rabbi had said something. "I beg your pardon?" Buck said.

"I am sorry, Cameron. I was praying."

Later Buck heard him singing. Later still, weeping. Well after midnight, Buck checked his map and noted that they were rolling through Haiheul, a small town just a tick north of Hebron. "Will the tourists be out at this time of night in Hebron?" Buck asked.

Tsion leaned forward. "No. But still, it is a populated area. I will be careful. Cameron, there is something I would like to talk to you about."

"Anything."

"I want you to know that I am deeply grateful that you have sacrificed your time and risked your life to come for me."

"No friend would do less, Tsion. I've felt a deep bond with you since the day you first took me to the Wailing Wall. And then we had to flee together after your television broadcast."

"We have been through some incredible experiences, it is true." Tsion said. "That is why I knew if I could merely get Dr. Rosenzweig to point you in the direction of the witnesses, you would find me. I did not dare let on to him where I was. Even my driver knew only to take me to Michael and the other brothers in Jericho. My driver was so distraught at what happened to my family that he was in tears. We have been together for many years. Michael promised to keep him informed, but I would like to call him myself. Perhaps I can use your secure phone once we have passed the border."

Buck didn't know what to say. He had more confidence than Michael that Tsion could take yet more bad news, but why did he have to be the one to bear it? The intuitive rabbi seemed to immediately suspect Buck was hiding something. "What?" he asked. "Do you think it is too late to call him?"

"It *is* very late," Buck said.

"But if the situation were reversed, I would be overjoyed to hear from him at any time of the day or night."

"I'm sure he felt—feels the same," Buck said lamely.

Buck peeked into the rearview mirror. Tsion stared at him, a look of realization coming over him. "Maybe I should call him now," he suggested. "May I use your phone?"

"Tsion, you are always welcome to whatever I have. You know that. I would not phone him now, no."

When Tsion responded, Buck knew that he knew. His voice was flat, full of the pain that would plague him the rest of his days. "Cameron, his name was Jaime. He had been with me since I started teaching at the university. He was not an educated man; however, he was wise in the ways of the world. We talked much about my findings. He and my wife were the only ones besides my student assistants who knew what I was going to say on the television broadcast. He was close, Cameron. So close. But he is no longer with us, is he?"

Buck thought about merely shaking his head, but he could not do that. He busied himself looking for road signs for Hebron, but the rabbi, of course, would not let it go.

"Cameron, we are too close and have gone through too much for you to hold out on me now. Clearly you have been told the disposition of Jaime. You must understand that the toll the bad news has taken on me can be made neither worse by hearing more, nor better by hear-

ing less. We believers in Christ, of all people, must never
fear any truth, hard as it may be."

"Jaime is dead," Buck said.

Tsion hung his head. "He heard me preach so many
times. He knew the gospel. Sometimes I even pushed
him. He was not offended. He knew I cared about him.
I can only hope and pray that perhaps after he delivered
me to Michael, he had time to join the family. Tell me
how it happened."

"Car bomb."

"Instantaneous, then," he said. "Perhaps he never
knew what hit him. Perhaps he did not suffer."

"I'm so sorry, Tsion. Michael didn't think you could
take it."

"He underestimates me, but I appreciate his concern.
I worry about everyone associated with me. Anyone who
appears they might know anything of my whereabouts
may suffer if they are not forthcoming. That includes so
many. I will never forgive myself if they all pay the ultimate price for merely having known me. Frankly, I
worry about Chaim Rosenzweig."

"I wouldn't worry about him just yet," Buck said.
"He's still closely identified with Carpathia. Ironically,
that's his protection for now."

Buck drove cautiously through Hebron, and he and
Tsion rode in silence all the way to Beersheba. In the
wee hours of the morning, about ten kilometers south
of Beersheba, Buck noticed the heat gauge rising. The oil
gauge still looked OK, but the last thing Buck wanted

was to overheat. "I'm gonna add some water to this radiator, Tsion," he said. The rabbi seemed to be dozing.

Buck pulled far off the road onto the gravel shoulder. He found a rag and climbed out. Once he got the hood propped up, he gingerly opened the radiator cap. It was steaming, but he was able to dump a couple of liters of water in before the thing boiled over. While he was working he noticed a Global Community peacekeeping force squad car slowly drive past. Buck tried to look casual and took a deep breath.

He wiped his hands and dropped the rag into his water can, noticing the squad car had pulled over about a hundred feet in front of the bus and was slowly backing up. Trying not to look suspicious, Buck tossed the water can into the bus and came back around to shut the hood. Before he shut it, the squad car backed onto the road and turned to face him on the shoulder. With the headlights shining in his eyes, Buck heard the Global Community peacekeeper say something to him in Hebrew over his loudspeaker.

Buck held out both arms and hollered, "English!"

In a heavy accent, the peacekeeper said, "Please to remain outside your vehicle."

Buck turned to lower the hood, but the officer called out to him again, "Please to stand where you are."

Buck shrugged and stood awkwardly, hands at his sides. The officer spoke into his radio. Finally the young man emerged. "Happy evening to you, sir," he said.

"Thank you," Buck said. "Just had some overheating problems is all."

The officer was dark and slender, wearing the gaudy uniform of the Global Community. Buck wished he'd had his own passport and papers. Nothing sent a GC operative running more quickly than Buck's 2-A clearance. "Are you alone?" the officer asked.

"Name's Herb Katz," Buck said.

"I asked you are you alone?"

"I'm an American businessman, here on pleasure."

"Your papers, please."

Buck pulled out his phony passport and wallet. The young man studied them with a flashlight and pointed the light into Buck's face. Buck didn't think that was necessary with the headlights already blinding him, but he said nothing.

"Mr. Katz, can you tell me where you got this vehicle?"

"I bought it tonight. Just before midnight."

"And you bought it from?"

"I have the papers. I can't pronounce his name. I'm an American."

"Sir, the plates on this vehicle trace to a resident of Jericho."

Buck, still playing dumb, said, "Well, there you go! That's where I bought it, in Jericho."

"And you say you purchased it before midnight?"

"Yes, sir."

"Are you aware of a manhunt in this country?"

"Tell me," Buck said.

"It happens that the owner of this vehicle was

detained, just over an hour ago, in connection with aiding and abetting a murder suspect."

"You don't say?" Buck said. "I just took a boat ride with this man. He runs a tour boat. I told him I needed a vehicle to just get me from Israel to Egypt so I could fly home to America. He told me he had just the rig, and this is it."

The officer moved toward the bus. "I'm going to need to see those papers," he said.

"I'll get them for you," Buck said, stepping in front of him and jumping onto the bus. He grabbed the papers and waved them as he came down the steps. The officer backed away and into the light of his own headlamps again.

"The papers seem to be in order, but it's just too coincidental that you purchased this vehicle only hours before this man was arrested."

"I don't see what buying a bus has to do with what some guy is messed up with," Buck said.

"We have reason to believe that the man who sold you this vehicle has been harboring a murderer. He was found with the suspect's papers and those of an American. It will not be long before we persuade him to tell us where he has harbored the suspect." The officer looked at his own notes. "Are you familiar with a Cameron Williams, an American?"

"Doesn't sound like the name of any friend I've got. I'm from Chicago."

"And you are leaving tonight, from Egypt?"

"That's right."

"Why?"

"Why?" Buck repeated.

"Why do you need to leave through Egypt? Why do you not fly out of Jerusalem or Tel Aviv?"

"No flights tonight. I want to get home. I've chartered a flight."

"And why didn't you simply hire a ride?"

"If you look closely at that title and bill of sale, you'll see I paid less for the bus than I would have for a ride."

"One moment, sir." The officer went back to his squad car and sat talking on the radio for several minutes.

Buck prayed he would think of something that would keep the peacekeeper from searching the bus.

Soon the young man emerged again. "You claim to never have heard of Cameron Williams. We are now determining if the man who sold you this vehicle will implicate you in his scheme."

"His scheme?" Buck said.

"It will not take us long to find out where he has hidden our suspect. It will be in his best interest to tell us the whole truth. He has a wife and children, after all."

For the first time in his life, Buck was tempted to kill a man. He knew the officer was just a pawn in a cosmic game, the war between good and evil. But he represented evil. Would Buck have been justified, the way Michael had felt justified, in killing those who might kill Tsion? The officer heard squawking on his radio and hurried back to the squad car. He returned in a moment.

"Our techniques have worked," he said. "We have extracted the location of the hiding place, somewhere between Jericho and Lake Tiberius off the Jordan River. But under the threat of torture and even death, he swears you were merely a tour guest to whom he sold the vehicle."

Buck sighed. Others might consider that mutual ruse a coincidence. To him it was as much a miracle as what he had seen at the Wailing Wall.

"Just for safety's sake, however," the officer said, "I have been asked to search your vehicle for any evidence of the fugitive."

"But you said—"

"Have no fear, sir. You are in the clear. Perhaps you were used to transport some evidence out of the country without your knowing it. We simply need to check the vehicle for anything that might lead us to the suspect. I will thank you to stand aside and remain here while I search your vehicle."

"You don't need a warrant or my permission or anything?"

The officer turned menacingly toward Buck. "Sir, you have been pleasant and cooperative. But do not make the mistake of thinking that you are talking with local law enforcement here. You can see from my car and my uniform that I represent the peacekeeping forces of the Global Community. We are restricted by no conventions or rules. I could confiscate this vehicle without so much as your signature. Now wait here."

Wild thoughts ran through Buck's mind. He considered trying to disarm the officer and racing away in the man's squad car with Tsion. It was ludicrous, he knew, but he hated inaction. Would Tsion jump the officer? Kill him? Buck heard the officer's footsteps move slowly to the back of the bus and then to the front again. The flashlight beam danced around inside the bus.

The officer rejoined him. "What did you think you were going to do? Did you think you were going to get away with this? Did you think I was going to allow you to drive this vehicle across the border into Egypt and to simply dump it? Were you going to leave it at an airport somewhere for local authorities to clean up?"

Buck was dumbfounded. This was what the officer was worried about now? Had he not seen Tsion Ben-Judah on the bus? Had God supernaturally blinded him?

"Uh, I, uh, actually had thought of that. Yes, I understood that many of the locals who try to pick up extra money helping with baggage and the like, that they, uh, would be thrilled to have such a vehicle."

"You must be a very wealthy American, sir. I realize this bus is not worth much, but it sure is a big tip for a baggage handler, wouldn't you say?"

"Call me frivolous," Buck said.

"Thank you for your cooperation, Mr. Katz."

"Well, you're welcome. And thank you."

The officer reentered his vehicle and pulled across the road, heading north back into Beersheba. Buck, his knees like jelly and his fingers twitching, slammed the hood shut and boarded the bus. "How in the world did you pull that off, Tsion? Tsion! It's me! You can come out now, wherever you are. No way you fit up in the luggage rack. Tsion?"

Buck stood on a seat and scanned the racks. Nothing. He lay on the floor and looked beneath the seats. Nothing but his own bag, the pile of clothes, the foodstuffs, and the water, oil, and gasoline. If Buck hadn't known better, he'd have thought Tsion Ben-Judah had been raptured after all.

Now what? No traffic had passed while Buck was engaged with the officer. Did he dare shout into the darkness? When had Tsion left the bus? Rather than make a scene for anyone who might happen along, Buck merely climbed aboard, restarted the engine, and drove down the shoulder of the road. After about two hundred yards, he tried to pop a U-turn and found that he had to accomplish it with a three-point turn instead. He drove down the other shoulder, clouds of dust rising behind him, illuminated by the red taillights. *C'mon, Tsion! Tell me you didn't start off walking all the way toward Egypt!*

Buck thought of honking the horn. Instead he drove another couple of hundred yards north and turned around yet again. This time his lights picked up the small, furtive wave of his friend from a grove of trees in the distance. He slowly rolled the bus to the area and opened the door. Tsion Ben-Judah leaped aboard and lay on the floor next to Buck. He was panting.

"If you have ever wondered what the saying meant about the Lord working in mysterious ways," Tsion said, "there was your answer."

"What in the world happened?" Buck said. "I thought we'd had it for good."

"So did I!" Tsion said. "I was dozing and barely understood that you were going to do something with the engine. When you raised the hood, I realized I needed to relieve myself. You were pouring the water when I got off. I was only about fifteen feet off the road when the squad car rolled by. I did not know what you would do, but I knew I could not be on that bus. I just started walking this way, praying you would somehow talk your way out of it."

"Did you hear our conversation, then?"

"No. What all was said?"

"You won't believe it, Tsion." And Buck told him the whole story as they rolled on toward the border.

As the old bus putted along in the darkness, Tsion apparently grew brave. He sat in the front seat, directly behind Buck. He was not hiding, not leaned over. He bent forward and spoke earnestly into Buck's ear. "Cameron," he said, his voice quavery and weak, "I am going nearly mad wondering who will take care of the disposition of my family."

Buck hesitated. "I don't quite know how to ask you this, sir, but what generally happens in cases like this? When pseudo-official factions do something like this, I mean."

"That is what bothers me. You never see what happens to the bodies. Do they bury them? Do they burn them? I do not know. But the mere imagining of it is deeply troubling to me."

"Tsion, far be it from me to advise you spiritually. You are a man of the Word and of deep faith."

Tsion interrupted him. "Do not be foolish, my young friend. Just because you are not a scholar does not mean you are any less mature in the faith. You were a believer before I was."

"Still, sir, I am at the end of my insight in knowing how to deal with such personal tragedy. I could not have remotely handled what you're going through in any way near how you're handling it."

"Do not forget, Cameron, that I am mostly running on emotion. No doubt my system is in shock. My worst days are yet to come."

"Frankly, Tsion, I have feared the same thing for you. At least you have been able to cry. Tears can be a great release. I fear for those who go through such trauma and find it impossible to shed tears."

Tsion sat back and said nothing. Buck prayed silently for him. Finally, Tsion leaned forward again. "I come from a heritage of tears," he said. "Centuries of tears."

"I wish I could do something tangible for you, Tsion," Buck said.

"Tangible? What is more tangible than this? You have been of such encouragement to me I cannot tell you. Who else would do this for a man he hardly knows?"

"It seems I've known you forever."

"And God has given you resources that even my closest friends do not have." Tsion seemed deep in thought. Finally he said, "Cameron, there is something you can do that would be of some comfort to me."

"Anything."

"Tell me about your little group of believers there in

America. What did you call them? The core group, I
mean?"

"The Tribulation Force."

"Yes! I love hearing such stories. Wherever I have
gone in the world to preach and to help be an instrument
in converting the 144,000 Jews who are becoming the
witnesses foretold in the Scriptures, I have heard wonderful tales of secret meetings and the like. Tell me all about
your Tribulation Force."

Buck began at the beginning. He started on the plane
when he was merely a passenger and Hattie Durham was
a flight attendant, Rayford Steele the pilot. As he talked,
he kept glancing in the rearview mirror to see if Tsion
was really listening or merely tolerating a long story.
Buck had always been amazed that his own mind could
be on two tracks at once. He could be telling a story and
thinking of another at the same time. All the while he
told Tsion of hearing Rayford spill his own story of a
spiritual quest, of meeting Chloe and traveling back
from New York to Chicago with her on the very day she
prayed with her father to receive Christ, of meeting and
being counseled by Bruce Barnes and mentored and
tutored by him whenever possible, Buck was trying to
hold at bay his fear of facing the border crossing. At the
same time he was wondering whether he should complete his story. Tsion did not know yet of the death of
Bruce Barnes, a man he had never met but with whom he
had corresponded and with whom he hoped to minister
one day.

Buck brought the story up to just a few days before,

when the Tribulation Force had reunited in Chicago, just before war erupted. Buck sensed Tsion growing more nervous as they neared the border. He seemed to move more, to interrupt more, to talk more quickly, and to ask more questions.

"And Pastor Bruce had been on the church staff for many years without having truly been a believer?"

"Yes. That was a sad, difficult story even for him to tell."

"I cannot wait to meet him," Tsion said. "I will grieve for my family, and I will miss my mother country as if she truly were my parent. But to get to pray with your Tribulation Force and open the Scriptures with them, this will be balm for my pain, salve for my wound."

Buck took a deep breath. He wanted to stop talking, to concentrate on the road, on the border ahead. Yet he could never be less than fully honest with Tsion. "You will meet Bruce Barnes at the Glorious Appearing," he said.

Buck peeked in the mirror. Clearly Tsion had heard and understood. He lowered his head. "When did it happen?" he asked.

Buck told him.

"And how did he die?"

Buck told him what he knew. "We're probably never going to know whether it was the virus he picked up overseas or the impact of the blast on the hospital. Rayford said there seemed to be no marks on his body."

"Perhaps the Lord spared him from the bombing by taking him first."

Buck considered that God was providing Rabbi Ben-Judah to be the new scriptural and spiritual mentor for the Tribulation Force, but he didn't dare suggest that. No way an international fugitive could become the new pastor of New Hope Village Church, especially if Nicolae Carpathia had his sights trained on him. Anyway, Tsion might consider Buck's idea a crazy one. Was there not some easier way God could have put Tsion in a position to help the Tribulation Force without costing him his wife and children?

In spite of his nervousness, in spite of his fear, in spite of the distraction of driving in unknown, dangerous territory with a less-than-desirable conveyance, suddenly Buck saw it all laid out before him. He wouldn't call it a vision. It was simply a realization of the possibilities. Suddenly he knew the first use for the secret shelter beneath the church. He envisioned Tsion there, supplied with everything he needed, including one of those great computers Donny Moore was dolling up.

Buck grew excited just thinking about it. He would provide for the rabbi every software package he needed. He would have the Bible in every version, every language, with all the notes and commentaries and dictionaries and encyclopedias he needed. Tsion would never again have to worry about losing his books. They would all be in one place, on one massive hard drive.

And what might Donny come up with that would allow Tsion to broadcast surreptitiously on the Internet? Was it possible his ministry could be more dramatic and wider than ever? Could he do his teaching and preaching and Bible studies on the Net to the millions of computers and televisions all over the world? Surely there must be some technology that would allow him to do this without being detected. If cell phone manufacturers could provide chips allowing a caller to jump between three-dozen different frequencies in seconds to avoid static and interception, surely there was a way to scramble a message over the Net and keep the sender from being identified.

In the distance Buck saw GC squad cars and trucks near two one-story buildings that straddled the road. The buildings would be the exit from Israel. Up the road would be the entrance into the Sinai. Buck downshifted and checked his gauges. The heat was starting to rise only slightly, and he was convinced if he drove slowly and was able to shut off the vehicle for a while at the border crossing, that would take care of it. He was doing fine on fuel, and the oil gauge looked OK.

He was irritated. His mind was engaged with the possibilities of a ministry for Tsion Ben-Judah that would outstrip anything he had ever been able to accomplish before, but it also reminded him that he too could, in essence, broadcast over the Internet the truth about what was going on in the world. For how long could he pretend to be a cooperative, if not loyal employee, of Nicolae Carpathia? His journalism was no longer objective. It was propaganda. It was what George Orwell would have called "newspeak" in his famous novel *1984*.

Buck didn't want to face a border crossing. He wanted to sit with a yellow pad and noodle his ideas. He wanted to excite the rabbi over the possibilities. But he could not. Apparently his rattletrap and its vulnerable personal cargo would have the full attention of the border guards. Whatever vehicles had preceded them were long gone, and none appeared in the rearview mirror.

Tsion lay on the floor beneath the seats. Buck pulled up to two uniformed and helmeted guards at a lowered crossbar. The one on the driver's side of the bus signaled that he should slide open the window and then spoke to him in Hebrew.

"English," Buck said.

"Passport, visa, identification papers, vehicle registration, any goods to declare, and anything on board you want us to know about before we search should be passed through the window or told to us before we raise the gate."

Buck stood and retrieved from the front seat all the papers related to the vehicle. He added his phony passport, visa, and identification. He slipped back behind the wheel and passed everything out to the guard. "I am also carrying foodstuffs, gasoline, oil, and water."

"Anything else?"

"Anything else?" Buck repeated.

"Anything else we need to see, sir! You will be interrogated inside, and your vehicle will be searched over there." The guard pointed just beyond the building on the right side of the road.

"Yes, I have some clothing and some blankets."

"Is that all?"

"Those are the only other things I am carrying."

"Very good, sir. When the bar is raised, please pull your vehicle to the right and meet me in the building on the left."

Buck slowly drove under the angled crossbar, keeping the bus in first gear, the noisiest. Tsion reached past Buck's chair and grabbed his ankle. Buck took it as encouragement, as thanks, and, if necessary, farewell. "Tsion," he whispered, "your only hope is to stay as far in the back as possible. Can you scoot all the way to the back?"

"I will try."

"Tsion, Michael's wife said something to me when I left. I didn't understand it. It was in Hebrew. The last two words were something like *Y'shua Hama*-some-thing."

"*Y'shua Hamashiach* means 'Jesus the Messiah,'" Tsion said, his voice quavery. "She was wishing you the blessing of God on your trip, in the name of *Y'shua Hamashiach.*"

"The same to you, my brother," Buck said.

"Cameron, my friend, I will see you soon. If not in this life, then in the everlasting kingdom."

The guards were approaching, obviously wondering what was keeping Buck. He shut off the engine and opened the door, just as a young guard approached. Buck grabbed a water can and shouldered his way past the guard. "Been having a little trouble with the radiator," he said. "You know anything about radiators?"

Distracted, the guard raised his eyebrows and followed Buck to the front of the bus. He raised the hood and they added water. The older guard, the one who had talked to him at the gate, said "Come on, let's go, let's go!"

"Be right with you," Buck said, aware of every nerve in his body. He made a huge noise, slamming the hood. The younger guard moved toward the door, but Buck passed him, excused himself, put one foot on the steps, and tossed the water can into the bus. He thought about "helping" the guard search the bus. He could stand with him and point out the blankets and cans of gas, oil, and water. But he had already come dangerously close, he feared, to making them suspicious. He came back off the bus and into the face of the young guard. "Thanks so much for your help. I don't know much about engines, really. Business is my game. America, you know."

The young guard looked him in the eyes and nodded. Buck prayed he would merely follow him into the building on the other side of the border crossing. The older guard was waiting, staring at him, now waving for him to come over. Buck had no choice now. He left Rabbi Tsion Ben-Judah, the most recognizable and notorious fugitive in Israel, in the hands of border guards.

Buck hurried into the processing building. He was as distracted as he'd ever been, but he couldn't let it show. He wanted to turn and see if Tsion was dragged off the bus. No way he could escape on foot as he had on the road not long before. There was nowhere to go here, nowhere to hide. Barbed wire fences lined each side. Once you got in the gate, you had to go one way or the other. There was no going around.

The original guard had Buck's papers spread out before him. "You entered Israel through what entry point?"

"Tel Aviv," Buck said. "It should all be there—"

"Oh, it is. Just checking. Your papers seem to be in order, Mr. Katz," he added, stamping Buck's passport and visa. "And you are representing . . . ?"

"International Harvesters," Buck said, making it plural because he meant it.

"And you're leaving the area when?"

"Tonight. If my pilot meets up with me at Al Arish."

"And how will you dispose of the vehicle?"

"I was hoping to sell it cheap to someone at the airport."

"Depending upon how cheap, that should be no problem."

Buck seemed frozen into place. The guard looked over his shoulder and out across the road. What was he looking at? Buck could only imagine Tsion detained, handcuffed, and led across the road. What a fool he had been to not try to find some secret compartment for Tsion. This was madness. Had he driven a man to his death? Buck couldn't stand the thought of losing yet another member of his new family in Christ.

The guard was on the computer. "This shows you were detained near Beersheba earlier this morning?"

"Detained is overstating it a bit. I was adding water to the radiator and was questioned briefly by a GC peacekeeping officer."

"Did he tell you the previous owner of your vehicle

has been arrested in connection with the escape of Tsion
Ben-Judah?"

"He did."

"You might be interested in this, then." The guard
turned and pointed a remote control device at a television up in the corner. The Global Community Network
News was reporting that a Michael Shorosh had been
arrested in connection with the harboring of a fugitive
from justice. "Global Community spokesmen say that
Ben-Judah, formerly a respected scholar and clergyman,
apparently became a radical fanatic fundamentalist, and
point to this sermon he delivered just a week ago as evidence that he overreacted to a New Testament passage
and was later seen by several neighbors slaughtering his
own family."

Buck watched in horror as the news ran a tape of
Tsion speaking at a huge rally in a filled stadium in
Larnaca, on the island of Cyprus. "You'll note," the
newsman said, as the tape was stopped, "the man on
the platform behind Dr. Ben-Judah has been identified
as Michael Shorosh. In a raid on his Jericho home
shortly after midnight tonight, peacekeeping forces found
personal photos of Ben-Judah's family and identification
papers from both Ben-Judah and an American journalist,
Cameron Williams. Williams's connection to the case has
not been determined."

Buck prayed they would not show his face on television. He was startled to see the guard look over his
shoulder to the door. Buck whirled to see the young
guard come in, staring at him. The young man let the

door close behind him and leaned back against it, his arms folded over his chest. He watched the news report with them. The tape showed Ben-Judah reading from Matthew. Buck had heard Tsion preach this message before. The verses, of course, had been taken out of context. "Whoever denies Me before men, him I will also deny before My Father who is in heaven.

"Do not think that I came to bring peace on earth. I did not come to bring peace but a sword. For I have come to 'set a man against his father, a daughter against her mother, and a daughter-in-law against her mother-in-law'; and 'a man's enemies will be those of his own household.' He who loves father or mother more than Me is not worthy of Me. And he who loves son or daughter more than Me is not worthy of Me. And he who does not take his cross and follow after Me is not worthy of Me."

The news reporter said solemnly, "This just a few days before the rabbi murdered his own wife and children in broad daylight."

"That's something, isn't it?" the older guard said.

"That's something all right," Buck said, fearing his voice betrayed him.

The guard at the desk was stacking Buck's papers. He looked past Buck to the young guard. "Everything all right with the vehicle, Anis?"

Buck had to think quickly. Which would look more suspicious? Not turning to look at the young man, or turning to look at him? He turned to look. Still standing before the closed door, arms over his chest, the rigid young man nodded once. "All is in order. Blankets and supplies."

Buck had been holding his breath. The man at the desk slid his papers across. "Safe journey," he said.

Buck nearly wept as he exhaled. "Thank you," he said.

He turned toward the door, but the older guard was not finished. "Thank you for visiting Israel," he added.

Buck wanted to scream. He turned around and nodded. "Yeah, uh, yes. You're welcome."

He had to will himself to walk. Anis did not move as Buck approached the door. He came face-to-face with the young man and stopped. He sensed the older guard watching. "Excuse me," Buck said.

"My name is Anis," the man said.

"Yes, Anis. Thank you. Excuse me, please."

Finally Anis stepped aside and Buck shakily left. His hands trembled as he folded his papers and stuffed them into his pocket. He boarded the rickety old bus and fired it up. If Tsion had found somewhere to hide, how would Buck find him now? He executed the fragile dance between clutch and accelerator and got the rig moving. Finally up to speed, he shifted into third, and the engine smoothed out a bit. He called out, "If you're still on board, my friend, stay right where you are until the lights of that border crossing disappear. Then I want to know everything."

THIRTEEN

RAYFORD was tired of being awakened by the phone. However, few people in New Babylon outside of Carpathia and Fortunato ever called him. And they usually had the sense not to disturb him in the middle of the night. So, he decided, the ringing phone was either good news or bad news. One chance out of two, in this day and age, wasn't bad.

He picked up the phone. "Steele," he said.

It was Amanda. "Oh, Rayford, I know it's the middle of the night there, and I'm sorry to wake you. It's just that we've had a little excitement here, and we want to know if you know anything."

"Know anything about what?"

"Well, Chloe and I were just going over all these pages from Bruce's computer printout. We told you about that?"

"Yeah."

"We got the strangest call from Loretta at the church. She said she was just working there alone, taking a few phone calls. She said she just had an overwhelming urge to pray for Buck."

"For Buck?"

"Yes. She said she was so overcome with the emotion of it that she quickly stood up from her chair. She said she thought that made her lightheaded, but something made her fall to her knees. Once she was kneeling, she realized she wasn't dizzy but was just praying earnestly for Buck."

"All I know, hon, is that Buck is in Israel. I think he's trying to find Tsion Ben-Judah, and you know what's happened to his family."

"We know," Amanda said. "It's just that Buck has a way of getting himself into trouble."

"He also has a way of getting himself out of trouble," Rayford said.

"Then what do you make of this premonition, or whatever it was, of Loretta's?"

"I wouldn't call it a premonition. We all could use prayer these days, couldn't we?"

Amanda sounded annoyed. "Rayford, this was no fluke. You know Loretta is as levelheaded as they come. She was so upset she shut the office and came home."

"You mean before nine o'clock at night? What has she become, a slacker?"

"Come on, Ray. She didn't go in until about noon

today. You know she often stays till nine. People call at all hours."

"I know. I'm sorry."

"She wants to talk to you."

"To me?"

"Yes. Will you talk to her?"

"Sure, put her on." Rayford had no idea what to say to her. Bruce would have had an answer for something like this.

Loretta indeed sounded shaken. "Captain Steele, I'm so sorry 'bout troubling you at this time of the night. What is it, goin' on like three o'clock over there?"

"Yes ma'am, but it's all right."

"No, it's not all right. There's no reason to raise you out of a sound sleep. But sir, God told me to pray for that boy, I just know it."

"Then I'm glad you did."

"Do you think I'm crazy?"

"I've always thought you were crazy, Loretta. That's why we love you so much."

"I know you're sporting with me, Captain Steele, but seriously, have I lost my marbles?"

"No ma'am. God seems to be working in much more direct and dramatic ways all the time. If you were led to pray for Buck right then, you remember to ask him what was happening."

"That's just the thing, Mr. Steele. I had this over-whelming sense that Buck was in deep trouble. I just hope he makes it out of there alive. We're all hoping he can be back here in time for the Sunday service. You'll be here, won't you?"

"The Lord willing," Rayford said, stunned to hear from his own lips a phrase he had always considered silly when Irene's old friends had used it.

"We want everybody together Sunday," Loretta said.

"It's my highest priority, ma'am. And Loretta, would you do me a favor?"

"After gettin' you up in the middle of the night? You name it."

"If the Lord prompts you to pray for me, would you do it with all your might?"

"'Course I will. You know that. I hope you're not just bein' funny now."

"I've never been more serious."

———————————

When the lights of the border crossing disappeared behind him, Buck pulled the bus off the road, shifted into neutral, set the brake, turned sideways in his seat, and sighed heavily. He could barely produce volume in his voice. "Tsion, are you on this bus? Come out now, wherever you are."

From the back of the bus came an emotion-filled voice. "I am here, Cameron. Praise the Lord God Almighty, Maker of heaven and earth."

The rabbi crawled out from under the seats. Buck met him in the aisle and they embraced. "Talk to me," Buck said.

"I told you the Lord would make a way somehow,"
Tsion said. "I don't know if the young Anis was an angel
or a man, but he was sent from God."

"Anis?"

"Anis. He walked up and down the aisle of the bus,
shining his flashlight here and there. Then he knelt and
shined it under the seats. I looked right into the beam.
I was praying that God would blind his eyes. But God
did not blind him. He came back to where I was and
dropped to his elbows and knees. He kept the flashlight
in my face with one hand and reached with the other
to grab me by the shirt. He pulled me close to him.
I thought my heart would burst. I imagined myself
dragged into the building, a trophy for a young officer.

"He whispered hoarsely to me through clenched teeth
in Hebrew, 'You had better be who I think you are, or
you are a dead man.' What could I do? There was no
more hiding. No more future in pretending I wasn't
here. I said to him, 'Young man, my name is Tsion
Ben-Judah.'

"Still holding my shirt in his fist and with his flashlight
blinding me, he said, 'Rabbi Ben-Judah, my name is
Anis. Pray as you have never prayed before that my
report will be believed. And now may the Lord bless you
and keep you. May the Lord make His face shine upon
you and give you peace.' Cameron, as God is my witness,
the young man stood and walked out of the bus. I have
been lying here, praising God with my tears ever since."

There was nothing more to say. Tsion slumped into a

seat in the middle of the bus. Buck returned to the wheel and drove off to the border crossing in Egypt.

Half an hour later Buck and Tsion pulled up to the entrance into the Sinai. This time, God merely used the carelessness of the system to allow Ben-Judah to slip through. The only crossing gate was on the other side of the border into the Sinai. When Buck was told to stop, one guard immediately boarded and began barking orders in his own tongue. Buck said, "English?"

"English it is, gentlemen." He looked back at Tsion. "You'll be able to go back to sleep in a few minutes there, old-timer," he said. "You've got to come in and be processed first. I'll search your bus while you're in there, and you'll be on your way."

Buck, emboldened by the most recent miracle, looked at Tsion and shrugged. He waited as Tsion made way for the guard to get past him and begin the search, but Tsion motioned to Buck that he should get going. Buck hurried off the bus and into the building. As his papers were being processed, the guard said, "No trouble at the Israeli checkpoint then?"

Buck nearly smiled. *No problem? There's no problem when God is on your side.* "No, sir."

Buck couldn't help himself. He kept looking over his shoulder for Tsion. Where had he gone now? Had God made him invisible?

This was a much easier and quicker process. Apparently the Egyptians were used to simply rubber-stamping whatever the Israelis had approved. You couldn't get to this checkpoint without going through the previous, so unless the Israelis were trying to dump their castoffs, it was usually smooth sailing. Buck's papers were stamped and stacked and handed back to him with just a few questions. "Less than a hundred kilometers to Al Arish," the guard said. "No commercial flights scheduled out of there at this time, of course."

"I know," Buck said. "I have made my own arrangements."

"Very good then, Mr. Katz. All the best."

All the best is right! Buck thought.

He turned to hurry out to the bus. There was no sign of Tsion. The original guard was still on the bus. As Buck began to board, Tsion came from behind the bus and stepped in front of him. They boarded together. The guard was going through Buck's bag. "Impressive equipment, Mr. Katz."

"Thanks."

Tsion casually moved past the guard and went back to where he had been sitting when they arrived. He stretched out on the seat.

"And you work for whom?" the guard asked.

"International Harvesters," Buck said. Tsion rose up briefly in his seat, and Buck nearly laughed. Surely Tsion appreciated that.

The guard closed the bag. "You're both all processed then and ready to proceed?"

"All set," Buck said.

The guard looked toward the back. Tsion was snoring. The guard turned toward Buck and spoke quietly, "Carry on."

Buck tried not to be too eager to drive off, but he popped the clutch when the guard was clear of the front of the bus, and soon he was out onto the road again. "All right, Tsion, where were you that time?"

Tsion sat up. "Did you like my snore?"

Buck laughed. "Very impressive. Where were you when the guard thought you were being processed with me?"

"Merely standing behind the bus. You got off and went one way, I got off and went the other."

"You're joking."

"I did not know what to do, Cameron. He was so friendly, and he had seen me. I certainly wasn't going to walk into the processing center with no papers. When you returned, I figured I had been gone an appropriate time."

"The question now," Buck said, "is how long before that guard mentions he saw *two* men on the bus."

Tsion carefully made his way up to the seat behind Buck. "Yes," he said. "First he will have to convince them that he was not seeing things. Maybe it will not come up. But if it does, they will soon give chase."

"I trust the Lord to deliver us, because he has promised he will," Buck said. "But I also think we had better be as prepared as possible." He pulled off to the side of the road. He topped off the water in the radiator and dumped nearly two liters of oil into the engine. He filled the gas tanks.

"It is like we are living in the New Testament," Tsion said.

Buck, clutching and shifting, said "They might be able to overtake this old bus. But if we can make it to Al

Arish, we'll be on that Learjet and out over the Mediterranean before they know we're gone."

For the next two hours, the road grew worse. The temperature rose. Buck kept an eye on the rearview mirror and noticed that Tsion kept looking back as well. Occasionally a smaller, faster car would appear on the horizon and fly past them.

"What are we worried about, Cameron? God would not bring us so far only to have us captured. Would he?"

"You're asking me? I never had anything like this happen to me until I ran into you!"

They rode in silence for half an hour. Finally, Tsion spoke, and Buck thought he sounded as strong as he had since Buck first saw him in the hideout. "Cameron, you know I have had to force myself to eat up until now, and I have not done a good job at it."

"So eat something! There's lots of stuff in here!"

"I believe I will. The pain in my heart is so deep that I feel as if I will never do anything again only for the sake of my own enjoyment. I used to love to eat. Even before I knew Christ, I knew that food was God's provision for us. He wanted us to enjoy it. I am hungry now, but I will eat only for sustenance and energy."

"You don't have to explain it to me, Tsion. I only pray that sometime between now and the Glorious Appearing, you'll get some relief from the deep wound you must feel."

"You want anything?"

Buck shook his head, then thought better of it. "Anything there with lots of fiber and natural sugar?"

He didn't know what was ahead, but he didn't want to be physically weak, regardless.

Tsion snorted. "High in fiber and natural sugars? This is food from Israel, Cameron. You just described everything we eat."

The rabbi tossed Buck several fig bars that reminded him of granola and fruit. Buck had not realized his own level of hunger until he began to eat. He suddenly felt supercharged and hoped Tsion felt the same. Especially when he saw flashing yellow lights on the horizon far behind them.

The question now was whether to try to outrun the official vehicle or to feign innocence and merely let it pass. Perhaps it was not after them anyway. Buck shook his head. What was he thinking? Of course this was probably their Waterloo. He was confident God would bring them through, but he also didn't want to be naïve enough to think an emergency vehicle would be coming at them from the border crossing without Buck and Tsion in its sights. "Tsion, you'd better secure everything and get out of sight."

Tsion leaned to stare out the back. "More excitement," he muttered. "Lord, have we not had enough for one day? Cameron, I will put most of it away, but I am taking a few morsels with me to my bed."

"Suit yourself. From the looks of those cars at the border, they're small and have very little power. If I step on it, it will take them a long time to catch us."

"And when they do?" Tsion said, from beneath the seats in the back.

"I am trying to think of a strategy now."

"I will be praying," Tsion said.

Buck nearly laughed. "Your praying has resulted in a lot of mayhem tonight," he said.

There was no response from the back. Buck pushed the bus for all it was worth. He got it up to over eighty kilometers an hour, which he guessed was in the fifty mile-an-hour range. It rattled and shook and bounced, and the various metal parts squeaked in protest. He knew that if he could see the border patrol car, its driver could see him. There was no sense cutting the lights and hoping they assumed he had pulled off the road.

It seemed he might be pulling away from them. He could not judge distances well in the darkness, but they didn't appear to be coming at high speed. The lights were flashing, and he was convinced they were after him, but he pushed ahead.

From the back: "Cameron, I think I have the right to know. What is your plan? What will you do when they overtake us, as they surely will?"

"Well, I'll tell you one thing, I'm not going back to that border. I'm not even sure I'll let them pull me over."

"How will you know what they want?"

"If it's the man who searched the bus, we'll know what they want, won't we?"

"I suppose we will."

"I will holler at him from the window and urge him to deal with us at the airport. There's no sense driving all the way back to the border."

"But will that not be *his* decision?"

"I guess I'll have to engage in civil disobedience then," Buck said.

"But what if he forces you off the road? Makes you pull over?"

"I'll try to avoid hitting him at all costs, but I will not stop, and if I am forced to stop, I will not turn around."

"I appreciate your resolve, Cameron. I will pray, and you do as God leads you."

"You know I will."

Buck guessed they were thirty kilometers from the airport outside Al Arish. If he could even keep the bus close to sixty kilometers per hour, they could make it in half an hour. The border patrol car would surely overtake them before that. But they were so much closer to the airport than to the border, he was certain the officer would see the wisdom of following them to the airport rather than leading them back to the border.

"Tsion, I need your help."

"Anything."

"Stay down and out of sight, but find my phone in my bag and get it to me."

When Tsion crawled next to Buck with his phone, Buck asked him, "Sir, how old are you?"

"That is considered an impolite question in my culture," Tsion said.

"Yeah, like I care about that now."

"I'm forty-six, Cameron. Why do you ask?"

"You seem in pretty good shape."

"Thank you. I work out."

"You do? Really?"

"Does that surprise you? You would be surprised at the number of scholars who work out. Of course there are many who do not, but—"

"I just want to make sure you'll be able to run if you need to."

"I hope it does not come to that, but yes, I can run. I am not as fast as I was as a young man, but I have surprising endurance for one of my vintage."

"That's all I wanted to know."

"Remind me to ask *you* some personal question sometime," Tsion said.

"Seriously, Tsion. I did not offend you, did I?"

Buck was strangely warmed. The rabbi actually chuckled. "Oh, my friend, think about it. What would it take to offend me now?"

"Tsion, you'd better get back where you were, but can you tell me how much gasoline we have left?"

"The gauge is right there in front of you, Cameron. You tell me."

"No, I mean in our extra cans."

"I will check, but surely we do not have time to fill our tanks while we are being chased. What do you have in mind?"

"Why do you ask so many questions?"

"Because I am a student. I will always be a student. Anyway, we are in this together, are we not?"

"Well, let me just give you a hint. While you're tapping on the sides of those gas cans to tell me how much we have left, I'm going to be checking the cigarette lighter on the dashboard."

"Cameron, cigarette lighters are the first to go in old vehicles, are they not?"

"For our sakes, let's hope not."

Buck's phone buzzed. Startled, he flipped it open. "Buck here."

"Buck! It's Chloe!"

"Chloe! I really can't talk to you now. Trust me. Don't ask any questions. For right now I'm OK, but please ask everybody to pray and pray now. And listen, somehow, on the Internet or something, find the phone number for the airport at Al Arish, south of the Gaza Strip on the Mediterranean in the Sinai. Get hold of Ken Ritz, who should be waiting there. Have him call me at this number."

"But Buck—"

"Chloe, it's life or death!"

"You call me as soon as you're safe!"

"Promise!"

Buck clapped the phone shut and heard Tsion from the back. "Cameron! Are you planning to blow up this bus?"

"You really are a scholar, aren't you?" Buck said.

"I just hope you wait until we get to the airport. I mean, a flaming bus may get us there faster, but your pilot friend may just ferry our remains to the States."

"That's all right, Chloe," Rayford said, "I long since gave up trying to sleep. I'm up reading anyway."

Chloe told him of her strange conversation with Buck.

"Don't waste time on the Internet," Rayford said, "I've got a guide to all those phone numbers. Hang on."

"Daddy," she said, "it's gotta be a closer phone call for you anyway. Call Ken Ritz and tell him to call Buck."

"I'm tempted to fly over there myself, if I had a small enough craft."

"Daddy, we don't need both you and Buck endangering your lives at the same time."

"Chloe, we do that every day."

"Better hurry, Dad."

Buck guessed the border patrol car was less than half a mile behind him. He put the accelerator to the floor and the bus lurched. The steering wheel shook and bounced as they hurtled down the road. The gauges still looked OK for the moment, but Buck knew it was only a matter of time before the radiator overheated.

"I am guessing we have about eight liters of gasoline," Tsion said.

"That will be plenty."

"I agree, Cameron. That will be more than enough to make martyrs of us both."

Buck eased off the throttle just enough to smooth out the ride. Smooth, of course, was a misnomer. Buck felt it in his back and hips as they bounced along. The border patrol car had closed to within a quarter mile.

Tsion called out from the back: "Cameron, it is clear we are not going to outrun them to the airport, do you agree?"

"Yes! So?"

"Then it makes no sense to push this vehicle to its limit. It would be smarter to conserve water, oil, and gasoline to be sure we make it to the airport. If we break down, all your resolve means nothing."

Buck couldn't argue with that. He immediately slowed to about fifty kilometers per hour and sensed he had bought several miles. However, this also allowed the border patrol car to pull right up behind him.

A siren sounded and a spotlight flashed in his outside rearview mirror. Buck merely waved and drove on. Soon it was yellow flashing lights, the spotlight, the siren, and the horn of the patrol car. Buck ignored them all.

Finally, the squad car pulled even with him. He glanced down to see the very guard who had searched the bus. "Fasten your seat belt, Tsion!" Buck hollered. "The chase is on!"

"I wish I *had* a seat belt!"

Buck continued at his modest speed as the patrol car stayed with him and the guard pointed that he should pull over. Buck waved at him and drove on. The guard pulled in front of the bus and slowed, again pointing to the side of the road. When Buck made no attempt to pull off, the car slowed even more, forcing him to swerve around it. He had no acceleration, however, and the patrol car, now on the other side of him, sped up to keep him from passing. Buck merely backed off and got behind the car again. When it stopped, he stopped.

When the guard got out, Buck backed up and drove around him, building about a hundred-yard gap before the guard jumped back in and quickly caught up again. This time, the guard pulled alongside and showed Buck a handgun. Buck opened his window and hollered, "If I stop, this bus will stall! Follow me to Al Arish!"

"No!" came the reply. "You follow me back to the border!"

"We are much closer to the airport! I don't think this bus can make it back to the border!"

"Then leave it! You can ride back with me!"

"I'll see you at the airport!"

"No!"

But Buck slid his window shut. When the guard pointed his weapon at Buck's window, Buck ducked but kept going.

Buck's phone was buzzing. He clicked it open. "Talk to me!"

"This is Ritz. What's the deal?"

"Ken, have you passed through customs there?"

"Yeah! I'm ready when you are."

"You ready for some fun?"

"I thought you'd never ask! I haven't had any real fun for ages."

"You're gonna risk your life and break the law," Buck said.

"Is that all? I've been there before."

"Tell me your position and all, Ken," Buck said.

"Looks like I'm the only plane going out of here tonight. I'm just outside of a hangar at the end of the runway. My plane is, I mean. I'm talking to you from the little terminal here."

"But you've been processed, and you're ready to leave Egypt?"

"Yeah, no problem."

"What did you tell them as far as other passengers and cargo?"

"I figured you wouldn't want me to talk about anybody but you."

"Perfect, Ken! Thanks! And who do they think I am?"

"You're exactly who I say you are, Mr. Katz."

"Ken, that's great. Hang on just a second."

The guard had pulled in front of the bus and now slammed on his brakes. Buck had to swerve almost all the way off the road to miss him, and when he pulled back on, the bus fishtailed and nearly went over.

"I am rolling back here!" Tsion said.

"Enjoy the ride!" Buck said. "I'm not stopping, and I'm not turning around."

The guard had turned off his flashing yellow lights and his spotlight. The siren was silent now too. He quickly caught up with the bus and tapped it from behind. He tapped it again. And again.

"He's afraid to hurt that squad car, isn't he?" Buck said.

"Do not be so sure," Tsion said.

"I'm sure." Buck slammed on the brakes, making Tsion slide forward and cry out. Buck heard the screeching tires behind him and saw the squad car lurch off the right side of the road and down into loose gravel. Buck punched the accelerator. The bus stalled. As he tried to start it he saw the squad car, still in the gravel, coming up along his right side. The engine kicked in, and Buck popped the clutch. He picked up the phone. "Ken, you still there?"

"Yeah, what in the world's going on?"

"You wouldn't believe it!"

"You bein' chased or something?"

"That's the understatement of the year, Ritz! I don't think we're gonna have time to go through customs there. I need to know how to get to your plane. You need to be cleared, engines running, door open, and stairs down."

"This *is* gonna be fun!" Ritz said.

"You have no idea," Buck said. The pilot quickly told Buck the layout of the airstrip and the terminal and precisely where he was. "We're within about ten minutes of you," Buck said. "If I can keep this thing rolling, I'll try to get as close to the runway and your plane as possible. What am I gonna run into?"

The squad car came up onto the road, spun, and now faced the bus. Buck swerved left, but the car cut him off. Buck couldn't avoid smashing him. The impact turned the car around in the road and knocked the hood off. Buck sensed little damage to the big old bus, but the temperature gauge was rising.

"Who's chasing you anyway?" Ritz said.

"Egyptian border patrol," Buck said.

"Then you can bet they're gonna radio ahead here. There'll be some kind of a roadblock."

"I just hit the squad car. Is this going to be a roadblock I can blast through?"

"You'll have to play that one by ear. If you're as close as you say you are, I'd better get out to my plane."

"The cigarette lighter works!" Buck hollered to Tsion.

"I am not sure I wanted to hear that!"

The smashed patrol car resumed pursuit. Buck saw the lights of the airstrip in the distance. "Tsion, come up here. We need to strategize."

"Strategy? It is lunacy!"

"And what would you call what else we've been through?"

"The lunacy of the Lord! Just tell me what to do, Cameron, and I will do it. Nothing will be able to stop us tonight."

The guard in the squad car had apparently radioed ahead not only for a roadblock but also for help. Two sets of headlights, side-by-side and covering both lanes of the road, headed toward the bus. "Have you heard the phrase 'playing chicken'?" Buck asked.

"No," Tsion said, "but it is becoming clear to me. Are you going to challenge them?"

"Don't you agree they have more to lose than we do?"

"I do. I am hanging on. Do what you have to do!"

Buck pressed the accelerator to the floor. The heat gauge was pressed to the maximum and quivering. Steam billowed from the engine. "Here's what we're going to do, Tsion! Listen carefully!"

"Just concentrate on your driving, Cameron! Tell me later!"

"There will be no later! If these cars don't back down, there's going to be a tremendous crash. I think we'll be able to keep going either way. When we get to whatever roadblock they have for us at the airport, we have to make a quick decision. I need you to pour all those gas containers into the one big water bucket, the one that's wide open at the top. I'll have the cigarette lighter hot and ready to go. If we come upon a roadblock I think I can smash through, I'll just keep going and get as close to the runway as possible. The Lear is going to be off to our right and about a hundred yards from the terminal. If the roadblock is not something we can smash through, I'll try to go around it. If that's impossible, I'm going to pull the wheel hard to the left and slam on the brakes. That will make the back end swing around into the roadblock and anything loose will slide to the back door. You must put that bucket of gasoline in the aisle about eight feet from the back door, and when I give you the signal, toss that cigarette lighter into it. It needs to be just enough ahead of the collision so it's burning before we hit."

"I do not understand! How will *we* escape that?"

"If the roadblock is impenetrable, it's our only hope! When that back door blows open and that burning gasoline flies out, we have to be hanging on up here with all our might so we don't get thrown back into it. While they're concentrating on the fire, we jump out the front and run toward the jet. Got it?"

"I get it, Cameron, but I am not optimistic!"

"Hang on!" Buck shouted as two cars from the airport closed on him. Tsion hooked one arm around the metal pole behind Buck and wrapped his other around

Buck's chest, grabbing the back of the chair like a human seat belt.

Buck gave no indication of slowing or swerving and headed straight for the two sets of headlights. At the last instant he closed his eyes, fully expecting a huge collision. When he opened his eyes, the road was clear. He looked first one way then the other behind him. Both cars had gone off the road, one of them rolling. The original pursuit car was still behind him, and Buck heard gunfire.

Less than a mile ahead the small airport loomed. Huge fences of mesh and barbed wire flanked the entrance, and just inside sat a blockade of a half-dozen vehicles and several armed soldiers. Buck could see he would not be able to blast through it or go around.

He pressed in the cigarette lighter as Tsion lugged the gas cans and the bucket to the back. "It is sloshing around!" Tsion called out.

"Just do the best you can!"

As Buck raced toward the open gate and the huge blockade, the patrol car still following close behind, the cigarette lighter popped out. Buck grabbed it and tossed it back to Tsion. It bounced and rolled under a seat. "Oh no!" Buck shouted.

"I have got it!" Tsion said. Buck peeked in the rearview mirror as Tsion climbed out from under a seat, tossed the cigarette lighter into the bucket, and scrambled to the front.

The back of the bus burst into flames. "Hang on!" Buck shouted, pulling hard to the left and slamming on the brakes. The bus whirled so fast it nearly tipped over. The back smashed into the stockade of cars, and the back door burst open, flaming gasoline splashing everywhere.

Buck and Tsion jumped out and ran, low as they could, around the left side of the blockade as guards began firing into the bus and others screamed and ran from the flames. Tsion was limping. Buck grabbed the older man and dragged him around the dark side of the terminal near the runway.

There was the Learjet, ready for takeoff. Never had a plane looked like such an oasis of safety. Buck looked back twice, but no one seemed to have seen them escape. It was too good to be true, but it fit with everything else that had happened that night.

Fifty feet from the plane, Buck heard shots and turned to see a half-dozen guards racing toward them, firing high-powered weapons. When they reached the steps, Buck grabbed Tsion by the belt in the back and threw him aboard. As Buck dived into the plane, a bullet ripped through the bottom of the heel of his right boot. Pain shot through the side of his foot as he yanked the door shut, Ritz already rolling.

Buck and Tsion crawled up to behind the cockpit.

Ritz muttered, "Those rascals shoot my plane, I'm gonna be really mad."

The plane took off like a rocket and rose quickly. "Next stop," Ritz announced, "Palwaukee Airport, State of Illinois, in the U.S. of A."

Buck lay on the floor, unable to move. He wanted to

look out the window, but he didn't dare. Tsion buried his face in his hands. He wept and seemed to be praying.

Ritz turned. "Well, Williams, you sure left a mess down there. What was that all about?"

"It would take a week to tell," Buck said, panting.

"Well," Ritz said, "whatever it was, that was sure fun."

An hour later, Buck and Tsion sat in reclining seats, assessing the damage. "It is only sprained," Tsion said. "I caught my foot under one of the seat supports when we first hit. I was afraid I had broken it. It will heal quickly."

Buck slowly took off his right boot and held it up so Tsion could see the trajectory of the bullet. A clean hole had been blasted from the sole to the ankle. Buck took off a bloody sock. "Would you look at that?" he said, smiling. "I won't even need stitches. Just a nick there."

Tsion used Ken Ritz's first-aid kit to treat Buck's foot and found an Ace bandage for his own ankle.

Finally settled back with their wounded limbs elevated, Tsion and Buck looked at each other. "Are you as exhausted as I am?" Buck said.

"I am ready to sleep," Tsion said, "but we would be remiss, would we not, if we did not return thanks."

Buck leaned forward and bowed his head. The last thing he heard, before he slipped into a sleep of sweet relief, was the beautiful cadence of Rabbi Tsion Ben-Judah's prayer, thanking God that "the glory of the Lord was our rear guard."

FOURTEEN

BUCK awoke nearly ten hours later, pleased that Tsion was still sleeping. He checked Tsion's Ace bandage. The ankle was swollen, but it didn't look serious. His own foot was too tender to go back into his boot. He limped forward. "How are you doing, Cap?"

"A lot better, now that we're over American airspace. I had no idea what you guys got yourselves into, and who knew what kind of fighter pilots might have been on my tail."

"I don't think we were worth all that, with World War III going on," Buck said.

"Where'd you leave all your stuff?"

Buck whirled around. What was he looking for? He had brought nothing with him. Everything he brought had been in that leather bag, which by now was charred and melted. "I promised to call my wife back, too!" he said.

"You'll be happy to know I already talked to your people," Ritz said. "They were mighty relieved to hear you were on your way home."

"You didn't say anything about my wound or about my passenger, did you?"

"Give me some credit, Williams. You and I both know your wound isn't worth worrying about, so no wife needs to hear about that until she sees it. And as for your passenger, I have no idea who he is or whether your people knew you were bringing him home for dinner, so, no, I didn't say a word about him either."

"You're a good man, Ritz," Buck said, clapping him on the shoulder.

"I like a compliment as much as the next guy, but I hope you know you owe me battle pay on top of everything else."

"That can be arranged."

Because Ritz had carefully documented his plane and passenger on the way out of the country a few days before, he was on record and easily made it back through the North American radar net. He did not announce his extra passenger, and because personnel at Palwaukee Airport were not in the habit of processing international travelers, no one there paid any attention when an American pilot in his fifties, an Israeli rabbi in his forties, and an American writer in his thirties disembarked. Ritz was the only one not limping.

Buck had finally reached Chloe from the plane. It sounded to him as if she might have bitten his head off

for keeping her up all night worrying and praying, had
she not been so relieved to hear his voice. "Believe me,
babe," he said, "when you hear the whole story, you'll
understand."

Buck had convinced her that only the Tribulation
Force and Loretta could know about Tsion. "Don't tell
Verna. Can you come alone to Palwaukee?"

"I'm not up to driving yet, Buck," she said. "Amanda
can drive me out there. Verna isn't even staying with us
anymore. She has moved in with friends."

"That could be a problem," Buck said. "I may have
made myself vulnerable to the worst possible person in
my profession."

"We'll have to talk about that, Buck."

It was as if Tsion Ben-Judah was in some international
witness protection program. He was smuggled into
Loretta's home under the cover of night. Amanda and
Chloe, who had heard from Rayford the news about
Tsion's family, greeted him warmly and compassionately
but seemed not to know how much to say. Loretta had a
light snack waiting for all of them. "I'm old and not too
up on things," she said, "but I'm quickly getting the picture here. The less I know about your friend, the better,
am I right?"

Tsion answered her circumspectly. "I am deeply grateful for your hospitality."

Loretta soon trundled off to bed, expressing her
delight in offering hospitality as her service to the Lord.

Buck, Chloe, and Tsion limped into the living room,
followed by a chuckling Amanda. "I wish Rayford were

here," she said. "I feel like the only teetotaler in a car full of drunks. Every chore that requires two feet is going to fall to me."

Chloe, characteristically direct, leaned forward and reached for Tsion's hand with both of hers. "Dr. Ben-Judah, we have heard so much about you. We feel blessed of God to have you with us. We can't imagine your pain."

The rabbi took a deep breath and exhaled slowly, his lips quivering. "I cannot tell you how deeply grateful I am to God that he has brought me here, and to you who have welcomed me. I confess my heart is broken. The Lord has shown me his hand so clearly since the death of my family that I cannot deny his presence. Yet there are times I wonder how I will go on. I do not want to dwell on how my loved ones lost their lives. I must not think about who did this and how it was accomplished. I know my wife and children are safe and happy now, but it is very difficult for me to imagine their horror and pain before God received them. I must pray for relief from bitterness and hatred. Most of all, I feel terrible guilt that I brought this upon them. I do not know what else I could have done, short of trying to make them more secure. I could not have avoided serving God in the way he has called me."

Amanda and Buck each moved to put a hand on Tsion's shoulders, and with the three of them touching him, they all prayed as he wept.

They talked well into the night, Buck explaining that Tsion would be the object of an international manhunt, which would likely have even Carpathia's approval. "How many people know about the underground shelter at the church?"

"Believe it or not," Chloe said, "unless Loretta has read the printouts from Bruce's computer, even she thinks it was just some new utility installation."

"How was he able to keep that from her? She was at the church every day while it was being excavated."

"You'll have to read Bruce's stuff, Buck. In short, she was under the impression that all that work was for the new water tank and parking lot improvements. Just like everyone else in the church thought."

Two hours later, Buck and Chloe lay in bed, unable to sleep. "I knew this was going to be difficult," she said. "I guess I just didn't know how much."

"Do you wish you'd never gotten involved with somebody like me?"

"Let's just say it hasn't been boring."

Chloe then told him about Verna Zee. "She thought we were all wacky."

"Aren't we? The question is, how much damage can she do to me? She knows completely where I stand now, and if that gets back to people at the *Weekly,* it'll shoot up the line to Carpathia like lightning. Then what?"

Chloe told Buck that she and Amanda and Loretta had at least persuaded Verna to keep Buck's secret for now.

"But why would she do that?" Buck said. "We've never liked each other. We've been at each other's throats. The only reason we traded favors the other night was that World War III made our skirmishes look petty."

"Your skirmishes *were* petty," Chloe said. "She admitted she was intimidated by you and jealous of you. You were what she had always hoped to be, and she even confessed that she knew she was no journalist compared to you."

"That doesn't give me confidence about her ability to keep my secret."

"You would have been proud of us, Buck. Loretta had already told Verna her entire story, how she was the only person in her extended family not taken in the Rapture. Then I got my licks in, telling her all about how you and I met, where you were when the Rapture happened, and how you and I and Daddy became believers."

"Verna must have thought we were all from another planet," Buck said. "Is that why she moved out?"

"No. I think she felt in the way."

"Was she sympathetic at all?"

"She actually was. I took her aside once and told her that the most important thing was what she decided to do about Christ. But I also told her that our very lives depended upon her protecting the news of your loyalties from your colleagues and superiors. She said, 'His *superiors?* Cameron's only superior is Carpathia.' But she also said something else very interesting, Buck. She said that as much as she admires Carpathia and what he has done for America and the world—gag—she hates the way he controls and manipulates the news."

"The question, Chloe, is whether you extracted from her any promises of my protection."

"She wanted to trade favors. Probably wanted some sort of a promotion or raise. I told her you would never work that way, and she said she figured that. I asked if she would promise me that she would at least not say anything to anyone until after she had talked to you. And then, are you ready for this? I made her promise to come to Bruce's memorial service Sunday."

"And she's coming?"

"She said she would. I told her she'd better be there early. It'll be packed."

"It sure will. How foreign is all this going to be to her?"

"She claims she's been in church only about a dozen times in her life, for weddings and funerals and such. Her father was a self-styled atheist, and her mother apparently had been raised in some sort of a strict denomination that she turned her back on as an adult. Verna says the idea of attending church was never discussed in her home."

"And she was never curious? Never searched for any deeper meaning in life?"

"No. In fact, she admitted she's been a pretty cynical and miserable person for years. She thought it made her the perfect journalist."

"She always gave me the willies," Buck said. "I was as cynical and negative as any, but hopefully there was a balance of humor and personality there."

"Oh yeah, that's you all right," Chloe teased. "That's why I'm still tempted to have a child with you, even now."

Buck didn't know what to say or think. They had had this discussion before. The idea of bringing a child into the Tribulation was, on the surface, unconscionable, and yet they had both agreed to think about it, pray about it, and see what Scripture said about it. "You want to talk about this now?"

She shook her head. "No. I'm tired. But let's not shut the door on it."

"You know I won't, Chlo'," he said. "I also need to tell you I'm on a different time zone. I slept all the way back."

"Oh, Buck! I've missed you. Can't you at least stay with me until *I* fall asleep?"

"Sure. Then I'm going to sneak over to the church and see how Bruce's shelter turned out."

"I'll tell you what you ought to do," Chloe said, "is finish reading Bruce's stuff. We've been marking passages we want Daddy to read at the memorial service. I don't know how he'll get through all of it without taking the whole day, but it's astounding stuff. Wait till you see it."

"I can't wait."

———

Rayford Steele was having a crisis of conscience. Packed and ready to go, he sat reading the *Global Community International Daily* while awaiting word from Hattie Durham's driver that he was in front of the building.

Rayford missed Amanda. In many ways, they still

seemed strangers, and he knew that in the little more than five years before the Glorious Appearing, they would never have the time to get to know each other and develop the lifelong relationship and bond he had shared with Irene. For that matter, he still missed Irene. On the other hand, Rayford felt guilty that in many ways he was closer to Amanda already than he had ever been to Irene.

That was his own fault, he knew. He had not known nor shared Irene's faith until it was too late. She had been so sweet, so giving. While he knew of worse marriages and less loyal husbands, he often regretted that he was never the husband to her that he could have been. She had deserved better.

To Rayford, Amanda was a gift from God. He recalled not even having liked her at first. A handsome, wealthy woman slightly older than he, she was so nervous upon first meeting him that she gave the impression of being a jabberer. She didn't let him or Chloe get a word in, but kept correcting herself, answering her own questions, and rambling.

Rayford and Chloe were bemused by her, but seeing her as a future love interest never crossed his mind. They were impressed with how taken Amanda had been with Irene from her brief encounter. Amanda had seemed to catch the essence of Irene's heart and soul. The way she described her, Rayford and Chloe might have thought she had known her for years.

Chloe had initially suspected Amanda of having designs on Rayford. Having lost her family in the Rapture, she was suddenly a lonely, needy woman. Rayford had not sensed anything but a genuine desire to let him know what his former wife had meant to her. But Chloe's suspicion had put him on guard. He made no attempt to pursue Amanda and was careful to watch for any signs coming the other way. There were none.

That made Rayford curious. He watched how she assimilated herself into New Hope Village Church. She was cordial to him, but never inappropriate, and never—in his mind—forward. Even Chloe eventually had to admit that Amanda did not come off as a flirt to anyone. She quickly became known around New Hope as a servant. That was her spiritual gift. She busied herself about the work of the church. She would cook, clean, drive, teach, greet, serve on boards and committees, whatever was necessary. A full-time professional woman, her spare time was spent in church life. "It's always been all or nothing with me," she said. "When I became a believer, it was lock, stock, and barrel."

From a distance, having hardly socialized with her after that first encounter when she merely wanted to talk to him and Chloe about Irene, Rayford became an admirer. He found her quiet, gentle, giving spirit most attractive. When he first found himself wanting to spend time with her, he still wasn't thinking of her romantically. He just liked her. Liked her smile. Liked her look. Liked her attitude. He had sat in on one of her Sunday school classes. She was a most engaging teacher and a quick study. The next week, he found *her* sitting in *his* class. She was complimentary. They joked about someday team-teaching. But that day didn't come until after they had double-dated with Buck and

Chloe. It wasn't long before they were desperately in love. Having been married just a few months before in a double ceremony with Buck and Chloe had been one of the small islands of happiness in Rayford's life during the worst period of human history.

Rayford was eager to get back to the States to see Amanda. He also looked forward to some time with Hattie on the plane. He knew the work of drawing her to Christ was that of the Spirit and not his responsibility, but still he felt he should maximize every legitimate opportunity to persuade her. His problem that Saturday morning was that every fiber of his being fought against his role as pilot for Nicolae Carpathia. Everything he had read, studied, and learned under Bruce Barnes's tutelage had convinced him and the other members of the Tribulation Force, as well as the congregation at New Hope, that Carpathia himself was the Antichrist. There were advantages to believers to have Rayford in the position he found himself, and Carpathia knew well where Rayford stood. What Nicolae did not know, of course, was that one of his other trusted employees, Cameron Williams, was now Rayford's son-in-law and had been a believer nearly as long as Rayford.

How long could it last? Rayford wondered. Was he endangering Buck's and Chloe's lives? Amanda's? His own? He knew the day would come when what Bruce referred to as "tribulation saints" would become the mortal enemies of the Antichrist. Rayford would have to choose his timing carefully. Someday, according to Bruce's teaching, to merely have the right to buy and sell, citizens of the Global Community would have to take the "mark of the beast." No one knew yet exactly what form this would take, but the Bible indicated it would be a mark on the forehead or on the hand. There would be no faking. The mark would somehow be specifically detectable. Those who took the mark could never repent of it. They would be lost forever. Those who did not take the mark would have to live in hiding, their lives worth nothing to the Global Community.

For now, Carpathia seemed merely amused by and impressed with Rayford. Perhaps he thought he had some connection, some insight to the opposition by keeping Rayford around. But what would happen when Carpathia discovered that Buck was not loyal and that Rayford had known all along? Worse, how long could Rayford justify in his own mind that the benefits of being able to eavesdrop and spy on Carpathia outweighed his own culpability in abetting the work of the evil one?

Rayford glanced at his watch and speed-read the rest of the paper. Hattie and her driver would be there in a few moments. Rayford felt as if he had undergone sensory overload. Any one of the traumas he had witnessed since the day the war broke out might have institutionalized a normal man during normal times. Now, it seemed, Rayford had to take everything in stride. The most heinous, horrible atrocities were part of daily life. World War III had erupted, Rayford had discovered one of his dearest friends dead, and he had heard Nicolae Carpathia give the word to destroy major cities and then announce his grief and disappointment on international television.

Rayford shook his head. He had done his job, flown his new plane, landed it thrice with Carpathia aboard, had gone to dinner with an old friend, gone to bed, had several phone conversations, rose, read his paper, and was now ready to blithely fly home to his family. What kind of a crazy world had this become? How could vestiges of normality remain in a world going to hell?

The newspaper carried the stories out of Israel, how the rabbi who had so shocked his own nation and culture and religion and people—not to mention the rest of the world—with his conclusions about the messiahship of Jesus, had suddenly gone mad. Rayford knew the truth, of course, and looked forward with great anticipation to meeting this brave saint.

Rayford knew Buck had somehow spirited him out of the country, but he didn't know how. He would be eager to get the details. Was this what they all had to look forward to? The martyrdom of their families? Their own deaths? He knew it was. He tried to push it from his mind. The juxtaposition between the easy, daily, routine life of a jumbo-jet pilot—the Rayford Steele he was a scant two years ago—and the international political pinball he felt like today was almost more than his mind could assimilate.

The phone rang. His ride was here.

Buck was astonished at what he found at the church. Bruce had done such a good job camouflaging the shelter that Buck had almost not been able to find it again.

Alone in the cavernous place, Buck headed downstairs. He walked through the fellowship hall, down a narrow corridor, past the washrooms, and past the furnace room. He was now at the end of a hallway with no light—it would have been dark there at noon. Where was that entrance? He felt around the wall. Nothing. He moved back into the furnace room and flipped on the switch. A flashlight rested atop the furnace. He used it to find the hand-sized indentation in one of the concrete blocks on the wall. Setting himself and feeling the nagging sting in his right heel from his recent wound, he pushed with all his might, and a section of block wall slid open slightly. He stepped in and pulled it closed behind him. The flashlight illuminated a sign directly in front of him and six stair steps down: "Danger! High Voltage. Authorized Personnel Only."

Buck smiled. That would have scared him off if he hadn't known better. He moved down the steps and took a left. Four more steps down was a huge steel door. The sign at the landing of the stairs was duplicated on the door. Bruce had shown him, the day of the weddings, how to open that seemingly locked door.

Buck gripped the knob and turned it first right and then left. He pushed the handle in about a quarter of an inch, then back out half an inch. It seemed to free itself, but still it didn't turn right or left. He pushed in as he turned it slightly right and then left, following a secret pattern devised by Bruce. The door swung open, and Buck faced what appeared to be a man-sized circuit-breaker box. Not even a church the size of New Hope would carry that many circuit breakers, Buck knew. And as real as all those switches were, they led to no circuits. The chassis of that box was merely another door. It opened easily and led to the hidden shelter. Bruce had done an amazing amount of work since Buck had seen it just a few months before.

Buck wondered when Bruce had had the time to get in there after hours and do all that work. No one else knew about it, not even Loretta, so it was a good thing Bruce was handy. It was vented, air-conditioned, well-lit, paneled, ceilinged, floored, and contained all the necessities. Bruce had sectioned the twenty-four-by-twenty-four-foot area into three rooms. There was a full bath and shower, a bedroom with four double bunk beds, and a larger room with a kitchenette on one end and a combination living room/study on the other. Buck was struck by the lack of claustrophobia, but he knew that with more than two people in there—and being aware of how far underground you were—it could soon become close.

Bruce had spared no expense. Everything was new. There was a freezer, a refrigerator, a microwave, a range and oven, and it seemed every spare inch possible had been converted into storage space. *Now,* Buck wondered, *what did Bruce do about connections?*

Buck crawled along the carpet and looked behind a sleeper sofa. There was a bank of telephone jacks. He traced the wiring up the wall and tried to spot where it would come out in the hallway. He turned off the lights, closed the circuit-breaker door, closed the metal door, jogged up the steps, and slid the brick door shut. In a

dark corner of the hallway he shined the flashlight and
saw the section of conduit that led from the floor up
through the ceiling. He moved back into the fellowship
hall and looked out the window. From the lights in the
parking lot, he could make out that the conduit went
outside at the ceiling level and snaked its way up toward
the steeple.

Bruce had told Buck that the reconditioned steeple had
been the one vestige of the old church, the original building that had been torn down thirty years before. In the
old days it actually had bells that beckoned people to
church. The bells were still there, but the ropes that had
once extended through a trapdoor to a spot where one of
the ushers could ring them from the foyer had been cut.
The steeple was now just decorative. Or was it?

Buck lugged a stepladder from a utility room up into
the foyer and pushed open the trapdoor. He hoisted himself above the ceiling and found a wrought-iron ladder
that led into the belfry. He climbed up near the old bells,
which were covered with cobwebs and dust and soot.
When he reached the section open to the air, his last step
made his hair brush a web, and he felt a spider skitter
through his hair. He nearly lost his balance swatting it
away and trying to hang on to the flashlight and to the
ladder. It was just yesterday that he had been chased
across the desert, rammed, shot at, and virtually chased
through flames to his freedom. He snorted. He would
almost rather go through all that again than have a spider
run through his hair.

Buck peeked down from the opening and looked for

the conduit. It ran all the way up to the tapered part of the steeple. He reached the top of the ladder and stepped out through the opening. He was around the side of the steeple not illuminated from the ground. The old wood didn't feel solid. His sore foot began to twitch. *Wouldn't this be great?* he thought. *Slip off the steeple of your own church and kill yourself in the middle of the night.*

Carefully surveying the area to be sure no cars were around, Buck briefly shined the flashlight at the top of where the conduit ran up the steeple. There was what appeared to be a miniature satellite dish, about two-and-a-half inches in diameter. Buck couldn't read the tiny sticker applied to the front of it, so he stood on tiptoe and peeled it off. He stuck it in his pocket and waited until he was safely back inside the steeple, down the ladder, and through the trapdoor to the stepladder before pulling it out. It read "Donny Moore Technologies: Your Computer Doctor."

Buck put the stepladder away and began shutting off the lights. He grabbed a concordance off the shelf in Bruce's office and looked up the word *housetop*. Bruce's installing that crazy mini-satellite dish made him think of a verse he once heard or read about shouting the good news from the housetop. Matthew 10:27-28 said, "Whatever I tell you in the dark, speak in the light; and what you hear in the ear, preach on the housetops. And do not fear those who kill the body but cannot kill the soul. But rather fear Him who is able to destroy both soul and body in hell."

Wasn't it just like Bruce to take the Bible literally?

Buck headed back to Loretta's house, where he would read Bruce's material until about six. Then he wanted to sleep until noon and be up when Amanda brought Rayford home from Mitchell Field in Milwaukee.

Would he ever cease to be amazed? As he drove the few blocks, he was struck by the difference between the two vehicles he had driven within the last twenty-four hours. This, a six-figure Range Rover with everything but a kitchen sink, and that probably still-smoldering bus he had "bought" from a man who might soon be a martyr.

More amazing, however, was that Bruce had planned so well and prepared so much before his departure. With a little technology, the Tribulation Force and its newest member, Tsion Ben-Judah, would soon be proclaiming the gospel from a hidden location and sending it via satellite and the Internet to just about anybody in the world who wanted to hear it, and to many who didn't.

It was two-thirty in the morning, Chicago time, when Buck returned from the church and sat before Bruce's papers on the dining room table at Loretta's home. They read like a novel. He drank in Bruce's Bible studies and commentary, finding his sermon notes for that very Sunday. Buck couldn't speak publicly in that church. He was vulnerable and exposed enough already, but he could sure help Rayford put together some remarks.

Despite his years of flying, Rayford had never found a cure for jet lag, especially going east to west. His body told him it was the middle of the evening, and after a day of flying, he was ready for bed. But as the DC-10 taxied toward the gate in Milwaukee, it was noon Central Standard Time. Across the aisle from him, the beautiful and stylish Hattie Durham slept. Her long blonde hair was in a bun, and she had made a mess of her mascara trying to wipe away her tears.

She had wept off and on almost the entire flight. Through two meals, a movie, and a snack, she had unburdened herself to Rayford. She did not want to stay with Nicolae Carpathia. She had lost her love for the man. She didn't understand him. While she wasn't ready to say he was the Antichrist, she certainly was not as impressed with him behind closed doors as most of his public was with him.

Rayford had carefully avoided declaring his starkest beliefs about Carpathia. Clearly Rayford was no fan and hardly loyal, but he didn't consider it the better part of wisdom to state categorically that he agreed with most Christian believers that Carpathia fit the bill of the Antichrist. Of course, Rayford had no doubt about it. But he had seen broken romances heal before, and the last thing he wanted was to give Hattie ammunition that could be used against him with Carpathia. Soon enough it wouldn't matter who might bad-mouth him to Nicolae. They would be mortal enemies anyway.

Most troubling to Rayford was Hattie's turmoil over her pregnancy. He wished she would refer to what she was carrying as a child. But it was a pregnancy to her, an unwanted pregnancy. It may not have been at the beginning, but now, given her state of mind, she did not want to give birth to Nicolae Carpathia's child. She didn't refer to it as a child or even a baby.

Rayford had the difficult task of trying to plead his case without being too obvious. He had asked her, "Hattie, what do you think your options are?"

"I know there are only three, Rayford. Every woman has to consider these three options when she's pregnant."

Not every *woman,* Rayford thought.

Hattie had continued: "I can carry it to term and keep it, which I don't want to do. I can put it up for adoption, but I'm not sure I want to endure the entire pregnancy and birth process. And, of course, I can terminate the pregnancy."

"What does that mean exactly?"

"What do you mean 'what does that mean?'" Hattie had said. "Terminate the pregnancy means terminate the pregnancy."

"You mean have an abortion?"

Hattie had stared at him like he was an imbecile. "Yes! What did you think I meant?"

"Well, it just seems you're using language that makes it sound like the easiest option."

"It *is* the easiest option, Rayford. Think about it. Obviously, the worst scenario would be to let a pregnancy run its entire course, go through all that discomfort, then go through the pain of labor. And then what if I got all those maternal instincts everybody talks about? Besides nine months of living in the pits, I'd go through all that stuff delivering somebody else's child. Then I'd have to give it up, which would just make everything worse."

"You just called it a child there," Rayford had said.

"Hmm?"

"You had been referring to this as your pregnancy. But once you deliver it, then it's a child?"

"Well, it will be *someone's* child. I hope not mine."

Rayford had let the matter drop while a meal was served. He had prayed silently that he would be able to communicate to her some truth. Subtlety was not his forte. She was not a dumb woman. Maybe the best tack was to be direct.

Later in the flight, Hattie herself had brought up the issue again. "Why do you want to make me feel guilty for considering an abortion?"

"Hattie," he had said, "I can't make you feel guilty. You have to make your own decisions. What I think about it means very little, doesn't it?"

"Well, I care what you think. I respect you as someone who's been around. I hope you don't think that I think abortion is an easy decision, even though it's the best and simplest solution."

"Best and simplest for whom?"

"For me, I know. Sometimes you have to look out for yourself. When I left my job and ran off to New York to be with Nicolae, I thought I was finally doing something for Hattie. Now I don't like what I did for Hattie, so I need to do something else for Hattie. Understand?"

Rayford had nodded. He understood all too well. He had to remind himself that she was not a believer. She would not be thinking about the good of anyone but herself. Why should she? "Hattie, just humor me for a moment and assume that that pregnancy, that 'it' you're carrying, is already a child. It's your child. Perhaps you don't like its father. Perhaps you'd hate to see what kind of a person its father might produce. But that baby is *your* blood relative too. You already have maternal feelings, or you wouldn't be in such turmoil about this. My question is, who's looking out for that child's best interest? Let's say a wrong has been done. Let's say it was immoral for you to live with Nicolae Carpathia outside of marriage. Let's say this pregnancy, this child, was produced from an immoral union. Let's go farther. Let's say that those people are right who consider Nicolae Carpathia the Antichrist. I'll even buy the argument that perhaps you regret the idea of having a child at all and would not be the best mother for it. I don't think you can shirk responsibility for it the way a rape or incest victim might be justified in doing.

"But even in those cases, the solution isn't to kill the innocent party, is it? Something is wrong, really wrong, and so people defend their right to choose. What they choose, of course, is not just the end of a pregnancy, not just an abortion, it's the death of a person. But which person? One of the people who made a mistake? One of the people who committed a rape or incest? Or one of the people who got pregnant out of wedlock? No, the solution is always to kill the most innocent party of all."

Rayford had gone too far, and he had known it. He had glanced up at Hattie holding her hands over her ears, tears streaming down her face. He had touched her arm, and she had wrenched away. He had leaned further and grabbed her elbow. "Hattie, please don't pull away from me. Please don't think I said any of that to hurt you personally. Just chalk it up to somebody standing up for the rights of someone who can't defend him- or herself. If you won't stand up for your own child, somebody has to."

With that, she had wrenched fully away from him and had buried her face in her hands and wept. Rayford had been angry with himself. Why couldn't he learn? How could he sit there spouting all that? He believed it, and he was convinced it was God's view. It made sense to him. But he also knew she could reject it out of hand simply because he was a man. How could he under- stand? No one was suggesting what he could or could not do with his own body. He had wanted to tell her he understood that, but again, what if that unborn child was a female? Who was standing up for the rights of that woman's body?

Hattie had not spoken to him for hours. He knew he deserved that. *But,* he wondered, *how much time is there to be diplomatic?* He had no idea what her plans were. He could only plead with her when he had the chance. "Hattie," he had said. She hadn't looked at him. "Hattie, please let me just express one more thing to you."

She had turned slightly, not looking fully at him, but he had the impression she would at least listen.

"I want you to forgive me for anything I said that hurt you personally or insulted you. I hope you know me well enough by now to know that I would not do that intentionally. More important, I want you to know that I am one of a few friends you have in the Chicago area who loves you and wants only the best for you. I wish you'd think about stopping in and seeing us in Mt. Prospect on your way back. Even if I'm not there, even if I have to go on back to New Babylon before you, stop in and see Chloe and Buck. Talk to Amanda. Would you do that?"

Now she had looked at him. She had pressed her lips together and shook her head apologetically. "Probably not. I appreciate your sentiments, and I accept your apology. But no, probably not."

And that's the way it had been left. Rayford was angry with himself. His motives were pure, and he believed his logic was right. But maybe he had counted too much on his own personality and style and not enough on God himself to work in Hattie's heart. All he could do now was pray for her.

When the plane finally stopped at the gate, Rayford helped Hattie pull her bag from the overhead rack. She thanked him. He didn't trust himself to say anything more. He had apologized enough. Hattie wiped her face one more time and said, "Rayford, I know you mean well. But you drive me nuts sometimes. I should be glad nothing ever really developed between us."

"Thanks a lot," Rayford said, feigning insult.

"I'm serious," she said. "You know what I mean. We're just too far apart in age or something, I guess."

"I guess," Rayford said. So, that was how she summarized it. Fine. That wasn't the issue at all, of course. He may not have handled it the best way, but he knew trying to fix it now would accomplish nothing.

As they emerged from the gateway, he saw Amanda's welcome smile. He rushed to her, and she held him tight. She kissed him passionately but pulled away quickly. "I didn't mean to ignore you, Hattie, but frankly I was more eager to see Rayford."

"I understand," Hattie said flatly, shaking hands and looking away.

"Can we drop you somewhere?" Amanda said.

Hattie chuckled. "Well, my bags are checked through to Denver. Can you drop me there?"

"Oh, I knew that!" Amanda said. "Can we walk you to your gate?"

"No, I'll be fine. I know this airport. I've got a little layover here, and I'm just gonna try to relax."

Rayford and Amanda said their good-byes to Hattie, and she was cordial enough, but as they walked away, she caught Rayford's eye. She pursed her lips and shook her head. He felt miserable.

Rayford and Amanda walked hand-in-hand, then arm-in-arm, then arms around each other's waist, all the way to the escalators that led down to baggage claim. Amanda hesitated and pulled Rayford back from the moving stairway. Something on a TV monitor had caught her eye. "Ray," she said, "come look at this."

They stood watching as a CNN/GNN report summarized the extent of the damage from the war around the world. Already, Carpathia was putting his spin on it. The announcer said, "World health care experts predict the death toll will rise to more than 20 percent internationally. Global Community Potentate Nicolae Carpathia has announced formation of an international health care organization that will take precedence over all local and regional efforts. He and his ten global ambassadors released a statement from their private, high-level meetings in New Babylon outlining a proposal for strict measures regulating the health and welfare of the entire global community. We have a reaction now from renowned cardiovascular surgeon Samuel Kline of Norway."

Rayford whispered, "This guy is in Carpathia's back pocket. I've seen him around. He says whatever Saint Nick wants him to say."

The doctor was saying, "The International Red Cross and the World Health Organization, as wonderful and effective as they have been in the past, are not equipped to handle devastation, disease, and death on this scale. Potentate Carpathia's visionary plan is not only our only hope for survival in the midst of coming famine and plagues, but also it seems to me—at first glance—a blueprint for the most aggressive international health care agenda ever. Should the death toll reach as high as 25 percent due to contaminated water and air, food shortages, and the like, as some have predicted, new directives that govern life from the womb to the tomb can bring this planet from the brink of death to a utopian state as regards physical health."

Rayford and Amanda turned toward the escalator, Rayford shaking his head. "In other words, Carpathia clears away the bodies he has blown to bits or starved or allowed to become diseased by plagues because of his war, and the rest of us lucky subjects will be healthier and more prosperous than ever."

Amanda looked at him. "Spoken like a true, loyal, employee," she said. He wrapped his arms around her and kissed her. They stumbled and nearly tumbled when the escalator reached the bottom.

Buck embraced his new father-in-law and old friend like the brother he was. He considered it a tremendous honor to introduce Tsion Ben-Judah to Rayford and to watch them get acquainted. The Tribulation Force was together once more, bringing each other up-to-date and trying to plan for a future that had never seemed less certain.

FIFTEEN

RAYFORD forced himself to stay up until a normal bed-time Saturday night. He, Buck, and Tsion went over and over Bruce's material. More than once Rayford was moved to tears. "I'm not sure I'm up to this," he said.

Tsion spoke softly. "You are."

"What would you have done had I been unable to get back?"

Buck said, "I don't know, but I can't risk speaking in public. And certainly Tsion can't."

Rayford asked what they were going to do about Tsion. "He can't stay here long, can he?" he said.

"No," Buck said. "It won't be long before it gets back to Global Community brass that I was involved in his escape. In fact, it wouldn't surprise me if Carpathia already knows."

They decided amongst themselves that Tsion should be

able to come to New Hope Sunday morning, possibly
with Loretta, as a guest who appeared to be an old
friend. There was enough difference in their ages that,
except for his Middle Eastern look, he might appear to
be a son or a nephew. "But I wouldn't risk his exposure
any further than that," Rayford said. "If the shelter is
ready, we need to sneak him in there before the end of
the day tomorrow."

Late in the evening a bleary-eyed Rayford called a
meeting of the Tribulation Force, asking Tsion Ben-
Judah to wait in another room. Rayford, Amanda, Buck,
and Chloe sat around the dining room table, Bruce's
pages piled high before them. "I suppose it falls to me,"
Rayford said, "as the senior member of this little band of
freedom fighters, to call to order the first meeting after
the loss of our leader."

Amanda shyly raised her hand. "Excuse me, but I
believe I am the senior member, if you're talking age."

Rayford smiled. There was precious little levity anymore, and he appreciated her feeble attempts. "I know
you're the oldest, hon," he said, "but I've been a believer
longer. Probably by a week or so."

"Fair enough," she said.

"The only order of business tonight is voting in a new
member. I think it's obvious to all of us that God has
provided a new leader and mentor in Dr. Ben-Judah."

Chloe spoke up. "We're asking an awful lot of him,
aren't we? Are we sure he wants to live in this country?
In this city?"

"Where else could he go?" Buck asked. "I mean, it's

only fair to ask him rather than to make assumptions, I guess, but his options are limited."

Buck told the others about the new phones, the coming computers, how Bruce had outfitted the shelter for phone and computer broadcasting, and how Donny Moore was designing a system that would be interception- and trace-proof.

Rayford thought everyone seemed encouraged. He finalized preparations for the memorial service the next morning and said he planned to be unabashedly evangelistic. They prayed for the confidence, peace, and blessing of God on their decision to include Tsion in the Tribulation Force. Rayford invited him into the meeting.

"Tsion, my brother, we would like to ask you to join our little core group of believers. We know you have been deeply wounded and may be in pain for a long, long time. We're not asking for an immediate decision. As you can imagine, we need you not to just be one of us, but also to be our leader, in essence, our pastor. We recognize that the day may come when we might all be living with you in the secret shelter. Meanwhile, we will try to maintain as normal lives as possible, trying to survive and spread the good news of Christ to others until his Glorious Appearing."

Tsion rose at one end of the table and placed both hands atop it. Buck, who so recently had thought Tsion looked younger than his forty-six years, now saw him weary and spent, grief etching his face. His words came slowly, haltingly, through quivering lips.

"My dear brothers and sisters in Christ," he said in

his thick, Israeli accent, "I am deeply honored and moved. I am grateful to God for his provision and blessing to me in bringing young Cameron to find me and save my life. We must pray for our brothers, Michael and his three friends, whom I believe are among the 144,000 witnesses God is raising up around the world from the tribes of Israel. We must also pray for our brother Anis, whom Cameron has told you about. He was used of God to deliver us. I know nothing more about him, except that should it come out that he could have detained me, he too may be a martyr before we know it.

"Devastated as I am over my own personal loss, I see the clear hand of God Almighty in guiding my steps. It was as if my blessed homeland were a saltshaker in his hand, and he upended it and shook me out across the desert and into the air. I landed right where he wants me. Where else can I go?

"I need no time to think about it. I have already prayed about it. I am where God wants me to be, and I will be here for as long as he wishes. I do not like to live in hiding, but neither am I a reckless man. I will gratefully accept your offer of shelter and provisions, and I look forward to all the Bible software Cameron has promised to put on the new computer. If you and your technical adviser, young Mr. Moore, can devise a way to multiply my ministry, I would be thankful. Clearly, my days of international travel and speaking are over. I look forward to sitting with fellow believers in your church tomorrow morning and hearing more about your wonderful mentor, my predecessor, Bruce Barnes.

"I cannot and will not promise to replace him in your hearts. Who can replace one's spiritual father? But as God has blessed me with a mind that understands many languages, with a heart that seeks after him and always has, and with the truth he has imparted to me and which I discovered and accepted and received only a little too late, I will dedicate the rest of my life to sharing with you and anyone else who will hear it the Good News of the gospel of Jesus Christ, the Messiah, the Savior, my Messiah, and my Savior."

Tsion seemed to collapse into his chair, and, as one, Rayford and the rest of the Tribulation Force turned and knelt before theirs.

Buck felt the presence of God as clearly as he had during his escapade in Israel and Egypt. He realized his God was not limited by space and time. Later, when he and Chloe went up to bed, leaving Rayford alone in the dining room to put the final touches on his memorial service message, they prayed that Verna Zee would follow through on her promise to attend. "She's the key," Buck said. "Chloe, if she gets spooked and says anything to anybody about me, our lives will never be the same."

"Buck, our lives haven't been the same from one day to the next for almost two years."

Buck gathered her in, and she nestled against his chest. Buck felt her relax and heard her deep, even breathing as she fell asleep minutes later. He lay awake another hour, staring at the ceiling.

Buck awoke at eight in an empty bed. He smelled breakfast. Loretta would have already been at church. He knew Chloe and Amanda had bonded and frequently worked together, but he was surprised to find Tsion also putzing around in the kitchen. "We will add a little Middle Eastern flavor to our morning repast, no?" he asked.

"Sounds good to me, brother," Buck said. "Loretta will be back to pick you up at about nine. Amanda, Chloe, and I will head over as soon as we're finished with breakfast."

Buck knew there would be a crowd that morning, but he didn't expect the parking lots to be full and the streets lined with cars for blocks. If Loretta hadn't had a reserved spot, she might have done better to leave her car at home and walk to the church with Tsion. As it was, she told Buck later, she had to wave someone out of her spot when she got back with him.

It didn't make sense for Tsion to be seen with Buck at church. Buck sat with Chloe and Amanda. Loretta sat near the back with Tsion. Loretta, Buck, Chloe, and Amanda kept an eye out for Verna.

———

Rayford would not have known Verna if she was standing in front of him. He was occupied with his own thoughts and responsibilities that morning. Fifty minutes before the service he signaled the funeral director to move the casket into the sanctuary and open it.

Rayford was in Bruce's office when the funeral director hurried back to him. "Sir, are you sure you still want me to do that? The sanctuary is full to overflowing already."

Rayford didn't doubt him but followed him to look for himself. He peeked through the platform door. It would have been inappropriate to open the casket in front of all those people. Had Bruce's body been on display, waiting for them when they arrived, that would have been one thing. "Just wheel the closed coffin out there," Rayford said. "We'll schedule a viewing later."

As Rayford headed back to the office, he and the funeral director came upon the casket and the attendants in an otherwise empty corridor that led to the platform. Rayford was overcome with a sudden urge. "Could you open it just for me, briefly?"

"Certainly, sir, if you would avert your eyes a moment."

Rayford turned his back and heard the lid open and the movement of material.

"All right, sir," the director said.

Bruce looked less alive and even more like the shell Rayford knew this body to be than he had under the shroud outside the demolished hospital where Rayford had found him. Whether it was the lighting, the passage of time, or his own grief and fatigue, Rayford did not know. This, he knew, was merely the earthly house of his dear friend. Bruce was gone. The likeness that lay here was just a reflection of the man he once was. Rayford thanked the director and headed back to the office.

He was glad he had taken that last look. It wasn't that he needed closure, as so many said of such a viewing. He had simply feared that the shock of Bruce appearing so lifeless at a corporate viewing might render him speechless. But it didn't now. He was nervous, yet he felt more confidence than ever about representing Bruce and representing God to these people.

———————

The lump in Buck's throat began the moment he entered the sanctuary and saw the crowd. The number didn't surprise him, but how early they had assembled did. Also, there was not the usual murmuring as at a normal Sunday morning service. No one here seemed even to whisper. The silence was eerie, and anyone could have interpreted it as a tribute to Bruce. People wept, but no one sobbed. At least not yet. They simply sat, most with heads bowed, some reading the brief program that included Bruce's vital statistics. Buck was amazed by the verse someone, probably Loretta, ran along the bottom of the back page of the program. It read simply, "I know that my Redeemer lives."

Buck felt Chloe shudder and knew she was near tears. He put his arm around her shoulder and his hand brushed Amanda just beyond her. Amanda turned, and

Buck saw her tears. He put a hand on her shoulder, and there they sat in their silent grief.

At precisely ten o'clock, just the way (Buck thought) a pilot would do it, Rayford and one other elder emerged from the door at the side of the platform. Rayford sat while the other man stepped to the pulpit and motioned that all should rise. He led the congregation in two hymns sung so slowly and quietly and with such meaning that Buck could barely get the words out. When the songs had concluded, the elder said, "That is the extent of our preliminary service. There will be no offering today. There will be no announcements today. All meetings will resume next Sunday, as scheduled. This memorial service is in memory of our dear departed pastor, Bruce Barnes."

He proceeded to tell when and where Bruce was born and when and where he died. "He was preceded by his wife, a daughter, and two sons, who were raptured with the church. Our speaker this morning is Elder Rayford Steele, a member of this congregation since just after the Rapture. He was a friend and confidant of Bruce. He will deliver the eulogy and a brief message. You may come back at 4:00 P.M. for a viewing if you wish."

Rayford felt as if he were floating in another dimension. He had heard his name and knew well what they were about that morning. Was this a mental defense mechanism? Was God allowing him to set aside his grief and his emotions so he could speak clearly? That was all he could imagine. Were his emotions to overcome him, there would be no way he could speak.

He thanked the other elder and opened his notes. "Members and friends of New Hope Village Church," he began, "and relatives and friends of Bruce Barnes, I greet you today in the matchless name of Jesus Christ, our Lord and Savior.

"If there is one thing I have learned out there in the world, it is that a speaker should never apologize for himself. Allow me to break that rule first and get it out of the way, because I know that despite how close Bruce and I were, this is not about me. In fact, Bruce would tell you, it's not about him either. It's about Jesus.

"I need to tell you that I'm up here this morning not as an elder, not as a parishioner, and certainly not as a preacher. Speaking is not my gift. No one has even suggested that I might replace Bruce here. I am here because I loved him and because in many ways—primarily because he left a treasure trove of notes behind—I am able in a small way to speak for him."

Buck held Chloe close, as much for his own comfort as for hers. He felt for Rayford. This had to be so hard. He was impressed with Rayford's ability to be articulate in this situation. He himself would have been blubbering, he knew.

Rayford was saying, "I want to tell you how I first met Bruce, because I know that many of you met him in much the same way. We were at the point of the greatest need in our lives, and Bruce had beat us to it by only a few hours."

Buck heard the story he had heard so many times before, of Rayford's having been warned by his wife that the Rapture was coming. When he and Chloe had been left behind and Irene and Raymie had been taken, at the end of himself he had sought out the church where she had heard the message. Bruce Barnes had been the only person left on the staff, and Bruce knew exactly why. He became, in an instant, an unabashed convert and evange-list. Bruce had pleaded with Rayford and Chloe to hear his own testimony of losing his wife and three young children in the middle of the night. Rayford had been ready. Chloe had been skeptical. It would be a while before she came around.

Bruce had provided them with a copy of a videotape his senior pastor had left behind for just this purpose. Rayford had been amazed that the pastor could have known in advance what he would be going through. He had explained from the Bible that all this had been pre-dicted and then had been careful to explain the way of salvation. Rayford now took the time, as he had on so many occasions in Sunday school classes and testimony meetings, to go through that same simple plan.

Buck never ceased to be moved by what Bruce had always called "the old, old story." Rayford said, "This has been the most misunderstood message of the ages. Had you asked people on the street five minutes before the Rapture what Christians taught about God and heaven, nine in ten would have told you that the church expected them to live a good life, to do the best they could, to think of others, to be kind, to live in peace. It sounded so good, and yet it was so wrong. How far from the mark!

"The Bible is clear that all our righteousnesses are like filthy rags. There is none righteous, no not one. We have turned, every one, to his own way. All have sinned and fall short of the glory of God. In the economy of God, we are all worthy only of the punishment of death.

"I would be remiss and would fail you most miserably if we got to the end of a memorial service for a man with the evangelistic heart of Bruce Barnes and did not tell you what he told me and everyone else he came in contact with during the last nearly two years of his life on this earth. Jesus has already paid the penalty. The work has been done. Are we to live good lives? Are we to do the best we can? Are we to think of others and live in peace? Of course! But to earn our salvation? Scripture is clear that we are saved by grace through faith, and that not of ourselves; not of works, lest anyone should boast. We live our lives in as righteous a manner as we can in thankful response to that priceless gift of God, our salvation, freely paid for on the cross by Christ himself.

"That is what Bruce Barnes would tell you this morning, were he still housed in the shell that lies in the box before you. Anyone who knew him knows that this message became his life. He was devastated at the loss of his family and in grief over the sin in his life and his ultimate failure to have made the transaction with God he knew was necessary to assure him of eternal life.

"But he did not wallow in self-pity. He quickly became a student of the Scriptures and a teller of the Good News. This pulpit could not contain him. He started house churches all over America and then began speaking throughout the world. Yes, he was usually here on Sundays, because he believed his flock was his primary responsibility. But you and I, all of us, let him travel because we knew that here was a man of whom the world was not worthy."

Buck watched closely as Rayford stopped speaking. He stepped to the side of the pulpit and gestured at the coffin. "And now," he said, "if I can get through this, I would like to speak directly to Bruce. You all know that the body is dead. It cannot hear. But Bruce," he said, raising his eyes, "we thank you. We envy you. We know you are with Christ, which Paul the apostle says is 'far better.'

"We confess we don't like this. It hurts. We miss you. But in your memory we pledge to carry on, to stay at the task, to keep on keeping on against all odds. We will study the materials you have left behind, and we will keep this church the lighthouse you made it for the glory of God."

Rayford stepped back into the pulpit, feeling drained. But he was not half done. "I would also be remiss if I did not try to share with you at least the core thoughts from the sermon Bruce had prepared for today. It is an important one, one none of us in leadership here would want you to have missed. I can tell you I have been over it many times, and it blesses me each time. But before I do that, I feel compelled to open the floor to anyone else who feels led to say anything in memory of our dear brother."

Rayford took one step back from the microphone and waited. For a few seconds he wondered if he had caught everyone off guard. No one moved. Finally, Loretta stood.

"Y'all know me here," she said. "I've been Bruce's secretary since the day everybody else disappeared. If you'll pray I can maintain my composure, I have just a few things to say about Pastor Barnes."

Loretta told her now-familiar story, of how she was the only one of more than a hundred blood relatives who was left behind at the Rapture. "There are only a dozen or so of us in this room who were members of this church before that day," she said. "We all know who we are, and grateful as we are to have finally found the truth, we live in regret for all the wasted years."

Buck, Chloe, and Amanda turned in their pew to hear Loretta better. Buck noticed tissues and handkerchiefs all over the sanctuary. Loretta finished with this: "Brother Barnes was a very bright man who had made a very huge mistake. As soon as he got right with the Lord and committed himself to serve him for the rest of his days, he became pastor to the rest of us. I can't tell you the countless numbers that he personally led to Christ. But I can tell you this: He was never condescendin', never judgmental, never short-tempered with anyone. He was earnest and compassionate, and he loved people into the kingdom. Oh, he never was polite to the point where he wouldn't tell people exactly how it was. There are enough people in here who can attest to that. But winnin' people to Christ was his main, whole, and only goal. I just pray that if there's anybody here who is still wonderin' or holdin' out, that you'll realize maybe you're the reason that we'll always be able to say that Bruce did not die in vain. His passion for souls continues beyond the grave." And Loretta broke down. She sat. The stranger next to her, the dark-complected man known only to her and the Tribulation Force, gently put his arm around her.

Rayford stood listening as people from all over the sanctuary stood and testified to the impact Bruce Barnes had had on their lives. It went on and on and on for more than an hour. Finally, when there seemed to be a lull, Rayford said, "I hate to arbitrarily end this, but if there is anyone else, let me ask you to stand quickly. After one more, I'll then allow any who need to leave to do so. Staying for my summary of what would have been Bruce's sermon this morning is optional."

Tsion Ben-Judah stood. "You do not know me," he said. "I represent the international community where your pastor toiled so long and so earnestly and so effectively. Many, many Christian leaders around the globe knew him, sat under his ministry, and were brought closer to Christ because of him. My prayer for you is that you would continue his ministry and his memory, that you would, as the Scriptures say, 'not grow weary in doing good.'"

Rayford announced, "Stand if you would. Stretch, embrace a friend, greet someone." People stood and stretched and shook hands and embraced, but few said anything. Rayford said, "While you are standing I would like to excuse any who are overcome, hungry, restless, or for any other reason need to leave. We are long past our normal closing time. We will tape the rest of this service for any who have to leave. I will be summarizing Bruce's message for this morning, apologizing in advance for reading some of it to you. I am not the preacher he was, so bear with me. We'll take a couple of minutes' break now, so feel free to leave if you need to."

Rayford backed away from the pulpit and sat. En masse, the congregation sat back down and looked expectantly at him. When it was clear no one was leaving, someone giggled, then another, and a few more. Rayford smiled and shrugged and returned to the pulpit.

"I guess there are things more important in this life than personal comfort, aren't there?" he said. A few amens resounded. Rayford opened his Bible and Bruce's notes.

Buck knew what was coming. He had been over the material nearly as many times as Rayford had and had helped condense it. Still, he was excited. People would be inspired by what Bruce believed had happened, what he predicted would happen, and what was yet to come.

Rayford began by explaining, "As best we have been

able to determine, these sermon notes were written onboard an aircraft while Bruce was returning from Indonesia last week. The name of the file is 'Sermon' with today's date, and what he has here is a rough outline and a lot of commentary. Occasionally he lapses into personal notations, some of which I feel free to share with you now that he is gone, others that I feel compelled to keep from you now that he is gone.

"For instance, shortly after outlining where he wants to go with this message, he notes, 'I was ill all night last night and feel not much better today. I was warned about viruses, despite all my shots. I can't complain. I have traveled extensively without problem. God has been with me. Of course, he is with me now, too, but I fear dehydration. If I'm not better upon my return, I'll get checked out.'

"So," Rayford added, "we get a glimpse of the ailment that brought him low and which led to his collapse at the church upon his return. As most of you know, he was rushed to the hospital, where it is our belief that he died from this ailment and not from the blast.

"Bruce has outlined a message here that he believed was particularly urgent, because, as he writes, 'I have become convinced we are at the end of the eighteen-month period of peace, which follows the agreement the Antichrist has made with Israel. If I am right, and we can set the beginning of the Tribulation at the time of the signing of the treaty between the nation of Israel and what was then known as the United Nations, we are perilously close to and must prepare for the next ominous and dire prediction in the Tribulation timeline: The Red Horse of the Apocalypse. Revelation 6:3-4 indicates that it was granted to the one who sat on it to take peace from the earth, and that people should kill one another; and there was given to him a great sword. In my mind, this is a prediction of global war. It will likely become known as World War III. It will be instigated by the Antichrist, and yet he will rise as the great solver of it, the great peacemaker, as he is the great deceiving liar.

"'This will immediately usher in the next two horses of the apocalypse, the black horse of plague and famine, and the pale horse of death. These will be nearly simultaneous—it should not surprise any of us to know that global war would result in famine, plague, and death.'

"Do any of you find this as astounding as I did when I first read it?" Rayford asked. All over the sanctuary, people nodded. "I remind you that this was written by a man who died either just before or just after the first bomb was volleyed in the global war we find ourselves in. He didn't know precisely when it would occur, but he didn't want to let one more Sunday pass without sharing this message with you. I don't know about you, but I'm inclined to heed the words of one who interprets the prophecy of Scripture so accurately. Here's what Bruce, in his own notes, says is yet to come:

"'The time is short now for everyone. Revelation 6:7-8 says the rider of the pale horse is Death and that Hades follows after him. Power was given to them over a fourth of the earth, to kill with sword, with hunger, with death, and by the beasts of the earth. I confess I don't know what the Scripture is referring to when it says the beasts of the earth, but perhaps these are animals that devour people when they are left without protection due to the war. Perhaps a great beast of the earth is some symbolic metaphor for the weapons employed by the Antichrist and his enemies. Regardless, in short order one-fourth of the world's population will be wiped out.'

"Bruce continues: 'I shared this with three close compatriots not long ago, and asked them to consider that there were four of us in the room. Was it possible that one of us would be gone in due time? Of course it was. Might I lose a fourth of my congregation? I pray my church will be spared, but I have so many congregations now around the world, it is impossible to imagine that all could be spared. Of the quarter of the earth's population that will perish, surely many, many of these will be tribulation saints.

"'Given the level of modern technology, global war will take little time at all to wreak its havoc and devastation. These three last horsemen of the apocalypse will gallop one right after the other. If people were horrified by the painless, bloodless, disappearance of the saints at the Rapture, which resulted in enough chaos of its own because of crashes and fires and suicides, imagine the desperation of a world ripped to shreds by global war, famine, plague, and death.'"

Rayford looked up from Bruce's notes. "My wife and I watched the news yesterday at the airport," he said, "as I'm sure many of you watched wherever you were, and we saw these very things reported from all around the world. Only the greatest skeptic would accuse us of having written this after the fact. But let's say that you're skeptical. Let's say you believe we are charlatans. Who then wrote the Bible? And when was it written? Forget Bruce Barnes and his present-day predictions, a week before the fact. Consider these prophecies made thousands of years ago. You can imagine the pain it brought Bruce to have to prepare this sermon. In a side note he writes, 'I hate preaching bad news. My problem in the past was that I always hated hearing bad news too. I shut it out. I didn't listen. It was there if I merely had ears to hear. I must share more bad news in this message, and though it grieves me, I cannot shirk the responsibility.'

"You'll note Bruce's turmoil here," Rayford said. "Because I'm the one who has to deliver this, I empathize totally with where he was. The next part of his outline indicates that the Four Horsemen of the Apocalypse, once they have visited their judgments on the earth, represent the first four of the seven Seal Judgments that Revelation 6:1-16 indicates will occur during the first twenty-one months of the Tribulation. According to Bruce's calculations, using as a reference point the treaty signed between Israel and the United Nations, which we now know as the Global Community, we are closing in on the end of that twenty-one-month period. Therefore, it behooves us to understand clearly the fifth, sixth, and seventh Seal Judgments predicted in Revelation. As you know from what Bruce has taught before, there are yet to come two more seven-part judgments that will carry us through to the end of the seven-year Tribulation and the glorious appearing of Christ. The next seven will be the Trumpet Judgments, and the seven following that will be the Vial Judgments. Whoever becomes your pastor-teacher will, I'm sure, carefully walk you through those as the time draws near. Meanwhile, let me, with Bruce's notes and commentary, make us all aware of what we have to look forward to just within the next few weeks."

Rayford was exhausted, but worse than that, he had gone over and over in his mind what he was about to share. It was not good news. He felt weak. He was hungry. He was enough in tune with his body to know he needed sugar. "I'm going to ask for just a five-minute break. I know many of you may need to use the facilities. I need to get a drink. We'll meet back here at precisely one o'clock."

He left the platform, and Amanda made a beeline for the side door, meeting him in the corridor. "What do you need?" she asked.

"Besides prayer?"

"I've been praying for you all morning," she said. "You know that. What do you want? Some orange juice?"

"You make me sound like a diabetic."

"I just know what I would need if I'd been standing up there that long between meals."

"Juice sounds great," he said. While she hurried off, Buck joined Rayford in the hallway.

"Do you think they're ready for what's to come?" Buck asked.

"Frankly, I think Bruce has been trying to tell them this for months. There's nothing like today's newscasts to convince you your pastor is right."

Buck assured Rayford he would continue praying for him. When he returned to his seat, he found that, again, it appeared not one person had left. It didn't surprise Buck that Rayford was back in the pulpit exactly when he said he would be.

"I won't keep you much longer," he said. "But I'm sure you all agree that this is life-and-death stuff. From Bruce's notes and teaching we learn that Revelation 6:9-11 points out that the fifth of the seven Seal Judgments concerns tribulation martyrs. The Scripture says, 'I saw under the altar the souls of those who had been slain for the word of God and for the testimony which they held. And they cried with a loud voice, saying, "How long, O Lord, holy and true, until You judge and avenge our blood on those who dwell on the earth?" Then a white robe was given to each of them; and it was said to them that they should rest a little while longer, until both the number of their fellow servants and their brethren, who would be killed as they were, was completed.'

"In other words," Rayford continued, "many of those who have died in this world war, and are yet to die until a quarter of the world's population is gone, are considered tribulation martyrs. I put Bruce in this category. While he may not have died specifically for preaching the gospel or *while* preaching the gospel, clearly it was his life's work and it resulted in his death. I envision Bruce under the altar with the souls of those slain for the word of God and for the testimony they held. He will be given a white robe and told to rest a while longer until even more martyrs are added to the total. I must ask you today, are you prepared? Are you willing? Would you give your life for the sake of the gospel?"

Rayford paused to take a breath and was startled when someone cried out, "I will!"

Rayford didn't know what to say. Suddenly, from another part of the sanctuary: "So will I!"

Three or four others said the same in unison. Rayford choked back tears. It had been a rhetorical question. He had not expected an answer. How moving! How inspiring! He felt led not to let others follow based on emotion alone. He continued, his voice thick, "Thank you, brothers and sisters. I fear we may all be called upon to express our willingness to die for the cause. Praise God you are willing. Bruce's notes indicate that he believed these judgments are chronological. If the Four Horsemen of the Apocalypse lead to the white-robed tribulation martyrs under the altar in heaven, that could be happening even as we speak. And if it is, we need to know what the sixth seal is. Bruce felt so strongly about this Seal Judgment that on his computer he cut and pasted right here into his notes several different translations and versions of Revelation 6:12-17. Let me just read you the one he marked as the most stark and easily understood:

" 'I looked when He'—and you'll recall that the *he* mentioned here is the Lamb, who is described in verse fourteen of the previous chapter as 'Him who lives forever and ever,' who is, of course, Jesus Christ himself—'He opened the sixth seal, and behold, there was a great earthquake; and the sun became black as sackcloth of hair, and the moon became like blood. And the stars of heaven fell to the earth, as a fig tree drops its late figs when it is shaken by a mighty wind. Then the sky receded as a scroll when it is rolled up, and every mountain and island was moved out of its place. And the kings of the earth, the great men, the rich men, the commanders, the mighty men, every slave and every free man, hid themselves in the caves and in the rocks of the mountains, and said to the mountains and rocks, "Fall on us and hide us from the face of Him who sits on the throne and from the wrath of the Lamb! For the great day of His wrath has come, and who is able to stand?" ' "

Rayford looked up and scanned the sanctuary. Some stared at him, ashen. Others peered intently at their Bibles. "I'm no theologian, people. I'm no scholar. I have had as much trouble reading the Bible as any of you throughout my lifetime, and especially over the nearly two years since the Rapture. But I ask you, is there anything difficult to understand about a passage that begins, 'Behold, there was a great earthquake'? Bruce has carefully charted these events, and he believed that the first seven seals cover the first twenty-one months of the seven-year tribulation, which began at the time of the covenant between Israel and the Antichrist. If you happen to be one who doesn't believe the Antichrist has appeared on the scene yet, then you don't believe there's an agreement between Israel and that person. If that is true, all this is still yet to come. The Tribulation did not begin with the Rapture. It begins with the signing of that treaty.

"Bruce taught us that the first four Seal Judgments were represented by the Four Horsemen of the Apocalypse. I submit to you that those horsemen are at full gallop. The fifth seal, the tribulation martyrs who had been slain for the word of God and for the testimony which they held, and whose souls are under the altar, has begun.

"Bruce's commentary indicates that more and more martyrs will be added now. Antichrist will come against tribulation saints and the 144,000 witnesses springing up all over the world from the tribes of Israel.

"Hear me, from a very practical standpoint. If Bruce is right—and he has been so far—we are close to the end of the first twenty-one months. I believe in God. I believe in Christ. I believe the Bible is the Word of God. I believe our dear departed brother 'rightly divided the word of truth,' and thus I am preparing to endure what this passage calls 'the wrath of the Lamb.' An earthquake is coming, and it is not symbolic. This passage indicates that everyone, great or small, would rather be crushed to death than to face the one who sits on the throne."

Buck was furiously taking notes. This was not new to him, but he was so moved by Rayford's passion and the

idea of the earthquake being known as the wrath of the
Lamb that he knew it had to be publicized to the world.

Perhaps it would be his swan song, his death knell, but
he was going to put in the *Global Community Weekly*
that Christians were teaching of the coming "wrath of
the Lamb." It was one thing to predict an earthquake.
Armchair scientists and clairvoyants had been doing that
for years. But there was something about the psyche of
the current world citizen that caused him or her to
become enamored of catchphrases. What better catch-
phrase than one from the Word of God?

Buck listened as Rayford concluded: "At the end of
this first twenty-one-month period, the mysterious
seventh Seal Judgment will usher in the next twenty-
one-month period, during which we will receive the
seven Trumpet Judgments. I say the seventh Seal Judgment is mysterious because Scripture is not clear what
form it will take. All the Bible says is that it is apparently
so dramatic that there will be silence in heaven for half
an hour. Then seven angels, each with a trumpet, prepare
themselves to sound. We will study those judgments and
talk about them as we move into that period. However,
for now, I believe Bruce has left us with much to think
and pray about.

"We have loved this man, we have learned from this
man, and now we have eulogized him. Though we know
he is finally with Christ, do not hesitate to grieve and
mourn. The Bible says we are not to mourn as do the
heathen, who have no hope, but it does not say we
should not mourn at all. Embrace the grief and grieve

with all your might. But don't let it keep you from the task. What Bruce would have wanted above all else is that we stay about the business of bringing every person we can into the kingdom before it is too late."

Rayford was exhausted. He closed in prayer, but rather than leaving the platform he merely sat and lowered his head. There was not the usual rush for the doors. Most continued to sit, while a few slowly and quietly began to make their way out.

SIXTEEN

Buck helped Chloe into the Range Rover, but before he could get around to the driver's side, he was accosted by Verna Zee.

"Verna! I didn't see you! I'm glad you made it."

"I made it all right, Cameron. I also recognized Tsion Ben-Judah!"

Buck fought to keep from covering her mouth with his hand. "I'm sorry?"

"He's going to be in deep trouble when the Global Community peacekeeping forces find out where he is. Don't you know he's wanted all over the world? And that your passport and ID were found on one of his accomplices? Buck, you're in as much trouble as he is. Steve Plank has been trying to get ahold of you, and I'm tired of pretending I have no idea what you're up to."

"Verna, we're going to have to go somewhere and talk about this."

"I can't keep your secret forever, Buck. I'm not going down with you. That was a pretty impressive meeting, and it's obvious everybody loved that Barnes guy. But do all these people believe that Nicolae Carpathia is the Antichrist?"

"I can't speak for everyone."

"But how about you, Buck? You report directly to the man. Are you going to write a story in one of his own magazines that says that?"

"I already have, Verna."

"Yeah, but you've always represented it as a neutral report of what some believe. This is your church! These are your people! You buy into all this stuff."

"Can we go somewhere and talk about this or not?" Buck said.

"I think we'd better. Anyway, I want to interview Tsion Ben-Judah. You can't blame me for going for the scoop of a lifetime."

Buck bit his tongue to keep from saying she wasn't enough of a writer to do justice to a story like Ben-Judah anyway. "Let me get back to you tomorrow," he said. "And then we can—"

"Tomorrow? Today, Buck. Let's meet at the office this afternoon."

"This afternoon is not good. I'm coming back here for the viewing at four."

"Then how about six-thirty?"

"Why does it have to be today?" Buck asked.

"It doesn't. I could just tell Steve Plank or Carpathia himself or anybody I want exactly what I've seen today."

"Verna, I took a huge risk in helping you out the other night and letting you stay at Loretta's home."

"You sure did. And you may regret it for the rest of your life."

"So none of what you heard here today made any impact on you?"

"Yes, it did. It made me wonder why I went soft on you all of a sudden. You people are wacko, Buck. I'm gonna need some compelling reason to keep quiet about you."

That sounded like extortion, but Buck also realized that Verna had apparently stayed for the entire service that morning. Something had to be working on her. Buck wanted to find out how she could relegate the prophecies of Revelation and what had happened in the world in the last twenty months or so to mere coincidence. "All right," he said. "Six-thirty at the office."

Rayford and the other elders had agreed there would be no more formality at the viewing. No prayer, no message, no eulogies, no nothing. Just a procession of people filing past the coffin and paying their last respects. Someone had suggested opening the fellowship hall for refreshments, but Rayford, having been tipped off by Buck, decided against it. A ribbon was draped across the stairway, from wall to wall, to keep everyone from going downstairs. A sign indicated the viewing would last from 4 to 6 P.M.

At about five, while a crowd of hundreds slowly moved past the casket in a line that stretched out the front door, through the parking lot, and down the street, Buck wheeled into Loretta's parking spot with the Range Rover full of people.

"Chloe, I promise this is the last time I take advantage of your ailment and use you as a decoy."

"A decoy for what? Do you think Carpathia is here and is going to grab you or Tsion?"

Buck chuckled. Rayford had been in the sanctuary since just before four. Now, Buck, Chloe, Amanda, Tsion, and Loretta emerged from the Range Rover. Amanda got on one side of Chloe and Loretta on the other. They helped her up the back steps as Buck opened the door. Buck peeked at the parishioners waiting in line to get into the church. Nearly all ignored his little group. Those who idly watched them seemed to be concentrating on the pretty young newlywed, her ankle cast, her sling, and her cane.

As the three women made their way to the office, planning to view the body when the crowd dissipated, Buck and Tsion slipped away. When Buck entered the office about twenty minutes later, Chloe asked, "Where's Tsion?"

"He's around," Buck said.

Rayford stood near Bruce's coffin, shaking hands with mourners. Donny Moore approached. "I'm sorry to bother you with a question right here," Donny said, "but would you know where I could find Mr. Williams? He ordered some stuff from me, and I've got it for him."

Rayford directed him to the office.

As Donny and dozens of others filed past, Rayford wondered how long Hattie Durham would be with her mother in Denver. Carpathia had scheduled a meeting with Pontifex Maximus Peter Mathews, who had recently been named Supreme Pontiff of Enigma Babylon One World Faith, a conglomeration of all the religions in the world. Carpathia wanted Rayford back to New Babylon by the Thursday after next to fly the Condor 216 to Rome. There he was to pick up Mathews and bring him to New Babylon. Carpathia had made noises about headquartering Mathews and One World Faith in New Babylon, along with almost every other inter-naional organization.

Rayford found himself numb, shaking hand after hand. He tried not to look at Bruce's body. He busied himself remembering what else he'd heard Carpathia saying through that ingenious reverse intercom bugging device the late Earl Halliday had installed in the Condor. Most interesting to Rayford was Carpathia's insistence on taking over leadership of several of the groups and committees that had been headed by his old friend and financial angel Jonathan Stonagal. Buck had told Rayford and the rest of the Tribulation Force that he was in the room when Carpathia murdered Stonagal and then brainwashed everyone else to believe they'd just witnessed a suicide. With Carpathia now angling his way into the leadership of international relations committees, commissions on international harmony, and, most important, secret financial cooperatives, his motives for that murder became clear.

Rayford let his mind wander to the good old days, when all he had to do was show up at O'Hare on time, fly his routes, and come home. Of course, he was not a believer then. Not the kind of husband and father he should have been. The good old days really hadn't been so good at all.

He couldn't complain about excitement in his life. While he despised Carpathia and hated to be in a position of actual service to the man, he had long since decided to be obedient to God. If this was where God wanted him, it was where he would serve. He just hoped Hattie Durham might come back through Chicago before he had to leave. Somehow, he and Amanda and Chloe and Buck had to pull her away from Nicolae Carpathia. It had been encouraging to him, in a perverse way, that she had found her own reasons to distance herself from Nicolae. But Carpathia might not be so easily dumped, considering that she was carrying his child and he was so jealous of his public image.

Buck was busy with Donny Moore, learning the incredible features of the new computers, when he heard Loretta on the phone.

"Yes, Verna," she was saying, "he's busy with someone right now, but I'll tell him you said Steve Plank called."

Buck excused himself from Donny for a second and mouthed to Loretta, "If she's at the office, ask her if my checks are there."

Buck had been away from both the New York and Chicago offices on paydays for several weeks and was pleased to see Loretta nodding after she had asked Verna about the checks. One thing he had seen in Bruce's printouts, and which had been corroborated by Tsion, was that he needed to start investing in gold. Cash would soon be meaningless. He had to start stockpiling some sort of financial resource because, even in the best-case scenario, even if Verna became a believer and protected him from Carpathia, he couldn't maintain this ruse for long. That relationship would end. His income would dry up. He would not be able to buy or sell without the mark of the beast anyway, and the new world order Carpathia was so proud of could virtually starve him out.

———————

By a quarter to six, the sanctuary was nearly empty. Rayford headed back to the office. He shut the door behind him. "We can have our moment alone with Bruce's body in a few minutes," he said.

The Tribulation Force, plus Loretta and minus Tsion, sat somberly. "So, that's what Donny Moore brought you?" Rayford said, nodding at the stack of laptops.

"Yep. One for each of us. I asked Loretta if she wanted one too."

Loretta waved him off, smiling. "I wouldn't know what to do with it. I probably couldn't even open it."

"Where's Tsion?" Rayford said. "I really think we ought to keep him with us for a while and—"

"Tsion is safe," Buck said, looking carefully at Rayford.

"Uh-huh."

"What does that mean?" Loretta asked. "Where is he?"

Rayford sat in a chair on wheels and rolled it close to Loretta. "Ma'am, there are some things we are not going to tell you, for your own good."

"Well," she said, "what would you say if I told you I didn't appreciate that very much?"

"I can understand, Loretta—"

"I'm not so sure you can, Captain Steele. I've had things kept from me all my life just because I was a polite, southern lady."

"A southern belle is more like it," Rayford said.

"Now you're patronizin' me, and I don't appreciate that either."

Rayford was taken aback. "I'm sorry, Loretta, I meant no offense."

"Well, it offends me to have secrets kept from me."

Rayford leaned forward. "I'm quite serious about doing this for your own good. The fact is, someday, and I mean someday very soon, very high-placed officials may try to force you to tell them where Tsion is."

"And you think if I know where he is, I'll crack."

"If you don't know where he is, you can't crack and don't even have to worry about it."

Loretta pursed her lips and shook her head. "I know y'all are livin' dangerous lives. I feel like I've risked a lot just by puttin' you up. Now I'm only your landlady, is that it?"

"Loretta, you're one of the dearest people in the world to us, that's who you are. We wouldn't do anything to hurt you. That's why, even though I know it offends you—and that's the last thing I want to do—I'm not going to let you intimidate me into telling you where Tsion is. You'll be able to communicate with him by phone, and we can communicate with him by computer. Someday you may thank us for withholding this from you."

Amanda interrupted. "Rayford, are you and Buck saying that Tsion is where I think he is?"

Rayford nodded.

"Is that necessary already?" Chloe asked.

"I'm afraid so. I wish I could say how long it will be for the rest of us."

Loretta, clearly peeved, stood and paced, her arms folded across her chest. "Captain Steele, sir, could you tell me one thing? Could you tell me that you're not keepin' this from me because you think I'd blab it all over?"

Rayford stood. "Loretta, come here."

She stopped and stared at him.

"Come on now," he said. "Come right over here and let me hug you. I'm young enough to be your son, so don't be taking this as condescending."

Loretta seemed to be refusing to smile, but she did slowly approach Rayford. He embraced her. "Ma'am, I've known you long enough to know that you don't tell secrets. The fact is, the people who might ask you about Tsion Ben-Judah's whereabouts wouldn't hesitate to use a lie detector or even truth serum if they thought you knew. If they could somehow force you to give him up against your will, it could really hurt the cause of Christ."

She hugged him. "All right then," she said. "I still think I'm a tougher bird than you people seem to think, but all right. If I didn't think you were doin' this with my best interests in mind, misguided as y'all are, I'd throw you out of my boardinghouse."

That made everybody smile. Everybody except Loretta.

There was a knock at the door. "Excuse me, sir," the funeral director said to Rayford. "The sanctuary is empty."

Buck was last in line as the five of them filed into the sanctuary and stood by Bruce's coffin. At first Buck felt guilty. He was strangely unmoved. He realized he had expended his emotion during the memorial service. He knew so well that Bruce was no longer there that he largely felt nothing by simply noting that his friend was, indeed, dead.

And yet he was able to use these moments, standing there with the people closest to him in the world, to think about how dramatically and specifically God had acted in his behalf even just within the last several hours. If there was one thing he had learned from Bruce, it was that the Christian life was a series of new beginnings. What had God done for him lately? What *hadn't* he done for him? Buck only wished he would feel the same compulsion to renew his commitment to the service of Christ when God didn't seem so close.

Twenty minutes later, Buck and Chloe pulled into the parking lot of *Global Community Weekly*. Only Verna's car was in the lot.

To Buck, it seemed Verna looked both surprised and disappointed to see Chloe hobbling in with him. Chloe must have noticed too. "Am I not welcome here?" she said.

"Of course," Verna said. "If Buck needs someone to hold his hand."

"Why would I need someone to hold my hand?"

They sat in a small conference room with Verna at the head of the table. She leaned back in her seat and steepled her fingers. "Buck, we both know I hold all the cards now, don't we?"

"What happened to the new Verna?" Buck asked.

"There was no new Verna," she said. "Just a slightly mellower version of the old Verna."

Chloe leaned forward. "Then nothing we've said, nothing you and I have talked about, nothing you've seen or heard or experienced at Loretta's house or at the church has meant anything to you whatsoever?"

"Well, I have to admit I appreciate the new car. It is better than the one I had. Of course, that was only fair, and the least Buck could do for me after ruining mine."

"So," Chloe said, "your moments of vulnerability, your admitting that you had been jealous of Buck, and your realization that you had been inappropriate in how you talked with him, that was all, what, made up?"

Verna stood. She put her hands on her hips and stared down at Buck and Chloe. "I'm really surprised at how petty this conversation has begun. We're not talking about office politics here. We're not talking about personality conflicts. The fact is, Buck, you're not loyal to your employer. It's not just a matter of worrying, because it isn't journalism the way it's supposed to be. I've got a problem with that myself. I even told Chloe that, didn't I, Chloe?"

"You did."

"Carpathia has bought up all the news outlets, I know that," Verna continued. "None of us old-fashioned journalists enjoy the prospect of covering news our owner is making. We don't like being expected to put his spin on everything. But, Buck, you're a wolf in sheep's clothing. You're a spy. You're the enemy. You not only don't like the man, you also think he's the Antichrist himself."

"Why don't you sit down, Verna?" Chloe said. "We all know the little negotiation hints from the books that teach you how to look out for number one. I can't speak for Buck, but your trying to tower over me doesn't intimidate me."

"I'll sit down, but only because I want to."

"So, what's your game?" Chloe said. "Are you about to engage in extortion?"

"Speaking of that," Buck said, "I'll thank you for my checks for the last several weeks."

"I haven't touched them. They're in your top drawer. And no, I'm not a blackmailer. It just seems to me your life depends on who knows or doesn't know that you're harboring Tsion Ben-Judah."

"That's something you think you know?"

"I saw him in church this morning!"

"At least you thought you did," Chloe said.

Buck flinched and looked at her. So did Verna. For the first time, Buck saw a flicker of uncertainty on Verna's face.

"You're telling me I didn't see Tsion Ben-Judah in church this morning?"

"It certainly sounds unlikely," Chloe said. "Wouldn't you say?"

"Not really. I know Buck was in Israel and that his papers were found with a Ben-Judah sympathizer."

"And so you saw Buck in church with Ben-Judah?"

"I didn't say that. I said I saw Ben-Judah. He was sitting with that woman who put me up the other night, Loretta."

"So Loretta's dating Tsion Ben-Judah, is that what you're saying?"

"You know what I'm saying, Chloe. Ben-Judah even spoke in that service. If that wasn't him, I'm no journalist."

"No comment," Buck said.

"I resent that!"

Chloe kept the pressure on. "You were sitting somewhere where we couldn't see you—"

"I was in the balcony, if you must know."

"And from the balcony you could see a man sitting in the back with Loretta?"

"I didn't say that. I meant I could tell he was sitting with her. They both spoke and it sounded like it was coming from the same area."

"So Ben-Judah escapes from Israel, apparently with Buck's help. Buck is brilliant enough to leave his official papers with some enemy of the state. When Buck gets Ben-Judah safely into North America, he brings him out in public at his own church, and then Ben-Judah stands and speaks in front of hundreds of people. This is your thought?"

Verna was sputtering. "Well, he, well, if that wasn't Ben-Judah, who was it?"

"This is your story, Verna."

"Loretta will tell me. I got the impression she liked me. I'm sure I saw him walking out the back with her. A small, kind of stocky Israeli?"

"And you could tell from behind who he was?"

"I'm gonna call Loretta right now." She reached for a phone. "I don't suppose you'd give me her phone number."

Buck wondered if that was a good idea. They had not prepped Loretta. But after the incident in the office with Rayford earlier, he believed Loretta could handle Verna Zee. "Sure," Buck said, scribbling the number.

Verna hit the speaker button and dialed.

"Loretta's phone, Rayford Steele speaking."

Apparently, Verna had not expected that. "Oh, uh, yes. Loretta please."

"May I ask—"

"Verna Zee."

When Loretta came on, she was her typical, charming self. "Verna, dear! How are you? I heard you were at the service today, but I missed you. Did you find it as moving as I did?"

"We'll have to talk about that sometime, Loretta. I just wanted to—"

"I can't think of a better time than now, sweetheart. Would you like to meet someplace, come over, what?"

Verna looked irritated. "No, ma'am, not now. Sometime, maybe. I just wanted to ask you a question. Who was that man with you in church this morning?"

"That man?"

"Yes! You were with a Middle Eastern man. He spoke briefly. Who was he?"

"Is this on the record?"

"No! I'm just asking."

"Well I'm just telling you that that's a personal, impertinent question."

"So you're not going to tell me?"

"I don't believe it's any of your business."

"What if I told you that Buck and Chloe said you'd tell me?"

"First off, I'd probably say you were a liar. But that would be impolite and more impertinent than the question you asked."

"Just tell me if that was Rabbi Tsion Ben-Judah of Israel!"

"It sounds like you've already named him. What do you need my input for?"

"So, it *was* him?"

"You said it. I didn't."

"But was it?"

"You want the honest truth, Verna? That man is my secret lover. I keep him under the bed."

"What? What? So, come on—"

"Verna, if you'd like to talk about how moved you were by our memorial service this morning, I'd love to chat with you some more. Do you?"

Verna hung up on Loretta. "All right, so you've all gotten together and decided not to tell the truth. I don't think I'll have much trouble convincing Steve Plank or even Nicolae Carpathia that it appears you're harboring Tsion Ben-Judah."

Chloe looked at Buck. "You think Buck would do something so royally stupid it would not only get him fired, but it would also get him killed? And you're going to use the threat of this news to the Global Community higher-ups in exchange for what?"

Verna stalked out of the room. Buck looked at Chloe, winked, and shook his head. "You're priceless," he said.

Verna rushed back in and slapped Buck's checks on the table. "You know your time is short, Buck."

"Truth to tell," Buck said, "I believe all of our time is short."

Verna sat down resignedly. "You really believe this stuff, don't you?"

Buck tried to change the tone. He spoke sympathetically. "Verna, you've talked with Loretta and Amanda and Chloe and me. We've all shared our stories. You heard Rayford's story this morning. If we're all wacko, then we're all wacko. But were you not in the least impressed with some of the things that Bruce Barnes garnered from the Bible? Things that are coming true right now?"

Verna, at last, was silent for a moment. Finally she spoke. "It *was* kind of strange. Kind of impressive. But isn't it just like Nostradamus? Can't these prophecies be read into? Can't they mean anything you want them to mean?"

"I don't know how you could believe that," Chloe said. "You're smarter than that. Bruce said that if the treaty between the United Nations and Israel was the covenant referred to in the Bible, it would usher in the seven-year tribulation period. First there would be the seven Seal Judgments. The Four Horsemen of the Apocalypse would be the horse of peace—for eighteen months—the horse of war, the horse of plague and famine, and the horse of death."

"That's all symbolic, isn't it?" Verna said.

"Of course it is," Chloe said. "I haven't seen any horsemen. But I have seen a year and a half of peace. I have seen World War III break out. I've seen it result in plagues and famine with more to come. I've seen lots of people die, and more will. What will it take to convince you? You can't see the fifth Seal Judgment, the martyred saints under the altar in heaven. But did you hear what Rayford said Bruce believes is coming next?"

"An earthquake, yes, I know."

"Will that convince you?"

Verna turned in her chair and stared out the window. "I suppose that would be pretty hard to argue with."

"I have some advice for you," Chloe said. "If that earthquake is as devastating as the Bible makes it sound, you may not have time to change your mind about all of this before *your* time is up."

Verna stood and walked slowly to the door. Holding it open, she said softly, "I still don't like the idea of Buck's pretending to Carpathia to be something he's not."

Buck and Chloe followed her out toward the front door. "Our private lives, our beliefs, are none of our employer's business," Buck said. "For instance, if I knew you were a lesbian, I wouldn't feel it necessary to tell your superiors."

Verna whirled to face him. "Who told you that? What business is that of yours? You tell anybody that and I'll—"

Buck raised both hands. "Verna, your personal life is confidential with me. You don't have to worry that I'll ever say anything to anybody about that."

"There's nothing to tell!"

"My point exactly."

Buck held the door open for Chloe. In the parking lot, Verna said, "So we're agreed?"

"Agreed?" Buck said.

"That neither of us is going to say anything about the other's personal life?"

Buck shrugged. "Sounds fair to me."

The funeral director was on the phone with Rayford. "So," he was saying, "with the backlog of deaths, the scarcity of grave sites, and so forth, we're estimating interment no sooner than three weeks, possibly as late as five weeks. We store the bodies at no charge to you, as this is a matter of public health."

"I understand. If you could simply inform us once the burial has occurred, we'd appreciate it. We will not have a service, and no one will attend."

Loretta sat at the dining room table next to Rayford. "That seems so sad," she said. "Are you sure not even one of us should go?"

"I've never been much for graveside services," Rayford said. "And I don't think anything more needs to be said over Bruce's body."

"That's true," she said. "It's not like that's him. He's not going to feel lonely or neglected."

Rayford nodded and pulled a sheet from a stack of Bruce's papers. "Loretta, I think Bruce would have wanted you to see this."

"What is it?"

"It's from his personal journal. A few private thoughts about you."

"Are you sure?"

"Of course."

"I mean, are you sure he'd want me to see it?"

"I can go only by my *own* feelings," he said. "If I had written something like this, I would want you to see it, especially after I was gone."

Loretta, her fingers shaking, pulled the sheet to where she could read it with her bifocals. She was soon overcome. "Thank you, Rayford," she managed through her tears. "Thank you for letting me see that."

"Buck! I had no idea Verna was a lesbian!" Chloe said.

"*You* had no idea? Neither did I!"

"You're kidding!"

"I'm not. You think that little revelation was of God too?"

"I'd sooner think it was a wild coincidence, but you never know. That tidbit may have saved your life."

"*You* may have saved my life, Chloe. You were brilliant in there."

"Just sticking up for my man. She rattled the wrong cage."

SEVENTEEN

A WEEK and a half later, as Rayford was preparing to head back to New Babylon to resume his duties, he got a call from Leon Fortunato. "You haven't heard anything from the potentate's woman, have you?"

"The potentate's woman?" Rayford repeated, trying to let his disgust show.

"You know who I'm talking about. She flew over there on the same flight you did. Where is she?"

"I wasn't under the impression I was responsible for her."

"Steele, you don't really want to withhold information about somebody Carpathia wants to know about."

"Oh, *he* wants to know where she is. In other words, he hasn't heard from her?"

"You know that's the only reason I'd be calling you."

"Where does he think she is?"

"Don't play games with me, Steele. Tell me what you know."

"I don't know precisely where she is. And I don't feel the liberty to be reporting on her whereabouts or even where I think she is, without her knowledge."

"I think you'd better remember who you work for, pal."

"How can I forget?"

"So, you want me to imply to Carpathia that you're harboring his fiancée?"

"If that's what you're worried about, I can put your mind at ease. The last time I saw Hattie Durham was at Mitchell Field in Milwaukee when I arrived."

"And she went on where?"

"I really don't think I should be sharing her itinerary if she chose not to."

"You could regret this, Steele."

"You know what, Leon? I'll sleep tonight."

"We're assuming she went to see her family in Denver. There was no war damage there, so we don't understand why we can't get through by phone."

"I'm sure you have many resources for locating her. I'd rather not be one of them."

"I hope you're financially secure, Captain Steele."

Rayford did not respond. He didn't want to get into more of a war of words with Leon Fortunato.

"There's been a slight change of plans by the way, as it relates to your picking up Supreme Pontiff Mathews in Rome."

"I'm listening."

"Carpathia will be going with you. He wants to accompany Mathews back to New Babylon."

"How does that affect me?"

"I just wanted to make sure you didn't leave without him."

———

Buck had already had his tongue-lashing by phone from Steve Plank about having allowed his passport and ID to fall into the wrong hands in Israel. "They tortured that Shorosh guy within an inch of his life, and he still swore you were just a passenger on his boat."

"It was a nice big, wood boat," Buck had said.

"Well, the boat is no more."

"What was the point of destroying a man's boat and torturing him?"

"Are we on the record?"

"I don't know, Steve. Are we talking as journalists, friends, or is this a warning from a colleague?"

Steve changed the subject. "Carpathia still likes the copy you're sending out from Chicago. He thinks *Global Community Weekly* is the best magazine in the world. Of course, it always has been."

"Yeah, yeah. If you forget about objectivity and journalistic credibility—"

"We all forgot about that years ago," Plank had said. "Even before we were owned by Carpathia, we still had to dance to somebody's tune."

Buck brought Amanda, Chloe, Rayford, and Tsion up to speed on their new laptop computers. Tsion had been using his secure phone to talk to everyone at Loretta's place, which they began calling their "safe house." More than once Loretta said, "That man sounds like he's next door."

"That's cellular technology for you," Buck said.

Tsion required daily visits from his fellow Tribulation Force members, just to keep his spirits up. He was fascinated by the new technology, and he spent much of his time monitoring the news. He was tempted to try to communicate via E-mail to many of his spiritual children around the world; however, he feared they might be tortured in attempts to determine his whereabouts. He asked Buck to ask Donny how he might go about communicating widely without the recipients of his missives suffering for it. The solution was simple. He would merely put his messages on a central bulletin board, and no one would know who was accessing them.

Tsion spent much of his days poring over Bruce's material and getting it into publishable shape. That was made easier by Buck's getting it to Tsion on disk. Frequently Tsion uploaded portions and in essence broadcast them to certain members of the Tribulation Force. He was especially impressed with what Bruce had to say about Chloe and Amanda. In his personal journal Bruce frequently mentioned his dream that they work together, researching, writing, and teaching cell groups and house churches. Eventually it was agreed that

354

Amanda would not return to New Babylon until after
Rayford got back from his flight to Rome. That would
give her a few more days with Chloe to plan a ministry
similar to what Bruce had outlined. They didn't know
where it would take them or what the opportunities
would be, but they enjoyed working together and
seemed to learn more that way.

Buck was glad Verna Zee was keeping her distance.
Much of the staff of the Chicago office was deployed
to various bombed-out cities to report on the resultant
chaos. There was no doubt in Buck's mind that the
black horse of plagues and famine and the pale horse
of death had come galloping in on the heels of the red
horse of war.

On Wednesday evening, Amanda drove Rayford to
Milwaukee for his flight to Iraq. "Why couldn't
Mathews fly on his own plane to see Carpathia?"
she said.

"You know Carpathia. He likes to take the upper
hand by being the most deferential and kind. He not
only sends a plane for you, he also comes along and
accompanies you back."

"What does he want from Mathews?"

"Who knows? It could be anything. The increase
in converts we're seeing has to be very troubling for
Mathews. We are one faction that doesn't buy into the
one-world faith routine."

———————

At six Thursday morning, Loretta's household was awakened by the phone. Chloe grabbed it. She put her hand over the mouthpiece and told Buck, "Loretta's got it. It's Hattie."

Buck leaned close to listen with her. "Yes," Loretta was saying, "you woke me, darlin', but it's all right. Captain Steele said you might call."

"Well, I'm flying through Milwaukee on my way back to New Babylon, and I purposely scheduled a six-hour layover. Tell anybody there who cares that I'll be at Mitchell Field if they want to talk to me. They shouldn't feel obligated, and I won't be offended if they don't come."

"Oh, they'll come, hon. Don't you worry about that."

———————

That same hour was three o'clock in the afternoon in Baghdad when Rayford's commercial flight landed. He had planned to stay onboard to wait for the short flight on to New Babylon a little over an hour later, but his cell phone vibrated in his pocket. He wondered if this would be the call from Buck, or from Carpathia about Buck, that would end the speculation and suspicion of the Tribulation Force. They all knew it couldn't be long before Buck's position was jeopardized past the point of safety.

Rayford also had a fleeting thought that this might be a call from Hattie Durham. He had waited as long as he could before heading back, hoping to connect with her before her return. Like Carpathia and Fortunato, he had no luck trying to reach her by phone in Denver.

But the call was from his copilot, Mac McCullum. "Get off that plane, Steele, and stretch your legs. Your taxi is here."

"Hey, Mac! What's that mean?"

"It means the big boss doesn't want to wait. Meet me at the helipad on the other side of the terminal. I'm coptering you back to headquarters."

Rayford had wanted to put off his return to New Babylon as long as possible, but at least a helicopter ride was a diversion. He envied McCullum's ability to easily switch back and forth between copiloting jumbo jets and flying whirlybirds. Rayford hadn't piloted a helicopter since his military days more than twenty years before.

Global Community Weekly was released to the public every Thursday, with the following Monday's date on the cover. Buck tingled with excitement merely anticipating that day's issue.

At the safe house it was decided that Amanda and Chloe would drive up to Milwaukee to pick up Hattie. Loretta would come home from the church office in time to host a small luncheon for her. Buck would go to the office to see the first copies of the magazine and head for Loretta's house when he got the call from Chloe that she and Amanda and Hattie were home.

Buck had gone out on a limb with his cover story.

Purporting, as usual, to take a neutral, objective, journalistic viewpoint, Buck started with much of the material Bruce would have preached the Sunday morning of his own funeral. Buck did the writing, but he assigned reporters from every *Global Community Weekly* office still standing in several countries to interview local and regional clergymen about the prophecies in the book of Revelation.

For some reason, his reporters—most of them skeptics—went at this task with glee. Buck was faxed, modemed, phoned, couriered, and mailed dispatches from all over the world. His cover story title, and the specific question he wanted his reporters to ask religious leaders, was "Will we suffer the 'wrath of the Lamb'?"

Buck had enjoyed this self-assigned task more than all the other cover stories he had ever done. That included his Man of the Year stories, even the one on Chaim Rosenzweig. He had spent nearly three days and nights, hardly sleeping, collating, contrasting, and comparing the various reports.

He, of course, could detect fellow believers in some of the comments. Despite the skepticism and cynicism of most of the reporters, tribulation-saint pastors and a few converted Jews were quoted that the "wrath of the Lamb" predicted in Revelation 6 was literal and imminent. The vast majority of the quotes were from clergy formerly representing various and sundry religions and denominations, but now serving Enigma Babylon One World Faith. Almost to a person, these men and women "faith guides" (no one was called a reverend or a pastor or a priest anymore) took their lead from Pontifex Maximus Peter Mathews. Buck himself had talked to Mathews. His view, echoed dozens of times, was that the book of Revelation was "wonderful, archaic, beautiful literature, to be taken symbolically, figuratively, metaphorically. This earthquake," Mathews had told Buck by phone, a smile in his voice, "could refer to anything. It may have happened already. It may refer to something someone imagined going on in heaven. Who knows? It may be some story related to the old theory of an eternal man in the sky who created the world. I don't know about you, but I have not seen any apocalyptic horsemen. I haven't seen anyone die for their religion. I haven't seen anyone 'slain for the word of God,' as the previous verses say. I haven't seen anyone in a white robe. And I don't expect to endure any earthquake. Regardless of your view on the person or concept of God, or *a* god, hardly anyone today would imagine a supreme spirit-being full of goodness and light subjecting the entire earth—already suffering from so recent a devastating war—to a calamity like an earthquake."

"But," Buck had asked him, "are you not aware that this idea of fearing the 'wrath of the Lamb' is a doctrine still preached in many churches?"

"Of course," Mathews had responded. "But these are the same holdovers from your right-wing, fanatical, fundamentalist factions who have always taken the Bible literally. These same preachers, and I daresay many of their parishioners, are the ones who take the creation account—the Adam and Eve myth, if you will—literally.

They believe the entire world was under water at the time of Noah and that only he and his three sons and their wives survived to begin the entire human race as we now know it."

"But you, as a Catholic, as the former pope—"

"Not just the former pope, Mr. Williams, also a former Catholic. I feel a great responsibility as leader of the Global Community's faith to set aside all trappings of parochialism. I must, in the spirit of unity and conciliation and ecumenism, be prepared to admit that much Catholic thought and scholarship was just as rigid and narrow-minded as that which I'm criticizing here."

"Such as?"

"I don't care to be too specific, at the risk of offending those few who still like to refer to themselves as Catholics, but the idea of a literal virgin birth should be seen as an incredible leap of logic. The idea that the Holy Roman Catholic Church was the only true church was almost as damaging as the evangelical Protestant view that Jesus was the only way to God. That assumes, of course, that Jesus was, as so many of my Bible-worshiping friends like to say, 'the only begotten Son of the Father.' By now I'm sure that most thinking people realize that God is, at most, a spirit, an idea, if you will. If they like to infuse him, or it, or her, with some characteristics of purity and goodness, it only follows that we are *all* sons and daughters of God."

Buck had led him. "The idea of heaven and hell then . . . ?"

"Heaven is a state of mind. Heaven is what you can

make of your life here on earth. I believe we're heading toward a utopian state. Hell? More damage has been done to more tender psyches by the wholly mythical idea that—well, let me put it this way: Let's say those fundamentalists, these people who believe we're about to suffer the 'wrath of the Lamb,' are right that there is a loving, personal God who cares about each one of us. How does that jibe? Is it possible he would create something that he would eventually burn up? It makes no sense."

"But don't Christian believers, the ones you're trying to characterize, say that God is not willing that any should perish? In other words, he doesn't send people to hell. Hell is judgment for those who don't believe, but everyone is given the opportunity."

"You have summarized their position well, Mr. Williams. But, as I'm sure you can see, it just doesn't hold water."

Early that morning, before the door was unlocked, Buck picked up the shrink-wrapped bundle of *Global Community Weekly*s and lugged them inside. The secretaries would distribute one to each desk, but for now Buck ripped off the plastic and set a magazine before him. The cover, which had been tweaked at the international headquarters office, was even better than Buck had hoped. Under the logo was a stylized illustration of a huge mountain range splitting from one end to the other. A red moon hung over the scene, and the copy read: "Will You Suffer the Wrath of the Lamb?"

Buck turned to the extra-long story inside that carried his byline. Characteristic of a Buck Williams story, he had covered all the bases. He had quoted leaders from Carpathia and Mathews to local faith guides. There was even a smattering of quotes from the man on the street.

The biggest coup, in Buck's mind, was a sidebar carrying a brief but very cogent and articulate word study by none other than Rabbi Tsion Ben-Judah. He explained who the sacrificed Lamb was in Scripture and how the imagery had begun in the Old Testament and was fulfilled by Jesus in the New Testament.

Buck had been suspicious about not having been called on the carpet by anyone but his old friend Steve Plank regarding his potential involvement in the escape of Tsion Ben-Judah. Quoting Tsion extensively in his own sidebar could have made it seem as if Buck were rubbing in the faces of his superiors his knowledge of Ben-Judah's whereabouts. But he had headed that off. When the story was filed and sent via satellite to the various print plant facilities, Buck added a note that "Dr. Ben-Judah learned of this story over the Internet and has submitted his view via computer from an undisclosed location."

Also amusing to Buck, if anything about this cosmic subject could be amusing, was that one of his enterprising young reporters from Africa took it upon himself to interview geological scholars in a university in Zimbabwe. Their conclusion? "The idea of a global earthquake is, on the face of it, illogical. Earthquakes are caused by faults, by underground plates rubbing against each other. It's cause and effect. The reason it happens in certain areas at certain times is, logically, because it's not happening other places at the same time. These plates move and crash together because they have nowhere else to go. You never hear of simultaneous earthquakes. There is not one in North America and one in South America at precisely the same time. The odds against one earth-wide geological event, which would really be simultaneous earthquakes all over the globe, are astronomical."

———————————

McCullum landed the chopper on the roof of the Global Community international headquarters building in New Babylon. He helped carry Rayford's bags into the elevator that took them past Carpathia's Suite 216, an entire floor of offices and conference rooms. Rayford had never understood its address, as it was not on the second floor at all. Carpathia and his senior staff occupied the top floor of the eighteen-story building.

Rayford hoped Carpathia would not know precisely when they arrived. He assumed he would have to face the man when he flew him to Rome to pick up Mathews, but Rayford wanted to get unpacked, freshen up, and settle in at his condo before getting back on board a plane again right away. He was grateful they were not intercepted. He had a couple of hours before takeoff. "See you on the 216, Mac," he said.

———————————

The phones began ringing at the *Global Weekly* office even before anyone else began to arrive. Buck let the answering machine take the calls, and it wasn't long before he rolled his chair to the receptionist's desk and just sat listening to the comments. One woman said, "So, *Global Community Weekly* has stooped to the level of the tabloids, covering every latest fairy tale to come out of the so-called church. Leave this trash to the yellow journalists."

Another said, "I wouldn't have dreamed people still believe this malarkey. That you could dig up that many weirdos to contribute to one story is a tribute to investigative journalism. Thanks for exposing them to the light and showing them what fools they really are."

Only the occasional call carried the tone of this one from a woman in Florida: "Why didn't somebody tell me about this before? I've been reading Revelation since the minute this magazine hit my doorstep, and I'm scared to death. What am I supposed to do now?"

Buck hoped she would read deep enough into the article to discover what a converted Jew from Norway said was the only protection from the coming earthquake: "No one should assume there will be shelter. If you believe, as I do, that Jesus Christ is the only hope for salvation, you should repent of your sins and receive him before the threat of death visits you."

Buck's personal phone buzzed. It was Verna.

"Buck, I'm keeping your secret, so I hope you're keeping your end of the bargain."

"I am. What's got you so agitated this morning?"

"Your cover story, of course. I knew it was coming, but I didn't expect it to be so overt. Do you think you've hidden behind your objectivity? Don't you think this exposes you as a proponent?"

"I don't know. I hope not. Even if Carpathia didn't own this magazine, I would want to come across as objective."

"You're deluding yourself."

Buck scrambled mentally for an answer. In one way, he appreciated the warning. In another, this was old news. Maybe Verna was just trying to find some point of contact, some reason to start a dialogue again. "Verna, I urge you to keep thinking about what you heard from Loretta, Chloe, and Amanda."

"And from you. Don't leave yourself out." Her tone was mocking and sarcastic.

"I mean it, Verna. If you ever want to talk about this stuff, you can come to me."

"With what your religion says about homosexuals, are you kidding?"

"My Bible doesn't differentiate between homosexuals and heterosexuals," Buck said. "It may call practicing homosexuals sinners, but it also calls heterosexual sex outside of marriage sinful."

"Semantics, Buck. Semantics."

"Just remember what I said, Verna. I don't want our personality conflict to get in the way of what's real and true. You were right when you said the outbreak of the war made our skirmishes petty. I'm willing to put those behind us."

She was silent for a moment. Then she sounded

almost impressed. "Well, thank you, Buck. I'll keep that in mind."

By late morning Chicago time it was early evening in Iraq. Rayford and McCullum were flying Carpathia, Fortunato, and Dr. Kline to Rome to pick up One World Faith supreme pontiff Peter Mathews. Rayford knew Carpathia wanted to pave the way for the apostate union of religions to move to New Babylon, but he wasn't sure how Dr. Kline fit into this meeting. By listening in on his bugging device, he soon found out.

As was his usual custom, Rayford took off, quickly reached cruising altitude, put the plane on autopilot, and turned over control to Mac McCullum. "I feel like I've been on a plane all day," he said, leaning back in his seat, pulling the bill of his cap down over his eyes, applying his headphones, and appearing to drift off to sleep. In the approximately two hours it took to fly from New Babylon to Rome, Rayford would get a lesson in new-world-order international diplomacy. But before they got down to business, Carpathia checked with Fortunato on the flight plans of Hattie Durham.

Fortunato told him, "She is on some kind of a multi-leg journey that has a long layover in Milwaukee, then heads for Boston. She'll fly nonstop from Boston to Baghdad. She'll lose several hours coming this way, but I think we can expect her tomorrow morning."

Carpathia sounded peeved. "How long before we get

the international terminal finished in New Babylon? I am tired of everything having to come through Baghdad."

"They're telling us a couple of months now."

"And these are the same building engineers who tell us everything else in New Babylon is state of the art?"

"Yes, sir. Have you noticed problems?"

"No, but it almost makes me wish this 'wrath of the Lamb' business was more than a myth. I would like to put the true test to their earthquake-proof claims."

"I saw that piece today," Dr. Kline said. "Interesting bit of fiction. That Williams can make an interesting story out of anything, can't he?"

"Yes," Carpathia said solemnly. "I suspect he has made an interesting story of his own background."

"I don't follow."

"I do not follow either," Carpathia said. "Our intelligence forces link him to the disappearance of Rabbi Ben-Judah."

Rayford straightened and listened more closely. He didn't want McCullum to realize he was listening on a different frequency, but neither did he want to miss anything.

"We are learning more and more about our brilliant young journalist," Carpathia said. "He has never been forthcoming about his ties to my own pilot, but then neither has Captain Steele. I still do not mind having them around. They may think they are in strategy proximity to me, but I am also able to learn much about the opposition through them."

So there it is, Rayford thought. *The gauntlet is down.*

"Leon, what is the latest on those two crazy men in Jerusalem?"

Fortunato sounded disgusted. "They've got the whole nation of Israel up in arms again," he said. "You know it hasn't rained there since they began all that preaching. And that trick they pulled on the water supply—turning it to blood—during the temple ceremonies, they're doing that again."

"What has set them off this time?"

"I think you know."

"I have asked you not to be circumspect with me, Leon. When I ask you a question, I expect—"

"Forgive me, Potentate. They have been carrying on about the arrest and torture of people associated with Dr. Ben-Judah. They are saying that until those suspects have been released and the search has been called off, all water supplies will be polluted by blood."

"How do they do that?"

"No one knows, but it's very real, isn't it Dr. Kline?"

"Oh yes," he said. "I have been sent samples. There is a high water content, but it is mostly blood."

"Human blood?"

"It has all the characteristics of human blood, although the type is difficult to determine. It borders on some cross between human and animal blood."

"How is morale in Israel?" Carpathia asked.

"The people are angry with the two preachers. They want to kill them."

"That is not all bad," Carpathia said. "Can we not get that done?"

"No one dares. The death count on those who've made attacks on them is over a dozen by now. You learn your lesson after a while."

"We are going to find a way," Carpathia said. "Meanwhile, let the suspects go. Ben-Judah cannot get far. Anyway, without being able to show his face in public, he cannot do us much harm. If those two rascals do not immediately purify the water supply, we will see how they stand up to an atomic blast."

"You're not serious, are you?" Dr. Kline said.

"Why would I not be?"

"You would drop an atomic bomb on a sacred site in the Holy City?"

"Frankly, I do not worry about the Wailing Wall or the Temple Mount or the new temple. Those two are giving me no end of grief, so mark my word: The day will come when they push me too far."

"It would be good to get Pontiff Mathews's opinion of all of this."

"We have enough of an agenda with him," Carpathia said. "In fact, I am sure he has an agenda for me as well, though perhaps a hidden one."

Later, after someone switched on the TV and the three men caught up on the international coverage of the war cleanup effort, Carpathia turned his attention to Dr. Kline.

"As you know, the ten ambassadors voted unani-mously to fund abortions for women in underprivileged countries. I have made an executive decision to make that unilateral. Every continent has suffered from the war, so all could be considered underprivileged. I do not anticipate a problem from Mathews on this, the way he might have protested were he still pope. However, should he express some opposition, are you prepared to discuss the long-term benefits?"

"Of course."

"And where are we on the technology for predetermining the health and viability of a fetus?"

"Amniocentesis can now tell us everything we want to know. Its benefits are so far-reaching that it is worth any risk the procedure might afford."

"And Leon," Carpathia said, "are we at a point where we can announce sanctions requiring amniocentesis on every pregnancy, along with an abortion requirement for any fetal tissue determined to result in a deformed or handicapped fetus?"

"Everything is in place," Fortunato said. "However, you are going to want as broad a base of support as possible before going public with that."

"Of course. That is one of the reasons for this meeting with Mathews."

"Are you optimistic?" Fortunato asked.

"Should I not be? Is Mathews not aware that I put him where he is today?"

"That's a question I ask myself all the time, Potentate. Surely you notice his lack of deference and respect. I don't like the way he treats you as if he's an equal."

"For the time being, he can be as pushy as he wants.

He can be of great value to the cause because of his
following. I know he is having financial difficulty
because he cannot sell surplus churches. They are single-
use facilities, so he will no doubt be pleading his case for
more of an allotment from the Global Community. The
ambassadors are already upset about this. For right now,
though, I do not mind having the upper hand financially.
Maybe we can strike a deal."

EIGHTEEN

BUCK was amused that his cover story was the hottest topic of the day. Every talk show, news show, and even some variety shows mentioned it. One comedy featured an animated short of a woolly lamb going on the rampage. They called it "Our View of the 'Wrath of the Lamb.'"

Glancing at the magazine before him, Buck suddenly realized that when he was exposed, when he would have to step down, when he possibly became a fugitive, it would be impossible to match the distribution of a magazine so well-established around the world. He might have a larger audience via television and the Internet, but he wondered if he would ever have the influence again that he had right now.

He looked at his watch. It was almost time to head for the safe house and the luncheon with Hattie.

———————

Rayford and Mac McCullum had about an hour's break after they hit the ground in Rome and before they were to head back to New Babylon. They passed Peter Mathews and one of his aides boarding the plane. Rayford was nauseated by Carpathia's obsequious deference to Mathews. He heard the potentate say, "How good of you to allow us to come and collect you, Pontiff. I am hoping we can have meaningful dialogue, profitable to the good of the Global Community."

Just before Rayford stepped out of earshot, Mathews told Carpathia, "As long as it's profitable to the One World Faith, I don't much care whether you benefit or not."

Rayford found reasons to excuse himself from McCullum and hurry back to the plane and into the cockpit. He apologized to Fortunato for "having to check on a few things" and was soon back in his customary spot. The door was locked. The reverse intercom was on, and Rayford was listening.

———————

Buck had not seen Hattie Durham in real distress since the night of the Rapture. He, like most other men, usually saw her only as striking. Now the kindest term he could think of for her was disheveled. She carried an oversized purse stuffed mostly with tissues, and she made use of every last one. Loretta pointed her to the head of the table, and when lunch was served, they all sat awkwardly, seeming to try to avoid meaningful conversation. Buck said, "Amanda, would you pray for us?"

Hattie quickly entwined her fingers under her chin, like a little girl kneeling at her bedside. Amanda said, "Father, sometimes in the situations we find ourselves, it's difficult to know what to say to you. Sometimes we're unhappy. Sometimes we're distraught. Sometimes we have no idea where to turn. The world seems in such chaos. However, we know we can thank you for who you are. We thank you that you're a good God. That you care about us and love us. We thank you that you're sovereign and that you hold the world in your hands. We thank you for friends, especially old friends like Hattie. Give us words to say that might help her in whatever decision making she must do, and thank you for the provision of this food. In Jesus' name, Amen."

They ate in silence, Buck noticing that Hattie's eyes were full of tears. Despite that, she ate quickly and was done before the rest. She grabbed yet another tissue and blew her nose.

"Well," she said, "Rayford insisted that I drop in on you on my way back. I'm sorry I missed him, but I think he really wanted me to talk to you anyway. Or maybe he wanted you to talk to me."

The women looked as puzzled as Buck felt. That was it? The floor was theirs? What were they supposed to do? It was hard to meet this woman at her point of need if she wasn't going to share that need.

Loretta began. "Hattie, what's troubling you the most just now?"

Either what Loretta said or how she said it unleashed a torrent of tears. "Fact is," Hattie managed, "I want an abortion. My family is encouraging me that way. I don't know what Nicolae will say, but if there's no change in our relationship when I get back there, I'm going to want an abortion for sure. I suppose I'm here because I know you'll try to talk me out of it, and I guess I need to hear both sides. Rayford already gave me the standard right-wing, pro-life position. I don't guess I need to hear that again."

"What do you need to hear?" Buck said, feeling very male and very insensitive just then.

Chloe gave him a look that implied he should not push. "Hattie," she said, "you know where we stand. That's not why you're here. If you want to be talked out of it, we can do that. If you won't be talked out of it, nothing we say will make any difference."

Hattie looked frustrated. "So, you think I'm here to get preached at."

"We're not going to preach at you," Amanda said. "From what I understand, you know where we stand on the things of God as well."

"Yes, I do," Hattie said. "I'm sorry to have wasted your time. I guess I have a decision to make about this pregnancy, and it was foolish of me to drag you into it."

"Don't feel like you have to leave, darlin'," Loretta said. "This is my house, and I'm your hostess, and you might risk offendin' me if you were to leave too early."

Hattie looked at her as if to be sure Loretta was teasing. It was clear that she was. "I can just as easily wait at the airport," Hattie said. "I'm sorry to have put you through all this inconvenience."

Buck wanted to say something but knew he couldn't communicate at this level. He looked into the eyes of the women, who intently watched their guest. Finally, Chloe stood and walked behind Hattie's chair. She put her hands on Hattie's shoulders. "I have always admired and liked you," she said. "I think we could have been friends in another situation. But Hattie, I feel led to tell you that I know why you came here today. I know why you followed my dad's advice, though you may have done it against your will. Something tells me your visit home was not successful. Maybe they were too practical. Maybe they didn't give you the compassion you needed along with their advice. Maybe hearing that they wanted you to end this pregnancy was not what you really wanted.

"Let me just tell you, Hattie, if it's love you're looking for, you came to the right place. Yes, there are things we believe. Things we think you should know. Things we think you should agree with. Decisions we think you should make. We have ideas about what you should do about your baby, and we have ideas about what you should do about your soul. But these are personal decisions only you can make. And while they are life-and-death, heaven-and-hell decisions, all we can offer is support, encouragement, advice if you ask for it, and love."

"Yeah," Hattie said, "love, if I buy into everything you have to sell."

"No. We are going to love you anyway. We're going to love you the way God loves you. We're going to love you so fully and so well that you won't be able to hide from it. Even if your decisions go against everything we believe to be true, and even though we would grieve over the loss of innocent life if you chose to abort your baby, we won't love you any less."

Hattie burst into tears as Chloe rubbed her shoulders. "That's impossible! You can't love me no matter what I do, especially if I ignore your advice!"

"You're right," Chloe said. "We are not capable of unconditional love. That's why we have to let God love you through us. He's the one who loves us regardless of what we do. The Bible says he sent his Son to die for us while we were dead in our sins. That's unconditional love. That's what we have to offer you, Hattie, because that's all we have."

Hattie stood awkwardly, and her chair scraped the floor as she turned to embrace Chloe. They held each other for a long minute, and then the entire party moved into the other room. Hattie tried to smile. "I feel foolish," she said, "like a blubbering schoolgirl."

The other women didn't protest. They didn't tell her she looked fine. They simply looked at her with love. For a moment Buck wished he was Hattie so he could respond. He didn't know about her, but this sure would have won him over.

"I'll get right to it," Peter Mathews told Carpathia. "If there are ways we can help each other, I want to know what you need. Because there are things I need from you."

"Such as?" Carpathia asked.

"Frankly, I need amnesty from One World Faith's debt to your administration. We might be able to pay back some of our allotment someday, but right now we just don't have the income."

"Having trouble selling off some of those surplus church buildings?" Carpathia said.

"Oh, that's part of it, but a very small part. Our real problem lies with two religious groups who not only have refused to join our union, but who are also antagonistic and intolerant. You know who I'm talking about. One group is a problem that you caused yourself by that agreement between the Global Community and Israel. The Jews have no need for us, no reason to join. They still believe in the one true God and a Messiah who's supposed to come in the sky by and by. I don't know what your plan is after the contract runs out, but I could sure use some ammunition against them.

"The other bunch are these Christians who call themselves tribulation saints. They're the ones who think the Messiah already came and raptured his church and they missed it. I figure if they are right, they're kidding themselves to think he'd give them another chance, but you know as well as I do they're growing like wildfire. The strange thing is, a whole bunch of their converts are

Jews. They've got these two nuts at the Wailing Wall telling everybody that the Jews are halfway there with their belief in the one true God, but that Jesus is his Son, that he came back, and that he's coming back again."

"Peter, my friend, this should not be strange doctrine to you as a former Catholic."

"I didn't say it was strange to me. I just never realized the depth of the intolerance that we Catholics had and that those tribulation saint–types have now."

"You have noticed the intolerance too?"

"Who hasn't? These people take the Bible literally. You've seen their propaganda and heard their preachers at the big rallies. There are Jews buying into this stuff by the tens of thousands. Their intolerance hurts us."

"How so?"

"You know. The secret to our success, the enigma that is One World Faith, is simply that we have broken down the barriers that used to divide us. Any religion that believes there's only one way to God is, by definition, intolerant. They become enemies of One World Faith and thus the global community as a whole. Our enemies are your enemies. We have to do something about them."

"What do you propose?"

"I was about to ask you that very question, Nicolae."

Rayford could only imagine Nicolae wincing at Mathews' referring to him by his first name.

"Believe it or not, my friend, I have already given this a great deal of thought."

"You have?"

"I have. As you say, your enemies are my enemies.

Those two at the Wailing Wall, the ones the so-called saints refer to as the witnesses, have meant no end of grief for me and my administration. I do not know where they come from or what they are up to, but they have terrorized the people of Jerusalem, and more than once they have made me look bad. This group of fundamentalists, the ones who are converting so many Jews, look to these two as heroes."

"So, what conclusion have you come to?"

"Frankly, I have been considering more legislation. Conventional wisdom says you cannot legislate morale. I happen not to believe that. I admit my dreams and goals are grandiose, but I will not be deterred. I foresee a global community of true peace and harmony, a utopia where people live together for the good of each other. When that was threatened by insurrection forces from three of our ten regions, I immediately retaliated. In spite of my long-standing and most sincere opposition to war, I made a strategic decision. Now I am legislating morale. People who want to get along and live together will find me most generous and conciliatory. Those who want to cause trouble will be gone. It is as simple as that."

"So, what are you saying, Nicolae? You're going to wage war on the fundamentalists?"

"In a sense I am. No, we will not do it with tanks and bombs. But I believe the time has come to enforce rules for the new Global Community. As this would seem to benefit you as much as it would benefit me, I would like you to cooperate in forming and heading an organization of elite enforcers, if you will, of pure thought."

"How are you defining 'pure thought'?"

"I foresee a cadre of young, healthy, strong men and women so devoted to the cause of the Global Community that they would be willing to train and build themselves to the point where they will be eager to make sure everyone is in line with our objectives."

Rayford heard someone rise and begin pacing. He assumed it was Mathews, warming to the idea. "These would not be uniformed people, I assume."

"No. They would blend in with everyone else, but they would be chosen for their insight and trained in psychology. They would keep us informed of subversive elements who oppose our views. Surely you agree that we are long past the time where we can tolerate the extreme negative by-product of free speech run amok."

"Not only do I agree," Mathews said quickly, "but I stand ready to assist in any way possible. Can One World Faith help seek out candidates? train them? house them? clothe them?"

"I thought you were running short of funds," Carpathia said, chuckling.

"This will only result in more income for us. When we eliminate the opposition, everyone benefits."

Rayford heard Carpathia sigh. "We would call them the GCMM. The Global Community Morale Monitors."

"That makes them sound a little soft, Nicolae."

"Precisely the idea. We do not want to call them the secret police, or the thought police, or the hate police, or any kind of police. Make no mistake. They will be secret. They will have power. They will be able to supersede normal due cause in the interest of the better good for the global community."

"To what limit?"

"No limit."

"They would carry weapons?"

"Of course."

"And they would be allowed to use these to what extent?"

"That is the beauty of it, Pontiff Mathews. By selecting the right young people, by training them carefully in the ideal of a peaceful utopia, and by giving them ultimate capital power to mete out justice as they see fit, we quickly subdue the enemy and eliminate it. We should foresee no need of the GCMM within just a few years."

"Nicolae, you're a genius."

———

Buck was disappointed. When it came time to run Hattie back up to Milwaukee, he felt little progress had been made. She had a lot of questions about just what it was these women did with their time. She was intrigued by the idea of Bible studies. And she had mentioned her envy of having close friends of the same sex who seemed to really care about each other.

But Buck had been hoping there would have been some breakthrough. Maybe Hattie would have promised not to have an abortion or broken down and become a believer. He tried to push from his mind that Chloe might get the idea of taking and raising as their own the unwanted baby Hattie was carrying. He and Chloe were close to a decision about whether to bring a baby into this stage of history, but he hardly wanted to consider raising the child of the Antichrist.

Hattie thanked everyone and climbed into the Range Rover with the women. Buck implied he was going to take one of the other cars back to the *Global Community Weekly* office, but instead he drove to the church. He stopped on the way for a treat for his friend, and within minutes he had gone through the labyrinth that took him to the inner sanctum of Rabbi Tsion Ben-Judah's personal study chamber.

Every time Buck sneaked into that place, he was certain that claustrophobia, loneliness, fear, and grief would have overcome his friend. Without fail, however, it was Buck who was warmed by these visits. Tsion was hardly gleeful. He did not laugh much, nor did he offer a huge smile when Buck appeared. His eyes were red, and his face showed the lines of the recently bereaved. But he was also staying fit. He worked out, running in place, doing jumping jacks, stretching, and who knew what else. He told Buck he did this for at least an hour a day, and it showed. He seemed in a better frame of mind each time Buck saw him, and he never complained. That afternoon Tsion seemed genuinely pleased to have a visitor. "Cameron," he said, "were I not living with a heaviness of soul right now, certain parts of this place, even its location, would be paradise. I can read, I can study, I can pray, I can write, I can communicate by phone and computer. It is a scholar's dream. I miss the interaction with my colleagues, especially the young students who helped me. But Amanda and Chloe are wonderful students themselves."

He greedily joined Buck in their fast-food snack.

"I need to talk about my family. I hope you don't mind."

"Tsion, you may talk about your family with me anytime you want. You should forgive me for not being more diligent in asking."

"I know you, like many others, wonder if you should bring up such a painful subject. As long as we do not dwell on how they died, I am most pleased to talk about my memories. You know I raised my son and daughter from the ages of eight and ten to fourteen and sixteen. They were my wife's children from her first marriage. Her husband was killed in a construction accident. The children did not accept me at first, but I won them over by my love for *her*. I did not try to take the place of their father or pretend I was in charge of them. Eventually they referred to me as their father, and it was one of the proudest days of my life."

"Your wife seemed like a wonderful woman."

"She was. The children were wonderful too, though my family was human just like anyone else. I do not idealize them. They were all very bright. That was a joy to me. I could converse with them about deep things, complicated things. My wife herself had taught at the college level before having children. The children were both in special private schools and were exceptionally good students. Most important of all, when I began to tell them what I was learning in my research, they never once accused me of heresy or of turning my back on my culture, my religion, or my country. They were bright enough to see that I was discovering the truth. I did not preach at them, did not try to unduly influence them. I would merely read them passages and say, 'What do you deduce from this? What is the Torah saying here about qualifications for Messiah?' I was so fervent in my Socratic method that at times I believe they came to my ultimate conclusions before I did. When the Rapture occurred, I immediately knew what had happened. In some ways I was actually disappointed to find that I had failed my family and that all three of them had been left behind with me. I would have missed them, as I miss them now, but it also would have been a blessing to me had any of them seen the truth and acted upon it before it was too late."

"You told me they all became believers shortly after you did."

Tsion stood and paced. "Cameron, I do not understand how anyone with any exposure to the Bible could doubt the meaning of the mass vanishings. Rayford Steele, with his limited knowledge, knew because of the testimony of his wife. I, above all people, should have known. And yet you see it all around you. People are still trying to explain it away. It breaks my heart."

Tsion showed Buck what he was working on. He had nearly completed the first booklet in what he hoped would be a series from Bruce's writings. "He was a surprisingly adept scholar for a young man," Tsion said. "He was not the linguist that I am, and so I am adding some of that to his work. I think it makes for a better final product."

"I'm sure Bruce would agree," Buck said.

Buck wanted to broach the subject of Tsion's helping the church, remotely of course, locate a new pastor. How perfect if it could be Tsion! But that was out of the question. Anyway, Buck did not want anything to interrupt Tsion's important work.

"You know, Tsion, that I will likely be the first to join you here on a permanent basis."

"Cameron, I cannot see you as content to hide out."

"It'll drive me crazy, there's no doubt about that. But I have begun to get careless. Riskier. It's bound to catch up with me."

"You will be able to do what I do on the Internet," Tsion said. "I am communicating with many hundreds already, just by learning a few tricks. Imagine what you can do with the truth. You can write the way you used to write, with total objectivity and seriousness. You will not be influenced by the owner of the paper."

"What was that you said about the truth?"

"You can write the truth, that's all."

Buck sat and began noodling on paper. He drew the cover of a magazine and called it simply "Truth." He was excited.

"Look at this. I could design the graphics, write the copy, and disseminate it on the Net. According to Donny Moore, it could never be traced back here."

"I don't want to see you forced into self-incarceration," Ben-Judah said. "But I confess I would enjoy the company."

NINETEEN

RAYFORD was proud of Hattie Durham. From what he could gather in New Babylon, she had pulled another fast one on Nicolae and his henchman Leon Fortunato. Apparently she had flown from Milwaukee to Boston, but rather than taking her connecting flight on to Baghdad, she had stopped somewhere.

Rayford had been out of hearing range, of course, when the meetings with Peter Mathews were continued at New Babylon headquarters. All he knew was that there was great consternation around the place, especially among Nicolae and Leon, that Hattie had slipped off schedule yet again. Though Nicolae had shown indifference to her, not knowing where she was made her a loose cannon and a potential embarrassment.

When word finally arrived that she had a new itinerary, Carpathia himself asked to see Rayford in private.

The new secretarial staff was in place and operational by the time Rayford entered Suite 216 and was granted audience with the potentate.

"It is good to see you again, Captain Steele. I fear I have not been as forthcoming with my thanks for your service as I used to be, before so many distractions have come about.

"Let me get straight to the point. I know that Ms. Durham once worked for you. In fact, you came to us based on her recommendation. I know also that she has at times confided in you. Thus, it should come as no surprise to you that there has been some trouble in paradise, as they say. Let me be frank. The fact is, I believe Ms. Durham always overestimated the seriousness of our personal relationship."

Rayford thought back to when Nicolae had seemed to proudly announce that Hattie was pregnant and that she was wearing his ring. But Rayford knew better than to try to catch the liar of liars in a lie.

Carpathia continued: "Ms. Durham should have realized that in a position such as the one I hold, there really is no room for a personal life that would enjoy the commitment required by a marriage and family. She seemed pleased with the prospect of bearing a child, my child. Thus, I did not discourage that or encourage some other option. Should she take the pregnancy to term, I would of course exercise my fiscal responsibility. However, it is unfair for her to expect me to devote the time that might be available to the normal father.

"My advice to her would be to terminate the pregnancy. However, due to the fact that this result of our relationship is really her responsibility, I will leave that decision to her."

Rayford was puzzled and didn't try to hide it. Why was Carpathia telling him this? What assignment was going to fall to him? He didn't have long to wait.

"I have needs like any other man, Captain Steele. You understand. I would never commit myself to just one woman, and I certainly made no such commitment to Ms. Durham. The fact is that I already have someone else with whom I am enjoying a relationship. Therefore, you can see my dilemma."

"I'm not sure I do," Rayford said.

"Well, I have replaced Ms. Durham as my personal assistant. I sense that she is distraught from that and from what she has to deduce is a relationship that has soured. I do not see it as souring; I see us both moving on. But, as I say, as she saw it as more important a commitment than I did, she is thus more upset and disappointed at the conclusion of it."

"I need to ask you about the ring you gave her," Rayford said.

"Oh, that is no problem. I will not be requiring that back. In fact, I always believed that the stone was much too large to be worn as an engagement ring. It clearly is decorative. She need not worry about returning that."

Rayford was getting the picture. Carpathia was going to call on him, as Hattie's old friend and boss, to deliver the news. Why else would he need all this information?

"I will do the right thing by Ms. Durham, Captain

Steele. You may be assured of that. I would not want her to become destitute. I know she is employable, probably not as a clerical person, but certainly in the aviation industry."

"Which has been devastated by the war, as you know," Rayford said.

"Yes, but with her seniority and perhaps with some gentle pressure on my part . . ."

"And so you're saying that you will give her some sort of severance or a stipend or settlement?"

Carpathia seemed to brighten. "Yes, if that will make it easier for her, I am happy to do that."

I should think you would be, Rayford thought.

"Captain Steele, I have an assignment for you—"

"I deduced that."

"Of course, you would. You are a bright man. We have received word that Ms. Durham is back on her itinerary and is expected in Baghdad on a flight from Boston on Monday."

It finally hit Rayford why Hattie might have delayed her return. Perhaps she knew of Amanda's plans. It would be just like Amanda to arrange to meet her somewhere and accompany her back. Amanda would have had an ulterior motive, of course: to keep Hattie from visiting a reproductive clinic. She also would have wanted to continue expressing love to her. Rayford decided against telling Carpathia he was headed to the airport in Baghdad Monday anyway to pick up his own wife.

"Assuming you are free, Captain Steele, and I will

make sure that you are, I would ask that you would meet Miss Durham's plane. As her old friend, you will be the right one to break this news to her. Her belongings have been delivered to one of the condominiums in your building. She will be allowed to stay there for a month before deciding where she would like to relocate."

Rayford interrupted. "Excuse me, but are you asking me to do something that you yourself should be doing?"

"Oh, make no mistake, Captain Steele. I am not afraid of this confrontation. It would be most distasteful for me, yes, but I recognize my responsibility here. It is just that I am under such crushing deadlines for important meetings. We have established many new directives and legislative encyclicals in light of the recent insurrection, and I simply cannot be away from the office."

Rayford thought Carpathia's meeting with Hattie Durham might have taken less time than the meeting they were conducting right then. But what was the sense of arguing with a man like this?

"Any questions, Captain Steele?"

"No. It's all very clear to me."

"You will do it then?"

"I was not under the impression I had a choice."

Carpathia smiled. "You have a good sense of humor, Captain Steele. I would not say your job depends on it, but I appreciate that your military background has trained you to realize that when a directive is given, it is to be carried out. I want you to know that I appreciate it."

Rayford stared at him. He willed himself not to say the obligatory, "You're welcome." He nodded and stood.

"Captain Steele, might I ask you to remain seated for a moment."

Rayford sat back down. *What now? Is this the beginning of the end?*

"I would like to ask you about your relationship with Cameron Williams." Rayford did not respond at first. Carpathia continued. "Sometimes known as Buck Williams. He was formerly a senior staff writer for *Global Weekly*, now *Global Community Weekly*. He is my publisher there."

"He's my son-in-law," Rayford said.

"And can you think of any reason why he would not have shared that happy news with me?"

"I suppose you'll have to ask him that, sir."

"Well, then perhaps I should ask you. Why would *you* not have shared that with me?"

"It's just personal family business," Rayford said, trying to remain calm. "Anyway, with him serving you at such a high level, I assumed you would become aware of it soon enough."

"Does it happen that he shares your religious beliefs?"

"I prefer not to speak for Buck."

"I will take that as a yes." Rayford stared at him. Carpathia continued, "I am not saying that this is necessarily a problem, you understand." *I understand all right,* Rayford thought. "I was just curious," Carpathia concluded. He smiled at Rayford, and the pilot read everything in that smile that the Antichrist implied. "I will look forward to a report of your meeting with Miss Durham, and I have full confidence that it will be successful."

Buck was at the Chicago office of *Global Community Weekly* when he took a call from Amanda on his private phone. "I got the strangest call from Rayford," she said. "He asked if I had hooked up with Hattie on her flight out of Boston to Baghdad. I told him no. I thought she was already back there. He said he thought she was on another schedule now and that we would likely be arriving at about the same time. I asked him what was up, but he seemed rushed and didn't feel free to take the time to tell me. Do you know what's happening?"

"This is all news to me, Amanda. Did your flight refuel in Boston as well?"

"Yes. You know New York is completely shut down. So is Washington. I don't know if these planes can go all the way from Milwaukee to Baghdad."

"What would have taken Hattie so long to get back there?"

"I have no idea. If I had known she was going to delay her return, I would have offered to have flown with her. We need to maintain contact with that girl."

Buck agreed. "Chloe misses you already. She and Tsion are working hard on some New Testament curriculum. It's almost as if they're in the same room, though they're at least a quarter of a mile apart."

"I know she's enjoying that," Amanda said. "I wish I could talk Rayford into letting me move back this way. I'd see less of him, but I don't see much of him in New Babylon either."

"Don't forget you can be in that 'same room' with Tsion and Chloe, no matter where you are now."

"Yeah," she said, "except that we're nine hours later than you guys."

"You'll just have to coordinate your schedules. Where are you now?"

"We're over the continent. Should be touching down in an hour or so. It's what there, just a little after eight in the morning?"

"Right. The Tribulation Force is about as spread out as it's been for a while. Tsion seems productive and contented, if not happy. Chloe is at Loretta's and excited about her study and her teaching opportunities, though she knows she may not always be free, legally, to do that. I'm here, you're there, and you'll be meeting up with Rayford before you know it. I guess we're all present and accounted for."

"I sure hope Rayford's right about Hattie," Amanda said. "It'll be handy if he can pick us both up."

———

It was time for Rayford to head for Baghdad. He was confused. Why had Hattie remained incommunicado in Denver for so long and then misled Fortunato about her return flight when she *did* reestablish contact? If it wasn't for the purpose of hooking up with Amanda, what was it? What would have interested her in Boston?

Rayford couldn't wait to see Amanda. It had been only a few days, but they were still newlyweds, after all.

He did not relish his assignment with Hattie, especially with Amanda getting in at the same time. One thing he could justify, however, based on what he had been told about Hattie's encounter with Loretta, Chloe, and Amanda at the safe house, was that Hattie would be comforted by Amanda's presence.

The question was, would this word from Rayford be bad news for Hattie? It might make her future easier to accept. She knew it was over. She feared Carpathia might not let her go. She would be offended, of course, insulted. She wouldn't want his ring or his money or his condo. But at least she would know. To Rayford's male mind, this seemed a practical solution. He had learned enough from Irene and Amanda over the years, however, to know that regardless of how unattractive Nicolae Carpathia had become to Hattie, still she would be hurt and would feel rejected.

Rayford phoned Hattie's driver. "Could you drive me, or could I borrow your car? I'm to pick up Miss Durham in Baghdad and also my—"

"Oh, sorry sir. I'm no longer Miss Durham's driver. I drive for someone else in the executive suite."

"You know where I could get wheels then?"

"You could try the motor pool, but that takes awhile. Lots of paperwork, you know."

"I don't have that kind of time. Any other suggestions?" Rayford was angry with himself for not planning better.

"If the potentate called the motor pool, you'd have a vehicle as quick as you wanted it."

Rayford phoned Carpathia's office. The secretary said he was unavailable.

"Is he there?" Rayford asked.

"He is here, sir, but as I said, he's not available."

"This is sort of urgent. If he's at all interruptible, I'd appreciate it if you'd let me talk to him for just a second."

When the secretary came back on the line, she said, "The potentate wants to know if you could drop by his office for a moment before you finish your assignment for him."

"I'm a little short of time, but—"

"I'll tell him you'll be here then."

Rayford was three blocks from Carpathia's building. He hurried down in the elevator and jogged toward headquarters. He had a sudden thought and grabbed his phone. As he ran, he called McCullum. "Mac? Are you free right now? Good! I need a chopper ride to Baghdad. My wife's coming in, and I'm supposed to meet Hattie Durham as well. Rumors about her? I'm not at liberty to say anything, Mac. I'll be in Carpathia's office in a few minutes. Meet you on the helipad? Good! Thanks!"

Buck was working on his laptop with his office door shut when the machine signaled that he had incoming, real-time mail. He liked this feature. It was like being on a chat line with just one person. The message was from Tsion. He asked, "Shall we try the video feature?"

Buck typed, "Sure." And he tapped in the code. It took a few minutes to program itself, but then Tsion's image flickered on the screen. Buck tapped in, "Is that you, or am I looking in the mirror?"

Tsion responded, "It's me. We could use the audio and talk to each other, if you're in a secure area."

"Better not," Buck tapped in. "Did you want something specific?"

"I would like a companion for breakfast," Tsion said. "I'm feeling much better today, but I'm getting a little claustrophobic here. I know you can't sneak me out, but could you get in without Loretta suspecting?"

"I'll try. What would you like for breakfast?"

"I have cooked up something American just for you, Buck. I'm turning my screen now to see if it can pick it up."

The machine was not really built to pan around a dark, underground shelter. Buck typed in: "I can't see anything, but I'll trust you. Be there as soon as I can." Buck told the receptionist he would be gone for a couple of hours, but as he was heading to the Range Rover, Verna Zee caught him. "Where are you going?" she asked.

"I'm sorry?" he said.

"I want to know where you'll be."

"I'm not sure where all I'll be," he said. "The desk knows I'll be gone for a couple of hours. I don't feel obligated to share specifics."

Verna shook her head.

———————

Rayford slowed as he reached the grand entrance of Global Community headquarters. The compound had been set in an unusual area where upscale residences surrounded it. Something had caught Rayford's attention. Animal noises. Barking. He had been aware of dogs in the area. Many employees owned expensive breeds they enjoyed walking and tethering outside their places. They were showpieces of prosperity. He had heard one or two barking at times. But now they were all barking. They were noisy enough that he turned to see if he could detect what was agitating them so. He saw a couple of dogs jerk away from their owners and race down the street howling.

He shrugged and entered the building.

———————

Buck considered swinging by Loretta's house and picking up Chloe. He would have to think of a story to tell Loretta at the church office. He wouldn't be able to park or walk into the church without her seeing him. Maybe he and Chloe would just spend some time with her and then appear to be leaving the church the back way. If no one was watching, they could slip down and see Tsion. It sounded like a plan. Buck was halfway to Mt. Prospect when he noticed something strange. Roadkill. Lots of it. And more potential roadkill skittering across the streets. Squirrels, rabbits, snakes. Snakes? He had seen few snakes in the Midwest, particularly this far north. The occasional garter snake was all. That's what these were, but why so many of them? Coons, possum, ducks, geese, dogs, cats, animals everywhere. He lowered the window of the Range Rover and listened. Huge clouds of birds swept from tree to tree. But the sky was bright. Cloudless. There seemed to be no wind. No leaf even shivered on a tree. Buck waited at a stoplight and noticed that, despite the lack of wind, the streetlights swayed. Signs bent back and forth. Buck blew the light and raced toward Mt. Prospect.

Rayford was ushered into Carpathia's office. The potentate had several VIPs around a conference table. He quickly pulled Rayford aside. "Thank you for stopping in, Captain Steele. I just wanted to reiterate my wish that I not have to face Ms. Durham. She may want to talk to me. That will be out of the question. I—"

"Excuse me," Leon Fortunato interrupted, "but Potentate, sir, we're getting some strange readouts on our power meters."

"Your power meters?" Carpathia asked, incredulous. "I leave maintenance to you and your staff, Leon—"

"Sir!" the secretary said. "An emergency call for you or Mr. Fortunato from the International Seismograph Institute."

Carpathia looked irritated and whirled to face Fortunato. "Take that, will you, Leon? I am busy here."

Fortunato took the call and appeared to want to keep quiet until he blurted, "What? What?!"

Now Carpathia was angry. "Leon!"

Rayford moved away from Carpathia and looked out the window. Below, dogs ran in circles, their owners chasing them. Rayford reached in his pocket for his cell phone and quickly called McCullum. Carpathia glared at him. "Captain Steele! I was talking to you here—"

"Mac! Where are you? Start 'er up. I'm on my way now!"

Suddenly the power went out. Only battery-operated lights near the ceiling shined, and the bright sun flooded through the windows. The secretary screamed. Fortunato turned to Carpathia and tried to tell him what he had just heard. Carpathia shouted above the din. "I would like order in here, please!"

And as if someone had flipped a switch, the day went black. Now even the grown men moaned and shrieked. Those battery-operated lights in the corner cast a haunting glow on the building, which began to shudder. Rayford made a dash for the door. He sensed someone right behind him. He pushed the elevator button and then smacked himself in the head, remembering there was no power. He dashed upstairs to the roof, where McCullum had the chopper blades whirring.

The building shifted under Rayford like the surf. The chopper, resting on its skis, dipped first to the left and then to the right. Rayford reached for the opening, seeing Mac's wide eyes. As Rayford tried to climb in, he was pushed from behind and flew up behind Mac. Nicolae Carpathia was scrambling in. "Lift off!" he shouted. "Lift off!"

McCullum raised the chopper about a foot off the roof. "Others are coming!" he shouted.

"No more room!" Carpathia hollered. "Lift off!"

As two young women and several middle-aged men grabbed the struts, Mac pulled away from the building. As he banked left, his lights illuminated the roof, where others came shrieking and crying out the door. As Rayford watched in horror, the entire eighteen-story building, filled with hundreds of employees, crashed to the ground in a mighty roar and a cloud of dust. One by one the screaming people hanging from the chopper fell away.

Rayford stared at Carpathia. In the dim light from the control panel he saw no expression. Carpathia simply appeared busy about strapping himself in. Rayford was ill. He had seen people die. Carpathia had ordered Mac away from people who might have been saved. Rayford could have killed the man with his bare hands.

Wondering if he wouldn't have been better off to have died in the building himself, Rayford shook his head and resolutely fastened his seat belt. "Baghdad!" he shouted. "Baghdad Airport!"

Buck had known exactly what was coming and had been speeding through lights and stop signs, jumping curbs, and going around cars and trucks. He wanted to get to Chloe at Loretta's house first. He reached for his phone, but he had not stored speed-dial numbers yet,

and there was no way he could drive this quickly and
punch in an entire number at the same time. He tossed
the phone on the seat and kept going. He was going
through an intersection when the sun was snuffed out.
Day went to night in an instant, and power went out
all over the area. People quickly turned on their headlights, but Buck saw the crevasse too late. He was heading for a fissure in the road that had opened before
him. It looked at least ten feet wide and that deep. He
figured if he dropped into it he would be killed, but he
was going too fast to avoid it. He wrenched the wheel
to the left and the Range Rover rolled over completely
before plunging down into the hole. The passenger-side
air bag deployed and quietly deflated. It was time to
find out what this car was made of.

Ahead of him the gap narrowed. There would be no
going out that way unless he could start going up first.
He pushed the buttons that gave him all-wheel drive and
stick shift, shifted into low gear, crimped the front
wheels slightly to the left, and floored the accelerator.
The left front tire bit into the steep bank of the crevasse,
and suddenly Buck shot almost straight up. A small car
behind him dropped front first into the hole and burst
into flames.

The ground shifted and broke up. A huge section of
sidewalk pushed up from the ground more than ten feet
and toppled into the street.

The sound was deafening. Buck had never raised his
window after listening to the animals, and now the thun-

derous crashing enveloped him as trucks flipped over and streetlamps, telephone poles, and houses fell.

Buck told himself to slow down. Speed would kill him. He had to see what he was encountering and pick his way through it. The Range Rover bounced and twisted. Once he spun in a circle. People who had, for the moment, survived this were driving wildly and smashing into each other.

How long would it last? Buck was disoriented. He looked at the compass on the dash and tried to stay pointed to the west. For a moment there seemed almost a pattern in the street. He went down then up then down then up as if on a roller coaster, but the great quake had just begun. What at first appeared as jagged peaks the Rover could handle quickly became swirling masses of mud and asphalt. Cars were swallowed up in them.

Horror was not a good enough word for it. Rayford could not bring himself to speak to Carpathia or even to Mac. They were headed toward Baghdad Airport, and Rayford could not keep from staring at the devastation below. Fires had broken out all over the place. They illuminated car crashes, flattened buildings, the earth roiling and rolling like an angry sea. What appeared a huge ball of a gasoline fire caught his eye. There, hanging in the sky so close it seemed he could touch it, was the moon. The bloodred moon.

Buck was not thinking of himself. He was thinking of Chloe. He was thinking of Loretta. He was thinking of Tsion. Could God have brought them through all this only to let them die in the great earthquake, the sixth Seal Judgment? If they all went to be with God, so much the better. Was it too much to ask that it be painless for his loved ones? If they were to go, he prayed, "Lord, take them quickly."

The quake roared on and on, a monster that gobbled everything in sight. Buck recoiled in horror as his head-lights shone on a huge house dropping completely underground. How far was he from Chloe at Loretta's? Would he have a better chance of getting to Loretta and Tsion at the church? Soon Buck found his the only vehicle in sight. No streetlights, no traffic lights, no street signs. Houses were crumbling. Above the road he heard screams, saw people running, tripping, falling, rolling.

The Range Rover bounced and shook. He couldn't count the times his head hit the roof. Once a strip of curb rolled up and pushed the Range Rover on its side. Buck thought the end was near. He was not going to take it lying down. There he was, pressed up against the left side of the vehicle, strapped in. He reached for the seat belt. He was going to unfasten it and climb out the passenger's-side window. Just before he got it unlatched, the rolling earth uprighted the Range Rover, and off he drove again. Glass broke. Walls fell. Restaurants disappeared. Car dealerships were swallowed. Office buildings stood at jagged angles, then slowly toppled. Again Buck saw a gap in the road he could not avoid. He closed his eyes and braced himself, feeling his tires roll over an uneven surface and break glass and crumple metal. He looked around quickly as he took a left and saw that he had driven over the top of someone else's car. He hardly knew where he was. He just kept heading west. If only he could get to the church or to Loretta's house. Would he recognize either? Was there a prayer that anyone he knew anywhere in the world was still alive?

———————

Mac had caught a glimpse of the moon. Rayford could see he was awestruck. He maneuvered the chopper so Nicolae could see it too. Carpathia seemed to stare at it in wonder. It illuminated his face in its awful red glow, and the man had never looked more like the devil.

Great sobs rose in Rayford's chest and throat. As he looked at the destruction and mayhem below, he knew the odds were against his finding Amanda. *Lord, receive her unto yourself without suffering, please!*

And Hattie! Was it possible she might have received Christ before this? Could there have been somebody in Boston or on the plane who would have helped her make the transaction?

Suddenly there came a meteor shower, as if the sky was falling. Huge flaming rocks streaked from the sky. Rayford had seen it go from day to night and now back to day with all the flames.

Buck gasped as the Range Rover finally hit something that made it stop. The back end had settled into a small indentation, and the headlights pointed straight up. Buck had both hands on the wheel, and he was reclining, staring at the sky. Suddenly the heavens opened. Monstrous black and purple clouds rolled upon each other and seemed to peel back the very blackness of the night. Meteors came hurtling down, smashing everything that had somehow avoided being swallowed. One landed next to Buck's door, so hot that it melted the windshield and made Buck unlatch his seat belt and try to scramble out the right side. But as he did, another molten rock exploded behind the Range Rover and punched it out of the ditch. Buck was thrown into the backseat and hit his head on the ceiling. He was dazed, but he knew if he stayed in one place he was dead. He climbed over the seat and got behind the wheel again. He strapped himself in, thinking how flimsy that precaution seemed against the greatest earthquake in the history of mankind.

There seemed no diminishing of the motion of the earth. These were not aftershocks. This thing simply was not going to quit. Buck drove slowly, the Range Rover's headlights jerking and bouncing crazily as first one side and then the other dropped and flew into the air. Buck thought he recognized a landmark: a low-slung restaurant at a corner three blocks from the church. Somehow he had to keep going. He carefully drove around and through destruction and mayhem.

The earth continued to shift and roll, but he just kept going. Through his blown-out window he saw people running, heard them screaming, saw their gaping wounds and their blood. They tried to hide under rocks that had been disgorged from the earth. They used upright chunks of asphalt and sidewalk to protect them, but just as quickly they were crushed. A middle-aged man, shirtless and shoeless and bleeding, looked heavenward through broken glasses and opened his arms wide. He screamed to the sky, "God, kill me! Kill me!" And as Buck slowly bounced past in the Range Rover, the man was swallowed into the earth.

———————

Rayford had lost hope. Part of him was praying that the helicopter would drop from the sky and crash. The irony was, he knew Nicolae Carpathia was not to die for yet another twenty-one months. And then he would be resurrected and live another three-and-a-half years. No meteor would smash that helicopter. And wherever they landed, they would somehow be safe. All because Rayford had been running an errand for the Antichrist.

———————

Buck's heart sank as he saw the steeple of New Hope Village Church. It had to be less than six hundred yards away, but the earth was still churning. Things were still crashing. Huge trees fell and dragged power lines into the street. Buck spent several minutes wending his way through debris and over huge piles of wood and dirt and cement. The closer he got to the church, the emptier he felt in his heart. That steeple was the only thing standing. Its base rested at ground level. The lights of the Range Rover illuminated pews, sitting incongruously in neat rows, some of them unscathed. The rest of the sanctuary, the high-arched beams, the stained-glass windows, all gone. The administration building, the classrooms, the offices were flattened to the ground in a pile of bricks and glass and mortar.

One car was visible in a crater in what used to be the parking lot. The bottom of the car was flat on the ground, all four tires blown, axles broken. Two bare human legs protruded from under the car. Buck stopped the Range Rover a hundred feet from that mess in the parking lot. He shifted into park and turned off the engine. His door would not open. He loosened his belt and climbed out the passenger side. And suddenly the earthquake stopped. The sun reappeared. It was a bright, sunshiny Monday morning in Mt. Prospect, Illinois. Buck felt every bone in his body. He staggered over the uneven ground toward that little flattened car. When he was close enough, he saw that the crushed body was missing a shoe. The one that remained, however, confirmed his fear. Loretta had been crushed by her own car.

Buck stumbled and fell facedown in the dirt, something gashing his cheek. He ignored it and crawled to the car. He braced himself and pushed with all his might, trying to roll the vehicle off the body. It would not budge. Everything in him screamed against leaving Loretta there. But where would he take the body if he could free it? Sobbing now, he crawled through the debris, looking for any entrance to the underground shelter. Small recognizable areas of the fellowship hall allowed him to crawl around what was left of the flattened church. The conduit that led to the steeple had been snapped. He made his way over bricks and chunks of wood. Finally he found the vent shaft. He cupped his hands over it and shouted down into it, "Tsion! Tsion! Are you there?"

He turned and put his ear to the shaft, feeling cool air rush from the shelter. "I am here, Buck! Can you hear me?"

"I hear you, Tsion! Are you all right?"

"I am all right! I cannot get out the door!"

"You don't want to see what's up here anyway, Tsion!" Buck shouted, his voice getting weaker.

"How is Loretta?"

"Gone!"

"Was it the great earthquake?"

"It was!"

"Can you get to me?"

"I will get to you if it's the last thing I do, Tsion! I need you to help me look for Chloe!"

"I am OK for now, Buck! I will wait for you!"

Buck turned to look in the direction of the safe house. People staggered in ragged clothes, bleeding. Some dropped and seemed to die in front of his eyes. He didn't know how long it would take him to get to Chloe. He was sure he would not want to see what he found there, but he would not stop until he did. If there was one chance in a million of getting to her, of saving her, he would do it.

———————

The sun had reappeared over New Babylon. Rayford urged Mac McCullum to keep going toward Baghdad. Everywhere the three of them looked was destruction. Craters from meteors. Fires burning. Buildings flattened. Roads wasted.

When Baghdad Airport came into sight, Rayford hung his head and wept. Jumbo jets were twisted, some sticking out of great cavities in the ground. The terminal was flattened. The tower was down. Bodies strewn everywhere.

Rayford signaled Mac to set the chopper down. But as he surveyed the area, Rayford knew. The only prayer for Amanda or for Hattie was that their planes were still in the air when this occurred.

When the blades stopped whirring, Carpathia turned to the other two. "Do either of you have a working phone?"

Rayford was so disgusted he reached past Carpathia and pushed open the door. He slipped out from behind Carpathia's seat and jumped to the ground. Then he reached in, loosened Carpathia's belt, grabbed him by the lapels, and yanked him out of the chopper. Carpathia landed on his seat on the uneven ground. He jumped up quickly, as if ready to fight. Rayford pushed him back up against the helicopter.

"Captain Steele, I understand you are upset, but—"

"Nicolae," Rayford said, his words rushing through clenched teeth, "you can explain this away any way you want, but let me be the first to tell you: You have just seen the wrath of the Lamb!"

Carpathia shrugged. Rayford gave him a last shove against the helicopter and stumbled away. He set his face toward the airport terminal, a quarter mile away. He prayed this would be the last time he had to search for the body of a loved one in the rubble.

EPILOGUE

"WHEN He opened the seventh seal, there was silence in heaven for about half an hour. And I saw the seven angels who stand before God, and to them were given seven trumpets. Then another angel, having a golden censer, came and stood at the altar. He was given much incense, that he should offer it with the prayers of all the saints upon the golden altar which was before the throne. And the smoke of the incense, with the prayers of the saints, ascended before God from the angel's hand. Then the angel took the censer, filled it with fire from the altar, and threw it to the earth. And there were noises, thunderings, lightnings, and an earthquake.

"So the seven angels who had the seven trumpets prepared themselves to sound."   Revelation 8:1-6

ACKNOWLEDGMENTS

SPECIAL thanks to Rennie Rees and Shannon Kurtz.

ABOUT THE AUTHORS

Jerry B. Jenkins (www.jerryjenkins.com) is the writer of the Left Behind series. He is author of more than one hundred books, of which ten have reached the *New York Times* best-seller list. Former vice president for publishing for the Moody Bible Institute of Chicago, he also served many years as editor of *Moody* magazine and is now Moody's writer-at-large.

His writing has appeared in publications as varied as *Reader's Digest, Parade,* in-flight magazines, and many Christian periodicals. He has written books in four genres: biography, marriage and family, fiction for children, and fiction for adults.

Jenkins's biographies include books with Hank Aaron, Bill Gaither, Luis Palau, Walter Payton, Orel Hershiser, Nolan Ryan, Brett Butler, and Billy Graham, among many others.

Seven of his apocalyptic novels—*Left Behind, Tribulation Force, Nicolae, Soul Harvest, Apollyon, Assassins,* and *The Indwelling*—have appeared on the Christian Booksellers Association's best-selling fiction list and the *Publishers Weekly* religion best-seller list. *Left Behind* was nominated for Book of the Year by the Evangelical Christian Publishers Association in 1997, 1998, and 1999.

As a marriage and family author and speaker, Jenkins has been a frequent guest on Dr. James Dobson's *Focus on the Family* radio program.

Jerry is also the writer of the nationally syndicated sports story comic strip *Gil Thorp,* distributed to newspapers across the United States by Tribune Media Services.

Jerry and his wife, Dianna, live in Colorado.

Limited speaking engagement information is available through speaking@jerryjenkins.com.

ABOUT THE AUTHORS

Dr. Tim LaHaye (www.timlahaye.com), who conceived the idea of fictionalizing an account of the Rapture and the Tribulation, is a noted author, minister, and nationally recognized speaker on Bible prophecy. He is the founder of both Tim LaHaye Ministries and The Pre-Trib Research Center. Presently Dr. LaHaye speaks at many of the major Bible prophecy conferences in the U.S. and Canada, where his nine current prophecy books are very popular.

Dr. LaHaye holds a doctor of ministry degree from Western Theological Seminary and a doctor of literature degree from Liberty University. For twenty-five years he pastored one of the nation's outstanding churches in San Diego, which grew to three locations. It was during that time that he founded two accredited Christian high schools, a Christian school system of ten schools, and Christian Heritage College.

Dr. LaHaye has written over forty books, with over 22 million copies in print in thirty-three languages. He has written books on a wide variety of subjects, such as family life, temperaments, and Bible prophecy. His current fiction works, written with Jerry B. Jenkins—*Left Behind, Tribulation Force, Nicolae, Soul Harvest, Apollyon, Assassins,* and *The Indwelling*—have all reached number one on the Christian best-seller charts. Other works by Dr. LaHaye are *Spirit-Controlled Temperament; How to Be Happy Though Married; Revelation Unveiled; Understanding the Last Days; Rapture under Attack; Are We Living in the End Times?;* and the youth fiction series Left Behind: The Kids.

He is the father of four grown children and grandfather of nine. Snow skiing, waterskiing, motorcycling, golfing, vacationing with family, and jogging are among his leisure activities.

THE FUTURE IS CLEAR

Left Behind®
A novel of the earth's last days . . .
In one cataclysmic moment, millions around the world disappear. In the midst of global chaos, airline captain Rayford Steele must search for his family, for answers, for truth. As devastating as the disappearances have been, the darkest days lie ahead.

0-8423-2911-0 Hardcover
0-8423-2912-9 Softcover

0-8423-1675-2 Audio book—Cassette
0-8423-4323-7 Audio book—CD

Tribulation Force
The continuing drama of those left behind . . .
Rayford Steele, Buck Williams, Bruce Barnes, and Chloe Steele band together to form the Tribulation Force. Their task is clear, and their goal nothing less than to stand and fight the enemies of God during the seven most chaotic years the planet will ever see.

0-8423-2913-7 Hardcover
0-8423-2921-8 Softcover

0-8423-1787-2 Audio book—Cassette
0-8423-4324-5 Audio book—CD

Nicolae
The rise of Antichrist . . .
The seven-year tribulation period is nearing the end of its first quarter, when prophecy says "the wrath of the Lamb" will be poured out upon the earth. Rayford Steele has become the ears of the tribulation saints in the Carpathia regime. A dramatic all-night rescue run from Israel through the Sinai will hold you breathless to the end.

0-8423-2914-5 Hardcover
0-8423-2924-2 Softcover

0-8423-1788-0 Audio book—Cassette
0-8423-4355-5 Audio book—CD

Soul Harvest
The world takes sides . . .
As the world hurtles toward the Trumpet Judgments and the great soul harvest prophesied in Scripture, Rayford Steele and Buck Williams begin searching for their loved ones from different corners of the world. *Soul Harvest* takes you from Iraq to America, from six miles in the air to underground shelters, from desert sand to the bottom of the Tigris River, from hope to devastation and back again—all in a quest for truth and life.

0-8423-2915-3 Hardcover
0-8423-2925-0 Softcover

0-8423-5175-2 Audio book—Cassette
0-8423-4333-4 Audio book—CD

Apollyon
The Destroyer is unleashed . . .
In this acclaimed *New York Times* best-seller, Apollyon, the Destroyer, leads the plague of demon locusts as they torture the unsaved. Meanwhile, despite growing threats from Antichrist, the Tribulation Force gathers in Israel for the Conference of Witnesses.

0-8423-2916-1 Hardcover   0-8423-1933-6 Audio book—Cassette
0-8423-2926-9 Softcover   0-8423-4334-2 Audio book—CD

Assassins
Assignment: Jerusalem, Target: Antichrist
As a horde of 200 million demonic horsemen slays a third of the world's population, the Tribulation Force prepares for a future as fugitives. History and prophecy collide in Jerusalem for the most explosive episode yet of the continuing drama of those left behind.

0-8423-2920-X Hardcover   0-8423-1934-4 Audio book—Cassette
0-8423-2927-7 Softcover   0-8423-3682-6 Audio book—CD

The Indwelling
The Beast takes possession . . .
It's the midpoint of the seven-year Tribulation. As the world mourns the death of a renowned man, the Tribulation Force faces its most dangerous challenges yet. Time and eternity seem suspended, and the destiny of mankind hangs in the balance.

0-8423-2928-5 Hardcover   0-8423-1935-2 Audio book—Cassette
0-8423-2929-3 Softcover   0-8423-3966-3 Audio Book—CD

The Mark
The Beast rules the world . . .
His Excellency Global Community Potentate Nicolae Carpathia, resurrected and indwelt by the devil himself, tightens his grip as ruler of the world. The battle is launched for the very souls of men and women around the globe as sites are set up to begin administering the mark.

0-8423-3225-1 Hardcover   0-8423-3231-6 Audio book—Cassette
0-8423-3228-6 Softcover   0-8423-3968-X Audio book—CD
  (available fall 2001)

Watch for book 9 in this best-selling series to arrive summer 2001

Left Behind®: The Kids

Four teens are left behind after the Rapture and band together to fight Satan's forces in this series for ten- to fourteen-year-olds.

#1 *The Vanishings* 0-8423-2193-4

#2 *Second Chance* 0-8423-2194-2

#3 *Through the Flames* 0-8423-2195-0

#4 *Facing the Future* 0-8423-2196-9

#5 *Nicolae High* 0-8423-4325-3

#6 *The Underground* 0-8423-4326-1

#7 *Busted!* 0-8423-4327-X

#8 *Death Strike* 0-8423-4328-8

#9 *The Search* 0-8423-4329-6

#10 *On the Run* 0-8423-4330-X

#11 *Into the Storm* 0-8423-4331-8

#12 *Earthquake!* 0-8423-4332-6

Watch for the next Left Behind®: The Kids books, available spring 2001

Have You Been Left Behind®?

Based on the video that New Hope Village Church's pastor Vernon Billings created for those left behind after the Rapture. This video explains what happened and what the viewer can do now.

0-8423-5196-5 Video

An Experience in Sound and Drama

Dramatic broadcast performances of the first four books in the best-selling Left Behind series. Original music, sound effects, and professional actors make the action come alive. Experience the heart-stopping action and suspense of the end times for yourself. . . . Twelve half-hour episodes, on four CDs or three cassettes, for each title.

0-8423-5146-9 *Left Behind®: An Experience in Sound and Drama* CD

0-8423-5181-7 *Left Behind®: An Experience in Sound and Drama* cassette

0-8423-3584-6 *Tribulation Force: An Experience in Sound and Drama* CD

0-8423-3583-8 *Tribulation Force: An Experience in Sound and Drama* cassette

0-8423-3663-X *Nicolae: An Experience in Sound and Drama* CD

0-8423-3662-1 *Nicolae: An Experience in Sound and Drama* cassette

0-8423-3986-8 *Soul Harvest: An Experience in Sound and Drama* CD

0-8423-3985-X *Soul Harvest: An Experience in Sound and Drama* cassette

0-8423-4336-9 *Apollyon: An Experience in Sound and Drama* CD
    (available spring 2001)

0-8423-4335-0 *Apollyon: An Experience in Sound and Drama* cassette
    (available spring 2001)

0-8423-4338-5 *Assassins: An Experience in Sound and Drama* CD
    (available spring 2001)

0-8423-4337-7 *Assassins: An Experience in Sound and Drama* cassette
    (available spring 2001)

Discover the latest about the Left Behind series
and interact with other readers at **www.leftbehind.com**